STAR TREK
THE NEXT GENERATION®

THE GENESIS WAVE
BOOK ONE

STAR TREK
THE NEXT GENERATION®

THE GENESIS WAVE
BOOK ONE

John Vornholt

POCKET BOOKS

New York   London   Toronto   Sydney   Singapore

This book is a work of fiction. Names, characters, places, and incidents are products of the author's imagination or are used fictitiously. Any resemblance to actual events or locales or persons, living or dead, is entirely coincidental.

POCKET BOOKS, a division of Simon & Schuster, Inc.
1230 Avenue of the Americas, New York, NY 10020

This book is published by Pocket Books, a division of Simon & Schuster, Inc., under exclusive license from Paramount Pictures.

Library of Congress Cataloging-in-Publication Data

Vornholt, John.
    The genesis wave / John Vornholt.
        p. cm. — (Star trek, the next generation)
    ISBN 0-7434-1180-3
        I. Title. II. Star trek, the next generation (Series)

PS3572.O564 G4 2000
813'.54—dc21
                                                                00-057134

First Pocket Books hardcover printing September 2000

10   9   8   7   6   5   4   3   2   1

Printed in the U.S.A.

For Ruth, who has saved us many times!

one

Waves lapped delicately at the blue pebbles and copper-colored sand of the lagoon, while ferns waved in the scented breeze. Their slender branches traced ripples in the tide pools, while sleek, black shapes teemed in the deepest part of the lagoon. Beyond the shore stretched an endless turquoise sea filled with whitecaps, dancing to the music of the waves. Heat and light radiated from the red midday sun, bathing the quiet seascape in a golden halo.

The sun felt good on the old woman's wrinkled skin. It seemed to penetrate into her aged bones and joints, making them feel good, too. Her hair was white and thinning, but it had once been vibrantly blond, matching her square-jawed Scandinavian face. She covered her eyes with a spotted hand and squinted into the glare, noting only a whisper of clouds in the azure sky.

The old woman bent down and ran her hand through the copper sand—it felt like a combination of bath water and hot ashes. With fingers that were spotted with age but still nimble, she probed the granules until she uncovered a tiny filament, no wider than a hair. Patiently she kept digging, ignoring a twinge of pain that rippled from her back down to her thighs. The glitches of advanced age were old acquaintances at this point in her life. She was 135 years old. Or was it 136? She often lost track in this sunny paradise, where every day was much like the day before.

The longer she kept digging, the older she felt, but her careful labor was slowly rewarded. One by one, she collected more fibers, stretching them across her palm, careful not to uproot them from the underground connectors. Her digging didn't stop until she had unearthed seven of the delicate filaments, and she hunched over to study them more closely.

"None of these are damaged," she said with relief, sinking back on her haunches. The woman recalled how fierce the storm had been last night, knocking out their sensor array. By midmorning, the sky over the island had reverted back to its usual crystal clarity.

"Sometimes this place is almost too sunny," the old woman complained. "It's not exactly the real world."

No one agreed or disagreed. The breeze whispered a reply, saying it didn't matter one whit, because the great work of her life was behind her. The old woman sighed at her foolishness and replanted the delicate fibers in the sand.

She stood up, groaning at the creak in her back. "I should take my medicine." Then she quickly added. "Computer, erase that last sentence from the log."

"Sentence erased," repeated a tinny voice coming from the combadge on her white jumpsuit.

The old woman snorted a laugh. "Is anybody really *listening* to me? Does anybody *care* that I've turned this entire beach into a giant solar-energy collector? And I did it without upsetting the ecosystem. Is everybody in the Federation just trying to humor an old lady?"

Once again, no one answered, except for the gentle lapping of the waves. The computer back in the lab was simply capturing her remarks in a log, to be transmitted to her correspondents in other locations. She missed having live colleagues around. Oh, they came to visit every so often, but they seldom stayed for long. They were intimidated by her bodyguards and her monastic lifestyle, neither of which was her choosing. Over the years, she had come to accept her quiet life until it had become the norm.

The old woman could travel if she wished, but it was too difficult taking her entourage with her. As the years passed, she traveled less and less. Her isolation in the watery expanses of Pacifica wasn't due to her experiments—it was necessary for that other part of her life, the part which often dominated. The old woman was a prisoner of the past, still suffering from acts of pride, ambition, and selfishness.

On days like this, it seemed as if her punishment and grief would be endless—as endless as the turquoise sea that surrounded her. Of all her grievous mistakes, the worst was leaving her son behind in that terrible place. The bloodstains from the past could never be cleansed, not by all the waves and torrential rain in the universe.

Why leave my island? thought the old woman bitterly. *I have no one out there, no one who cares about me. It's not respect or love my keepers feel for me—it's fear. I'm valuable because I have a secret. They'll be glad when I'm gone. . . . Then they can stop protecting information they don't even want to know.*

"Dr. Marcus?" asked a helpful male voice.

She whirled around to confront Ensign Martin Dupovitz, the youngest and newest member of her four-person security detail. "Don't sneak up on me like that!" she snapped, instantly regretting her hasty reaction.

"I'm . . . I'm sorry, Doctor," stammered the lad. In this setting and his gold-hued Starfleet uniform, he looked like some exotic waiter at a beach resort. "You sounded distressed over the comlink, and you were . . . talking to yourself."

"I was not talking to myself," insisted Carol Marcus impatiently. "I was making a log entry . . . talking to the computer."

"Of course, Doctor," answered Martin, trying not to sound condescending, but failing. "It's just that—with our sensor array down—we have to be extra careful."

"Go ahead and call me Carol," said the old woman, trying to muster some of the personality that used to charm the Federation Council and young suitors, such as James T. Kirk. "We don't stand on formality around here."

Martin lowered his eyes and kicked at a blue pebble in the sand. "Well, I prefer to maintain a professional demeanor, Dr. Marcus. I want to get good reports from Commander Quay'to—"

"So you can get out of here all the sooner," replied Carol, finishing his thought. He looked at her, abashed, having been found out.

"Don't worry about it," she said warmly. "Everybody leaves here eventually—we haven't lost an officer yet. And it's not so bad. The scuba diving is quite good, and so is weather watching. You don't know anything about solar flares, do you?"

The young man shook his head. "No, that's not my field of study. I have a black belt in karate, and I'm rated for tactical weaponry."

"Hmmm," said Carol with mild disapproval, having never liked the militaristic side of Starfleet. "What exactly do they think is going to happen to me out here? It's been ninety years since . . . the incident . . . and no one has come after me yet. Someday I'm just going to blurt out everything I know, and you people can spend eternity guarding *each other*!"

Martin blanched and took a step back. "Please, Dr. Marcus, it's not my job to question orders. And I don't want to know *anything* about what happened to you—or why you're here. All Starfleet says is that you have to be protected, and I'm here to do that job."

The old woman gazed wistfully at the pastel ocean. "I used to think that children would read about me in their science classes, maybe in their history classes. But, no. They wiped all traces of my early work from Starfleet records. Some people have duplicated small parts of it by accident, but not the way I did it. Nobody will ever learn about me. It's all too dangerous . . . too controversial. There are too many curious parties."

Martin shifted his feet uncomfortably. "They tell me your solar-energy experiments are very important."

"Glorified make-work." Marcus sniffed. "Oh, I've made some strides here, but hundreds of others could have done the same thing. My *real* work—no one else could have done that but me. And David." Her voice faltered and cracked at the mention of her son. He had been about the age of this young officer when he was brutally murdered.

"I'm sorry," said Martin. "But with respect, Doctor, I still don't want to hear about it."

"You won't." With effort, Carol mustered a smile. "I've kept my secrets this long. I think I can keep them a little while longer. There's nothing left of that other project, except for what I carry up here." She tapped her forehead.

"We'll protect you," vowed the young man. "Even the president of the council doesn't have around-the-clock security like you do."

"I know," said Marcus with a trace of melancholy. "If your professional demeanor permits it, could you please offer an old woman a steady arm for the walk back to the lab?"

"Certainly, Doctor." Gallantly the officer extended a brawny arm, and she grasped it with relief. It was difficult breaking in these new bodyguards, only to lose them quickly if they showed any ambition or skill. How many hundreds of security officers had drifted through her life in the last ninety years? What did they think about their time spent with the Mystery Woman of Pacifica? Maybe all they remembered was the endless sea and the searing sun, which could be exhilarating and sedating at the same time.

In the first years of her banishment, she had gotten too friendly with a few of her guards, believing that she had a right to still live a normal life, despite everything that had happened to her. That had been a mistake, which had cost the career of a man she loved. Or thought she loved. The truth was, she had been grasping for tenderness and forgiveness in the wake of David's death and the spectacular destruction of Project Genesis. Jim Kirk had disappeared again, and there was no one to console her while they erased her life's work from recorded history.

If it had been tough for her, it had also been tough on her guards. She remembered the despondency of the officers assigned to protect her during the Dominion war. They craved to be on the front lines—in the action—not beachcombing with a strange old lady. They could see her solar-energy research, but they didn't know why she should be valuable to the Dominion. In the end, Pacifica had avoided attack, but that only made their incomprehensible assignment seem more futile. Even now, she often overheard hushed conversations, discussing transfers. As a lot, Starfleet officers weren't happy sitting around on the beach.

How many times had she wanted to burst into their midst and tell them to go away? Just to leave her alone! But she had learned to play her role as well. It was a role scientists had played throughout the ages—the outcast who possessed forbidden knowledge.

As Dr. Marcus and Ensign Dupovitz walked from the beach toward a cluster of low-slung, green buildings, she admired the natural beauty of her island. Massive yellow succulent plants covered the ground, and they sprouted ten-meter-high pistils of a flaming burgundy color. Brilliantly colored insects, as big as birds and shaped like dragonflies, darted among the pistils in their furtive mating dance. Behind the row of buildings, giant ferns and trees towered into the sky, waving their wispy branches back and forth to the buzzing harmony of the waves and insects. Clumps of purple labano fruit hung from the trees in her orchard, and the bohalla bushes were in bloom with waxy lavender buds. Everywhere there was abundance and the sweet smell of the ocean.

That was all she had wanted to create with Project Genesis—beauty and life. Even now, it seemed a noble dream to turn barren matter into a thriving paradise that could rival this one. Of course, that was in a perfect universe, where people thought of progress and altruism before they thought of weapons and revenge. After years of reflection, Carol had come to admit to herself that she had been naïve those many years ago. No one had been prepared for Genesis to be a success, least of all her.

Yet ultimately it had been a failure . . . a planet formed from a nebula . . . erratic and unstable. *And I sacrificed my son trying to find out why,* thought Marcus miserably. *If only I had taken David home with me, instead of letting him go back there! If only I had told him to stay with his father . . . go anywhere, do anything but that!*

The toe of her boot hit the first step of the walkway, and she was jolted out of her melancholy. Now Carol was glad to be holding onto the ensign's arm, and she tightened her grip to steady herself.

He looked at her with concern, and she managed a smile. "I'm all right," she assured him. "You know us absent-minded scientists— can't walk and think at the same time."

Martin lowered his voice to say, "I don't understand why you have to live way out here. I think we could protect you in a rural town or a space station, someplace like that. And you could still do your experiments."

"Trust me, Martin, I deserve to be here." She patted his arm and started up the winding walkway. "Besides, I work best away from prying eyes—I hate interference. But I'm sure you would prefer to be out there in space, zooming around. I hate to tell you though, space travel is usually more boring than this island."

The young ensign smiled and was smart enough not to argue with her. They climbed the hill to the entrance of the compound, which required them to pass through a security gate in an electrified fence about eight meters high. Carol Marcus straightened her spine and peered into the retina scanner, trying not to blink her tired eyes. After a moment, the computer voice announced, "Carol Marcus, identity verified. You may pass."

"Thank you," she drawled. The woman stepped through the fence and waited while the young ensign completed the security procedure. While she stood on the short sidewalk between the fence and the first building, she noticed something odd on the ground. It looked like a sprig of moss, and she bent down to pick it up.

The waxy, gray sprig was unlike any vegetation she had ever seen on the island, and she studied it closely, trying to identify the plant. It looked something like mistletoe. "Is everything okay?" asked Martin.

"Except for this," she answered, holding up the sprig for him to see. He looked at it and shrugged blankly.

"Maybe somebody was planning a Christmas party," said Marcus with a smile. She dropped the sprig into an empty pocket on her jumpsuit and stepped toward a double door, which slid open at her approach.

Followed by Ensign Dupovitz, Carol Marcus strode into the common room of the Big House, as they called it. The Big House was really the dormitory where she lived with her four bodyguards. Other buildings housed her laboratory, their security and communication center, the water purification plant, a small infirmary, and equipment storage. All of their electricity was generated by various solar-energy collectors, and they had much more than they needed. Microwaves dispersed some of the excess power to nearby islands.

In the common room, Commander Quay'to and Lieutenant Jaspirin were seated at a card table, playing a game of three-dimensional chess. They looked up from their game at the new arrivals, feigning disinterest. Although they tried not to act like zealous babysitters, her protectors were nervous whenever she was out of their sight. This was doubly true with the sensor array down. The old woman had long ago ceased to be annoyed by their constant attention, but her guards still went out of their way not to appear overbearing.

Quay'to was a Zakdorn with an impassive, scaled face. A brilliant tactician, she seldom lost at three-dimensional chess unless she was badly distracted. Marcus could tell from the pieces she had lost to Jaspirin that she was not playing her best game.

"The beach hasn't washed away, has it?" asked Jaspirin, a Tarkannan whose red uniform was beginning to bulge a bit around his waistline. He seemed to be enjoying the leisurely life on the island more than any of his fellows.

"No, it's still there," answered Marcus, sitting down at the dining table to catch her breath. "How is the array?"

"Wilson's working on it," said Quay'to. With a swift movement, she made a decisive quadruple jump spanning three different planes of the chess board and capturing three of her opponent's pieces.

Jaspirin stared at her in mock shock. "Commander, I resent that move. I think you were setting me up."

"Not at all," replied the Zakdorn. "I merely saw an opening I hadn't noticed before."

"Do you want me to take a look at the array?" asked Carol helpfully.

Quay'to shook her head. "No, that's not necessary. We've got a repair crew on the way—they should be here by tonight. In the meantime, Wilson is trying to rig together something with the tricorders—at least we can have short-range sensors." The studious calm in the Zakdorn's voice barely masked her annoyance at this interruption in their routine.

"If we don't get another storm," said Martin Dupovitz, glancing out a window.

"Can't do anything about the weather," remarked Jaspirin, "although everyone keeps trying."

Carol smiled to herself, thinking that she had once been able to do a great deal about the weather. But that was in the past, in another lifetime. She rose slowly from her chair, feeling a twinge of pain in her lower back. Weariness overcame the scientist, reminding her that she had awakened well before dawn, fretting over the possibility of the storm damaging her experiments. In the end, it had turned out to be just another beautiful day on Pacifica.

"Is there anything on the local dish?" asked Jaspirin, glancing at a nearby viewscreen. "When are the yacht races from Pacifica Prime?"

"Not for another six months," answered Quay'to, pointing to the chess game. "Your move."

Carol Marcus yawned broadly and made a decision. "I'm going to take a quick nap."

"Go right ahead, Doctor." The commander nodded her approval, then went back to her chess game.

"We'll have lunch ready for you when you wake up," promised Martin.

Marcus nodded gratefully at the young ensign. One of the happy prerogatives of old age was that one could take a nap whenever one felt like it, without eliciting any resentment. She caught the three of them watching her as she made her way to her quarters; they were undoubtedly relieved that she would be inactive for a while.

Lying in her bed felt as luxurious as lying in a weightless mud bath on Rigel II. Marcus felt all of her worries and pain melting away as her body sank into the mattress. Faintly she could hear the gentle lapping of the waves, lulling her into tranquility. She also heard the muffled voices of her guards, greeting Wilson, who had just joined them in the common room.

I don't know when I've ever been so tired, Carol marveled to herself. She must have slept, although she wasn't sure. All she knew was that a strange mist seemed to enter her bedroom, filling it with shadows. Everything became deathly quiet, except for the rhythmic hush of the waves, and her body felt paralyzed, but comfortably so.

Then a warm hand touched hers, and the mattress dipped as someone alighted beside her. Stirring gently from her dreamy reverie, Carol Marcus looked up to see the most wonderful sight in the whole world: *David!* Her son's angelic face was framed by unruly blond curls, and he smiled at her with those delicate dimples and intense brown eyes. How all the girls, young and old, had loved to run their fingers through those curly locks of his.

"David," rasped Carol with tears brimming in her eyes. She lifted a trembling hand to touch his face, certain there would be nothing to feel but an old woman's illusion. To her astonishment, her hand touched real flesh, and she ran her fingers over his nose, mouth, and eyes.

"David . . . you . . . how?" she sputtered.

"Don't worry about that now," cooed David, cupping her hands in his. "The universe is full of strange and wondrous things. I'd like to show them to you, Mother. Are you ready to leave this pointless life behind and come with me? Father is anxious to see you, too."

"Jim?" she asked in astonishment. "But he's dead. *You're both dead!*" Carol shook her head and screwed her eyes shut, not wanting to consider the obvious. "Or maybe I'm the one who's dead."

"Even in death, there is life," said David, grabbing her slender shoulders and pulling her into a sitting position.

"I killed you!" said the old woman, weeping. "I left you behind!" She buried her face in his gray tunic and sobbed loudly, inconsolably. David stroked her matted ivory hair, the child comforting the mother.

Suddenly Carol looked up in a panic, certain that her loud crying would bring all four bodyguards running. She gazed out the open door toward the common room and saw Martin lying on the floor and Quay'to slumped in her chair.

"What's the matter—"

David touched her lips, silencing her. "Nothing is the matter . . . not anymore. It's taken me a long time to find you, Mother, but now we're going home."

"Home!" said Marcus with a gush of emotion. "Yes, home. Do you mean—"

David nodded happily. "Yes, back to the Regula I lab—to finish your work."

The old woman gulped and looked at him with a combination of joy and disbelief. She didn't feel dead, so she had to be dreaming. But if this was a dream, it was an exceedingly cruel one, because she couldn't stand to be torn away from David again.

He smiled with understanding. "I know you have questions, but you've just got to accept what is. I'm here, you're here, and we can be together just like always. We can start over, do it right. Just come with me . . . and trust. Will you do that?"

Carol nodded, tears of happiness streaming down her face. "Oh, yes, David! If you forgive me—"

"I forgive you, Mother. We'll never be apart again. Come along—Father is waiting." He smiled radiantly and wrapped his arms around her. From the corner of her eye, Carol saw the mists and shadows creeping back into the room, and she had a momentary lapse of doubt. *This can't be happening!* David's solid arms reassured her, and the old woman surrendered to her bliss. Her consciousness seeped away until all she felt was oblivion.

two

"The yacht races on Pacifica came to an exciting conclusion today," said the sportscaster on the audio feed, his voice wafting across the open-air market, along with the smells of a hundred different foods and perfumed oils. Everywhere signs proclaimed "Happy Terran Day," a celebration marking the day when the first human colonists had arrived on Seran to join the Camorites, Deltans, and other species. Aurora Square was filled with shoppers and revelers, picking up fresh produce, spices, gifts, and tasty delicacies for the holiday dinner.

The announcer went on, "With fireworks in the sky and a grand flotilla on the waves, the winners were honored today on Pacifica. A Bynar catamaran, the *Gemini*, won for the second year in a row in the freestyle category. A replay will be broadcast at twenty-two hundred hours on the All-Sport video transponder."

"I'll have to try to catch that," said Mikel Gordonez as he hefted a melon from a nearby stand and sniffed its dewy freshness. "I'll come back to the club tonight and watch it with the boys."

Leah Brahms lifted her blue eyes from a selection of squashes and tubers and looked curiously at her husband. Gray-haired, paunchy, Mikel was twenty years older than she, and he sometimes treated her like his subordinate, which she had been at the Theoretical Propulsion Group. Lately Mikel had been coming to the planet's surface almost every night, frequenting his athletic club.

She couldn't help herself—she had to ask, "Why would you want to watch a yacht race from the other side of the quadrant? You never pay any attention to the yacht races here."

"This is the Pacifica Invitational," he protested. "It's famous. All the other ones are just . . . the minor leagues." Mikel scowled and walked away from her. "If you don't want me to come to town tonight, just say so."

Leah followed him through the throng, brushing her chestnut-colored hair out of her eyes. For years, she had worn her hair long, usually pinned up in a bun, but now it was cut short. Mikel hated it. Although she was determined not to fight with him, she was equally determined to make her case. They had a ton of work left to do, and he acted as if they were on vacation.

As Leah charged after her husband, she realized that she didn't want to start an argument in public, surrounded by hundreds of residents of the capitol city. Leah Brahms and Mikel Gordonez were respected scientists, known to everyone on the planet as the landlords of Outpost Seran-T-One. Fighting in public wouldn't win them any friends, and they needed friends now that a vote on their funding was coming up before the council. They had enough enemies already.

She didn't want to blame Mikel for all of their problems, but his attention had been drifting for some time, from both the research and her. Even now, her husband strode through the crowded market ten paces ahead of her, oblivious to her struggle to keep up. She was carrying all of their purchases, an armful of bundles.

Stop! she wanted to scream, but she didn't. Leah was always the one who worried about appearances, the one who kept quiet when people were watching. She could be outspoken and opinionated on her own turf, but she maintained decorum when it came to the two of them. Where he was frivolous and childish, she was serious and adult. Where he was a people person, she was a techie. They were a good partnership on the face of it, but she still didn't understand him. *Why does he want to watch a yacht race when we're in the middle of running tests?*

He's just trying to get away from work, she concluded. *Or me.*

Leah didn't know everything in life, but she knew that Mikel couldn't get away from her. They worked together all day long, and their names were linked on hundreds of papers, proposals, and studies. It was impossible to tell where her life ended and his began. Colleagues and customers depended upon them—escape wasn't an option.

Finally Leah Brahms slowed down, took a deep breath, and paused to look at the colorful booths and luscious wares for sale. It had been Mikel's idea to come shopping in the market today, not hers. Leah had to admit that she seldom took time to admire the pottery or smell the bread pudding. *Maybe I should be the one who changes*, she thought with a start. *Maybe I should watch yacht races.*

A Deltan woman walked by, pushing a double stroller containing two beautiful, dark-haired children. Leah was suddenly aware of the laughter and gaiety of children all around her, running through the square, chasing their hoops and robotic pets.

It would have been different if we'd had children, thought the scientist. *Never had time*, came the familiar reply. She was still young enough, just approaching forty, and she could attempt it yet. But Leah didn't know whether having a child would balance her life and help the marriage or put undue stress on everyone. She knew that Mikel would be horrified at the idea.

The truth was, she didn't have as many other interests and people in her life as she should have. Everything revolved around work, even her marriage, which probably made her boring. She didn't work very hard at her marriage either, except to stay monogamous when confronted by the rare temptation. There had been moments of unwanted attention, such as Geordi La Forge's crush on her. At least that was over, and they had become friends. But who could make time for romance, with a husband or anyone else?

Yes, I'm boring, she decided. *If I'm boring to myself, what must I be to Mikel?*

A gangly Camorite bumped into her, and he politely nodded his plume of yellow hair. "Excuse me. Happy Terran Day."

"Yes, it is!" Leah replied cheerfully. She gazed up at the indigo sky, ablaze with the brilliance of a double-star system. There was a slight chill in the air, but midyear was coming soon with its dry, warm weather. All around them towered shimmering skyscrapers and sinewy monorails, stretching into the depths of the metropolis. Two joyous children cut through the crowd, waving streamers over their heads. A flotilla of hot-air balloons floated overhead, affording scores of Serans a lofty view of the festivities. On a glorious day like this, what was the point of fighting?

She tapped her combadge. "Brahms to Gordonez."

His voice didn't sound happy when he answered. "What are you doing? I'm ten meters away from you."

"Yes, and you're going to stay ten meters ahead of me unless you slow down. I just wanted to catch up with you." She cut through the crowd and bumped into him before he had time to react. After a grin, she said, "Brahms out."

He looked down at her, suppressing a smile despite his anger. "Listen, why don't you come with me to the club tonight? We'll watch the race together. You don't get out of the lab enough."

"All right, I will," she answered. "Here, help me carry this stuff."

While Mikel gaped at her, she shoved packages into his arms. "Are you kidding?" he asked.

"No, I'm not kidding," she said. "You have to help me carry this stuff."

"No, do you really want to go to the club with me tonight?" Suddenly he sounded doubtful.

"Yes, already—I'm going." Leah was more resolute than ever, because she sensed an odd reticence on his part. Mikel had asked her to go to his club many times before, but she had never said yes. Maybe she should have gone with him before now.

"Are we about done shopping?" asked Mikel, swiftly changing the subject. "Have we got enough for that special dinner tonight?"

"I think so. If not, we'll make do." But Leah suddenly felt a sort of panic, realizing that the entire day would be lost to shopping, cooking, eating, watching yacht races, and who knew what else? That was the problem with having a life—work always suffered.

"Let me just check in," she said, tapping her combadge. "Brahms to Outpost Seran-T-One." She tried to ignore the way Mikel smirked and rolled his eyes at her attention to duty.

"Henricksen here," came a high-pitched, harried response. "Is everything all right, Doctor?"

"Yes, it's all right with us," answered Brahms, speaking above the din of the crowd. She knew every nuance of voice and mannerism in her assistants, and she sensed that Ellen Henricksen was upset. "What's wrong up there?"

"It's nothing we can't handle."

"Go ahead and tell me," said Leah Brahms. "I'll find out sooner or later."

"Well, it's the test site—" began the worried assistant. "The Civil Guard showed up an hour ago, and they've held up our tests. Paldor is trying to talk them out of it, but they won't budge. They say we're not allowed to use radiation with any of the local subjects."

"What?" demanded Mikel angrily, yelling over Leah's shoulder. "That's the whole point of it! What's the matter with those rubes?"

Leah looked around at the crowd in the marketplace, wondering how many had overheard Mikel's remark. A few people glanced their way, but most were worried about holiday preparations and getting the last bit of Saurian sylph butter.

"Maybe we should go there," concluded Leah. "We're done here, anyway. Get ready to receive us."

"Paldor didn't want to call you," whined Ellen miserably. "We can handle it. *Really* we can!"

"We're on our way." Leah gripped her husband's hand and was soon dragging him and all their packages through the crowd, headed toward the outskirts of the square. She kept glancing at the signposts overhead, trying to find one which indicated a transporter kiosk. Mikel kept barking about "superstitious locals" and "bureaucrats on a power trip," but Leah did her best to ignore him.

Finally she located a transporter kiosk in the corner of the square, but there was a line of about twenty Serans waiting to get in. On a normal day, there wouldn't be anyone waiting, but this was hardly a normal day.

She hated doing it, but she had to pull rank. "Get out your I.D. card," she told Mikel.

He smiled slyly as he pulled the card from beneath his tunic and let it dangle from the cord around his neck. "They're going to hate you."

"I don't care." Leah whipped out her own badge and waved it at the people in line as she plowed past them. "Medical emergency! Coming through! Medical emergency! We need to use the transporter."

The Serans eyed their packages and attire doubtfully, as if thinking they didn't appear to be on any kind of emergency. Nevertheless, the customers at the front of the line stepped back to allow Leah and Mikel to enter the kiosk first. Such was the power of the Science Service badges they wore, which marked them as members of the elite on Seran.

Leah stamped her foot impatiently as she waited for the forcefield to clear, then she charged inside the circular room and took her place on the transporter platform. The interior of the kiosk was hardly any bigger than a Jefferies tube, and Mikel struggled to drag all their packages inside. "Hurry up," she urged him.

Breathing heavily, the gray-haired man finally took his place beside her on the platform. He looked ruefully at her. "Did anybody ever tell you that you're a slave driver?"

"All the time," answered Leah, knowing it was the truth. She had driven herself and others mercilessly all her life, and she had never learned how to relax. The current emergency probably wasn't much of one, but it had served the purpose of ending their brief shore leave before it became uncomfortable. She glanced at Mikel, who was busy keeping all the packages in his hands. She had never thought that he could hide anything from her, but maybe he wasn't as predictable as she thought.

The most disturbing part of this realization was the fact that it meant so little to her. As usual, her worry was for the work—always the work. Today they were testing the prototype of new, vastly improved radiation suit.

"Destination?" queried a polite computer voice.

"Outpost Seran-T-One," she answered. "Authorization code: five-zero-eight-one-nine."

"Prepare to energize."

Leah stared straight ahead, waiting for the familiar tingle to grip her spine. The sensation quickly faded, as the walls of the kiosk morphed into a shadowy cargo bay inside the largest of Seran's eight moons. The hidden outpost had been built as a Starfleet observation post over two centuries ago on the edge of Federation space. After observing the planet for thirty years and finding no high-level life, Starfleet issued permission to colonize. The Camorites had been first, followed by Deltans, Saurians, and others. In time, Federation borders had moved a bit closer to the center of the Milky Way, and the Federation had turned the outpost over to the science branch.

Leah stepped off the transporter platform, feeling a bounce in her step from the decrease in gravity. Mikel stumbled off the platform and promptly dropped all of their packages. Before Leah could help him, doors opened at the end of the bay, and Ellen Henricksen rushed toward them, bounding in the low gravity like an ostrich.

Ellen waved a padd over her head. "I've got the site permissions, environmental studies, and waivers right here!"

"Thanks," said Leah, taking the handheld device from her. She glanced guiltily at Mikel, who was chasing a rolling melon across the cargo bay. "Ellen, could you please round up the food for us and start dinner, as best you can."

Ellen flapped her long arms helplessly. "I guess so." She was a good kid, but just a kid, and this was her first real job since leaving the Daystrom Institute. Leah was often inclined to cut fellow Daystrom graduates more slack than the others. Ellen bounced over to the transporter console and busied herself checking coordinates.

Mikel stood up, rubbing his back. "Something tells me that tonight will be another meal from the replicator."

"Not if I can help it," vowed Leah. "Did we do the maintenance on the shuttlecraft?"

"Did the maintenance," answered Mikel, "and we're going to need it tomorrow."

"Let's settle this bit with the Civil Guard once and for all." Leah Brahms climbed back onto the transporter, her jaw set resolutely. She looked expectantly at Mikel, who wasn't moving quickly enough.

With a shrug, he dutifully followed. "They probably resent the fact that we're working on a holiday."

Leah shook the padd at him. "These people know they have no authority, they just want to meet the ones in charge. If they had left us alone, the test would be done already."

"The more tests, the better," said Mikel, snidely repeating a familiar litany. "We'll set them straight. Energize, Miss Henricksen."

"Yes, Doctor." The young woman plied the controls with authority, and Leah again felt the tingle of the transporter beam. A moment later, she and her husband materialized in a meadow on the outskirts of the capitol city. A muddy stream ran through the middle of the field, and tiny yellow flowers sprinkled its banks. The city and its monorails were nestled in the foothills beyond, looking like strands of pearls strewn among green velvet. On the jagged horizon rose the Tinkraw Mountains—shrouded, snow-dusted peaks which guarded the glistening city.

Sixteen tall coral pillars stood in the center of the meadow, forming a circle around a clearing. The pillars had been built to resemble the fertility temples of the Deltans, so as not to disrupt the natural beauty of the meadow. But this was no temple—it was a monitoring station. The pillars housed test equipment, scanners, monitors, force-field generators, and a particle accelerator. What had once been a remote area was getting more popular all the time, with a couple dozen people in attendance.

In the center of the pillars stood what appeared to be a white sculpture representing a humanoid. This stoic figure was the center of attention, with people milling around it. As Leah and Mikel strode toward the gathering, she could see that the bulky radiation suit was empty. Standing beside it was a young Deltan woman wearing an oversized robe and a chagrined expression.

Their assistants, Paldor and Gershon, were arguing vociferously with about twenty members of the Civil Guard, as denoted by their distinctive purple sashes. On a peaceful planet with no standing police or army, the Civil Guard was a volunteer organization that enforced laws. Sometimes they couldn't resist meddling.

At their approach, the warring parties broke off from each other and charged the new arrivals, waving their hands. Leah started to say something, but Mikel's voice boomed over her head. "I'll thank you to stop harassing my technicians! We've got all of our permissions, and this site has been cleared for these tests. Unless you're standing right on top of the emitter, it won't be any more dangerous than getting an X ray!"

"That's what I've been telling him!" bawled Paldor, a chubby Tellarite with a piglike snout, bristly orange beard, and shock of orange hair.

A tall, plumed Camorite approached Mikel, looking very grave. He was also armed with a padd full of data, so Leah handed her padd to Mikel. The Camorite spoke with authority. "According to common ordinance six-three-seven-point-nine, this facility is not to be used for class-three experiments on an official holiday when local citizens are endangered by their presence in the area."

Mikel turned to Leah and grinned triumphantly. "You see, it *was* because of working on a holiday." His expression grew somber as he turned back to the Civil Guard. "Okay, then no locals will be endangered, because we'll keep them away. We'd like to start by keeping *you* away, so please leave."

The Camorite craned his scrawny neck and looked at the Deltan shivering beside the radiation suit. "*She* is a local, endangered by your experiments."

Mikel sputtered indignantly, "But . . . but surely that doesn't mean we can't *hire* people as subjects! We have to collect data with a variety of different—" He caught sight of one of the Civil Guards touching the radiation suit, and he rushed toward him, waving his arms like a madman.

"Get away from there!" screamed Mikel, startling the man. "Get away! *Shoo!*"

The scientist hugged the hard-shelled suit as if it were a long-lost friend, then he gently wiped a smudge of dirt from the curved face-plate of its built-in helmet. "Do you know what this equipment is going to do? It's going to save hundreds of lives—maybe the life of *your* son or daughter. With this, starship engineers won't have to risk their lives trying to save the main engines. In this suit, they can work in the middle of a distressed warp core, surrounded by antimatter leaks, and they'll be safe. It's got medical monitoring, life support, a communications array, and phase-shifting."

Leah cringed. The phase-shifting technology was supposed to be a secret, because they had cribbed it from the Romulans without their permission. Even though it had only the standard shielding and reflective materials, what made the suit special was its interphase generator. An oscillating temporal displacement allowed the wearer to be effective in a dangerous environment but slightly removed from it as well. On a much larger scale, the Romulans used the same technology to cloak their ships.

Mikel pointed to her. "My wife here has spent her whole life designing warp engines and propulsion systems, only to see how dangerous her creations became when things went wrong. So she did something about it—she invented this suit. We have to test it under every known condition, including planetary atmosphere, before we can present this prototype to Starfleet. Every day we delay, lives are at risk."

The head of the Civil Guard scoffed. "Self-important, aren't you?"

Bounding on his feet beside her, Paldor could stand no more. The Tellarite's orange hair stood on end, and he wrinkled his snout and puffed out his chest. "No, that would be *you*, Sir, delaying our work over a *technicality*! This test is perfectly safe, and we need a female subject."

"This is Terran Day," complained one of the human members of the Civil Guard. "Have some respect for our heritage."

The Tellarite snorted loudly, and Leah Brahms laid a calming hand on his beefy shoulder. "Don't fight with them, Paldor. Go back to the base and relieve Ellen—send her down here. Then we'll have *two* females to finish the test, and none of them will be locals."

The feisty Tellarite wrinkled his nose with distaste. "But that's giving into them! There's a principle involved here."

"There's work that's not getting done," answered Brahms curtly.

"Electricity always takes the path of least resistance, and so do I. Now get going."

"Yes, Doctor." Paldor bowed politely to her, then swiveled on his heel and marched out of the clearing.

"And see if you can do something with the food we brought home!" Leah called after him. She had a lot more faith in Paldor's cooking than in Ellen's, which was the main reason she had sent him back. The Tellarite waved to her as he strode beyond the pillars into the open meadow. He was still walking when the transporter beam whisked his molecules away.

Mikel continued to argue with the Civil Guard, while extolling the virtues of the radiation suit. But that was Mikel, thought Leah with quiet frustration: *Always so stubborn.* Once the argument became about winning the argument, then all was lost. Leah couldn't think that way. What was the point of winning an argument if it meant wasting time and losing an opportunity?

She approached the Deltan woman who had volunteered to be their subject. "Thanks for sticking around, Margala, but this isn't going to work. Go ahead and enjoy the holiday—we'll pay you for your trouble."

"Are you sure?" asked the woman hesitantly.

Leah nodded, and the young subject hurried away before she could change her mind. Then Leah unsnapped the collar of her tunic and began to take off her clothes.

Mikel and the Civil Guard stopped their pointless conversation to stare at her. "What are you doing?" asked Mikel.

"I'm getting into the suit," answered Leah. She looked pointedly at their tormentors. "After you leave, there won't be any more locals to endanger."

The popinjay with his yellow plume and purple sash looked stunned that he could be dismissed so easily, while a grin spread across Mikel's face. "Yes, take your posse and go bother somebody else. We've got work to do."

After Leah began to remove her trousers, most of the Civil Guard turned on their heels and politely wandered off. Their spokesman flashed a scowl at Leah, but he eventually turned and strode away, too. Within a few minutes, there was no one left in the meadow except for Leah, her husband, and three technicians. That number swelled to four when Ellen Henricksen walked into the group.

"Where is everybody?" she asked puzzledly. "I thought we had a standoff here."

"Nope," said Mikel, proudly hugging his wife. "Leah took care of them. Are you really getting into that thing?"

"For the first trial," she answered. "Then Ellen is going to take over for me." The young woman gulped upon hearing that she would be a guinea pig, too.

"Are you sure?" For the first time, Mikel sounded a little nervous as he considered his wife donning the imposing suit during live radiation tests.

"I was the first one to wear it, remember?" Leah took off her pants and handed them to Mikel, having stripped down to her conservative underwear. She wasn't overly modest in front of this group of people, with whom she lived and worked in close confinement, but she didn't linger in the chill air. She opened the back of the suit like someone cracking open a giant lobster claw, then climbed in.

Leah mashed her forehead against the clear faceplate as she shoehorned her limbs inside; her grunts echoed loudly in her own ears. The gel interior of the suit molded to the contours of her body, shrinking or expanding as needed. The arms and legs retracted slightly, because she was smaller than the Deltan. Settling into the suit felt like entering a cocoon or jumping into the water—it was alien, disconnected from reality. In the fingers of the gloves, she found the controls, and she turned the suit on.

The upper right corner of the faceplate illuminated, giving her a reflective viewscreen full of instructions. Then she heard a slight whirring noise as the opening in the rear sealed itself tightly. It tickled when the interior molded itself to her buttocks, but that was over in a moment.

Leah felt a flash of claustrophobia when she realized she was completely encased, but she tried to breathe evenly and relax. Although space travel was her business, the scientist didn't have much cause to wear protective suits, even ones she designed. She tried to tell herself it was no different than wearing a cleanroom suit and hood, although it was completely different. Those lightweight suits were designed to protect the environment from the wearer, not the other way around.

Her uneasiness quickly passed when she remembered all the resources at her disposal, resources she had made sure to include. Leah often imagined the suit as a wearable escape pod, with its own life support, communications, and computer. It contained enough food and water for three days of moderate exertion. She tapped her little finger upward, activating the medical artificial intelligence.

"Systems are normal, Dr. Brahms," said the suit, recognizing her physiology. "Your pulse rate is elevated thirty-two percent from the rate on your last examination. Would you like me to administer a mild sedative?"

"No thanks," answered Leah with a smile. Maybe the suit was a little *too* friendly.

The next voice to cut in was Mikel's. "Are you all right in there?" She glanced up to see him striding toward her, adjusting his communications headset.

"Just fine," she answered, giving him a thumbs up. It felt cumbersome to move around, but there wasn't anything anyone could do about that in normal gravity. In microgravity, the suit could float free or be anchored in any number of positions by embedded magnets. She had tried to think of everything, but it was still daunting to consider the conditions under which the suit would be used. The engine room in chaos, ruptures in the hull, life support failing, core meltdown imminent. But in this suit, an engineer at least had a chance of staying at his post and doing some good.

Leah looked around at the brilliant blue sky, lush green meadow, and short-sleeved workers, thinking this really wasn't much of a test. Oh, well, Starfleet wanted to see results under every possible condition, including picnic weather.

"Your medical data is coming through," said Mikel's voice in her ear. "Just relax, Hon."

"Okay." Leah took a deep breath and shook her arms, which barely moved inside the constrictive suit. "Shall I put on phase-shift?"

"Let me get the gel-pack reading first," answered Mikel, who stepped behind one of the picturesque pillars surrounding the clearing. "Yes, power levels are normal. Go ahead."

Leah knew the power levels were good, because she could see the readout reflected on her faceplate. But she said nothing. In production models, phase-shifting would be automatic, coming on as soon as the suit was activated. In the prototype, it had to be activated manually for testing purposes.

"Computer, phase-shifting on," she ordered.

"Phase-shifting on," answered a voice matter-of-factly.

The lack of any sort of sensation startled Leah, considering that she was wavering in and out of the temporal plane. Here—not quite here—back and forth like a sine wave. In instances when she was present in the real world, she could interact with objects, and those instances blended together to form coherence. It was like a bad singer who used vibrato to make sure she hit the right note at least some of the time.

"Before we go live," said Mikel, "let's do some dexterity tests. Logs are recording. Okay, Ellen, toss her the ball."

The young woman picked up a colorful play ball and stepped closer to the immobile white figure. "Five years at the Daystrom Institute to toss a ball," muttered Ellen with a smile. Her voice sounded tinny and distant, even though she was only four meters away.

"Ready?"

Leah Brahms nodded, and Ellen bounded forward, tossing the ball with both hands. As it floated through the air on a high arc, the sky above them completely changed colors, shifting from a pale blue to a vivid green. Leah took her eyes off the ball to watch something curious on the horizon. A flaming curtain swept over the distant mountains, throbbing and mutating as if distorted by heat. The snowy peaks erupted in fury, disappearing into rolling clouds of ash and steam. And the ground trembled.

In the peaceful valley, buildings and monorails writhed like snakes on fire, and the city was consumed by the flaming green embers. A squeal sounded in her ears, and columns of readouts on her faceplate began to scroll at a madcap pace. Leah thought there was a malfunction in her suit, and she let the ball bounce off her chest and land at her feet.

As the ball hit the ground, it exploded, and the soil under her feet began to twist and churn. Leah looked up to see the ungodly wave pass over Ellen Henricksen. Caught in midscream, her skin flared like fire and turned a mottled green before it liquefied. Tissue dripped off her skeleton, which became brittle and crumbled, and her body contracted into a brackish, quivering puddle.

Eyes agape, Leah looked up to see Mikel stagger toward her, the gruesome transformation already ravaging his body. The squeal in her ears might have been his screams as his body contracted into a lumpen mass.

"No!" she yelled in panic. "Mikel! I'm hallucinating! Help me—"

Leah staggered to stay on her feet, because the ground was still erupting, shooting geysers and flaming green embers. *This isn't real, is it?* She clomped forward, trying to reach her husband, but there was no trace of him in the churning, twisting inferno.

All across the planet, millions of souls died the same ignominious death, as their flailing limbs were sucked into the seething morass. Towering mountains and tiny pebbles all crumbled into molten, fiery sludge. The seas erupted and boiled, shooting monstrous plumes of steam into the mottled skies. The wind roiled, and great forests of trees flew through the air like so much burnt kindling. The atmosphere became a choking, blood-streaked miasma, and the entire planet throbbed like a sun going nova.

three

Leah Brahms gritted her teeth and tried to hold onto her sanity as the ground convulsed all around her. She looked for the remains of her husband and friends, but their bodies had been absorbed in the cataclysm. Khaki clouds swirled in the sky, quivering vines shot from the ground, and obscene, wormy life-forms writhed in the detritus of a planet in agony.

She sniffed back a wad of mucus and tears, staggering to stay on her feet in the bulky radiation suit. Readouts on her faceplate screen were back to a semblance of normal, although she and the suit were the only things unchanged on the churning landscape. *The moonbase!* she thought in panic. *It might be all right.*

Trying to remain calm, she used the glove controls to turn on the comm system. "Leah Brahms," she said shakily, "to Outpost Seran-T-One."

Certain there would no response, she jumped when Paldor's voice responded loudly in her ears, "Doctor! Doctor!" gasped the Tellarite. "We've lost contact . . . what's happening down there?"

"They're dead . . . all dead," she rasped. "I'm only alive because

I'm in the suit." As slimy grubs tried to wrap around her foot, Leah stepped back and shook them off, suppressing her revulsion.

"Dead," muttered Paldor in disbelief.

With effort, Leah shook off grief and despair long enough to keep thinking. "What hit us? Did you see anything on sensors?"

"I didn't see anything before, but I see it now," answered Paldor. "An energy wave of some sort. It's past Seran . . . on its way to the moon!"

"Beam me up! Now!" shouted Leah.

She waited, while the ground continued to spew forth obscene, writhing life-forms unlike anything she had ever seen, even in her nightmares. Monstrous stalks and vines sprouted into the swirling sky, towering above her like prehistoric beasts. "Get me out of here!" she shouted.

"I can't," he answered. "There's something wrong . . . I can't get a lock!"

Leah tried to remain calm, even as slimy tentacles and vines curled around her feet, trying to absorb her into the mad convulsions of the planet. The wave might be causing interference, but their comm signal was strong.

"Maybe it's the phase-shifting," she said evenly. "I'll turn it off."

"But you might—"

There was no point thinking about what might happen, because she knew she couldn't stay here. With a gulp, Leah flicked off the interphase generator and held her breath. Although the soil continued to mutate beneath her feet, she found that she could still escape from the twitching slime, but the soles of her feet were starting to smolder. Leah yelled, "Now try it! Hurry!"

She would try to remember that the wave's effect, awful as it was, apparently did its damage and left. As her encased body escaped from the graveyard of her husband and friends, Leah made a desperate vow. She had to stay alive long enough to warn others of this cataclysmic disaster.

When she materialized in the cargo bay, she found Paldor running around, stuffing tins of food into a shoulder bag. "The wave will be here in a few seconds!" he shouted.

"Direct-beam us to the shuttlecraft! Punch it in, and get up here!"

Nostrils flared, eyebrows bristling, the Tellarite rushed to the transporter controls and entered the coordinates. Then he leaped onto the platform, moving swiftly for a big fellow. A moment later, they were deposited inside the roomy cabin of a type-8 personnel shuttlecraft. Leah needed the extra space in order to thrash about in the bulky suit until she got her bearings.

Paldor immediately rushed to the controls. "Should I start the ignition sequence?"

"Yes, and start the sensors and video log!" responded Leah, even though Paldor was hardly a shuttlecraft pilot. She pressed the escape button, opening the suit with a pop, then she pried her sweaty body out. As Leah tumbled to the deck, she heard the faint whine of the impulse engines powering up. "Open the space doors!"

Paldor did as he was told, opening the launch doors. Through the black expanse of space, they could see a rippling green wave reaching toward them.

"Oh, Mizerka!" cried the Tellarite, gaping at the awesome sight. Leah dropped into the seat beside him and punched the thrusters. They were both thrown back in their seats as the sleek shuttlecraft zoomed toward the hangar doors. The craft raked the doorway on its way out, shearing off a shielding cowl and a subspace dish. But the dent in the door didn't matter, because the entire moonbase was consumed in hellish green flame a second later.

The shuttlecraft banked away from the shimmering curtain as it rippled across the moon, turning pitted rock into living tissue, pulsing with freakish energy. Explosions ripped the planetoid, and the resulting clouds were also consumed in the churning maw. Leah watched this remarkable transformation in her viewscreen, as she pushed the shuttlecraft to top impulse speed. Even with her grief and shock, the scientist in her wanted to understand this phenomenon. What kind of alchemy turned a peaceful planet into a seething quagmire in a few seconds?

They were still outrunning the unknown wave, but not by much. It seemed to pick up speed as it left the devastated planet and her moons for the vacuum of open space. At the very least, it wasn't diminishing in size or force.

"Getting ready to enter warp drive," she said.

"Yes, warp!" agreed the Tellarite, nodding his approval. "Good idea."

Leah punched in maximum warp for the shuttlecraft, and they soared away from the solar system. For the first time, she sat back in her seat and paused to take stock . . . and reflect.

Paldor cleared his throat. "Are you sure . . . I mean, there's no way—"

"They're all dead," she answered numbly. "All dead." Like a robot, Leah rose from her seat and went to the locker, taking out a standard blue jumpsuit. She pulled the clothing over her shivering body, hoping it would staunch the chill, but it didn't.

Leah sniffed, thinking about the mate she had loved, and taken for granted. Mikel was gone now, and it was too late to do the things and say the things she should have said. He was struggling to get back to her when he died, even though she was the only one who was safe. Just like that, everything in the universe could be turned upside-down, until nothing mattered but a moment's worth of survival.

"What *is* that thing?" grumbled Paldor, studying the scanner readouts. "I've never seen anything like it. It must stretch across a hundred thousand kilometers!"

"I don't know what it is, and I've seen it up close." Leah sighed and looked gratefully at the radiation suit that had saved her life, functioning just as it was supposed to. But her survival was small consolation, unless it served a larger purpose. "We've got to warn the Federation."

"That won't be easy," said the Tellarite, working the board. "Our communications are out. Probably from that launch . . . it was a little rough."

Leah nodded solemnly and stared out the window at the endless starscape, looking slightly blurred and unreal at warp two. She could feel a tightness under her eyes where her tears had dried. How could something as vast as space be vulnerable? Yet it was. How many planets, stars, and moons would be consumed by the relentless force behind them?

"The distress signal may still be working," said Leah hopefully. She took her seat at the pilot's console and brought up a damage report. She had never claimed to be the greatest shuttlecraft pilot—Mikel did most of the flying—and she needed more practice. She would get that now.

"You know, there are a lot of my people in this part of the quadrant," said Paldor, wrinkling his snout.

"A lot of everybody's people." Brahms studied her readouts and made sure they were headed into the heart of the Federation. Then she began calculating how she could coax a little more speed from the shuttlecraft. "We'll keep running until we find somebody," she promised.

"Or until it catches us," muttered the Tellarite.

Ship's pipes sounded softly in the bowels of the *Enterprise*-E, noting the end of the second watch in main engineering. Geordi La Forge looked up from a display of schematics, adjusting his perception to deal with ambient light instead of digitized images. He checked the chronometer over the door to make sure it was time to quit, and it was. Not that Commander La Forge kept regular hours as chief engineer of the *Enterprise*, but he had to make sure that he scheduled time for other pursuits. If not, he was prone to worka-holism. He rubbed his eyes, something he could do now that he wore ocular implants instead of a VISOR.

Geordi glanced around the bustling engine room. Nearly twice as big as the old one on the *Enterprise*-D, it had multitiered access points to the warp drive, a dozen control rooms, twenty worksta-tions, and three master situation displays. But he still missed his old engine room, with its tight corners, bright lights, and cramped dis-plays. This room was more efficient and ergonomically correct, but it lacked that homey feeling of a place that had been wrecked, repaired, and refitted many times.

Montgomery Scott had once told him that he felt the same way about the engine room on the first *Enterprise*. There was something about your first command that always stayed with you.

He heard the distinctive squeak of Data's footsteps a moment before he heard the android's clipped voice. "Geordi, you asked me to—"

"I remember," said the engineer with a smile. "Time to knock off. Thanks for reminding me."

The yellow-skinned android nodded thoughtfully. "I, too, am leaving engineering. The lateral arrays and the torque sensors appear to be operating within accepted parameters."

"That's what I tried to tell the captain," said Geordi, lowering his voice. "But he still thinks he can hear the torque sensors go out of alignment."

Data cocked his head. "His hearing did improve during the time we spent with the Ba'ku."

"Yes, but that was months ago, and we're back to normal now. At least, *I'm* back to normal now. Aren't you?"

Data considered the question. "As I am a unique being, there is no 'normal' to which I may compare myself. As for appearing nor-mal, you almost always appear normal to me."

"I think that's a compliment," said Geordi with amusement.

Then he frowned and looked back at his friend. "Exactly when are the times I *don't* appear normal?"

"When you are trying to make small talk with a suitable, available woman."

"Okay," muttered Geordi irritably. "We don't need to get *that* specific." He moved quickly to the exit, acknowledging the nods from his subordinates, many of whom had just come on duty. "Lieutenant Keenayle, take over."

"Yes, Sir," answered the white-haired Argelian, snapping to attention. "Computer, log Commander La Forge off duty. Direct hails to me."

"Change in command noted," answered the computer.

The door slid open as La Forge strode into the corridor, followed by Data. To his relief, Geordi saw that there was no one around, and he could talk freely to his best friend. "I guess you mean Dolores Linton."

"Yes," agreed Data, "Mission Specialist Linton. At the reception, I skillfully drew you into our conversation, turned the topic to one of mutual interest to both of you, made a witty parting remark, then left. What more could I do?"

Geordi scowled and looked around again to make sure they weren't being overheard. "Okay, so I froze and didn't know what to say. *You* were programmed to make small talk; some of us weren't so lucky."

"I have adjusted my programming over the years," replied Data as if confiding a secret. "As I was originally programmed, I was deficient in conversational skills. Standard replies often do not fit the context or the occasion, so I made a conscious effort to improve my programming."

"And you're saying I haven't?" snapped Geordi, realizing it was true.

"Specialist Linton is only going to be onboard for sixty days," observed Data. "As they say, you should move with alacrity."

La Forge groaned. "Maybe the problem is that I'm getting romantic advice from an android."

"If you prefer Commander Riker—"

"No, no," sputtered Geordi. "I couldn't take a single one of his lines and make it come out right. I can't smile like he can."

"But you also have dimples."

"That's not the point." Exasperated, Geordi stopped at the turbolift door and folded his arms. It took a few moments for the door to open, and when it did, Mission Specialist Dolores Linton stood inside the lift all alone. She was a few years younger than Geordi and quite a vibrant woman; stocky and muscular, she looked as if she could break him in half. He had no problem believing that she was a geologist who spent her life hiking and climbing.

"Specialist Linton," said Data cheerfully, as he grabbed Geordi's arm in a viselike grip and ushered him inside. "We were just discussing you."

"Oh, you were?" she said warily.

Geordi tried to wave off this conversation or find some way to escape from the turbolift, but the door closed behind him. "Level ten," he muttered to the computer.

"Level six," said Linton.

"Bridge." Without mercy, Data plowed onward. "Yes, Commander La Forge was saying that he planned to come to my violin recital at twenty-two-hundred hours, and he wondered if you would enjoy it."

"Yes, I love violin music." Linton glanced politely at Geordi, but her eyes returned to Data. "What are you playing?"

"Bach's Sonata in G Major, on baroque violin."

"Oh," she said, sounding impressed. "Are you using real gut strings?"

"Yes, I constructed them myself according to seventeeth-century techniques."

Geordi tried to figure out how he could enter this conversation, but the turbolift door opened before he did. He did manage to say, "I'll pick you up at your cabin fifteen minutes before."

"Thank you, Commander." At least she was polite, if totally uninterested.

On his way out, Geordi whispered to Data, "You still need work." The android gave him a quizzical expression, but the engineer had left the lift.

As the door shut behind him, La Forge breathed a sigh of relief. He knew his friend was well-meaning, and he had certainly spotted an area that needed improvement. But Geordi had been trying to improve his love life since he was a teenager, with very little success. He could be perfectly okay around women once he got to know them, but making small talk with strange women was beyond his ken. He probably could have taken advantage of his position to woo the young engineers under him, most of whom were unattached, but that wasn't his style.

No, being a lonely nice-guy is my style, he thought ruefully.

After a slow stroll down the corridor, Geordi stopped at the entrance to his quarters and touched a panel to identify himself and open the door. He stepped inside a friendly suite of rooms that were decorated in the earth tones of Africa—dark green, rust, red, and yellow. There were masks from Africa, but Geordi's art collection was eclectic, reflecting his taste in modern sculpture and mixed-media works made from a variety of materials. Their tactile and infrared qualities were as important to him as the way they looked to others.

The sofa, tables, and chairs were homey and comfortable, because Geordi wouldn't put up with furnishings that weren't functional. The room was soothingly dark, because he didn't need visible light to see. But he left minimal lights on for any guests who might accompany him. *Always hopeful*, thought Geordi, chuckling to himself.

Although he had just left a bank of viewscreens in engineering, he went immediately to his desktop terminal and sat down in his old armchair. "Computer, check new messages, personal file." He loosened his collar and put his feet up on a hassock.

"Twenty-two new messages," said the computer dryly. His compact viewscreen gave him a page of headings, and he read them over, amazed that he had fallen so far behind in his correspondence. He found that he had missed a meeting of the Physicists Society, failed to respond to two invitations, including one from Data for tonight's recital, and had ignored a great many polite queries for papers or engineering advice. But he would make it up to his friends. Which apology should he issue first?

Geordi kept scrolling down until his implants caught a name that stopped him cold. *Leah Brahms.* It was probably a thank-you note for the gift he had sent, but any contact from Leah was a major occasion, even if it left him feeling like an also-ran. He said hoarsely, "Computer, play message nineteen."

La Forge sat forward in his chair as Leah's angelic face and form appeared on the screen, surrounded by the jumbled accoutrements of her laboratory. There was something new—a hulking white form loomed behind her, looking like an abominable snowman about to attack. Geordi also liked her short haircut, because it finally let her delicate cheekbones stand out. Now that Leah was older, her face had more character and less of that cherubic baby fat that had made her seem so young for her wisdom.

"Hi, Geordi," she said cheerfully. "I've just got to tell you about the new project we've been working on—and thank you for sending the fresh kiwi! I know we can replicate it, but it's not even close to the same."

Another person strolled through the background then stepped out of the frame. "Is that Geordi?" asked a male voice. "Tell him to send more kiwi. And guavas!"

Her husband, thought La Forge with a pang. Mikel was always in the background, and Geordi could never quite get a clear picture of him. He knew he worked with Leah and handled most of the political and paperwork aspects of the operation, but La Forge had a hard time imagining Leah needing anyone's help. She had started to explain about the radiation suit standing behind her, but he had been so lost in his own thoughts that he didn't catch it.

"Freeze playback," he said.

Now Leah Brahms was frozen on the screen, looking both radiant and excited, her delicate hands hovering in the air, trying to explain her enthusiasm. This frozen image, in all its glory, told Geordi all he needed to know about his love life. Not only had he made every possible wrong move with Leah, including turning her into a holodeck character, but he had fallen hopelessly in love with her—a married woman! It sounded like something Reg Barclay would do.

There you have it, as many boneheaded mistakes as one fool can make. Geordi shook his head, realizing he had only himself to blame. He persisted in comparing every woman he met to Leah Brahms, an exercise in futility if there ever was one. Maybe he could move on in that part of his life, if he could just get over her.

With determination, he had maintained a long-range friendship with Leah by concentrating on their mutual interests instead of his feelings, which he kept hidden. This piecemeal friendship over hundreds of parsecs was better than nothing, and he felt as if he had to prove to her he was an okay guy, after the rocky start to their relationship.

It had not been *this* Leah which had gone to the beach with him and held his hand under the palm trees. No, that had been a dream from a holodeck, created to help him solve a problem—only to create a bigger one. *This* Leah was a real person with a husband and a busy life that only peripherally included him. Still she was here in front of him, talking to him; that was consolation enough for the moment.

"Rewind and resume playback," said Geordi, paying attention this time. Yes, the radiation suit sounded fascinating, and it was exactly the kind of thing that would challenge her mind. When she talked about the interphase generator, he felt a shiver, because he'd had personal experience with that Romulan device.

"But keep that hush-hush about the phase-shifting technology," she said in a sly aside. "We don't really have permission from the Romulans, but I've always been good at reverse engineering. I think that with the Alliance, maybe we can get permission after the fact."

"We'd better!" said the disembodied voice of Mikel, somewhere in the background.

"Anyway, it's worked in all the trials, and we're doing more today," concluded Leah. "I really feel happy about this project, because it's going to do some good and save lives. So take care, Geordi. Keep the *Enterprise* running. And thanks for all the kiwi!"

Her beaming face blinked off the screen, taking part of his heart with it. "End transmission," added the computer.

La Forge sat back in his chair, wondering what he would say to her in reply. As always, it would be carefully worded to be innocuous. "Computer, record reply to message nineteen."

"Begin when ready."

Geordi plastered a smile on his face. "Hi, Leah . . . and Mikel. I'm glad you like the kiwi. When you've been around the fleet as long as I have, you learn how to pull a few strings. Everything is fine here on the big E, and we're almost back to full staff again. We're supporting a geological survey on Itamish III to see if it's stabilized enough to support a mining colony. It beats fighting a war. It's been months since we've had any real excitement, but nobody's complaining. Uh, Data has a violin recital tonight."

He twisted his hands, trying not to get tongue-tied. "I'm going to try to go to more conferences next year. Maybe I'll bump into you somewhere or other. I'll send you a schedule. Good-bye, Leah. End transmission." He cringed as soon as he signed off, wondering if he had sounded too forward. Meeting her at a conference somewhere was probably *his* fantasy but not hers.

"Message sent, delayed subspace relay," said the computer.

Geordi tried to shrug it off, because, after all, Leah already knew he was a hopeless goof. *I should just forget about her and never see or hear from her again,* he decided, knowing he would be better off. But he wouldn't do that, because he didn't have a lot of sense where Leah was concerned.

The off-duty engineer went on to answer a dozen more messages and do a little technical reading. He was thinking about getting a quick bite to eat when his terminal beeped at him.

"Message undeliverable," said the computer.

"Which message?" asked Geordi.

"Reply to message nineteen, Leah Brahms at Outpost Seran-T-One. Outpost not responding."

Now Geordi sat forward with interest. "That can't be—we've got a million relays out there. Why isn't the outpost responding?"

"No response from sector 4368."

"No response from the entire sector?" asked Geordi incredulously. "What is the explanation?"

"None reported."

"Keep trying," said the chief engineer, rising to his feet. He fastened the collar of his tunic as he strolled toward the door. It looked like his free time would include a trip to the bridge.

four

A grizzled old Klingon sat alone at a table in the back of a dark tavern, staring into space. He had wild salt-and-pepper hair that tumbled past his shoulders, craggy forehead ridges split diagonally by an old scar, eyebrows that bristled like weeds, a broken nose, and a pointy white beard, streaked with black. But the most frightening thing about him was his blurry eyes, which stared straight ahead in abject terror.

With a twitch, the Klingon broke out of his fearsome reverie and realized where he was. He quickly grabbed a mug studded with *targ* knuckles and drained it lustily, letting half of the amber liquid course down his beard. Without warning, the Klingon pounded his fist on the table, shaking the whole establishment. "More ale!" he roared.

Fortunately, the dim tavern was mostly empty, except for two lovers giggling in a corner booth and a drunk Tellarite sleeping at the bar. The customer at the bar woke up and blinked, as Pasoot the bartender scurried from behind the counter, hefting another huge mug of foaming ale.

"More ale!" thundered the voice, shaking the glasses hanging above the bar.

"Coming!" shouted Pasoot, weaving gracefully among the empty tables and chairs. Pasoot was also a Tellarite and a large one, but he had learned to negotiate the tavern furniture like a ballet dancer.

"Here you go!" said Pasoot, presenting the mug he had specially ordered for this customer. "Anything else, Sir?"

"No," muttered the Klingon in a guttural voice, again staring straight ahead. "You didn't see it coming, did you?"

"See what?"

The elder's eyes blazed. "The green fire . . . it eats *everything*! Then there's the lava and the geysers . . . and the wind . . . that awful wind—"

"Uh, didn't see it today, Sir," answered Pasoot cheerfully. "The weather looks nice outside. You sure you don't want some skull stew?"

The Klingon laughed insanely for a moment, then grew somber once more. "Go away," he grumbled.

Pasoot didn't wait to be told twice. He grabbed the empty mug and scooted across the room and back behind the bar.

His other customer was now awake and indignant at the loud-mouth who had woken him up. "Who's he?"

Pasoot whispered, "The Klingon consul. Drunk again as usual."

"He's in shameful condition," sniffed the Tellarite, his speech slurred.

Pasoot considered that for a moment, then shook his head. "Not for a Klingon. He's pretty peaceful for a Klingon. I used to serve a lot of them, and believe me, we could do worse. He's quite reasonable when he isn't getting nostalgic."

The Klingon muttered into his mug of ale, "Don't leave them! No chance . . . not with the lava—"

"What's he yelling?"

"I don't know . . . it's this kind of nightmare he has. Something about the 'green fire eating everything.' Then he talks about the lava and the wind. Always with the wind."

"The wind! The wind!" roared the Klingon.

Pasoot nodded sagely. "See what I mean."

"Why do you put up with that?"

"Because he's my best customer." The bartender picked up a glass and thoughtfully dried it with his towel. "I guess I feel sorry for him, because he must have messed up really badly to be sent to Hakon. In fact, a Klingon that old should either be a general, an ambassador . . . or dead."

He prodded his indignant customer. "So are you going to order another drink, or are you just going to complain?"

Before the tipsy Tellarite could reply, the outer door opened, and a ray of light sneaked into the darkness. The sunlight realized it didn't belong and quickly vanished, but a young Tellarite female was left in its wake. She was short and shapely, and her bristly hair was a rich auburn shade, not the orange of most males. She peered around the tavern, squinting into the dim light.

"Is he here?" she asked irritably.

"I don't know who *he* is," said the drunk at the bar. "But *I'm* here, and I'm all you need."

She wrinkled her snout. "Just tell me, Pasoot, is he here?"

"Maltz? Yes, he's way in the back." The bartender pointed with his towel. "He must be asleep, or else you'd hear him."

She snorted and put her hands on her hips. "Do you know how to sober up a Klingon?"

"Well, you can always impugn their honor, but I wouldn't recommend it." With a sigh of resignation, Pasoot finally moved from behind the bar. "Come on, Solia, I'll help you."

They warily approached the rear table, where the Klingon was indeed sleeping and snoring harshly, his face immersed in a puddle of spilt ale. Pasoot asked, "What's the emergency?"

"A trade delegation from the neutral worlds has landed, and they're demanding to see somebody important," answered Solia.

"And *this* is the best you could do?" asked the bartender, shaking his head.

"A Klingon is always impressive," answered Solia, looking doubtfully at her charge. "Well, almost always. My orders are to bring him to this reception."

Pasoot shrugged. "I guess we don't have a lot of local celebrities. Okay, but I'm only going to do this once."

The bartender leaned over the fallen Klingon and said sharply, "Officer Maltz, to your feet! The enemy is near! *Jagh! Jagh!*"

The old Klingon lumbered to his feet, looking startled and wary. "It was that madman, Kruge, who got us captured! I could not do . . . Huh? Where am I?"

"Hello, Consul Maltz," said Solia soothingly, taking his arm and snatching his cloak from the back of his chair. "If you'll come with me now, we'll get you ready for your reception. More food . . . and *drink!* Come on."

Brave soul that she was, Solia dragged the stumbling, muttering Klingon out of the tavern into the blazing light of day. Pasoot could only shake his head and say to his other customers, none of whom were listening, "I have a bad feeling that old guy is not going to live long."

"But I tell you, Dr. Brahms, we can't let them all die!" whined Paldor, his snout flaring. The Tellarite sat in the cockpit of the shuttlecraft, banging on the star map on his console. "This Tellarite colony is right in the path of that thing back there, and we have time to go warn them. Besides, you say you want to get word to *somebody* in the Federation."

Leah gulped, although she kept her hands firmly on the controls, wondering how far the big Tellarite would go to save his people.

They still hadn't made their communications system work, although Leah thought the distress signal was getting out. Yes, they had to stop somewhere, but was this it?

"How much time do we really have?" she asked.

"I can't tell." Paldor shook his bushy head with frustration. "Its speed is variable, depending on how many solar systems and dust clouds it has to chew up along the way. Now that I know what to look for, I think I can spot it on sensors. At warp speed, we were traveling about three times faster, so I'm sure we've gained some time on it. Come on, Dr. Brahms, we've got to stop running and start *warning*!"

"Okay," said Leah, "you made your point. Do you think you can make your people believe their whole planet is in imminent danger of being destroyed?"

"What choice do we have?" asked Paldor grimly.

Leah nodded and glanced at his map. "Okay I'm changing course for—"

"Hakon in the Hivernia System," answered the Tellarite with relief. "Thank you, Dr. Brahms."

"You're going to do something for me," she replied. "You'll find isolinear chips in the media drawer."

"Okay," said the Tellarite, opening the small drawer and finding the compact storage devices. "What should I do with them?"

"Transfer all the data we've collected, plus your thoughts and recollections—anything you can think of—onto an isolinear chip. We've got to make a record of what we've seen . . . in case something happens to us."

"But how will we protect the chip?" asked Paldor.

"The same way I was protected—we'll put it into the suit." She glanced back at the radiation suit, hulking silently in the rear of the craft.

"Okay," said the Tellarite, inserting a slim rectangular device into the computer. "How would you describe the changes that this mysterious energy wave made to the planet?"

"Mutagenic, radical," answered Brahms with a shiver, trying not to visualize what she had seen all too closely. "Matter seems to be reorganized into an entirely different substance, but it's also alive. You saw what it did to the moonbase."

"Let's hope we get to Hakon in time," said the Tellarite, frowning so deeply that his bushy eyebrows knitted together.

"Let's hope somebody listens to us," added Leah.

Dressed in a laboratory gown and wearing rubber gloves, Captain Jean-Luc Picard carefully washed the clump of rock and sand with water and a small brush. He made certain to stand over the strainer, so that any small material which fell off would not be lost in the flow of water. It was meticulous work requiring patience, but it was also oddly satisfying. The captain of the *Enterprise* liked working with his hands, and he could be infinitely patient when dealing with antiquities.

It helped, too, that he was in a lab full of people doing the same work. Although he wasn't entirely sure what he was doing, there was plenty of expert help with whom to consult. Plus he felt useful when he saw the small piles of shells, fossils, and mineral specimens he had gleaned from the fist-sized chunks of river bottom in his basket.

He felt a presence looming behind him, and he turned to see the mission commander, Itakva Gedruva. Professor Gedruva was a Tiburon, so she had the dignified, bald head and enormous, leaf-shaped ears of her species.

"Thank you, Captain, for volunteering to do all this work," she said gratefully. "We normally have a hard time finding volunteers to clean and sort samples."

"Think nothing of it," said Picard magnanimously. "I enjoy working with antiquities. You can ask my crew; I welcome any mission that gets me poking around in some old dig." He lifted a delicate bit of rock that was full of clam-shell imprints. "How old do you think these fossils are?"

"I would guess the carbon dating would show them to be half-a-million in terran years," answered the professor. "Thus far, we haven't been surprised, but maybe you'll find an arrowhead and shock us."

"That would be shocking, wouldn't it?" asked Picard with amusement. Then his expression grew thoughtfully serious. "But what do you think happened to life on Itamish III? It was on track to be a garden planet, wasn't it?"

The elderly Tiburon shook her enormous ears. "We have theories, but we don't know exactly. That is what we hope to find out, to try to prevent it from happening again. Life is so delicate, Captain Picard. You realize that after you sort through the bones of a few hundred planets where life used to thrive and does no longer."

"Professor!" called someone else at a nearby table.

"Excuse me, Captain." With a polite nod, the mission commander was gone, leaving Picard to continue brushing and washing.

He was just starting to remove the clay from a new sample when his combadge chirped. "Bridge to Picard," said the familiar voice of Commander Riker. With gooey, gloved hands, the captain couldn't touch his combadge to answer it, and he had to set down his material and tools, remove a glove, and open his gown.

With relief, he finally answered the hail. "Picard here."

"I'm sorry to bother you, Captain," said Riker, "but we've got a situation."

The captain knew his first officer well enough to realize that he wouldn't interrupt his free time unless it was important. He was also not going to come out and say what it was when he could be overheard. Riker was confident enough to deal with almost anything on his watch, so this had to be something well beyond the scope of their peaceful mission.

"On my way," said the captain, rising from his stool. He removed his other glove and his lab gown, shrugging helplessly at Professor Gedruva. Her brief smile told him that she quite understood the requisites of command.

A few moments later, he strode onto the circular bridge of the *Enterprise* and looked curiously at the clutch of senior officers gathered around the tactical station: Riker, Data, and La Forge. Neither Data nor La Forge were supposed to be on duty, yet both of them were poring over data.

"Status?" he asked Commander Riker.

"As Mister La Forge discovered, we've lost contact with almost an entire sector of Federation space, 4368. That's fairly close to us, toward the center of the galaxy."

Picard frowned. "What about ships in the area?"

"We've tried, but we can't raise any ships, outposts, or any relays out there. Unaffected areas nearby don't report anything amiss."

Data looked up from the tactical station. "The communications blackout spans several inhabited solar systems, and there was no advance warning. Starfleet can offer no explanation."

"You can't raise anyone at all?" asked Picard incredulously. He knew that region of space, and it was one of the sleepiest, most peaceful parts of the Federation, far removed from the Demilitarized Zone and sites of recent conflicts.

La Forge lifted his head up. "We think we've found a faint distress signal, but that's it. We can't even get a signature from it."

"Can you read me the last message from Starfleet?" asked Picard.

"Yes," said Riker, leaning over the small terminal built into the arm of the captain's chair. "Communications outage in sector 4368 confirmed, reason undetermined. Unable to reach other ships in area, so no ships dispatched at present time. *Enterprise*, use captain's discretion to investigate, but please advise of decision. Signed, Admiral Nechayev."

Picard rubbed his chin thoughtfully, well remembering one of the more prickly members of the admiralty, Alynna Nechayev. It was odd that she should be involved in such a day-to-day matter, since she was usually more concerned with counterespionage tactics and secret missions. She had spearheaded their espionage efforts against the Maquis, Bajoran terrorists, and Cardassians, for instance. Not that those situations didn't call for extreme tactics, but Picard still felt guilty over having recruited Ro Laren, Sito Jaxa, and others for such dangerous missions, many of which had not ended well.

The captain couldn't help himself—whenever Admiral Nechayev was involved, he felt the warning hackles rise on the back of his neck. He said nothing to any of his subordinates, but they knew. After all, they had seen the admiral chew him out for one of their risky failures. All of this was just one more reason to take "captain's discretion" very seriously. He had a strong feeling that Nechayev wanted the *Enterprise* to go but wouldn't come out and say so.

"We're trying to get a fix on that distress signal," said La Forge. "It's moving, and there's interference in the background—like solar flares or something."

"If you do get a fix, use it for a course setting," ordered the captain. "Otherwise, pick an inhabited planet. Maximum warp. Alert Starfleet of our intentions."

"Yes, Sir," answered Riker, his voice showing no surprise. "We've got to pick up a few people on the planet. Do you want me to tell the team that we're going to have to postpone our current mission?"

"No, I'll tell them," said Picard regretfully as he moved to the turbolift. "Get us moving as fast as you can."

"Thank you, Sir," added Geordi La Forge, sounding as if the engineer had a personal interest in sector 4368.

"Keep trying to raise them," ordered the captain. "I don't want to waste our time on a wild-goose chase."

five

A dry wind crackled across the baked-clay walls and rambling, earthen dwellings of Patoorgiston, the capital of Hakon's sole inhabitable continent. The hand-molded walls had wide arches every twenty meters or so, and inside the arches were clay pots full of flowers and candles, swaying in the searing breeze.

Most of the dwellings were two story and looked like children's blocks, piled one upon another. The upper levels were smaller, allowing the outer edge of the lower roof to be a balcony. Children played fearlessly on these narrow labyrinths, which were connected by ladders and stairs; the Tellarites had good balance and seldom had accidents despite their bulk. Although the earthen houses looked similar in color and shape, they were distinguished by curtains, banners, and laundry in large, bright plaids, flapping from every window and balcony.

The inhabitants themselves wore these same kind of brilliant, often clashing squares of color as they bustled up and down the rambling streets. Some of them rode solar-powered, two-wheeled scooters, which breezed along the bumpy thoroughfares, narrowly missing the pedestrians. The Tellarites were vocal, and their loud voices carried on the wind, which was hot and dry, just the way they liked it.

Every so often, a face appeared in the crowd which did not have orange hair and a prominent snout, but the outsiders were few in number. Most of them were headed toward the only four-story building in town, the Cultural Affairs Center, which was a hub of interplanetary commerce. A bushy crown of salt-and-pepper hair towered above the Tellarites, Ferengi, Valtese, and the rest of the pedestrians. He was the lone Klingon, and the others gave him and his handler wide berth.

"We're almost there," said the cultural affairs attaché, Solia, guiding the grizzled Klingon down the walkway.

Maltz squinted into the bright sunlight, thinking that if he had any *klin* at all, he would shake off this simpering flunky and crawl back into a dark tavern. But that old call to duty still stirred him, even though everything he did in this post was pointless. Most days he felt like a sideshow attraction. *Look at the Klingon! Hakon is important enough to have one of its very own.*

Maltz couldn't believe it had taken them this long to walk a few blocks, but he hadn't been paying attention. It seemed it was now afternoon, and he had left home that morning, hadn't he? His keeper must have led him on a merry stroll, trying to sober him up. Well, it hadn't worked! He was still drunk.

He looked down at the small figure holding him up. Well, she was small for a Tellarite. The Klingon knew he ought to take her in his arms and protect her, instead of the other way around. But he was beyond offering protection to anyone, including himself. Now he had to be guided around like an old fool, propped up against the wall to be admired like the relic he was. Maltz was old enough to remember fighting against these people on a daily basis, before the Khitomer Accords. How had he turned from a proud warrior to a broken-down souvenir for the conquering enemy?

"When did we lose?" he muttered.

"What did you say, Consul?"

"When did we *lose!*" he thundered. "When did a pack of puny do-gooders take over our lives and our heritage and turn us into *diplomats?* A whore you dress up and show off for dinner—not a warrior. But this is what I've been reduced to by the Federation."

Solia laughed nervously as she tried to ignore the stares of passersby. "Why, Sir, you haven't lost anything. The Klingon Empire is still as powerful and respected as ever. You're her representative—you should know."

"Yes, I know very well," grumbled Maltz. "The niceness and even-handedness of the Federation has spilled over, infecting us. There is no way to die with honor anymore." He swallowed hard and rasped, "No way to redeem myself."

"Now, Sir, you can't blame every misfortune in life on the Federation."

Maltz laughed harshly. "In my case, I can. Although I should blame Kruge as much as Kirk."

"Kruge and Kirk?" asked the young Tellarite doubtfully.

"Before you were born," snapped the Klingon with a derisive snort. "That was when the captain of a starship was a force unto himself, a sovereign with no equal. It's not diplomats and massive fleets who decide history, it's out there . . . where two captains meet in the eye of the storm!" He shook his head miserably. "And destroy my career."

"I'm sure it's not that bad," replied Solia briskly, her patience running out at the same time the assignment was mercifully coming to an end. "We're here. Now watch it, because there are some steps."

Maltz finally had enough of this simpering lackey. He straightened his cloak and yanked his gleaming chain-mail sash across over his gaunt frame. Then he leaped up the stairs to the landing. "I can make it from here. There must be some other infants somewhere who need your attention."

"I'm sure," she answered with a smile. "Straight ahead to the reception desk and sign in with . . . Consul Maltz!"

But the Klingon was already headed toward the refreshments, his nostrils flaring at the smell of food. With a few long strides, he was across the lobby and into the ballroom, where a gathering of notables from the city and many surrounding planets were enjoying the hastily assembled soiree. Tellarite servers bustled among them with steaming trays of food and tinkling glasses of blue Saurian ale. The old Klingon skidded to a stop and licked his cracked lips.

A Tellarite waiter passed by with a tray full of fluted glasses containing the bluish liquid, and Maltz quickly seized him. "Don't be in such a hurry."

"Of course, Sir!" said the young Tellarite with a trace of awe and fear in his voice at being waylaid by a Klingon. He started to offer a glass to the dignitary when the Klingon grabbed the whole tray of glasses.

"Get another one," he grumbled. "I'm thirsty."

The Tellarite nodded and hurried off, while Maltz looked around the demurely decorated ballroom. From a nearby serving table, he grabbed a vase full of flowers, dumped the flowers and the water under the table, and began to pour the contents of the fluted glasses into the vase. When he was done, he finally had a warrior-sized receptacle that fit his hand, and it was already full of ale.

As he mingled among the crowd, looking for servers with food, Maltz heard a voice call, "And there he is! Maltz, our esteemed Klingon representative!"

The old warrior froze in his tracks and slumped his shoulders. He knew that voice—it was Bekra, the Capellan consul and self-appointed social director of the diplomatic community. Maltz turned around to face the elaborately dressed consul and his retinue, softening his scowl to a mild frown. On his head, Bekra wore a conical turban the shape of a tornado, and its rich fabric trailed seamlessly into his bejeweled turquoise jumpsuit.

"Consul Maltz," said Bekra, sliding unctuously toward him. "We have some distinguished visitors from the Neutral Worlds. They're making a swing through the Federation colonies, discussing trade opportunities. We're so glad you could come on such short notice."

"I would not miss it," grumbled Maltz, taking a long drink of ale as he surveyed the half-dozen newcomers to their midst. A grinning Orion, plus two unsightly Talavians, a bug-eyed Dopterian, a sinewy Mikulak, and a green-skinned Rutian. Bekra assigned them all names as he introduced them, but the names flew right out of Maltz's head the moment he heard them.

"Pleased to meet you," he grumbled, mustering very little sincerity.

"Does the Klingon Trade Council do much business here on Hakon?" asked the Rutian, whose long, stringy hair had more streaks of white than Maltz's.

The Klingon dug deep in the recesses of his memory for an innocuous response. "We would like to do more, which is why we are all here, right?"

"As you know, the Klingons require more security controls than are typical," said Bekra, the know-it-all. "Consul Maltz spends a great deal of his time checking to make sure that all the conditions are met."

"Yes, I do," lied the Klingon, who rubber-stamped everything that crossed his desk. He took a long swig of ale and wiped the excess from his beard with the back of his gauntlet. "How long are you staying on Hakon?"

The Orion answered, "Long enough to see what the populace needs, and what they have to offer in trade."

Bekra broke in, "The locals manufacture a natural cloth here that is unlike anything else in the Federation. It's strong, tough, resistant to mildew, and—"

He went on, but Maltz managed to corral a passing waiter and confiscate about half a tray of truffles. He tuned out the conversation while he ate, but he caught the Orion looking intently at him. He wasn't surprised when the visitor sidled up to his elbow a moment later.

"There's something familiar about you," said the Orion in a low voice. "Maybe it's that scar. Have we met before?"

Maltz tapped the crooked dent in his forehead ridge and peered down at the snaggletoothed trader. "I have met a lot of people," he said warily. "And my memory is not so good."

"I'm sure of it." The Orion tugged thoughtfully on a giant earlobe as his beady eyes studied the Klingon's face. "What did you do during the war?"

"That is none of your business," answered Maltz defensively.

"He was right here with the rest of us," said Bekra. "Sweating it out."

But the Orion was shaking his finger and smiling with satisfaction. "Yes, I remember it now. I never forget a face, especially not a distinctive one like yours! It was probably thirty years ago, when I was in the prison supply business."

"I am not interested," grumbled Maltz. Actually he had no idea what the Orion was about to say, but he truly didn't want to hear anything about his past, whether it was factual or not.

"You were a bounty hunter."

Now the Klingon's stomach heaved, and he felt the bile of almost a century of dodging the past come surging up his throat. Maltz gripped his larynx and caught the bile before it spilled out, then he caught the snide Orion by the throat and lifted him off the tiled floor.

"Yes, I have been a bounty hunter," he snarled, "and worse than that. But I have never been a freeloader who drifts in here out of nowhere expecting to be wined and dined for free!"

"Maltz!" shouted Bekra with alarm, trying to pry his grip from the gagging Orion. "Set him down!"

It was then the Mikulak and the Dopterian attacked Maltz, with the Mikulak wrapping long tentacles around his neck, while the shorter Dopterian punched him rapidly in the stomach. The Klingon had to drop the Orion, but he smashed his vase over the Dopterian's head, coating the bug-eyed creature in blue ale. Then he grabbed the tray of truffles and smashed the Mikulak into submission, while he laughed with delight.

The two Talavians tackled Maltz from the rear and propelled him into a serving table, which crumpled under their weight, spilling punch and desserts over all of them. The melee continued on the floor in a churning heap of limbs and foamy punch. Maltz was all elbows, fists, and hobnailed boots, smashing anything that came within range.

Ah, it felt good to fight! There were no friends or enemies, just the enemy—he had to silence them all! Maltz barely noticed when three beefy constables rushed in from the street and joined the fray.

"Cowards!" he roared.

The old Klingon was still hollering and kicking when the exasperated constables leaped to their feet, drew phaser pistols, and shot him with pinpoint blue beams.

Peace at last, thought Maltz as his body stilled and consciousness drifted away.

"Geordi," said Data, tapping his friend on the shoulder. He kept his voice low in the efficient hum of activity on the bridge. "I must speak with you."

"Just a minute," answered the engineer impatiently as he gazed at his readouts. "The long-range sensor scan is just coming in, and it's pretty bizarre. I can't figure out what's going on out there."

"We should know in twelve hours and forty-five minutes," said the android. "Meanwhile, I have a recital to perform, and you have a date."

Geordi scowled and finally looked up from his console among

the circle of stations on the *Enterprise* bridge. Commander Riker was conferring with the officer on the conn, probably refining their course setting. "Can't you pick her up?" whispered Geordi. "She's interested in seeing *you*, anyway."

The android leaned closer. "We are enroute at maximum warp, and your concern will not make us reach Outpost Seran-T-One any faster."

Geordi blinked at his friend, feigning ignorance. "What do you mean . . . Seran-T-One? Why there?"

"Is that not where Dr. Leah Brahms lives?" asked Data with sympathy. "In addition, every long-range scan you have done has been centered on Outpost Seran-T-One."

Geordi smiled, thinking that Data didn't miss much. "Okay, so I'm worried about her. Do you think we'll get back to the bridge fairly soon?"

Data cocked his head thoughtfully. "I will play the violin six percent faster and cut out my curtain call."

"Okay, it's a deal." Geordi rose from the station and crossed the center clearing to Commander Riker. "Sir, Data and I will be back in a little while."

"Get some rest," suggested Riker. "We'll let you know if we find out anything of interest, but I kind of doubt it. Data, sorry I'll miss the show."

The android nodded with tacit understanding, and he waited by the turbolift until La Forge caught up. The two of them boarded the lift and went hurtling down to level six, where there was a wing devoted to guest quarters, close to the main shuttlebay for convenience sake.

For once, Data didn't practice his small talk, and Geordi was grateful for the silence. The engineer tried to tell himself there were a million logical—or even implausible—reasons for the communications to be out while the population was still fine. They weren't at war, and there hadn't been any unusual activity reported by any of the posts or settlements. Still, he had seen enough in his twenty years in Starfleet to be worried about things that weren't seen or reported.

He parted company with Data and quickly found the corridor devoted to guest quarters. Normally Geordi would have been nervous, but he had so much on his mind that this date seemed like an afterthought. He chimed her door and waited.

When the door opened, Dolores Linton was standing about a meter away from him, an intense look in her sultry eyes. She was dressed in a formfitting black evening gown that a regular crew member wouldn't have dared to wear. A slit up to her thigh showed her muscular legs, while the sleeveless gown revealed an impressively developed upper body, too. Geordi could see an aura of vibrant energy about her, and he sincerely regretted that he would have to shortchange her on this date.

"Hello," he said, trying to muster as much charm and enthusiasm as he could under a cloud of worry. "I'm sorry I'm a few minutes late."

"Don't worry about that. Come in." With a firm grip, she took his arm and pulled him into the small single quarters. The room was cluttered with climbing gear, collection boxes, chemicals, stasis bags, tricorders, and other tools of her profession, and there was barely room to stand.

The geologist put her hands on her hips and demanded. "Okay, what is the deal with them canceling our mission?"

Geordi was caught off guard by this topic of conversation, but of course that had to be a big disappointment to the visiting team of specialists. Plus they probably hadn't been told very much about the circumstances.

"Well, it's only been postponed while we check something out," he answered. "This kind of thing happens, especially to the *Enterprise*."

"What are we checking out?" she asked bluntly.

"Loss of contact with a sector not far from here." He shrugged. "It will probably turn out to be nothing, and we'll only lose a couple of days. Are you ready to go see Data perform?"

"Looking forward to it," she answered, taking his arm and gazing at him with those disconcerting dark eyes. "In fact, I have a lot of free time now, so tell me about everything there is to do on the *Enterprise*."

"Well, we have a large library, an exercise facility, recreation room, and holodecks, although you need a reservation for those." The door opened, and they strolled into the corridor.

"Holodecks aren't my cup of tea," said Dolores, shaking her medium-length brown hair. "I prefer real thrills and real fresh air. Please don't tell the ship's doctor, but I suffer from a bit of claustrophobia. I'm always glad to get out of these tin cans and back to solid ground, even if it's a Class-H planetoid."

"A Class-H planetoid?" asked Geordi, only half-listening.

"You're a million light-years from here, Commander," said the woman with bemusement. "Usually when I wear this dress, I have my date's undivided attention."

"I'm sorry, really," he stammered. "I have to admit that I'm concerned about this detour we're taking, because I have a good friend who lives out there. I'll be happier than anyone when we find out it's nothing."

She nodded sympathetically. "By the worry lines on your face, I think it must be a lady friend."

"No, Leah is a . . . a fellow engineer." Geordi lowered his head and plowed down the corridor, embarrassed by the direction of the conversation. Dolores Linton seemed to be one of those people who said anything she felt like saying. Maybe that was a luxury enjoyed by those who flitted from one place to another, disappearing in the wilds for weeks at a time.

"This way to the turbolift," he said, motioning to the color encoded lines which ran the length of the corridor.

"Oh, there's a turbolift down there?" remarked Dolores in amaze-ment. "I didn't know. I get so lost on ships. When you caught me today, I was just riding around on the lift, seeing how many decks there were. I've been on a lot of space stations smaller than this ves-sel. Seriously, Commander, if you get any free time at all, I'd love a tour of the *Enterprise*. Might as well, if I'm going to spend some time on shoreleave."

"We'll see," he answered with a half-smile. "And call me Geordi."

"You had to go and smash up the Cultural Affairs Center," said a chiding voice, followed by tongue clicking. "You're going to get a nasty bill."

"Aarghh," murmured the Klingon as he shuddered awake and stared at a brown ceiling carved with thousands of chit marks. With a grunt, Maltz swung his legs over the edge of the bed and finally succeeded in sitting up. "I thought I was dead."

"You sound disappointed," said Consul Bekra, standing outside a holding cell in an earthen room with a low ceiling and no windows. A shimmering force-field guarded the cell door.

"I am," grumbled Maltz.

"Come on, it's not that bad." The Capellan chuckled with amusement. "You'll be glad to know, none of our guests were seri-ously injured, and I think they relished the opportunity to tangle with a Klingon. At least you lived up to your advance billing. Not everything in life does."

"I'm gratified the tourists were happy," rasped the old Klingon. "How long do I have to stay in here?"

"You know how it works—you have to see the magistrate." Bekra stepped away from the wall and walked toward the door. "I'll do what I can to move the process along."

"Thanks."

"Hey! Hey, out there!" The Capellan stood by the door, trying to attract someone's attention to let him out. He finally gave up and turned back to Maltz. "Is it true you were once a bounty hunter?"

"Yes," muttered the Klingon. "I thought somebody would kill me back then, too. But nobody ever did."

The outer door suddenly opened, allowing more light and a cacophony of voices to flood into the quiet holding cell. It sounded as if a full-scale melee was taking place in the waiting room. Maltz tried to ignore it and concentrate on his thumping headache, but the voices were too loud and insistent. A Tellarite constable dressed in a red-and-white plaid uniform ducked into the room, looking as if he were trying to escape from the racket.

"What is going on out there?" asked Bekra.

"Two people have landed in a damaged shuttlecraft," answered the constable. "They're claiming that some kind of strange energy wave destroyed Seran and is coming after us."

"An energy wave destroyed a whole planet?" asked Bekra doubtfully. "Did they say what it was?"

The Tellarite shrugged. "Something about a green fire consuming the planet, turning it into sludge."

Maltz gasped and nearly fell out of his bed. "What!" he shouted, rushing the door. "What did they say *exactly*?" In his enthusiasm, he got too close to the door, and the force-field shocked him, hurling him to the floor.

"Careful there!" called the guard angrily. "You just sit tight until the magistrate gets here."

"I've got to see those people!" shouted Maltz desperately. He staggered to his feet, careful not to trip the force-field again. "Please, Officer, you've got to let me see them."

"You're in enough trouble already," scolded Bekra. "Would it help if *I* talked to them?"

The constable shrugged. "Well, they are asking to speak to important people, but we don't know what to tell them. They claim we haven't got any time, that we have to evacuate the planet." He snorted a laugh. "As if we could."

"Please!" roared the Klingon. "I know what they're talking about. Let me see them!"

With a scowl, the angry guard pushed Bekra out the door and slammed it shut behind him. Maltz could still hear muffled voices, but he couldn't hear any specifics. He howled like a wounded animal and dropped to his knees, beating his fists against his craggy skull.

"Listen to me!" he moaned. "I knew someone would use the device again . . . I *know* what it is!"

But no one was listening.

six

"Listen! Listen to me, please!" begged Leah Brahms, pushing up the sleeves on her jumpsuit and leaning over the amber desk to stare at an enormous Tellarite. She still couldn't believe this quaint hovel was the regional police station. "You've got to get ready to evacuate," she told them. "How many space vehicles have you got?"

The chief Tellarite raised his beefy hands and smiled condescendingly at her. According to a plate on his desk, he was a proctor. "Now you listen for a second . . . what did you say your name was?"

"Dr. Leah Brahms," she answerd impatiently for the nineteenth time. "I'm in the Science Service, I was once in the Theoretical Propulsion Group, I run the lab on Outpost Seran-T-One." With a lump in her throat, she correctd herself. "I mean, I *ran* it before it was totally destroyed about fourteen hours ago."

"That's what we're trying to ascertain," said the proctor importantly as he shuffled papers and motioned to his confederates. "We've got to discover the facts in the matter. So far, the only fact we know is that the two of you landed in a shuttlecraft, which isn't all that unusual."

Leah turned with exasperation to her colleague, Paldor, but the Tellarite was in shock. He'd had no idea that Hakon was such a sleepy backwater of a place, where no one would pay any attention to their anguished cries of warning. She could see from the despair on his face that he realized all of these people were going to die, and no doubt the two of them as well.

"Paldor," she said, trying to wake him from his reverie. "Tell them it's true! That a destructive wave is coming."

"Huh?" he said, blinking at her like a person coming out of a trance. "All they have are farms and a small village. They haven't got any labs here."

"A subspace radio," she told the officer at the desk. "There's got to be *some* way for you to contact other planets. Try contacting Seran, where we came from." She snapped her fingers. "Or better yet, let us try to contact Starfleet! We've got to warn the rest of the Federation."

Several of the smug constables chuckled at her earnestness. "We don't have any reason to contact other planets from this station," said the proctor slowly, as if talking to a child. "The spaceport probably has that capability. So do the ships in orbit."

"The spaceport!" exclaimed Leah, clinging to any semblance of advanced civilization in this provincial hamlet. "Yes, how can we get there?"

"It's about forty kilometers on the outskirts of town," explained the constable, pointing out the window at a row of mudflats.

"They can't help you," said a cultured voice coming from behind Leah. She whirled around to see an elegantly dressed Capellan; he shook his lofty turban sadly. "The spaceport is nothing but an automated system to handle our freighter and passenger traffic, which isn't much."

"Who are you?" asked Brahms, hoping he was the mayor or someone of enough rank to get things done.

"Capellan Trade Consul Bekra, at your service," he answered with a smart bow.

She gripped his turquoise collar, which brought a grimace of distaste to his dignified face. "Listen, Bekra, you've got to believe me—everyone on this planet is going to *die*! Do you understand me?"

"Do you have proof of this?" he asked gravely.

From the pocket of her jumpsuit, Leah removed an isolinear chip, which she waved in his face. "I've got this and another copy back in our shuttlecraft. But this is raw data—sensor readings, vidlogs, and recollections—you'd have to spend some time analyzing it. And you don't *have* any time."

"Let me see that!" ordered the constable, reaching across his desk and snatching the isolinear chip from her fingers. "You say this contains evidence?"

"Not evidence . . . data!" The human rolled her eyes in exasperation. "No crime's been committed—this is more like a natural disaster, I think. Do you have someone who can analyze our data?"

"We've got our medical examiner and the professors at the agricultural college," said the constable proudly. "First thing in the morning, we'll take this to them and—"

"No, no!" shouted Leah, balling her hands into fists and shaking them at the dense constable. "You're not listening to me! You won't be here 'first thing in the morning.' This entire planet will be pulverized into something . . . some kind of new life-form. You, your wife, your kids, your friends—"

"Now, you listen to *me*!" roared the proctor, jumping to his feet and shaking a beefy fist at her. "Around here, we don't tolerate people creating a public disturbance, and you're doing just that. We're a simple people—we don't look kindly on doomsday cults. We've got a sensor warning system in place from the war, and it hasn't put out so much as a *peep*."

"This is pointless," said Paldor, shaking his head miserably. "You're all doomed."

"That's quite enough of that!" bellowed the belligerent chief. As his fellows moved from behind the counter and surrounded them with a bulky phalanx, the proctor pointed toward the door. "Now get out of here, both of you. We've got your data, and we'll study it. And don't leave town."

"Come along," said the Capellan, putting a protective arm around Leah Brahms. She was so disillusioned—and fearful—that she let the consul lead her out of the building into the street, where the cheery sunshine did seem to belie their dire warnings. The weather had been just as beautiful on Seran seconds before the ungodly fire scourged everything, she recalled. How much time did they have? Hours? Seconds?

Paldor stumbled after Leah and bumped into her. "I'm sorry, Doctor. You were right—we should have kept running."

She turned again to the popinjay in his conical turban. "Have *you* got a ship, some way we can contact the Federation? Or at the very least some equipment, so we can repair our shuttlecraft?"

"Speaking of which, I should get back to the shuttlecraft," said Paldor, rousting himself from his stupor. "I'll keep our sensors running."

"Stay in contact via combadge," ordered Brahms, "and be ready to beam me back." Intellectually, she knew she had to fight through the locals' ignorance and make them understand, but part of her just wanted to get the hell out of there. Most of her reasons to live were gone, but the urge to save herself was still amazingly strong. Some internal motor wouldn't let her stand still and have that nightmarish wave strip her flesh off her bones.

"You're in charge, Doctor," Paldor gave her a grave bow, acknowledging that he had been wrong. He was also assigning his life to her hands, a fact which weighed heavily on her.

"I'll do what I can," she promised. "Go on."

With a nod, the Tellarite scurried off, glancing suspiciously around him. And well he might, because it looked as if the constables had been watching them from the station. Two of them took off in pursuit of Paldor, rushing right by Leah and the Capellan consul.

"Your ship," she told the Capellan. "We've got to contact somebody."

"All I've got is a shuttlecraft, too," he answered apologetically. "It doesn't even have warp drive, I'm afraid, but there is a subspace relay to my homeworld."

"Will they believe me?"

"Even if they do, what can they do to help?" asked Bekra rhetorically. "They're two thousand light-years away. You know, this planet *does* have sensors. If there was anything—"

"It's not like anything we've seen before," cut in Leah, shaking her head. "I've got to make *somebody* believe."

The Capellan grimaced. "Well, there is somebody who might be inclined to believe you, but he couldn't do much to help you either."

"Why is that?" she asked impatiently. "Who is this person?"

"Another consul. A Klingon. Unfortunately, he's a prisoner in the station we just left."

She blinked at the stranger. "Why should he believe me? Is he a scientist?"

"No, but he's old, and he's seen many things in his life. He thinks he's seen this energy wave of yours—I've heard him talking about it." The diplomat shrugged. "Then again, he may be insane."

"If he's seen what I saw, he has every right to be insane." Leah shuddered and looked back at the station, wondering if anything she could do on Hakon would make any difference. Evacuating entire planets on the spur of the moment was not going to work, not unless she had the whole Federation behind her. To get support, she needed more information. If there was any chance to find out more about that awesome force, she had to take it.

"Can we see this Klingon?" she asked.

Bekra sighed, as if realizing he was getting himself deeper into a quagmire. "You'd better not be getting me into trouble. I have to work with these people."

"Believe me, by tomorrow, that will be the least of your worries." Leah fixed him with a doleful stare.

The Capellan took her elbow and guided her back toward the station. "I wish I weren't starting to believe you, because you're frightening me."

"So far you're the only one." Leah Brahms made a concerted effort to soften her expression as they reentered the two-story police station. The half-dozen Tellarite officers in the waiting room regarded them warily as they approached the desk, and the big proctor snorted and tugged on his bristling orange beard.

"I thought I told you to leave?" he said gruffly.

"Our visitor . . . she thinks she may know Consul Maltz," answered Bekra quickly.

The big Tellarite smiled and glanced at his fellows. "She thinks she knows Maltz? Why does *that* not surprise me?"

"Listen," said Bekra, leaning across the desk and lowering his voice, "when the magistrate gets here, I'll make it easy on everyone by vouching for Maltz and paying any fines."

"Oh, he's not getting out of here so easy," said the proctor with satisfaction. "He attacked three constables and tore up a peaceful gathering. I've got a dozen witnesses who say it was his fault, and we'd like to teach that big oaf a lesson."

"I doubt if he even knew he was fighting three constables," answered the Capellan. "Can't you let her see him for a moment? I'll go with her."

"Why should I?"

"Because I'd be willing to take Maltz away from here," answered Leah forcefully. "Take him clear off the planet, out of your hands."

The Tellarite considered that for a moment, then pointed a chubby finger at her. "You'd better not get him riled up." He motioned to one of his underlings. "Let them in. Ten minutes, no more."

"Yes, Sir." A constable motioned to them, and Leah and Bekra dutifully followed. He opened a door, and they entered a room that seemed even more clammy and oppressive than the waiting room, due to its windowless, earthen walls. It was unusually cool in here, too, and Leah shivered and hugged her arms. The four small cells were all empty, except for the one on the end, wherein stood a tall, wild-eyed, bushy-haired Klingon, glaring at them.

He was grizzled and old, but he also looked defiant and vibrantly alive, like a wild animal kept in a zoo. The Klingon cautiously approached the door, shimmering with a force-field barrier, as Leah Brahms warily approached him.

"Did you see it?" he rasped.

"What is it?" she asked dubiously. "Describe it."

His big hands gestured in the air and his eyes blazed with the remembrance of a tale he had been told, or perhaps a tape he had seen. "It sweeps across the land like a burning curtain, ripping up everything. But it leaves new life—strange life—growing in its place. There are geysers, a terrible wind, mountains shooting up, awful things . . . growing in the muck."

"Yes! Yes! What is it?" she gasped. At last she would know that nameless force that killed her husband and colleagues.

The Klingon glanced suspiciously at the Capellan, who was leaning against the wall near the door. "I should not tell you. Your own government considers it top secret."

Leah gaped at him. "Are you telling me that *we* invented this thing? That it's *artificial?*"

"Is it a weapon?" asked Bekra, suddenly interested.

"It did not start out that way," the Klingon answered enigmatically. "You say, they set it off on Seran?"

"Nobody set it off . . . I don't think." Leah shook her head, unable to believe this explanation. "What you described sounds right, but this was an energy wave—moving through space. It hit Seran and all of her moons, and it's coming right this way, expanding as it goes."

"Moving through space," said Maltz, scratching his long white beard. "Maybe they improved it."

"Who is *they?*" demanded Leah. "Who controls this thing?"

"You do!" growled the Klingon. "You are the only ones who know the technology."

Leah's shoulders slumped, and the scowl returned to her face. "You're wrong. Nobody would unleash this against their own people. Like they say, maybe you *are* crazy."

The old Klingon howled with laughter, then he held up a triumphant finger, his eyes blazing. "I know the code word—what your people called this device many years ago. The Klingon High Council has our reports, but we never learned how to make it. All this time, I have *feared* it would be used again, and now it has."

"Ridiculous!" snapped Leah, marching toward the door. "Get me out of here, Bekra. He is mad."

"Mad?" said the Klingon, stifling a laugh. "Such great power you have never seen, have you? Such a force for change you have never seen. It takes matter and *guts* it, leaving behind something chaotic and loathsome."

Leah turned again and stared at the wild Klingon. If he hadn't seen it, then he had seen something eerily close. But the notion that this horror might be an invention fostered by her own government—a weapon—was repulsive in the extreme.

The door opened, and Maltz yelled one more thing. "How much time do we have?"

"A few hours," she answered, pausing in the doorway. "Maybe ten. Maybe one."

At that, the Klingon grew somber and gaunt, and Leah could see desperation and fear working in his rheumy eyes. It was the same desperation and fear that she felt churning in her stomach. She didn't want to believe him any more than the Tellarites wanted to believe her, but at that moment, she feared the old Klingon spoke the truth.

"The performance was lovely," gushed Dolores Linton, shaking Data's outstretched hand. The android was dressed in tuxedo and tails and looked very dapper, thought La Forge. Despite the high spirits at the end of the performance, most of the audience dispersed swiftly from the Antares Theater on deck fifteen. It was if everyone realized their mission had assumed an element of the unknown, and they had better stay close to their posts.

Geordi wanted to escape quickly, too, but Dolores Linton wanted to stay behind and congratulate Data. To people who had never heard the violin played to weeping perfection, a performance by Data was sheer magic. Geordi was fortunate enough to have heard him play many times. Although he wanted to get back to the bridge, he couldn't deny his friend a chance to hear a new fan tell him how wonderful he was. Geordi tried not to fidget, but the recital had lasted longer than he expected. Plus Data had been forced to take a curtain call, captain's prerogative.

"And your sustains are sublime," said the vivacious geologist as she studied Data's hands. "Your finger strength must be phenomenal. I bet you could do anything you wanted to do with these hands."

"When I first started," said the android, "I broke many strings. The fragility of the violin is a large part of its appeal."

"Yes, you have to handle fragile things with care," replied Dolores, gently stroking Data's palm.

"You should see his paintings," added Geordi, just trying to enter into the flow of the small talk.

"I would like to," answered the geologist, sounding in awe of the android.

"Another time," replied Data with a pointed nod to Geordi as he withdrew his hand and backed off.

Thankfully, there were only a handful of well-wishers left, and Geordi could edge toward the door without feeling guilty. "I'd like to give you that tour I promised," he began slowly, "but we don't know what we're getting into."

"Duty calls," said Dolores, shaking her pert brown hair and flexing a sizable bicep. "I really appreciate your bringing me to hear Data play. I wouldn't have come otherwise. I probably just would've sat in my room, stewing over the messed-up schedule."

"What is our delay going to mean to you?" asked Geordi as they strolled down the corridor.

"We were already on a tight schedule, and if we can't get done with Itamish III in eight weeks, then the team is going to have to delay another start. Then another. And we're booked a year in advance." Dolores smiled and batted her eyes playfully. "We're real popular."

"I can see that," said Geordi, reaching the turbolift and holding it for her. They stepped inside, and he added, "We hardly ever know what we're doing two months from now, or even two days from now. We're always in scramble mode."

The turbolift door shut, and Dolores said, "Level six." Then she turned to Geordi and smiled warmly. "Thank you for a great evening."

"I'm sorry it has to end so soon," he answered apologetically.

"Does it have to end so soon?" Dolores asked pointedly. "I heard them say that we're not going to reach the area for about ten hours."

"Uh, yes," stammered Geordi. "That's true." The door opened, and Dolores gave him a sly smile and stepped out. La Forge took a gulp of air and followed the sauntering figure in the skintight black dress.

She led the way to her quarters, letting him trail along behind her like a puppy dog. Since he didn't know what to say to her, he didn't catch up until she had reached her door. Then she turned to him, not with a sultry look but with doe-eyed sympathy.

"You know," said Dolores softly, touching his cheek, "there's something very appealing about a man in love . . . with someone else." She raised an eyebrow. "I hope she's worth all the anguish you're going through, worrying about her. Good night, Geordi. Thanks for the lovely evening."

Her hand touching his cheek wasn't exactly a kiss, but it felt like one as she pulled her fingertips away.

"I could check with the bridge," said Geordi uncertainly.

"Good night. Just don't forget my tour." With a whoosh of the door sliding shut, Dolores Linton was gone.

Geordi immediately hit his combadge. "La Forge to bridge."

"Riker here," came the answer.

"Have there been any developments?"

"Well, one small one," answered the first officer. "In addition to the other distress signal, we're now picking up a Capellan distress signal from a planet named Hakon. We're changing course now, because it's not much out of our way."

"Changing course?" asked Geordi with alarm. "I thought we were headed to Outpost Seran-T-One." He began charging down the corridor.

"It's on the edge of sector 4368," answered Riker. "There isn't a lot of traffic out here, so we've got to follow these distress signals, now that they've converged. They're our only clue that something's wrong."

La Forge bit his lip, knowing that he couldn't argue with his superior, and Riker read the silence perfectly. "Don't worry, Geordi, we'll find out what's going on. I've got Data on ops running ten times as many scans as you can, and I really don't need you on the bridge. Isn't there somewhere else you can go?"

The engineer stopped and looked back down the corridor at

Dolores Linton's door. He took a deep breath and finally said, "I promise I won't pace too much."

"Okay, see you on the bridge. Riker out."

His brow furrowed with worry, the chief engineer strode toward the turbolift. He could almost hear Data berating him for his hapless handling of Mission Specialist Linton. This was all just one more reason to regret his obsession with Leah Brahms, an obsession Data could never understand.

seven

"Here's your shopping list," said Leah Brahms, handing a padd to her comrade, Paldor, who stood outside the open hatch of the shuttlecraft. "If we can get these parts, I think we can fix the comm array."

Looking dismayed, the young Tellarite glanced at her and then at the gawkers who surrounded the vacant field where they had landed. Three of them were constables in red-and-white checked uniforms, and he lowered his voice to say, "I don't know where to begin. I doubt if they have *half* this stuff."

"Come on, they're your people, and you wanted to come here," Leah reminded him, instantly regretting her testiness. "It may be a farming community, but they're still part of the Federation. Ask around. I saw some sophisticated gear for monitoring the weather, so they must have antennas and dish arrays. We've also seen replicators."

"And money? What am I supposed to use for money?" asked the Tellarite skeptically.

Leah pointed to the screen of the handheld padd. "I have a blank purchase order right there on behalf of the Science Service. They should honor it anywhere in the Federation."

The Tellarite's orange beard bristled. "But this hasn't been requisitioned. That's illegal."

"You and I are probably already presumed dead," said Leah through clenched teeth. "Chances are we're really going to be dead unless we get some help. Now get me the stuff on that list."

"Yes, Doctor," said the Tellarite, recoiling from her gaze. He took a few steps from the shuttlecraft but turned back to her, pain etched in his small, black eyes. "I can't stand to talk to them . . . knowing they're all going to die."

"I know it's hard," admitted Leah. "Maybe your calculations were wrong, and it'll miss here."

"No," said Paldor grimly. "But even if they believed us, I don't know what they could do on such short notice."

"Just get our stuff," ordered Brahms, growing exasperated. She didn't want to be cold to the plight of these people, but she had seen her husband and friends perish in the consuming flame. Strangers were important, but she had no emotions left to grieve for them. Maybe living their last day in ignorant bliss instead of panic was a blessing.

"I'll be back as soon as I can," said Paldor. He hurried off, taking with him two of the constables, who followed at a discreet distance.

Leah couldn't worry about that now, because her associate's departure would finally let her try something she'd been eager to do. She hurried back into the shuttlecraft and shut the door behind her, blocking out the prying eyes surrounding the field. Then she sat at the pilot's console and ran a sensor scan of the constable station a couple of blocks away. She wanted to see if she could locate the Klingon in his cell, or at least find the force-field that marked his door. Then she would get a lock on him with the transporter.

No such luck. Surrounding the entire station was a dampening field, making it impossible to beam people in or out. These folks weren't the hayseeds they appeared, and she had to forget about pulling off a painless jailbreak. Although the dampening field worked against her, it wouldn't do anything to stop the monstrous force headed their way.

It would, however, keep her from getting easy access to the Klingon and whatever he knew. So all she could do now was watch the sensors and the darkening sky, wondering how much time they really had left.

Maltz paced in his cell, suddenly more sober than he had been in the last fifty years. All he knew was that he had to get out of this place and help that poor, deluded human. He should have helped her more when she was standing in front of him, but if she persisted in thinking it was a natural disaster, then she was a bigger fool than those fat constables. They had to be honest about what they were fighting. Like most objects of true horror, the Genesis Device was artificially designed.

But who had control of it now? Who had turned it into an energy wave that could sweep across space? One thing was certain: he wasn't going to get any answers sitting in this cell. He had to get out of here—or he'd be left to die like a caged animal.

Unfortunately, Maltz knew how long it took to roust the magistrate, if they even knew which bars to search. He glanced around at the brown earthen walls and shimmering force-field, realizing he had to arrange his own release. The Klingon had thought about breaking out of here before, but his rashness was always tempered by the knowledge that he would have to deal with these people the next day. Now there would be no tomorrow.

Although they had taken his knife, they had left him with his ceremonial chain-mail sash, not knowing what a treasure trove a Klingon's sash could be. He surveyed the room again, thinking those rustic walls and ceiling could house video-log equipment. But he decided that even if they were recording him, he was the only prisoner, and they probably weren't paying very much attention. Besides, he would look as if he were repairing his clothing, and it certainly needed it, after that brawl.

Maltz removed his sash at the same time that he removed his cloak. He wanted to look as if he were just getting comfortable, preparing to stay for a while. He sat on his cot and hunched his broad back, trying to shut off their view, while he turned over his sash and unsnapped the back lining. From hidden crevices and folds, he drew forth his arsenal: three small throwing daggers, a garrote and fishing line, a stiletto, a vial of deadly poison, a vial of acid, a wad of gel explosive, knuckle armor, lockpicks, sewing kit, Klingon communicator badge, and five strips of latinum.

The last object he withdrew was a small signal mirror, only it wouldn't be used for signaling today. Carefully he returned all the other objects to their hiding places, except for the explosives, the mirror, and the armor to fortify his knuckles.

Maltz palmed these objects while he put his cloak and sash back on. Then he strolled over to the door of his cell and bent down, as if fixing something on his boot. In his experience, every force-field had blind spots near the edge, between the field emitters. These blind spots were only a few centimeters across, which didn't do a normal-sized person a lot of good. But Maltz also knew that a force-field wall was actually thousands of criss-crossing beams, and that a beam reflected back onto itself caused all sorts of havoc.

Using his knuckle armor, he slowly pushed the mirror across the floor, probing for a blind spot between the emitters. The mirror bounced off the shimmering barrier a few times, but each time he caught it in midair and patiently tried again. Finally he succeeded in slipping the reflective glass under the pulsing shield, and he gave a satisfied grunt. Now penetration in the right spot would change the direction of the beams just enough that they would strike the mirror on the floor and be deflected upward. When that happened, the force-field would be attacking itself.

He couldn't conceal what he would do next, but if he moved quickly enough, perhaps his jailers wouldn't notice. He ran to his cot and grabbed his threadbare mattress. Holding it in front of him like a battering ram, the Klingon gritted his teeth and charged the door of his cell. The mattress hit the force-field and was propelled back into his face, but the Klingon kept charging forward as a lightning bolt rippled across the doorway. With a burst of smoke and sparks, the force-field imploded, and the shimmering curtain blinked erratically. Maltz's momentum carried him and the mattress through the opening into a heap on the floor. He was free—then a siren screamed directly over his head.

Maltz leaped to his feet, slipping the knuckle armor over his fist just as the outer door opened. The first one through happened to be the haughty proctor, and he received a crushing blow straight to the snout that sent him reeling into the wall. Before the big Tellarite even hit the floor, the Klingon had ripped the disruptor from his holster, and he sent a wild beam streaking through the outer doorway—just to keep the others at bay.

Maltz quickly slammed the outer door shut and propped the Tellarite's unconscious body against it. He chuckled at the shouting and commotion outside in the waiting room, and he ignored them when they began to demand that he give himself up.

"You can't get past us!" they shouted.

He had no intentions of going past them. Gingerly, he retrieved his mirror from the doorway of the cell, which was attempting to return to normal. With his newly acquired disruptor, he drilled a small hole about waist-high in a wall which abutted the outdoors. The Klingon stuffed his tiny wad of gel explosive into the hole he had made, then stepped back. With steely-eyed fearlessness, he adjusted the disruptor to maximum and blasted the charge he had planted.

The resulting explosion rocked the neighborhood and sent a cloud of dust and debris spewing twenty meters into the air. It also blew open a hole in the wall about a meter across, through which staggered a bedraggled Klingon, his clothes and facial hair still smoldering. With shouts and whistles, concerned citizens began converging on the smoky site, and Maltz had to shake himself off and run for it. He covered his head with his cloak, hoping no one would be able to give a good description of him.

As he rounded a corner and dashed down a side street, Maltz tried to figure out where he could go or what he could do. He had to find the strange woman and her shuttlecraft, that much was sure. But he didn't know where she was, and he couldn't very well start asking; in fact, he had to stay out of sight, if possible. The constables would really be after him now.

As the Klingon staggered into the shadows and slumped behind a trash vaporizer, he remembered someone who knew where she was. His old colleague, Consul Bekra. If he knew the Capellan, he was probably taking measures to save his own skin. That would mean a trip to the hangar where he kept his shuttlecraft.

"Urgh, why don't I have a shuttlecraft like everyone else?" muttered the old Klingon. He knew the reason—they didn't trust him with one.

Maltz unfolded the hood from his cloak and pulled it over his head, hoping to hide his head ridges and shock of hair. But he glanced at himself in his signal mirror and realized it wasn't enough, so he took the sewing kit from his sash. Using a pair of small scissors and the mirror, he clipped off most of his distinctive beard and moustache. A lot of it was singed, anyway, and it wasn't hair that made a Klingon.

Now when he looked at himself in the mirror, he looked sufficiently different to fool people at a glance. With a groan, Maltz dragged himself to his feet and wrapped the cloak around his gaunt frame. He had a long walk through back streets to reach the shuttle hangar, but at least the sky was darkening. Soon it would be night on this part of Hakon.

Rubbing her arms in the suddenly chill air, Leah Brahms stepped out of the shuttlecraft and looked at the crimson clouds backlighting the skyline. Light shifted on the earthen walls of the rustic dwellings, making them look like an eroded slope deep in the desert; and for the first time, Leah appreciated the naturalistic architecture. However, she wasn't too thrilled about the idea of night falling in this quaint village.

That was silly, because the awful force which chased them moved almost too swiftly to be seen. Still, she didn't want it to sneak up on her in the darkness. With a gulp, the scientist stepped closer to the open hatch of the shuttlecraft, so that she could hear the sensor alert she had programmed. Once the wave came within sensor range, they would only have a few minutes. How many minutes, it was anyone's guess.

A furry animal about the size of a goat strolled through the vacant lot, a bell ringing from its collar. It stopped to consider her for a moment, then shook its bell and walked on. She had noticed a decline in the presence of the onlookers, who had probably gone home to eat the food she smelled wafting on the breeze. The police presence was still high, hovering around six or seven ever since that explosion an hour ago. No one had explained what the explosion was about, but it had obviously cast suspicion upon the doomsayers.

Leah figured even more constables were following Paldor, who had yet to return from his shopping trip. This was bad, because she didn't know if they could effect repairs before they had to run for it. The Tellarite had checked in via combadge to say that he was making progress, albeit slowly, but that wasn't much consolation. She still couldn't do anything but wait, and Leah had never been good at waiting.

Leah glanced inside the shuttlecraft at the radiation suit, hulking silently in the rear. She didn't want to put it on again, but that gnawing, mindless drive for survival was urging her to don the suit. But to put on the suit meant that she had given up and was willing to watch another planet die. Besides, she needed full dexterity to pilot the shuttlecraft, because if they lost the shuttlecraft, there would be no escape at all. No way to warn anyone else. At the moment, the shuttlecraft and the data they had collected were more important than anything.

I'll have enough warning, Leah told herself, not really believing it was true. She stepped inside the shuttlecraft and shut the door, blocking out the crimson sunset that was bathing the mud-colored street in a warm glow.

As Maltz pushed open the window, which he had unlocked with his lockpicks, he could smell the scent of something burning. Choking smoke didn't fill the cavernous shuttlecraft hangar, but he could see light at the far end of the building, silhouetting a dozen boxy shuttlecraft. In fact, that was the only light in the whole building, now that night had fallen. He sniffed again, deciding that *something* was burning at the far end of the building.

As he stalked through the dark hangar, moving from one shuttlecraft to another, the Klingon drew his disruptor from his belt. There were windows on every wall, but the only light came from a work light hanging in the far corner, illuminating a shuttlecraft with its hatch open. It looked like somebody was packing to leave.

He drew closer, keeping to the shadows. To no surprise, it was the Capellan consul, Bekra, and he was burning papers, transparencies, and isolinear chips in a trash receptacle, where he had a considerable fire going. Bekra wasn't dressed in his usual finery, but instead wore a simple black jumpsuit as well as his ubiquitous turban. Duffel bags and boxes of gear sat outside the hatch, ready to be loaded into the waiting shuttlecraft.

"Going somewhere?" asked Maltz, stepping out of the shadows. He kept the disruptor trained on his old colleague.

"Ahh!" shouted Bekra with alarm, having been taken by surprise. He squinted into the wavering light, uncertain who the hooded visitor was. "Is that you, Maltz?"

The old Klingon scratched the stubble on his chin and grinned. "Makes me look younger, I think."

The Capellan laughed nervously. "You don't need that weapon, my old friend. If you want to escape with me in my shuttlecraft, that's no problem. But I have to warn you—I don't have warp drive. I'm thinking that if I leave now, I can get out of the path of that thing . . . if it's really out there."

"It is really out there," said Maltz, stepping toward the small bonfire. "What are you burning up in that can?"

"Oh, nothing of interest," said Bekra, edging toward the open hatch of his shuttlecraft.

"Stop there," ordered the Klingon, aiming his weapon at the Capellan's chest. "Just so you know, I never set weapons to stun. So who have you been spying for all these years?"

"Spying?" Bekra forced a laugh. "You are getting melodramatic in your old age."

Maltz smiled wistfully and kicked the trash can over, spilling its flaming contents on the floor of the hangar. Hoping he was distracted, Bekra bolted for the hatch of his shuttlecraft, but Maltz drilled him in the leg, shearing it off just below the knee. Howling with pain, the Capellan dropped to the floor and writhed, gripping his burnt stump.

He screamed incoherently, while Maltz carefully picked through the smoldering debris.

"I always suspected you," said the Klingon. "Too much brains for this post—you had to have ambitions."

"The first-aid kit!" sputtered the Capellan, twisting in agony.

"You will not die," said the Klingon, scoffing at him. "Unless I have to shoot you again. Now who do you spy for?"

Without warning, the windows all around the enormous hangar imploded, showering them with debris; and a ferocious wind ripped half the corrugated roof off the building, revealing a blazing field of stars in the sky.

The wind churned through the metal cavern, whipping the burning embers from the fire into a glowing funnel cloud. Maltz rocked unsteadily on his feet, while Bekra cried out with fear and rolled under his shuttlecraft.

"The wind!" roared Maltz, holding his ears and gaping at the hole in the roof. "*The wind!*"

eight

Leah Brahms felt the shuttlecraft shake as if it were being vandalized by a mob of hooligans. That was her first thought—that the citizens of Hakon had attacked her for some stupid reason. She punched her board to open the hatch, bolted to her feet, and charged outside, ready to give them hell. Instead she was met by an icy blast of wind—so frigid, it was like being in the Antarctic. It staggered her, and she felt the skin of her face stiffening. She looked up, expecting to see the worst, but the starlit sky was so brilliant that it was like viewing it from space. The distant moon seemed to have a strobe light on it.

She had heard of it getting colder at night in some places, but this was ridiculous. As she shivered and tried to stand her ground in the freezing wind, she noticed that the Tellarites and constables were also running for cover. Their vacant lot was suddenly deserted, and there was a frightened buzzing sound, as if the populace were crying with alarm. This wasn't normal weather.

She ducked back inside the shuttlecraft and shut the hatch, at the same moment that her sensor alarm went off. Without even checking what it was, Leah started the transporter sequence to lock onto Paldor's combadge and bring him back to their tiny refuge, which was shuddering like a grass shack in a hurricane.

The Tellarite appeared on the small transporter pad at the back of the craft, his arms full of dishes and electronic parts, which dropped to the deck as he shivered uncontrollably. "What's . . . happening?" he asked, barely getting the words out.

Leah studied her readouts, and her eyes grew wide with fright. "Oh, my God! The wave attacked the sun first, and it's eating its way around it. This solar system could be without a sun!"

"Will we start to go out of orbit?" asked Paldor, dropping the rest of the spare parts and dashing up the aisle.

Leah shook her head in frustration. "Who knows? The sun should maintain its mass, and it might even remain a star—but what kind of star? Anyway, it will hit us soon. We've got to get out of here."

"But all these people!" said Paldor.

"If you want to stay here and die with them, get out now," said Brahms coldly. "Otherwise, sit down and prepare for launch."

His face ashen, the Tellarite slid into his seat beside her. But he didn't do anything to prepare for launch; he just stared at the blank front screen, weeping. Leah put everything else out of her mind as she plotted a course for the heart of the Federation and set the computer to work on compensating for the wind.

Moments later, the shuttlecraft roared out of the vacant lot, streaking over the tops of the earthen buildings, which were already beginning to crack and fall apart from the extreme cold and gravitational changes. In a panic, people rushed into the street, only to be blasted by the wind and flying debris. There wasn't anything anyone could do for them now, thought Leah grimly.

"I feel alive!" bellowed the old Klingon, shaking his fists into the savage wind as it wreaked havoc in the shuttlecraft hangar. Nothing was left of the roof, and the air was cold and bracing, like a firm slap to the face. Maltz stood tall against the debris which pelted him, shouting down the wind.

"Yes, you Genesis Wave . . . you're a worthy adversary! Come and get me."

The wind was trying to get him, but he wouldn't go down without a fight. His jaw set with determination, Maltz strode toward the shuttlecraft just as a blue phaser beam streaked past him, tearing a hole in his cloak. He ducked down and zigzagged in a crouch, dodging streaks as Bekra continued to shoot wildly at him. Maltz finally reached the injured Capellan and kicked the phaser out of his hand.

"Stop being a pet Q!" shouted the Klingon over the din. "I hate these Federation toadies and all they stand for, so I do not care who your masters are! But you tell me what you have done, or I will leave you here. Understood?"

"Romulans," said Bekra, lowering his head. "I send dispatches to the Romulans. It started out innocently enough, when I—"

Maltz smacked him across the face, setting off another round of whimpering. Then he spit on the Capellan and said, "Romulans! I should kill you, anyway. But you brought the human to me, and she gave me the warning."

The old Klingon pointed a crooked finger into the howling wind. "Somewhere out there is an enemy worse than any we have ever faced. To have unleashed this weapon on us . . . they are worse than the Borg or the Dominion."

But Bekra was too busy whimpering and clutching his cauterized stump, so Maltz heaved a sigh, grabbed the injured consul, and threw him into his own shuttlecraft. He threw in a few of his bags and boxes for good measure, but he left most of them behind.

The Klingon climbed aboard the shuttlecraft and sat at the controls, cracking his knuckles. He had flown similar vessels many times—there was nothing to it. Most shuttlecraft hadn't changed much in a hundred years, and this one in particular looked old-fashioned. Maybe Bekra wasn't as important as he thought he was, having only this pathetic vessel with no warp capability.

He went into a vertical launch and zoomed straight up through the torn roof of the massive hangar. Paying no attention to the instruments, the Klingon punched the membrane board repeatedly until he got the craft to keep going up. There was no subtlety in this launch—it was thrusters blasting against the monstrous wind, with the craft straining and creaking to gain every centimeter in altitude. Finally they broke through the stratosphere of the planet into calm sailing, spiraling upward at a breakneck speed.

As they reached their maximum impulse speed, which was more suited to continent hopping than solar-system hopping, he turned on the sensors to take a look around.

The first thing he picked up was a distress signal about four thousand kilometers ahead of him, and he locked onto the signal and used it for a course heading. Ignoring Bekra's moans and heartfelt pleas for assistance, Maltz opened several Federation frequencies and broadcast on all of them.

"Hello, fellow shuttlecraft," he said jovially. "This is Consul Maltz and Consul Bekra on Bekra's shuttlecraft. We have escaped from the planet, but we do not have warp drive."

"That's too bad," came the woman's unfriendly response, accompanied by static. "The wave is working its way through the sun in this solar system, and we don't have a lot of time. I may save your worthless hides, but you'll have to play by *my* rules."

The Klingon grunted with distaste at having to be tactful to a human. "You could put a tractor beam on us, and both ships could go into warp."

"Listen to me, Maltz—I'm the only one who has warp drive, so your shuttlecraft is worthless. Unless you'd care to face that demon behind us, you'll do exactly as I say. I've got shields up, and I'll leave you here unless you give me your word that I'm the commander."

The Klingon clenched his teeth and grunted, although his admiration for this human woman had soared tremendously.

"Take the deal!" rasped Bekra, writhing on the deck.

"I agree," said Maltz, bowing his head and slamming his fist to his chest. "I pledge to follow your command if we unite crews. But I must report to a Klingon base as soon as possible."

"Fine with me," answered Leah. "I think it's a little grandiose to say we're 'uniting crews,' but——" Her voice broke up in a crackle of static.

"We have interference," said Maltz.

After several moments of useless noise, her voice came back forcefully. "I've stopped. We only have short-range communications, and the anomaly is affecting it. Lower your shields and prepare to transport."

"All my gear . . . my records," said Bekra, suddenly alarmed at the finality of what they were doing.

The Klingon scowled as he punched the board. "Your deeds in the next few days will mean more than anything you've done before. We're going to go down in history, my friend . . . if there is any history after this."

One at a time, their bodies turned into shimmering columns of suspended molecules, only to disappear entirely, while the empty shuttlecraft hurtled toward its doom.

Captain Picard paced within the circle of workstations on the bridge of the *Enterprise*, trying not to show his concern. They weren't making any headway—this process was moving too slowly over too vast an area. They were on the defensive, waiting. And he never liked to wait.

La Forge looked up from his engineering console and said, "Captain, the planet Hakon is sending all kinds of distress signals and subspace chatter. Something must be happening there."

"I concur," said Data on ops. "We are picking up unusual readings from solar system SY-911 on long-range sensors. It appears the sun in that solar system is in distress."

"Distress?" asked Captain Picard curiously, taking a step toward Data's station. "It is going nova? Dark corona syndrome?"

Data shook his head. "No, sir. The sun appears to be decreasing rapidly in temperature and size—among other radical changes. It is oscillating and emitting variable gravity waves and solar winds, which must be affecting the planets in the solar system. These readings are troubling, because there is no recognized phenomenon that would cause them. One thing is certain—unless the inhabitants of Hakon have a reliable shelter system, they are not going to survive the drastic changes in climate."

Picard gritted his teeth and looked at the concerned faces all around him. "How many inhabitants?"

"Eight million, Sir, most of them Tellarites," answered Data. "The colony was settled on agrarian principles and has relatively small population centers spread out over one large continent."

"Captain!" called La Forge with urgency in his voice. "Most of the messages from Hakon have now stopped, although we're still getting distress signals from a few ships in the area . . . freighters and shuttlecraft."

The captain stepped toward the tactical station, where a pale Antosian, Ensign Coltak, busily worked the board. "Did you try to answer their hails?"

"Yes, sir," answered Coltak, sounding frustrated, "but they haven't responded. There's a great deal of interference, but we captured what we could before the channels went dead."

"ETA, Mister Data?" asked Picard, helplessness gnawing in the pit of his stomach.

"Two hours and twenty-three minutes before we reach the solar system," answered the android.

Picard's shoulders slumped as he turned toward the tactical station. "Mister Coltak, it would appear that we have time to view some of those messages from Hakon. Maybe we can get an idea what we're facing."

"A thing that can blight a star," answered the Antosian in amazement as he studied his readouts. "I'm sorry, Sir, I'll start isolating the messages."

"That's all right, Ensign," said the captain, knowing how he felt.

A few moments later, the main viewscreen blinked on, showing what appeared to be the interior of a spaceport. A few panicked people dashed across the screen, covering their heads from flying debris. The walls and ceiling of the building appeared to be crumbling all around them, and wind ripped the furnishings. Finally a frightened Tellarite staggered in front of the chaotic scene; although he was large, he was shivering uncontrollably, and Picard could see his icy breath.

"Dispatcher Makolis from Cloud Spaceport on Hakon . . . calling whoever's out there!" shrieked the Tellarite, his voice barely audible over the ferocious din. "Something is happening . . . strange weather, without warning. Help us, please!"

The distraught Tellarite went on, begging futilely for help, but Picard barely listened, he was so deep in thought. "They did have warning," he said to himself. "Somebody went all the way there from Seran to warn them, but it didn't do any good."

Suddenly a mass of debris fell upon their poor commentator, and the screen went blank. "Bringing up another one," said Ensign Coltak without comment.

Now they saw a Ferengi on the bridge of his vessel, gripping the captain's chair as his ship was rocked back and forth by some mysterious force. His eyes were wide with fear as he stared down at them from the viewscreen. "Mayday! Mayday! Captain Baldoru on the freighter *Rich Prize*, and we're under attack!"

One of his crew members shouted something to him, and the Ferengi seemed to reconsider, despite the obvious pounding his craft was taking. "We're not under attack, but . . . we don't know what it is. Temperatures falling, gravity fluctuating—it's some kind of natural disaster! We've got to try to lift off the planet." He waved frantically at his subordinates. "Eject cargo!"

There was a flurry of activity and barked orders as the frightened Ferengi crew tried to get their launch together. Picard felt his hands balling into fists as he watched the dramatic effort, because he had a bad feeling it was not going to turn out well.

"Full thrusters! Manual launch at one-quarter impulse." The Ferengi captain looked with hope and confidence at his helmsman, who intently worked his board. Interference streaked the image on the viewscreen, and the freighter shuddered mightily as it tried to lift off. Picard imagined that they were on a giant outdoor landing pad, thrusters lifting them upward like a big helicopter.

"Stabilizers weakening!" yelled the ops officer.

"Divert emergency power to shields," ordered the captain.

Picard drew a sharp intake of breath, thinking that *he* would divert all power to thrusters. They were either going to get off the ground or they weren't—worry about damage later. "Altitude," he said softly, rooting for them.

"We're hitting solar winds!" called a voice a second before the image on the viewscreen disappeared in a slash of static. Just before the scene faded to complete darkness, they heard the screams of the Ferengi crew, forming a dissonant chorus of death.

Silence commanded the bridge of the *Enterprise* for several seconds until Ensign Coltak softly asked, "Do you want to see more, Captain?"

Picard shook his head grimly. "Not at the moment. Even though someone went to Hakon to warn them, the message never got through."

"These records are consistent with the expected results of a failing sun," said Data. "Which should not have happened in this solar system for another three billion years."

"What could transform a star like that?" asked Geordi, peering at his readouts. "It's still there—it hasn't been blasted apart—but it's a lot different. A yellow giant turned into a red dwarf."

Data cocked his head curiously. "Long-range sensors show another planet in that system which does not match the description we have for it. SY-911 Alpha, closest planet to the sun, is supposed to be Class-H, but now it is Class-L, bordering on -M. It has an oxidizing atmosphere that it never had before."

"Are you sure about that?" asked Picard doubtfully. "Could it be an error in the readings?"

"Possibly," admitted the android, "but the data from the sun appear to be consistent with what we have seen on Hakon. I agree, these readings are so unusual as to be questionable."

"Forward all of this data to Admiral Nechayev," ordered Picard. "Maybe she can make something out of it."

"Let's do a long-range scan of Seran," said La Forge, grimly plying his console. "We'll see if we get more weird readings."

Weird readings or not, thought Picard, there were beings out there dying by the millions, perhaps the billions. Not just highly intelligent beings but animals, birds, fish, microbes—ecosystems vanishing in the blink of an eye. It would be nice to pin it all on interference and erroneous sensor readings, but in his mind he could still hear that Ferengi crew screaming.

nine

From the cockpit of her shuttlecraft, Leah Brahms looked around at her motley crew, consisting of a Tellarite who would not stop crying, a Capellan who was suddenly missing a leg without any explanation, and a grizzled Klingon who hummed happily to himself as he gazed out a side viewport. Maltz seemed more clean-cut, too, and a few years younger, although his regal clothes were a wreck.

She had let everybody just find a seat and get comfortable while she plotted the course of the deadly wave. *Straight into the Federation, just like us. Only it's expanding and going faster, and we're not.* Without explaining it to anyone, Leah put the shuttlecraft into warp drive.

"How fast is her top speed?" asked Maltz, recognizing the change.

"Warp two, although I can get it close to three if I override our safeties." Leah wasn't eager for any conversation when her own thoughts were so heavy, but she recognized the need to communicate with this pathetic lot of survivors. "Paldor, will you do some first-aid on Consul Bekra? He's being stoic, but I think he's in pain."

The Tellarite sniffed and let out a sob that got caught several times in his throat. "Can you believe it? All of them *dead*. And us helpless! Oh, what was I thinking?" He began to blubber anew.

"We're all suffering," said Leah through clenched teeth, "but we've got a job to do—"

"What?" shrieked the Tellarite. "Flying somewhere else where they won't believe us . . . or move quickly enough? So we can watch this happen all over again!"

Behind them, Maltz muttered, "We've got to find out who set it off."

"What does he mean?" asked Paldor in confusion. "Who set *what* off?"

His turban askew, Bekra shifted in his seat and let out a groan. "Maltz has a theory that this is some sort of weapon. He has talked about a similar thing in the past." The Capellan grimaced. "I could use some of that first-aid, by the way."

When Paldor didn't move, Leah sighed wearily. "Maltz, can you pilot this shuttlecraft?"

"Aye, Captain." answered the Klingon, rising to his feet. "They're all the same. You learn one ship—you learn them all. I once knew a handful of humans who figured out how to fly a bird-of-prey."

"You really don't have to do anything," said Leah. "We're on course under computer control. Just watch the readouts for anything unusual."

"What about me?" asked Paldor, sounding hurt. "I could do that."

"When you get yourself together, maybe you will." Leah rose to her feet, feeling the lack of sleep and the overabundance of adrenaline and grief. She grabbed the first-aid kit from the locker and sat down to minister to Bekra's burnt stump of a leg.

"How did this happen?" she finally asked.

The Capellan grumbled, "I lost an argument to somebody who was a better shot."

Leah glanced pointedly at Maltz, sitting in the pilot's seat, but the consul's face remained stoic. She prepared a hypospray. "This will kill the pain."

"I'm going to need a lot of it to kill *all* the pain," replied the Capellan with a grim smile.

"I hear you," answered Leah softly. She put gloves on her hands and took a prepared dressing and a tube of antibiotic ointment from the kit. Thankfully, she wouldn't need the medical tricorder or surgical tools, because the wound had been cauterized by the disruptor.

"What about *this* planet?" asked Maltz from the front. "Pelleus V. It is on our way, and they have thirty-four million inhabitants. We could be there in six hours."

"You weren't supposed to do anything but watch the readouts," answered Leah testily.

"That planet isn't even in the Federation," said Paldor, glancing over his shoulder.

The Klingon scratched the white stubble on his chin and chuckled. "So you can let them *die* if they are not in the Federation? Hmmm, you people are more practical than I thought."

"We're doing the best we can!" snapped Paldor. "How would *you* save them?"

"I was only looking for a Class-M planet where we could set down and fix the communications array," answered Maltz. "We need to get help. It just so happens that the nearest place is inhabited; and by the graph you are running, I can see it is in the direct path of the wave."

"I saw the planet," answered Leah Brahms as she finished dressing Bekra's wound. "You should get some sleep," she told the Capellan.

"Thank you, I'll try," he promised.

The scientist stood and went to the cockpit, motioning Paldor to get up so that she could take the copilot's seat. She needed help, and this old Klingon seemed the most sane, competent, and energetic among them. Sobbing and grumbling, the Tellarite squeezed past her to get to the back of the craft, and Leah slid into the seat he had vacated.

She looked at her new first officer and lowered her voice. "If you were me, what you would do?"

Maltz scowled. "You cannot land on a strange planet and expect them to voluntarily leave their homes at a moment's notice—due to a threat you can't explain. That is, if they even have a way to leave. We need help. Where are the vaunted reinforcements of the Federation?"

"It hit too suddenly," Leah answered defensively, "and we lost a lot of ships during the war. Plus I hate to tell you, but this is a forgotten corner of the Federation. The wars, the wormholes—all of the action has been up by the zones. There aren't a lot of settlements this close to the middle of the Milky Way."

"But many settled worlds lie in the path of this thing," observed Maltz, pointing to his screen. "If I'm not mistaken—expanding on your chart—one of the targets is Earth."

"Earth?" asked Leah, leaning closer to the gaunt Klingon. She hadn't seen the latest updates on the computer projections, but Maltz had figured them out rather quickly. She had to go to three other screens to verify his quick analysis. Yes, it seemed, Earth itself was in the path of this awful scourge.

"You know better than I do where Earth is," remarked Leah.

He shrugged. "In my day, all of us learned those coordinates in basic training. We had to have some place to attack on the simulators and war games."

"Right," answered Leah dryly. "Exactly how many humans have you killed?"

The old warrior wrinkled his jagged brow. "Not enough, I can tell you. Had I killed just a few more, I would not be in this place." With a grunt, he pointed at the screen. "The enemy is going to cut a streak through the Romulan Star Empire, too. I also know those coordinates."

Bekra suddenly sat up, not sleeping as peacefully as he appeared. "Did you say the Romulans will get hit, too?"

"This is only a projection, but you can see its path widening through the Neutral Zone." The Klingon sighed and sat back in his seat. "It looks like you are going to need a lot of help to fight this thing."

"Are you ever going to tell us who built it, and what you think it is?" asked Bekra.

The Klingon shook his head forcefully. "No. I will know the right person to tell, and it will have to be someone who can verify what I say. No one on this ship can do anything but doubt my sanity. Now, do we change course for this planet . . . Pelleus V?"

Reluctantly, Leah Brahms nodded. "Yes."

"Doctor, you are making the same mistake I made," protested Paldor from the back.

"She is the captain—it is her mistake to make." The Klingon narrowed his eyes at the Tellarite. "If you want to debate that point, you can take it up with *me*. Now all of you sleep—I will inform you when we get there."

Leah nodded gratefully and rested her head on her arms, which were folded across the console. In a matter of seconds, she was asleep where she sat, her fate in the hands of the grizzled old Klingon.

In a sumptuously appointed stateroom on the namesake *Sovereign*-class flagship, the *U.S.S. Sovereign*, the gray-haired admiral turned off her viewscreen and lowered her reading glasses. In her sharp green eyes was an emotion seldom seen there—fear. She had witnessed many extraordinary events in her long career, but nothing like these reports and fragments from the *Enterprise*. It was hard to believe that this bitter fruit had been planted only six months ago. Someone had been busy making use of what they stole.

She tapped a companel on her desk. "Nechayev to bridge."

"Captain Tejeda here," came a prompt response. "What can I do for you, Admiral?"

"Set course for solar system SY-911 in sector 4368. Maximum warp."

"Sector 4368," repeated the captain, sounding a bit doubtful as to what could be important there. "That will take us about thirty-three hours. What kind of mission should we prepare for?"

"When you need to know, I'll tell you," answered the admiral in a tone of voice that brooked no discussion. While most people were in awe of veteran captains of great starships, Nechayev treated them like underlings. It kept them from getting too full of themselves and reminded them that they were only links in a chain.

"Yes, Sir," responded Captain Tejeda, properly chastened. "Should we alert Starfleet of our change in course?"

"I'll do that," she answered. "But you can alert the *Enterprise* that the *Sovereign* is en route to their general position, and tell them to keep sending me raw data."

"Yes, Admiral."

"Nechayev out." Taking a deep breath, the weary admiral activated her terminal one more time. "Computer, send a secure message to recipients list 'Nechayev Priority One.'"

"What is the password?" demanded the computer.

"Tulip bulbs in spring," answered Nechayev grimly.

"Proceed," suggested the computer.

"Tulips are blooming again sooner than expected," said Nechayev, her mouth feeling dry now that the dreaded words were finally out. "Weeding will require all hands. Blooms must be seen to be believed. Yours truly—A."

She closed her eyes. "End message. Send it."

"Message sent," the reasonable voice of the computer assured her.

Now a large part of the fleet was going to be mustered under some pretext and sent to the afflicted area. Other than seeing for herself how bad it was, there wasn't anything else she could do. But knowing that didn't ease Nechayev's mind—her response still seemed inadequate.

She told herself, *I have the best ship in the fleet on it, the second best coming for backup, and all the others getting ready to come. I'm hitting it with both barrels.* Unfortunately, she couldn't block out the knowledge that she had nothing in her arsenal which could stand up to what she feared was out there.

"If only I could see him once in a while," said Beverly Crusher, her watery blue eyes staring at a beige bulkhead. "At least . . . if I could get some kind of sign that he's okay, I'd feel better."

"Wesley is with extremely advanced beings," said Deanna Troi, leaning forward in her chair. The dark-haired Betazoid pushed the teapot and cup across the elegant coffee table in her office, but Beverly wasn't paying any attention to it. "I'm sure the Traveler is taking good care of him," the counselor continued, "but I'm not so sure they have the same sense of time we do."

"But why Wes?" asked Beverly, shaking her auburn hair with frustration. "There are billions of other humans—he could have taken anybody!"

The counselor smiled sympathetically. "Wes has a gift, and the Traveler got to know him. I think he chose well, too, because your son was bored with so much in Starfleet. He had basically mastered this job while he was still in high school. He was ready to move on."

"I know, but sometimes . . . it seems like he's dead." The distraught mother rose to her feet and paced the confines of the nondescript office. "I don't want to stop him . . . his development. But, dammit, I want to know where to send a birthday card! Is it too much to ask that he make contact with his mother?"

Troi sighed, thinking it was always hardest to make a good friend face harsh reality. "The Traveler said he was taking Wes to another plane of existence, so we have to assume that contact is difficult. He's your ambassador to a race that is light-years ahead of ours. We don't begin to understand how they get around."

"They have incredible powers," agreed Beverly, half in pride and half in fear. "I just want a sign that he's okay."

Troi's combadge sounded a second later, and she listened with relief to the interruption.

"Picard to Troi."

"Yes, Captain, Troi here."

"I'm sorry to interrupt your appointment. Is Dr. Crusher with you?"

"Yes, Sir."

"I need you both in transporter room two," ordered the captain. "We've made contact with a shuttlecraft of survivors who escaped from Hakon, and they may be injured or traumatized. We don't want to prolong their ordeal, but we do have to find out what they know. Their shuttlecraft is damaged, so we're taking them on as passengers."

"We're on our way. Troi out." The counselor rose from her chair and moved toward the door, stopping when she realized that Beverly was still in her seat, gazing at the bulkhead.

"You know," said Deanna softly, "we can send for a different medteam. I'll tell the captain you weren't feeling well."

"No," replied the doctor, rising to her feet and pushing back an errant strand of red hair. "I need to go and do my job. You're right— if I'm not going to hear anything, then I'm not going to hear anything."

"Are you sure you're okay?"

Beverly waved her off. "Yes, you go on. I'll pick up the medteam on the way."

Troi nodded and strode through the door into the corridor. She wished she could do more to comfort her friend, whose life had often been one of sacrifice, but she couldn't bring herself to worry about someone as competent as Wesley Crusher. Then again, she wasn't his mother.

After a quick trip in the turbolift, Deanna reached the broad corridor outside transporter room two at the same time that Captain Picard, Data, and La Forge came from the other direction. Of the three of them, only La Forge looked pleased, as if he were about to meet a friend coming for holiday. Both he and Data were carrying padds.

The door slid open, and the captain motioned her inside the transporter room. "We don't know what condition they'll be in. Tell me, Counselor, what do you know about our latest mission?"

"Commander Riker has told me a few things," she replied. "I know there have been a series of unexplained disasters."

"That's putting it mildly. Unfortunately, we don't know much more than that. At least we're close enough now that we can help." Picard gazed at the transporter operator, a tall, blue-skinned Andorian named Tyriden. "Do you have a lock on them?"

"Yes, sir. Four in total."

The doors opened again, and Beverly Crusher entered, leading a fully equipped medteam of five people. The captain smiled warmly at her for a moment, and she smiled back, then he motioned to the transporter operator. "Energize."

"Yes, Sir."

In a shimmering curtain of light, four bedraggled survivors appeared on the transporter platform. Two of them instantly collapsed, and Beverly and her team rushed forward to help them. All were male, and all were Tellarites, except for one, who appeared to be a Centaurian from his regal dress.

The most startling reaction was from Geordi La Forge, whose eager expression turned downcast and puzzled. He busied himself making entries on his padd, but Troi could tell that he was disappointed over the appearance of these survivors. Maybe he was expecting somebody else.

The healthiest of the Tellarites charged off the platform and gripped Captain Picard in an embarrassing embrace. "Oh, thank you, Captain! Thank you!"

Deanna rushed to aid the captain, pulling the overly grateful survivor away. "What happened to you?" she asked.

"Who knows?" he exclaimed. "We're a surveying team. One moment, we're laying out the boundaries of a wildlife refuge, and the next minute the trees are blowing over! And it's hailing and sleeting! We were able to take off, but not before a tree limb struck our craft. Then we hit a meteor shower on our way out—we were lucky to make it to warp."

"What did you see or get on your sensors?" asked Picard. "Anything unusual?"

"Nothing until we got into space," answered the Tellarite. "But we heard others on the emergency channels, and we saw what was happening to the sun." He buried his snout in his hands and began to weep.

"We ran for it," said the Centaurian defensively. "Is that so bad? Maybe I should've kept a video log, but I didn't."

"You weren't the shuttlecraft that came from Seran to Hakon just before this happened?" asked La Forge, stepping forward.

"No," said the Centaurian. "I'm their pilot, and it was strictly a day trip. We all left our families behind. Are they—"

Deanna hurriedly took his arm. "Before we deal with that, we'd like our medical personnel to take a look at you. The important thing is that you did right to get out of there."

"We've got to go back for them!" demanded the Tellarite, fighting through tears. Suddenly he grabbed the Centaurian pilot and shook him by the lapels of his flashy uniform. "I told you we had to go back for them!"

Troi and Picard reached in to try to pull the Tellarite off, but he was as big as both of them put together. Fortunately, Dr. Crusher made a timely arrival with a hypospray, getting the big Tellarite in the neck. A second later, he released the pilot, who dropped to the deck, coughing.

The big Tellarite stood as still as the bearded statue of an old general, but Crusher was able to move him toward the door. She motioned to her team to follow. "Let's all go to sickbay, shall we? Ogawa, Haberlee, I think everybody is ambulatory. Let's just walk."

"Beverly, will you need me?" asked Troi with concern.

"Not right now. I think we're looking at some sedation, rest, and a physical. I'll let you know." Under the doctor's direction, her team conducted the survivors from the transporter room. They looked more shell-shocked than anything else.

"They look like refugees from the war," said Troi, watching the last one exit.

"I was thinking the same thing," agreed Picard. "They *are* refugees. Unfortunately, there are only a handful, and they don't know anything."

"We've got to keep looking for the rest of the shuttlecrafts and freighters," insisted La Forge. "One of them came from Seran to Hakon to warn them, but we lost its signal when all hell broke loose. There was also the Capellan shuttlecraft that put out an early distress signal—"

"The Capellan shuttlecraft has been destroyed," said Data matter-of-factly.

"Are you sure?" asked Geordi in a hoarse voice.

The android nodded. "Yes, I was about to ask Commander Riker to continue tracking it when it disappeared."

"What destroyed it?" asked Picard, the frustration evident in his voice. "If it was safely in space, it couldn't have been the effects of the sun."

"That is unknown," answered Data. "It would appear the Capellan shuttlecraft did not have warp drive, and it remained in proximity to Hakon, where sensor readings have been unreliable."

"When you get back to the bridge, set course for solar system SY-911," ordered the captain. "Maximum warp."

"But, Sir!" pleaded La Forge. "If this mystery shuttlecraft is trying to warn people—and they know where to go next—we should keep looking for them. They manage to stay just ahead of this . . . trail of disaster."

"Get moving, Data." The captain nodded, and the android hurried off. Then Picard put his hand on La Forge's shoulder and said softly, "I know you have a personal interest in this. Since you have the opportunity, I wish you would take a moment to talk to Counselor Troi about it."

La Forge hung his head, knowing he had lost the argument, and the captain went on, "You've been on duty for about twenty hours straight, which I didn't deny you, because you discovered these irregularities. But now you need to talk to Counselor Troi and sleep."

The captain's lips thinned. "I'm afraid this is going to be a long haul. We can't go chasing after every small craft from Hakon, and we have to accept the fact that Seran and Outpost Seran-T-One are in the damage zone. What we need most are answers and firsthand observation."

"Yes, Sir," answered Geordi, trying to get control over his emotions.

The captain strode away, leaving La Forge and Troi alone in the transporter room. Even the operator was behind the platform, his head in an access panel.

"I still think we should track down that shuttle," insisted Geordi in a whisper. "Somebody out there *knows* what's going on—or at least where this thing is headed. We've got to find them. If I were really being selfish, I would want to go to Seran."

"Who's on Seran?" asked Deanna, moving toward the door.

"Remember Leah Brahms? We talked about her."

The counselor nodded sympathetically. "You really cared for her, didn't you? I'm sorry, Geordi."

The engineer swallowed hard, and she could see moisture in the corners of his opaque eyes. "I just can't believe that she could be gone . . . just like that. I mean, I knew she was married, but somewhere in the back of my mind, I always thought that someday there might be a chance—"

"Oh, Geordi," said Troi hoarsely, squeezing his shoulder. "I keep thinking that we've had these great lives aboard the *Enterprise*. We've had more adventures than anyone should have in ten lifetimes, but we've missed out on the ordinary parts of life. Sometimes I wonder how many of us could even have a normal relationship in an artificial world like this." She motioned around at the sleek, empty corridor.

He cleared his throat. "You and Will—"

"It's taken us a dozen years to be comfortable with each other in this small town we call the *Enterprise*." She gave him a wry smile. "You fell in love with the most brilliant woman you ever met, only it was on a holodeck. I sometimes think we should all be committed to a mental institution, considering what we've been through."

"You're just trying to cheer me up," said La Forge, "and I'm not buying it. Forgetting Leah, who is probably dead . . . we're up against something that's wiping out stars, planets, and nebulas like they're piles of dust! We don't even understand what it's doing to them, and now we're flying straight into the teeth of this thing."

"Okay, so you depressed me," admitted Troi. "And there are going to be a lot more refugees, like those people in sickbay."

"They're the lucky ones," said Geordi.

ten

Leah Brahms rustled in her sleep, muttering to herself. Finally she lifted her head groggily from the instrument panel and looked around the cramped shuttlecraft cabin. "Oh," she groaned, rubbing her head. "It's true."

"What is true?" asked the old Klingon sitting beside her.

"I had a dream that all of this *was* a dream . . . or rather a nightmare." She massaged her dry, cracked lips. "But, no, it's all true, isn't it? The thing behind us . . . it's still there."

"There is always an enemy," said Maltz with a shrug. "Sometimes it's boredom, but not today." He pointed to the back of the craft, where the Tellarite and the Capellan were sleeping among their luggage and the hulking radiation suit. "What is that unpleasant-looking device back there?"

"Oh, you mean the radiation suit?" Leah smiled despite her gloominess. "That suit saved my life. None of us would be here without it."

"It survived the wave?" asked Maltz, sounding impressed. "Can you do a space walk in it?"

"That's not what it's designed for, but you could. You would be using only half its capabilities."

The Klingon sat forward eagerly. "I have been looking at the parts you collected for your comm array, and I think we can repair it easily. The space walk should take no more than half an hour." He quickly added, "I can do it."

"No," said Leah forcefully. "I'll do it. I know the equipment better than you do."

"But the captain should not be at risk," grumbled the Klingon. "It should be someone expendable—what about Paldor?"

"Me!" squeaked the Tellarite, suddenly awake. "You want *me* to go outside and fix the shuttlecraft? I wouldn't even fit inside that suit. Are you sure we have to do this now?"

"Yes, because we need help." The old Klingon lowered his voice. "The first thing a captain should learn is this—when you are outnumbered, get help. If we do not, the next planet will be Hakon all over again."

"Listen to him," said a voice from the back. Leah turned to see Consul Bekra sitting up, trying to adjust his ornate turban and his bandaged stump. "We have to spread the word as fast as we can. A few hours could make a great deal of difference."

"Even if it means our lives?" asked Paldor in disbelief. "We don't know how far ahead of it we are, or how long it will take to fix the array. Dr. Brahms is not a welder by trade."

"That's enough, people. I don't know if we have enough time for this repair, but we sure as hell don't have time to argue about it. Besides," Leah added with a smile, "molecular bonding is easy, even for humans. We have everything we need in our supplies."

With a sigh, the engineer stood up and began removing her jumpsuit, which she had meant to change, anyway. If she were smart, she would just put the radiation suit on and leave it on, but she didn't want to be the only eyewitness survivor again. "Keep us on warp until I'm ready to exit the ship," she ordered. "I want as much distance between me and *it* as possible."

The young Tellarite began to weep all over again, and Leah surprised herself by grabbing his loud plaid shirt and shaking him. "Get ahold of yourself, Paldor! We don't have the luxury of grieving . . . not right now. I need you to help me get this suit ready, and monitor me . . . like we do in the tests. Get up!"

She yanked him to his feet, where he struggled to stand at attention, while bravely sniffing back tears. Behind her, she heard Maltz give a low chuckle.

"Now you are getting the hang of it," said the Klingon with satisfaction.

"Slow to one-quarter impulse," ordered Captain Picard as he hovered behind the young Bolian on the conn. He peered at the viewscreen with concern, not because he saw something which looked amiss; on the contrary, this part of space looked oddly tranquil, considering what it had gone through. Even the radically altered sun of system SY-911 looked like a natural part of the starscape when viewed from the safe distance of two million kilometers. At least Picard hoped this was a safe distance.

"Mister Data, where do we stand?"

"I would advise that we stop here," answered the android. "Radiation is very high in a field of particles about a hundred thousand kilometers from our position. This area also has trace readings of almost every element known to science, including organic components. I would almost conclude that a massive fleet of starships moved through here, expelling waste as they went, except we know that did not occur. Some extraordinary event has taken place, although I am unable to say what it was."

"Full stop," ordered the captain, concerned that they knew so little about this deadly menace. "Data, prepare three probes. A solar probe for the sun and two class-1 probes—one for Hakon and one for the planet with the strange readings."

"SY-911 Alpha," concluded Data, working his board with fingers moving so swiftly they were a blur. "Targeting probes."

"Launch when ready," ordered the captain.

"Probes launched."

On the viewscreen, the torpedoes streaked from the *Enterprise* across the peaceful starscape until they disappeared among the distant stars and the pulsing red sun. The transformed sun glowed with a brilliance that dared them to do something about it.

The turbolift door opened with a whoosh, startling the captain from his troubled reverie. He turned to see Counselor Troi enter the bridge, and he asked, "How are our passengers?"

"They're all sleeping now," she answered, "but we've got a lot of work to do. They're going to ask me what the chances are of going back to their homes. Will we mount a rescue effort, or at least recover the bodies?"

"I hope to know soon," answered Picard. "We've sent out probes, and we're trying to gather information. There's something destructive out here, but we don't know much about it."

"Captain," said Data from the ops station, "the first probe should be reaching the particle field. Peculiar."

"What is it, Data?"

"The probe ceased transmission." He worked his board furiously. "In fact, both probes have ceased transmission since they entered the particle field just ahead of us." The android looked up with concern. "I suggest we put up shields."

"Shields up," ordered Picard without a moment's hesitation.

"Shields up!" echoed the officer on tactical.

"What's the threat?" asked the captain.

Data shook his head. "Some sort of energy wave is following the deuterium trails of the probes—right back to us."

Picard looked up at the viewscreen to see two thin ripples—like green lightning bolts—come tearing from the darkness, headed straight toward them. "Brace for impact," said Data.

The captain wasn't expecting much of an impact since they had their shields up, and he wasn't disappointed. He felt nothing, although it was disturbing the way the mysterious strands seemed to remain attached to the ship, trailing off into the distance like giant vines.

He was shocked a moment later when the ship's alarms sounded, and the bridge went automatically to emergency lighting and Red Alert. "Hull breach on decks eleven and twelve," said the voice of the computer.

As he worked his console, Data added, "To be specific, the forward launch tubes."

"Our shields—" started Picard.

"Ineffective," answered Data.

"Conn, take us out of here, reverse course, full impulse," ordered Picard, striding to his command chair.

"Yes, Sir."

"Repair crews have been dispatched to the forward torpedo room," reported Data. "It was running under automated control—no casualties reported."

"Let's see what it's like. On screen." The captain sat stiffly in his chair, his brow furrowed, as the scene overhead switched to the cramped, elongated torpedo room. Torpedoes and probes were stacked top to bottom in robotic racks, ready to be moved into place, and rails ran the length of the deck, leading to the launch tubes. But the bank of launch tubes were gone—instead there was an amorphous green glow around a jagged hole which opened to the darkness of space. And the pulsing hole seemed to be growing larger.

The scene turned hectic a moment later when a team dressed in environmental suits charged in with fire extinguishers and foam guns blazing. They instantly attacked the breach, some of them erecting temporary force-field barriers, while the others battled the oddly glowing flames.

"I have isolated their audio," said Data. Suddenly, they heard a feminine voice saying, "What is that stuff? It's not working . . . it's not containing it! Kipnis, get a tricorder reading."

"Working on it, Sir." A moment later, his voice croaked when he said, "It's organic! Protomatter. It's eating through the hull . . . like acid!"

"Aagghhh!" screamed another voice. "It's got me! It's all over me! I can't get it off!"

Now there was real bedlam as a panicked officer staggered back from the breach in the hull, plowing through his coworkers trapped in the narrow room with him. He swatted and beat himself as if he were on fire, but Picard could see only a bit of the glowing vegetation on him. Anguished screams rent the air, and more of the repair team seemed to fall victim, scratching and clawing themselves. They began to tear off their environmental suits.

His jaw clenched, the captain rose from his chair. "Mr. Data, seal off the forward torpedo room."

"Yes, Sir." The android calmly worked his board. "Sealed off."

When some of the panicked repair crew tried to escape to the corridor, they realized they were shut off, and their screams became more urgent and frightful. Meanwhile, the cancerous hole in the hull kept growing, and the distraught workers scrambled and clawed over one another to get away from it.

"Patch me into them," ordered Picard. Data nodded to him, and he went on, "This is the captain. We are facing a quarantine situation in your position. Try to remain calm." He motioned to Data to cut off the transmission, then he said grimly, "Prepare to jettison forward torpedo module."

Deanna Troi sprang in front of him. "But, Sir, there are ten crew members trapped in there."

"We'll get them back," vowed Picard, "but we can't let that thing reach the main hull. Data, jettison the forward torpedo module."

"Yes, Sir."

On the viewscreen, the crew trapped in the torpedo room suddenly became weightless, and their panicked thrashing increased as they floated helplessly. With a jarring shudder, clamps released and powerful thrusters shot the entire module away from the Saucer Module of the *Enterprise*. One of the most dangerous parts of the ship, loaded with armaments, the torpedo module was designed to be ejected if its contents proved unstable. But it was never meant to be jettisoned with people in it.

"Patch me into them again," ordered Captain Picard, straightening his tunic. The image on the viewscreen was now obliterated by static, although the desperate struggles of the crew were plain to see . . . or imagine.

"Captain," said Data, "life support is failing in the module."

"Prepare to transport them," ordered Picard. "Data, can we surround the transporter room with a containment field?"

"That is inadvisable," answered the android. "If our battle shields had no effect on the intruder, we can assume our force-fields would not either."

Helplessly, the bridge crew gazed at the viewscreen, where the new image was more disturbing than the one inside the torpedo room. The trapezoid-shaped module was now misshapen and throbbing, which had to be an optical illusion, thought Picard. It hardly seemed possible that thick bulkheads could twist and mutate like that, no matter what power they were under. "Am I patched in?"

"Yes, Sir."

He stuck his jaw out. "This is Captain Picard to the members of the repair crew in the torpedo module. We're working on a way to rescue you from—"

"Captain," said Data, "the comlink has gone dead. No lifesigns either."

"Keep recording this," ordered Picard with a scowl, pointing to the abomination on the viewscreen. "But take us back another million kilometers, half impulse."

"Yes, Sir," answered the Bolian at the conn.

Feeling weary and saddened, the captain slumped into the captain's chair. Deanna Troi joined him in the center of the bridge, her face drawn with shock, and she lowered her head. "You tried, Captain. It all happened so fast—"

"You always think a miracle will happen . . . but sometimes it doesn't." The captain's gaze finally focused on the face of his longtime comrade. "I had to protect the ship."

"Yes, you did," agreed Troi. "You undoubtedly *saved* the ship."

Picard pointed to the ops station. "Data, make sure you send copies of this data to Admiral Nechayev. How much longer before the *Sovereign* is here?"

"Sixteen hours at our present position," answered the android, "although we could meet her sooner by backtracking."

"As long as we're collecting useful information, maintain position," said the captain. "I have to make a shipwide announcement."

He pressed a companel on the arm of his chair, and his voice reverberated throughout the ship. "Captain to all hands. I regret to announce that all members of the repair crew who answered the emergency in the forward torpedo room have been lost. There was a breach in the hull and a threat to the ship, for which we had no defense. So I made the decision to jettison the torpedo module.

"We will now all observe a moment of silence for our fallen comrades, who risked their lives many times on our behalf. Today they died valiantly on our behalf." Picard stood still for a moment, his hand resting on his chest, wishing there was more he could tell them about the peril which claimed their shipmates' lives.

"There will be an announcement about a memorial service later," he concluded. "That is all."

Picard slumped back in his chair and stared at the molten green object on the screen, an object which had once been part of his

ship. Had they been able to observe this phenomenon without losing any lives, it would have been fascinating. But now it was just
disgusting and frightening. "It almost looks alive," he said to no one
in particular.

"It *is* alive," agreed Data. "The mass which was formerly the torpedo module has generated into simple lifeforms, which continue to
evolve."

"What do you mean, evolve?" asked Deanna Troi.

"Single-celled animals are in a rapid state of growth," answered
the android, "forming more complex creatures as they develop. It is
like a hundred million years of evolution condensed into a few minutes. Without firsthand observation, I cannot be more specific than
that."

"We're not getting any closer," vowed Picard. "I feel rather helpless
just sitting here, but without more information, we can't do anything."
He tapped his fingers nervously on the arm of his chair. "What *is* that
thing?"

After floating in space for a while, cut off from her sullen crew
inside the shuttlecraft, Leah Brahms began to relax and enjoy the
excursion outside the ship. She was fairly dexterous, often wielding
a soldering iron or a laser torch in her normal routine, and
installing the makeshift comm array was just construction on a bigger scale. The work would have gone faster if she'd had real
Starfleet-approved replacement parts, but she didn't. So she had to
do some drilling, bending, and creative kludging, with advice from
Maltz and Paldor. She soon discovered that she knew as much
about the comm system as either one of them.

Fortunately, her radiation suit had been designed with the
expressed purpose of doing manual repairs, and the gloves worked
well. Also she was able to kneel on the outside of the boxy shuttlecraft, using the magnetic fields on the suit. Handling the bonding

gun was no problem, and Leah found the repetitive manual labor to be soothing. At least it felt as if she were *doing* something, rather than running for her life. Or mourning.

"How much longer, Captain?" came Maltz's gravelly voice over the intercom. He didn't sound frightened, exactly, but there was an urgency in his voice.

"It *might* work now," she said. "But if we want clean subspace on all channels, we'll have to get the signal preprocessor and the Doppler compensator working. But . . . what's the matter?"

"Do you remember that big asteroid belt we passed a while ago?"

"Yes," she answered, a sudden fear gripping in her stomach.

"It's gone!" cut in Paldor's voice. "And there's something that looks like a new planet in its place."

"I think I've done enough for now," said Leah, stuffing her floating tools and extra parts into a large net bag. "Reel me in. And make it quick!"

eleven

Geordi La Forge dragged himself out of his bed at the first alarm, still groggy from a deep sleep. As quickly as possible, he dressed in his uniform and was about to dash out of his quarters when he was stopped by Captain Picard's shipwide announcement. He didn't know offhand who was on that repair team, but he was sure there were people who had served with him in engineering, maybe some who currently served there. Despite the tragedy, it sounded like the *Enterprise* had dodged a bullet.

La Forge finished buttoning his collar and stepped toward the door, waving his hand at a panel to open it. He was so busy charging ahead that he nearly plowed into Dolores Linton, who was in the passageway just outside his door.

"Oh, my gosh, Geordi!" she exclaimed, grabbing him in a forceful hug. "I'm so afraid."

"It's okay," he said, returning the embrace and drawing some strength from her warm body. Her voluminous dark hair smelled fragrant and clean as it billowed just centimeters from his nostrils. He finally whispered hoarsely, "It sounds like the danger is over."

"But all those people!" She pulled slowly away from him and gazed at him with her sultry eyes. "How many?"

"In a crew like that, probably ten." He shook his head and felt guilty for having slept so soundly while the ship was in turmoil. He would hear the whole story later, but probably not from Dolores. "What were you doing out here?"

"I was pacing around," she admitted, straightening her khaki jumpsuit and looking ready to climb mountains that didn't exist on the *Enterprise*. "I don't really have any place to go—no station. I learned from the computer that you were off duty, and I was coming down here to bug you when the alert happened. I'm sorry if I behaved unprofessionally. I've been known to act very cool when there's a rockslide or a mudslide. I just feel a little helpless inside this ship."

Geordi gave her an encouraging smile. "We'll look out for you. But it's too bad you couldn't have picked a quieter time to travel with us." He stepped away from her, anxious to get to engineering.

"Are you still off duty?" she asked, following him down the corridor.

"Well, technically, yes. But we've just had a hull breach and casualties—and we've lost a chunk of the ship. I think I'd better check on things in engineering."

She smiled wistfully. "I was just going to ask if you wanted to have breakfast. It is breakfast time for you, isn't it?"

"Yes it is," he admitted, still moving to the turbolift. "Let's have a late breakfast in two hours. I'll give you that tour of the ship I promised. Meet you back here?"

"All right," answered the muscular brunette, mustering some bravado.

Maybe she is interested, thought Geordi as he dashed into the turbolift, *but her timing is nearly as bad as mine. It must be tough to be a passenger during a crisis like this, with nothing to do but sit and hope for the best.*

"Main engineering," he said to the computer. The turbolift had barely begun moving when his combadge beeped. "Bridge to La Forge," came the familiar clipped tones of Captain Picard.

"La Forge here," he answered. "Is everything all right?"

"As well as can be expected. I'm sorry to disturb you on break, but I doubt you were sleeping any longer."

"No, Sir, I'm on my way to engineering." The turbolift door opened, and Geordi stepped into his familiar workplace. It was bustling, the Red Alert having drawn plenty of hands to their posts. At the same time, the mood was subdued and somber after the tragedy.

"You might want to come to the bridge," said the captain. "We think we may have found your mystery shuttlecraft. They're broadcasting information about the nature of this disaster."

"I'm on my way. La Forge out." He glanced at the duty commander, Krygore, and waved. "I have to go to the bridge. Is everything under control?"

"We didn't take any damage," answered the dignified Kerelian. "But I guess there's nothing left of the forward torpedo module. The casualty list is just coming in. What's out there, Sir?"

"We don't know . . . yet. I'll look at the list on the bridge." With a troubled sigh, Geordi stepped back into the turbolift. "Stay alert down here."

"Yes, Sir."

A few moments later, he stepped off the turbolift onto the bridge, where it was also somber. The viewscreen was full of startling images: an entire planet wilting under vivid green flames; a shimmering curtain sweeping across space; a moon ripped apart by what looked like solar flares. The images were followed by columns of raw data, moving so swiftly that only Data could keep up with them.

"Where is that coming from?" asked Geordi.

"It's from Seran," answered Picard gravely. "We also saw images from Hakon which confirmed our fears about what happened there. Who knows how many planets and stars have been destroyed in between?"

"Can we talk to these people?" asked La Forge, stepping closer to the screen.

"We can't contact them at the moment," said the captain. "They're using all their bandwidth to broadcast raw data on every channel. It's gone through one cycle already. We're on course to intercept them."

"In approximately two hours," added Data. "Based on this new information, we are taking an elliptical course to stay out of the way of the phenomenon."

"Do we know who they are?" asked Geordi.

Data shook his head. "No. From the warp signature, it appears to be a type-8 shuttlecraft, but I am assuming their communications equipment is damaged. They appear to be on course for the inhabited planet, Pelleus V, which could indicate that Pelleus V is in danger."

"What else do thay say?" asked Geordi, leaning over his friend's shoulder.

"The most interesting thing is what they do *not* say," answered the android. "They claim to have more information—of a sensitive nature. And they do not identify themselves."

"Do you need help analyzing this stuff?" asked Geordi, sitting at an auxiliary console near his friend.

"Your perspective would be welcome," answered the android.

"What is their speed?" asked Captain Picard.

"Approximately warp three."

La Forge gave a low whistle. "Wow, that's fast for a type-8 shuttlecraft. They must have their foot to the floor."

Data cocked his head. "I fail to see how having their feet on the floor would make them go faster."

"It's an old analogy," answered Geordi. "It means they're not taking any precautions. They probably overrode the safeties."

"That is inadvisable," said Data with concern.

"Not when that thing is chasing you," concluded Captain Picard, gazing at the awesome destruction on the viewscreen. "Let's hope we reach them before *it* does."

"We need to get out of its path!" shouted Paldor, leaning uncomfortably over Leah Brahms' shoulder.

Leah tried to remain calm while she got a course correction from the computer, but panic had begun to sink in among her ragtag crew.

"We have to come out of warp to change course," she patiently explained. "It's right behind us—we don't know how far."

The Tellarite pressed forward, his ample stomach pushing the back of her head. "It can't take more than a few seconds. Maybe you can swing around a celestial body—"

"Will you back off!" she yelled at him, planting an elbow in his midsection.

The obstinate Tellarite pushed forward even more, which was a mistake. Maltz jumped to his feet, planted a fist in Paldor's chest and knocked him backwards; he sprawled in the aisle, bumping into Bekra's amputated leg. The Capellan groaned with pain, and Paldor shrieked as he thrashed about on the deck.

"The captain said to back off," explained the Klingon simply. "I will put you out the airlock next time." He sat down at the co-pilot's seat and continued to monitor the sensors.

Paldor jumped to his feet and sputtered in anger, shaking his fist. Leah tried to ignore him to concentrate on the job at hand. As long as they kept moving in their current course, she didn't think the wave could catch them, unless they stopped. If they changed course, they might flank the wave and get out of its path. Then they would be safe, but that was risky. They had estimates but no real idea how much the wave had expanded in girth, and if it caught them . . . there weren't any second guesses.

They continued to broadcast raw data on all channels, which had been Maltz's idea. He also suggested that they keep the information anonymous, so that everyone could take it at face value. As their projections increasingly showed, this was not just a Federation problem, and they didn't want it to sound that way.

From the corner of her eye, Leah saw Bekra motion to the Tellarite, and they were soon conversing in urgent whispers. Neither one of them liked the Klingon very much, but his lively presence was like a tonic to Leah, reminding her that there was nothing pretty about commanding a ship in the middle of a crisis. This desperation must have been what it was like for Geordi when he created a duplicate of her on the holodeck to consult with. A person could get crazy trying to operate under such stress, searching for a solution while death hovered all around. Leah suddenly had a great deal more compassion for Geordi and spacefaring engineers.

"Maintain course for Pelleus V?" asked Maltz, breaking into her troubled thoughts.

"Yes," she answered decisively. "And keep the message going out. Do you think it's getting through?"

The Klingon scowled, "If it isn't, it's not for lack of trying."

Suddenly the blackness of space lit up as if a thousand flares had gone off, and something streaked past their window, rocking the tiny ship. Leah had her hands full trying to control their rapid drop in speed, but she finally stabilized the small craft.

"That brought us out of warp," reported Maltz.

"What was it?" wailed Paldor behind them.

"A comet?" asked Bekra.

"No," answered the old Klingon. "Offhand, I would say it was a warning shot across our bow."

"From where?" asked Leah.

"Right there." Maltz pointed upward as a massive golden warship cruised overhead, blocking out the starscape. "I think we had better stop broadcasting and put on local two-way."

"Go ahead," rasped Leah with a squeak in her voice.

"We haven't got time for this!" shouted Paldor. "Unless they'll take us on board. Tell them to take us aboard!"

"Shut up," said Maltz as he fooled with his instruments. "Here we go. Let's see what they have to say."

After a screech of static, a deep voice which sounded stiff and mechanical came on the comlink. "Unknown spacecraft, you have entered Pellean space. Pelleus V is not a member of the Federation, and entry to the Pellean Principality is restricted. Please turn around and go back the way you came."

"We can't do that," said Paldor with alarm, echoing all of their thoughts.

"Come to a complete stop now," ordered the voice. Leah quickly obeyed him and brought the shuttlecraft to a full stop. But her eyes were on the sensor readings, and so were Maltz's. Although they couldn't pick up the exact location of the wave, they were learning to recognize the kind of incredible damage it left behind.

With anger and fear in her voice, she pressed a panel and responded. "Listen, we are running from a terrible energy wave that has already destroyed half a dozen solar systems. Millions of people on Seran and Hakon are dead, and *we're* going to be dead unless we both get out of here."

"Turn around and go back the way you came," ordered the stiff voice.

"Let me talk to him," said Bekra, sitting forward in his chair with effort. "After all, I'm a diplomat."

Maltz laughed. "It will not do any good. I ran sensors, and I do not see any life-forms on that whole ship."

"You mean, it's automated?" said Leah in amazement and distress.

"They're claiming an awfully big chunk of space," said Bekra indignantly.

"I heard they wanted a buffer zone during the war," said Maltz.

"The Federation was in no position to contest them, so they took it. Maybe they decided to hold onto it. *Now* might be a good time to try that course change we talked about."

"Okay," said Leah, working her board. "I want to skirt around their territory. I'll try a bearing of two-seven-zero and see if they let us get away with that." She piloted the shuttlecraft straight down, but the massive starship swiftly followed and barged in front of her, forcing her to stop.

"Insufficient," said the voice. "Resume bearing one-eight-zero or equivalent."

Bekra spoke up. "We're diplomats! This is Consul Maltz, and I'm Consul Bekra. There's been a terrible disaster, and your planet is right in the path of it. Escort us back to your leaders so we can talk. It's urgent!"

"Leave now!" ordered the voice. "Or we will put a tractor beam on your vessel and escort you from our space."

"I'm reversing course," said Leah, her heart thumping rapidly in her chest.

"Are you crazy?" shouted Paldor. "That's suicide!"

"No," she answered evenly, "suicide would be letting that big drone get a tractor beam on us. We'll stay on impulse."

"Then what will we do?" asked Bekra.

"I'll let you know when we get to that point." Leah Brahms swallowed hard, wishing she had a hologram of Captain Picard to consult. She glanced at her copilot. "Are they following us?"

"No," answered Maltz.

"That's good." Leah breathed a sigh of relief, and she peered into the endless distance. Only it didn't appear so endless today, with a glowing, spiral cloud blocking out the center of the starscape.

"What's that out there?" she asked. "A nebula?"

"No, not a nebula." Maltz stared intently at his instruments, then back at her. "It is moving rapidly toward us—at warp speed."

"Oh, no," whispered Leah. She heard Paldor wail in alarm, then

Bekra and Maltz began arguing about who was at fault for their being here. But the din in the shuttlecraft seemed to float over her head, and she felt as if she were back inside the radiation suit, removed from everything around her, concentrating only on the mission. Right now, the mission was to make a decision.

The right decision.

twelve

Without giving it a moment's thought—because she didn't have a moment—Leah reversed course again and slammed the shuttlecraft into warp two. Zooming into an elongated streak, the tiny craft hit warp just as a fiery green curtain wiped across their position, its fingers licking and lapping like solar flares. Ahead of them was a huge Pellean warship that was programmed to keep them from entering its space, which they did, anyway.

"Shields up," said Maltz with a wide grin. He shook his fists at the enemy and roared, "*qatlho*! It is a good day to die!"

"Speak for yourself!" exclaimed Paldor, slumping into his seat.

"At least we spread the alarm," muttered Brahms, hoping against crushing reality that it would do some good. Maybe the old Klingon was right, and it *was* a good day to die. Leah felt weary and miserable enough to die, but the old urge for self-preservation kept the adrenaline flowing, making her work to stay alive.

"Maltz," she asked, "do you think they'll fire another warning shot or go straight for us?"

"Perhaps they will be stupid enough to give us one more

chance." Suddenly the darkness in front of them erupted with a blaze of light, and the little ship was jolted hard. Once again, they spun out of warp.

"Unknown spacecraft, you have entered Pellean space," said the cold voice. "Pelleus V is not a member of the Federation, and entry to the Pellean Principality—"

Leah slammed the ship back into warp—this time warp three. Worrying about the safeties didn't seem to be a high priority under the circumstances. She was hoping they would underestimate her speed just enough to miss.

"Come to a complete stop now, or we will fire," warned the Pellean ship.

She increased their speed five percent just as another volley lit up the darkness and jarred them—but it didn't bring them out of warp.

"Ah, bad shots," said Maltz, rubbing his hands together with delight. "If I had just *one* aft torpedo, I would get them off our tail for good!"

"We've got warp-equipped sensor probes," said Leah.

Maltz scowled. "Sensor probes? What good is that?"

"They don't know they're sensor probes." She looked pointedly at the Klingon.

"Yes, Sir." The Klingon punched his board with enthusiasm. "I launched them all!"

"All two of them." She gave him a wry smile.

After studying his readouts for a few moments, the Klingon grinned and banged his fist on his console. "Well done, Captain! They are coming out of warp . . . taking evasive maneuvers. Humans are so devious." It almost sounded as if that were a compliment.

"Have we escaped them?" asked Paldor eagerly.

"I doubt if it will be that easy." As the Klingon continued to study his board, his expression drooped like his old moustache. "No . . . now they are powering up phasers."

"They can't miss with those, can they?" asked Leah with a gulp.

"Not at this range. Brace for impact!"

In the next instant, the tiny shuttlecraft was shaken like a rabbit in a wolf's mouth, and they were all dumped out of their seats, while lights in the cabin flickered and sparks spewed from the rear.

"There go the shields!" said Maltz over Paldor's screams and Bekra's groans. "The next shot, and we're space dust. It has been a pleasure serving with you, Captain!"

Leah dragged herself back into her seat. "Do we still have warp?"

Maltz rose to his knees to look at his console. "Yes."

The mechanized voice broke in. "You will cease hostilities, or we will destroy you. Prepare for our tractor beam to—" The voice suddenly became strangled and distorted, until it turned into a shrieking whine. Both Leah and Maltz stared at their screens, and they could see the ungodly curtain sweep over the golden starship, turning it into a lumpen mass.

"Full warp!" shouted Leah, working her console. The scorched shuttlecraft shot into space just as the fingers of the shimmering green curtain lapped at its stern.

"We are entering Pellean space," reported Data from the ops station on the bridge of the *Enterprise*. "We should have been hailed by now."

Geordi looked up from his console to watch Will Riker pace in front of the viewscreen, which showed what looked to be a peaceful stretch of space. The reality was far different, thought the engineer, because somewhere out there was a murderer, killing on a massive scale.

Captain Picard was getting some much-needed rest, and Riker was in charge. "What's the protocol with the Pelleans?" he asked.

Data cocked his head. "According to our treaty with them, we are not allowed to enter their space unannounced. If we are not hailed, we are to wait until we are met by an escort."

"There's no time for that," muttered Riker. "But we don't want to rush into an ambush either. Conn, slow to impulse but maintain course. Data, what's on long-range scans?" Geordi could see impatience etched on Riker's face, plus blotches of heated blood vessels under his skin, even if his tone of voice was relaxed.

After a moment, the android reported, "It would appear that Pelleus V has undergone the same sort of disaster and transformation that we have seen before. The particle field is also in evidence, as well as other indicators."

Riker pounded a fist into his palm, and La Forge knew how he felt. Once again, they were too late. An entire civilization—a billion souls—had vanished from existence along with every other form of life on the planet. They were one step behind this monster, and the only ones who were ahead of it had gone silent again.

"How is Paul Revere?" asked Geordi.

"Paul Revere?" queried Riker. "What's he got to do with it?"

Data spoke up, "That is Geordi's nickname for the mysterious shuttlecraft which has been trying to warn planets in this sector. We have been unable to identify it, other than that it is of Federation design and probably from the planet Seran. They are the ones who furnished us with the data you saw."

"And the captain's orders are to find them," added Riker, "not wait here for an escort who will likely never show up. So what is Paul Revere's position?"

"We are still picking up a faint distress signal from the other side of the Pellean solar system," answered Data. "But since they are no longer broadcasting on all frequencies, I cannot be one hundred percent certain that it is the *same* shuttlecraft."

"It's worth a try," said Riker. "Keep after them."

"Setting a course at warp speed is going to be tricky," broke in

Geordi. "We've got to avoid the energy wave, which seems to be expanding."

"Data, you take over the conn," ordered Riker. He nodded gratefully at the resident helmsman. "Sorry, Mr. Bollinger, but we need the best pilot we've got. You take ops."

"Understood," said the bald-headed Brekkian. Neither he nor Data had to move from their seats, because with a push of a button, the functions of their consoles were switched. Data was probably watching everyone's readouts, anyway, thought Geordi.

After a few dizzying moments of working his board, Data reported, "Course laid in. I suggest a maximum speed of warp 4, which will give me time to make needed course corrections to avoid the anomaly. I estimate we can intercept them in one hour."

"Sir," broke in the young Benzite on tactical, "I've received a message from the *Sovereign*." Now she had the attention of Riker, Data, La Forge, and everyone else on the bridge. With a slight tremor in her voice, she went on, "They want to know why we keep changing our position. It's making it difficult for them to rendezvous with us."

Riker stroked his clean-shaven chin for a moment, then said, "Tell them that Pelleus V appears to have been destroyed, and now we're on a rescue mission."

"Before you send that," said Geordi, cutting in, "can I make a suggestion?"

"Go ahead," answered Riker, "but make it good."

The engineer spoke quickly. "We've got a Stellar-class shuttlecraft that can catch them as well as the *Enterprise* can, under these circumstances. Why don't Data and I go chase them, and you stay here and wait for the admiral?"

Riker snapped his fingers and pointed to the turbolift. "Get going. I'll contact the captain and try to have his permission by the time you get to the shuttlebay."

La Forge and Data bounded out of their seats and rushed for the turbolift as relief personnel took their stations. It was a long shot, thought Geordi, and maybe a waste of time; but he couldn't sit around and do nothing while the people who had risked their lives to save others were in danger.

He and Data were soon speeding through the Saucer Module en route to the main shuttlebay. Data was unusually quiet, and La Forge noticed an electromagnetic haze around his friend, indicating a high degree of processing.

"What's the matter?" he asked.

"The nature of this threat has me puzzled," answered the android. "It defies most of what we know about natural science."

"Then it's *unnatural* science," said Geordi as the turbolift door opened.

"Artificial," concluded Data, cocking his head. "Manufactured. This theory supports the facts, yet it raises even more questions."

"I know somebody who has the answers," said Geordi, striding ahead of him through the cavernous main shuttlebay. "Paul Revere."

"You seemed convinced of that, yet they may prove to be nothing more than frightened refugees."

"I don't think so." La Forge strode past the front row of shuttle-craft nearest the launch doors, ready for immediate launch. He stopped at the biggest, sleekest, and newest craft, named the *Balboa*. "This one?"

"It's checked out, ready to go," said a voice behind them. They turned to see Chief Halstert, a curmudgeonly, gray-haired human who ran the shuttlebay like his own fiefdom. He practically lived in the place. But since he had been on duty for four years, no one had stolen a shuttlecraft—a new record.

"Commander Riker called down and said you were cleared to launch," reported the chief. "The Stellar-class is a real sweetheart, but watch your range if you spend a lot of time in warp. Good luck—I don't think I'd want to get to close to that thing."

"We intend to keep a safe distance," answered Data, stepping through the hatch into the cabin of the shuttlecraft.

"Thanks, Chief." With a wave, Geordi followed his friend onto the craft. He saw Halstert turn and jog away from them, seeking the safety of his observation booth. He must've remembered how quickly Data prepared for launch.

Less than a minute later, the great launch doors opened, and the doorstop-shaped *Balboa*, sporting twin warp nacelles, streaked into space.

The wind chimes tinkled merrily as a southernly breeze blew across the porch, bringing with it the sweet scents of lilac and honeysuckle, plus the gay laughter of children. Carol Marcus couldn't see the children, but she was certain they were out there . . . just beyond the high hedges and pink bougainvillea. She rocked contentedly on the old porch swing, watching the hummingbirds flit around the honeysuckle bushes, and she remembered sucking the nectar from those same sweet blossoms as a kid.

It was wonderful how little the old family home had changed over all these years. She vaguely remembered her parents selling it, but that couldn't be—or else they couldn't be here now. She must have been mistaken about that, but then so many things had been hazy lately. The present was incredibly vivid, but the past was like a book she had read years ago and only partially remembered.

Carol knew one thing—it was good to be on vacation after all the hard work of the last few months. When she looked at it, though, the work hadn't been that hard, thanks to her brilliant helpers.

She heard the screen door open with a creak, then slam shut, followed by footsteps crossing the porch. Carol recognized the sure footsteps right away, and she looked up to see Jim Kirk, holding a frosty glass of iced lemonade. When he gave her that winning smile, he looked impossibly handsome—about twenty-six years old with sandy hair and mirthful brown eyes. He was dressed in a tight-fitting gold lieutenant's uniform, just as he had been the day she first met him.

Jim touched her shoulder, and the old electricity still coursed between them. "I brought you a lemonade," he said.

"Thank you, Darling." She canted her head upward and closed her eyes, letting him kiss her longingly, yet gently. Finally Jim pulled away, still smiling at her with those dazzling dimples.

"Drink up," he suggested. "You must be thirsty."

"I am," she decided all of a sudden. Carol took a sip of the lemonade, and it was oddly flat, not having the usual biting tang she remembered. Then she took another sip, and it tasted much better—more lemony.

"How is that?" asked Jim with concern.

"Fine," she answered brightly. "It would be just perfect if David were here. When is he coming?"

"I talked to our son this morning," answered Kirk, "and the tests are going very well. He thinks he'll be able to join us tomorrow."

"Wonderful!" said Carol, clapping her hands together. "You can stay longer, too, can't you?"

"Of course, Sweetheart," he answered, kneeling in front of her and taking her free hand in his.

"Don't you have to report back to the *Farragut?*"

"No, I'm on special assignment," answered Jim. "Taking care of you is my only priority."

"And Genesis," she added.

"And Genesis," he agreed. "I haven't worked on it for as long as you and David, but I feel it's my baby, too."

"Well, it has changed so much, hasn't it?" she answered proudly. "The new delivery system . . . the carrier wave . . . the experimental life-forms. It means so much to me that Genesis is on the front burner again."

"But still a secret," Jim reminded her. "Not that you would ever tell anybody." He gently rocked her in the swinging porch chair, his voice taking on a soothing tone. "Nobody will know, not after you managed to keep it a secret for so many years. You are amazing."

"I was bursting to tell someone," said Carol with a yawn.

Jim gently took the glass of lemonade from her hand. "Honey, I can see in your eyes that you look a little tired. Don't feel that you have to stay awake on my account. You could take a nap right here on the porch. There's no one around—no one to worry about. Go ahead . . . sleep."

"Yes, I could," rasped Carol, immense drowsiness overcoming her. "Why not?"

He touched her forehead, and his hand felt as cool and dry as the breeze. Carol took his hand and held it to her face as she drifted off to sleep, the happiest woman in the universe.

Maltz grumbled and cursed in Klingon for several seconds, then crawled out from under the instrument panel and looked forlornly at Leah Brahms. "It's not going to work . . . we're still leaking plasma, and I can't fix the comm system."

Paldor and Bekra crowded around the cockpit of the shuttlecraft, shooting questions at the Klingon, but he ignored them while waiting for Leah to respond. In desperation, she finally turned to the Capellan and the Tellarite and shouted, "Be quiet! I can't hear myself *think*!"

Chagrined, Bekra retreated and hopped one-legged back to his seat, but Paldor pressed forward. "What's going on? We've got a right to know!"

Maltz growled and looked about ready to throttle the annoying Tellarite, but Leah put a calming hand on his shoulder. "It's okay. We have to face the truth."

She took a deep breath and turned to her shipmates. "It's like this—we already had damage, and we took more damage from the Pellean attack. We're leaking plasma, which means our fuel is going to run out sooner than expected."

"How soon?" asked Paldor.

"That depends whether we want to keep life support going."

"You mean, we can fly farther if we're all dead?" asked Bekra snidely.

Leah sighed. "I guess that's not an option, is it? I'd say we have twenty minutes . . . half an hour at the most."

"That does it!" shouted Paldor angrily. The Tellarite began to pace, making the cabin of the shuttlecraft seem even more cramped. "You should have listened to *me*! I never wanted to go to Pelleus V. I wanted to get out of the way of that thing! Now we don't have enough fuel to get out of the way—it's just going to eat us alive . . . like it did all the others!"

Maltz countered, "No, you will be spared that, because I am going to kill you!" The Klingon jumped to his feet and lunged for the Tellarite, but the big humanoid threw himself over a row of seats and crouched in the back.

"That's enough," snapped Leah, grabbing Maltz by the sash and pulling him gently back to his seat. "We're not going to spend our last few minutes bickering—we're going to find a way out. If we don't, we'll join lots of other good people."

"We're not all going to die," said Bekra with a sneer. "*One* of us is going to live."

The Capellan pointed to the hulking white radiation suit in the corner, and everyone's eyes followed his gesture. After a moment, Paldor timidly asked, "How will we choose who lives?"

"It's not *my* suit," said Maltz. He looked pointedly from Bekra to Paldor. "Not yours either."

Leah couldn't help herself—she laughed out loud at the absurdity of this argument, and the three males stared at her as if she were insane. Under their gaze, her deranged laughter trailed off. "I'm sorry; I lost it there. One of you can have it. I lived through seeing my husband and colleagues all die, and I'm not going to do *that* again. Besides, judging by how quickly we've been rescued so far, whoever is in that suit is just going to float in space for a few days longer before he dies, too."

"Still, it's a chance, isn't it?" said Bekra. "That's all we've been doing for the last day, trying to turn disaster into a fighting chance."

Leah nodded sadly, unable to argue with that. "Make sure you keep the isolinear chip in the pocket, so in a thousand years when they find your mummified body, they'll know what killed you."

"I think I should wear the suit," declard Maltz. "I need to tell someone what I know about this weapon."

"Why don't you tell me?" suggested Bekra. "Then I could wear the suit and survive."

"What about *me?*" wailed Paldor indignantly. "I work with Dr. Brahms, so I should be next in line. I'm also the youngest of everyone here. Most of my life is ahead of me."

Maltz grinned and slammed his fist into his palm. "What do you say we fight to the death for the honor? That way, even the losers will benefit from a valiant death. Come on, I will fight both of you at once!" He crouched down, waving his arms.

"Maltz, there's not enough room in this shuttlecraft for a brawl to the death," said Leah with disgust. "It's my invention, and I'll choose. Paldor is the youngest, and he already knows how the suit works. I haven't got time to train one of you."

The Tellarite leaped to his feet and rushed forward. "Oh, Dr. Brahms, thank you very much!" he gushed. "I won't forget this . . . or you."

"You have to get the suit on," she pointed out. "And it wasn't designed for someone your size."

"I'll get in," promised the Tellarite, rushing to the back of the cabin and starting to strip.

With a scowl, Maltz dropped into the seat beside her. "I can't believe you let that . . . that nuisance save himself."

"I'm still going to try to save us all," answered Leah.

Without warning, a beep sounded on her console, and the computer voice broke in, "Plasma injectors are depleted, and deuterium reserves are low. We are now operating on emergency gel-packs. We will come out of warp in one minute."

"Hurry!" shouted Leah. "The leak was worse than we thought!"

Grunting and groaning, Paldor tried to shoehorn himself into the hard-shelled suit, but he ended up crashing to the deck in a heap. Grumbling and cussing, Maltz rose to his feet and tried to help the Tellarite get into the armor. Having to keep her eyes on her instruments, Leah couldn't really watch them, but she heard howls of pain from Paldor.

"Keep going!" insisted the Tellarite through clenched teeth. "I'm almost in!"

"You people are fools!" shouted Bekra. "I should be the one who lives!" The one-legged Capellan suddenly lunged out of his seat, tackling Maltz and knocking Paldor over. The scene was surreal, although Leah only caught glimpses of it, with Maltz and Bekra grappling in the aisle while Paldor wrestled with the radiation suit. It looked as if the brawl to the death had broken out after all.

Maltz finally clawed his way to the top position, and he slugged the Capellan into unconsciousness. Without a word, the Klingon staggered to his feet and went back to helping Paldor, but the ruckus had cost them precious seconds. Paldor whimpered anxiously as he tried again to get into the suit.

With a low whine, the shuttlecraft dropped out of warp and began cruising at impulse speeds. Leah wished she knew some Klingon curses of her own, because she was all out of tricks. She fought the temptation to look for the wave, because she knew it was out there, churning through the heavens, bearing down on them.

She had a strong urge to call for help, which was futile, because all she had was local short-range communications, hardly better than a combadge. Still she opened up her comm channel and shouted, "Mayday! Mayday! We're out of fuel. We need help!"

"Maintain position," came a calm male voice, breaking through the crackle of static. "Stand by to transport."

"What?" she asked. No one else was paying the slightest attention, with Bekra sprawled unconscious on the deck and Paldor and Maltz still struggling to squeeze the Tellarite into the radiation suit. Maybe she had imagined that calm, efficient voice answering her hail, but it gave her the spark of hope she needed to keep thinking.

She stopped the shuttlecraft and checked her long-range sensors, certain the wave must be right behind them. Half-a-million kilometers away, there was nothing but the kind of destruction they had seen before, so it was almost on top of them. Behind her, she heard a howl of victory as Maltz finished fastening the back of the suit, encasing the Tellarite inside.

Brahms quickly hit her combadge. "Paldor, don't turn on the phase-shifting yet."

"Why not?" he demanded nervously.

"Because—" She felt a familiar tingle along her spine, or maybe it was delirium. "We're being rescued!" she cried.

Leah closed her eyes as her body was whisked away, and she didn't open them until she felt a deck under her feet. She looked up to see an angel with gleaming white eyes and outstretched hands, swooping in to catch her. Not only that, but he was an angel she *knew*. "Geordi!" Leah gasped with delight as she tumbled into his arms.

"Leah!" he shouted deliriously. "You're alive!" He gripped her and hugged her ferociously.

"More coming though!" called that calm, efficient voice.

Geordi immediately pulled her away from the small transporter platform, which was inside another shuttlecraft. She found herself weeping with relief, unable to do anything but shuffle along the aisle, going where he led her.

He guided her gently into a seat and grinned. "We'll talk in a second. The others—"

"Go, go!" she cried, anxiously gripping his arm. "Tell your pilot to go, too. There's no time to waste!"

thirteen

Geordi had to use every ounce of discipline and sense of duty in his being to pull himself away from Leah Brahms. Then he heard a clomping sound, and he turned to see a grizzled Klingon step off the transporter.

"At last you showed up," grumped the Klingon. "I am Maltz."

"Pleased to meet you," said Geordi, shoving past him to catch an injured man who staggered off the transporter platform. The man, a Capellan by the look of him, shot a glare at the Klingon as Geordi lifted him into a seat. He noticed that the Capellan's leg had been amputated at the knee and was freshly bandaged.

"The next one is a big one!" warned Maltz.

That was an understatement, decided Geordi, when an enormous being encased in white armor arrived on the transporter pad, thrashing around and filling up the rear of the shuttlecraft. Geordi rushed to calm him and keep him from breaking anything.

"Now!" called Leah. "Get out of here!"

"Very well," answered Data. He worked his instrument panel, and the shuttlecraft jumped into space.

"Here, I will get him out." The old Klingon stood at Geordi's side, and he waved through the faceplate at the inhabitant of the bulky suit. "He is a nuisance named Paldor, and that other one is a traitor named Bekra." The Klingon pointed to the surly Capellan. "You seem to know our captain."

"Captain?" said La Forge, glancing at Leah. "You got promoted?"

She shrugged. "It was my shuttlecraft."

La Forge knew he should take statements and get particulars from everyone, but only one person on the vessel commanded his attention. Since the Klingon seemed to know how to extricate the Tellarite from the suit, Geordi gave in and rushed to Leah's side.

"I . . . I just can't believe you're alive," he said, unable to stop grinning.

"That makes two of us." She looked beaten down, depressed, and he could guess why.

"Are you two the only ones who got away?"

She nodded and sniffed back the tears. Knowing Leah, this was probably one of the few times she had allowed herself to cry. "It was . . . It was horrible. I'd be dead, too, except for the radiation suit."

"I'm sorry," said Geordi, glancing behind him. The Tellarite was nearly out of the suit. "Yes, I remember the radiation suit from your last message. In fact, that's when we knew something was wrong." He quickly told her about his reply getting bounced, initiating the investigation which had brought the *Enterprise* here. But he could tell that she wasn't listening—she was in shock, grief-stricken, and exhausted. Soon she would have to describe what she had seen, but he wasn't going to make her do it now.

"I'm just glad that *you* were Paul Revere."

"Pardon me?" she asked with confusion.

"That was our nickname for you when we didn't know who you were." He patted her on the shoulder. "I know you've been through a lot, but you're all right now."

"No," she said, shuddering. "As long as that thing is out there, we're not all right. Everyone on Earth—"

"Earth?" echoed Geordi with alarm.

Data spoke up, "Which one of you claims to have secret information about this anomaly?"

"That would be me," said the gray-haired Klingon haughtily. "It is a weapon." He drew a bit closer to Data and peered curiously at him. "What kind of creature are you?"

"I am not a creature at all—I am an android."

"Are there many like you?"

"No." Data shook his head.

"Good." Maltz sat down beside him at the copilot's seat and studied the readouts. "Hmmm, this is a nicer shuttlecraft than she has. What ship did you say you were from?"

"The *Enterprise*. My captain would like to speak with you."

"I am sure he would," said the old Klingon with satisfaction. "The sooner, the better."

While Data contacted the ship, Geordi leaned forward to listen, but he discovered that Leah was asleep on his shoulder. So he sat still and listened, as did everyone else on the shuttlecraft. He could tell from the rapt attention that the Tellarite and the wounded Capellan were giving to Maltz that they also believed he knew what he was talking about.

"This is Captain Jean-Luc Picard of the Federation starship *Enterprise*."

The old Klingon lifted his stubbled chin and declared, "I am Maltz from the House of Grokan, formerly Klingon consul to Hakon. I have heard of you, Captain Picard. They say you respect our traditions."

"I do," replied the captain. "I would like to share a bottle of bloodwine with you, but right now we have more pressing matters. Do you know the origin of this destruction?"

"I do," said the old Klingon. "But are *you* the right one to tell?"

"Why is it such a secret?" asked Picard.

"I don't know—*you* tell me," said Maltz, holding up his palms. "This is the Federation's secret."

Frustrated, the captain scowled. "Listen, I'm about to meet with an admiral, and if you know anything that might be pertinent, it's your duty to tell me. If you don't, I have to conclude you're a *'yIH-mey SurghwI'*."

Maltz bristled and bolted upright; then he seemed to relax once again. "An admiral, eh? Listen, Picard, if this admiral seems to be hiding something from you, not being honest about what *they* know, all you have to do is say one word. That word is 'Genesis.'"

"Genesis?" asked Picard doubtfully. The word stirred a vague memory. Could this old Klingon mean *that* Genesis? If so . . .

Maltz nodded to himself, and there was a genuine look of fear in his eyes. "When I get to your ship, I will talk with you and your admiral. In the meantime, you could learn much armed with that word."

The Klingon sat back in his seat and made a regal motion to cut off the transmission. Data tapped his panel and said, "Captain, Dr. Leah Brahms is with us, and she believes Earth is in danger."

Picard nodded grimly. "We're working on those projections. We'll see you at the rendezvous. *Enterprise* out."

It suddenly became very quiet inside the shuttlecraft as everyone realized that *they* were safe but billions of people were not. But they had rescued four souls who would have been dead otherwise, and maybe one of them possessed the key to fighting this menace.

La Forge looked down at Leah, who was sleeping deeply, her head resting on his shoulder. He planned to live through this crisis, but if he had to die right this moment, he'd be a happy man.

Captain Picard rose slowly from his desk in his ready room, his lips thinning with distaste at the idea that Starfleet might know more about this peril than they let on. It was not beyond them to keep secrets, as he had learned recently. Nevertheless, Admiral Nechayev had always been straight with him, often brutally honest, in fact. When she had a dirty job for him, she told him it was a dirty job. If his crew would face extreme risk, she told him so.

His door chime sounded. "Come!" he said.

Will Riker poked his head in. "I thought you would like to know," said the first officer, "Admiral Nechayev is on her way up from the transporter room."

"We're meeting here?" asked the captain, slightly surprised. "Very well. How many aides does she have with her?"

"None," answered Riker. "It's just her."

Hmmm, thought Picard. It was odd that their conversation was to be private when they had so much they should be doing. He decided to follow the old Klingon's advice and look for other signs of secrecy.

"Stick around, Number One," he said. "I'd like you to sit in."

"Fine, Captain." Riker stepped inside, allowing the door to shut behind him. "We're running projections based on our new data, and it doesn't look good."

"Is Earth in its path?"

"It could be," agreed Riker with surprise. "How did you know?"

"One of the people on the Paul Revere shuttlecraft was Leah Brahms. She told Data that Earth was in the path."

"Leah Brahms," said Riker with a slight smile. "I bet Geordi is happy."

Another chime sounded at the door, and both Riker and Picard snapped to attention as the captain said, "Enter."

The door opened, and in walked a slight woman with grayish-blond hair, a cranberry uniform, and a bar on her collar with five pips. Alynna Nechayev was not the kind of woman you'd pay much attention to if you passed her on the street, but you couldn't get around her in Starfleet. If you were an enemy of the Federation, she would have your head on a platter, and she was not above fighting dirty.

"Admiral," said Picard, mustering a smile.

"Captain Picard, Commander Riker," she acknowledged. "I hope I haven't interrupted you during a briefing, but we haven't got much time."

Picard nodded. "I was hoping Commander Riker could sit in with us and be—"

"Out of the question," snapped Nechayev. "We're tying to avoid a panic, so our plans have to remain secret for the time being. I'm sure you understand, Commander."

Riker raised an eyebrow that made it clear he *didn't* understand, but he still moved toward the door. "I'll keep you posted, Captain," he said on his way out.

Okay, thought Picard, *two more strikes against full disclosure*. After the door shut, he motioned the admiral to a guest chair while he went behind his desk. Despite his intentions to let Nechayev do most of the talking, Picard found himself speaking up. "I don't see how we can keep this a secret. We have to muster fleets of ships, evacuate dozens of planets, convene a meeting of the council. Whatever it takes."

"I don't want to dampen your enthusiasm," said Nechayev, "but we don't know the first thing about this phenomenon."

"Haven't you been looking at the raw data we sent you?" asked the captain. "Do you mean that nobody in Starfleet has formed a theory about what this thing is?"

"Yes, there have been theories," admitted Nechayev. "But if you asked ten different scientists, you'd get ten different answers. Meanwhile, Captain Picard, I don't appreciate your tone of voice. We're all working just as hard as we can to react to this crisis—putting out incomplete and false information won't help the situation."

Picard screwed up his courage and said the magic word: "Genesis."

Nechayev's poker face didn't change, but she did flinch for a moment. A blush came to her face as she considered what to do with the word, and she shifted in her chair. *Damn if the old Klingon wasn't right*, thought the captain.

She finally asked, "What makes you mention Genesis? It is just a . . . space legend."

"A certain old Klingon we rescued," answered Picard. Since that was the only fact he knew for certain, he hoped he could bluff the rest of the way. "So if the Klingons know Genesis is not a myth, why don't your veteran captains know?"

"I doubt if every Klingon knows about it," answered the admiral. "There might be a few—"

"His name is Maltz," said Picard.

Nechayev nodded with the grim certainty of a bridge player who has just realized that she can't make her contract. "Then you might as well hear our side of it, too. Read this and tell me what you think we ought to do." She opened a small utility pouch on her belt and pulled out an isolinear chip, which she handed to Picard.

With that, the admiral rose from her seat and started for the door. "We'll talk later, Captain. Although you may be angry at me now, you'll see that these decisions were made many years ago."

The captain also stood, hefting the purple storage chip in his palm. Nechayev's somber, almost defeated attitude was more disturbing than anything else he had seen that day.

"Admiral, what makes you so certain that thing out there *is* Genesis?"

"You'll read a lot about Dr. Carol Marcus in those documents," said Nechayev. "She was kidnapped six months ago, by parties unknown. We've been expecting something like this ever since, because she's the only one who knows how to build it. After you digest that, you won't be in the dark anymore. I'll be on the *Sovereign*."

Picard nodded, feeling more troubled than ever. So this was some kind of dangerous technology which the Federation had failed to protect properly. He couldn't help but wonder why they had built it in the first place.

fourteen

After Admiral Nechayev left the ready room, Captain Picard sat with trepidation at his desk and inserted the isolinear chip into his computer terminal. Figuring he might need some soothing music, he requested a Beethoven sonata to play softly in the background. Then he leaned forward to read the documents given him by Admiral Nechayev.

THE GENESIS REPORT

CLASSIFIED TOP SECRET
by Executive Order of The President
of The United Federation of Planets
18 December 2286
(Stardate 8399.4)

SECURITY CLEARANCE
LEVELS 9 AND HIGHER ONLY

Unauthorized access punishable by mandatory life imprisonment

GENESIS REPORT—SUBJECT INDEX

01.00 TECHNICAL EVALUATION—03 November 2286
(Stardate 8411.2)
Dr. Carol Marcus, director, Project Genesis
    01.01 Project Overview
    01.02 The Mutara Nebula Detonation
    01.03 The Genesis Planet
    01.04 Findings & Recommendations

02.00 STRATEGIC EVALUATION—09 November 2286
(Stardate 8420.1)
Commander Stephen J. Klisiewicz,
Starfleet Intelligence
    02.01 Civilian Applications
    02.02 Scientific Applications
    02.03 Military Applications
    02.04 Potential Countermeasures
    02.05 Findings & Recommendations

03.00 POLITICAL EVALUATION—16 December 2286
(Stardate 8426.9)
Xev Chiana, Secretary of State, UFP
    03.01 Diplomatic Ramifications
    03.02 Pacification of Federation Rivals
    03.03 Threat of External Duplication
    03.04 Findings & Resolutions
    03.05 Addendum—Final Determination

04.00 PROJECT REASSESSMENT—12 May 2374
(Stardate 53303.4)
Lt. David Mack, Starfleet Research & Development

01.00 PROJECT GENESIS—TECHNICAL EVALUATION

Dr. Carol Marcus, director, Project Genesis
Regula I Space Laboratory
Transmission Received via Secure Subspace Channel Zed-328
03 November 2286 (Stardate 8411.2)

01.01 PROJECT OVERVIEW

Project Genesis was a scientific research program whose goal was to develop a process whereby uninhabitable planets could be transformed into worlds suitable for sustaining a variety of life-forms. The project began its preliminary research in August 2270, under my direction, as a purely voluntary effort by more than a dozen scientists from throughout the Federation.

The first challenge of the project was to harness the power, and control the behavior, of a wide variety of subatomic particles. The second, and far more daunting challenge, was to prevent the premature degradation of matter generated by the matrix. Because of the extremely high energy level of a Genesis Wave reaction, the strong and weak nuclear forces essential to normal subatomic cohesion are annihilated. Controlling the behavior of subatomic particles was only the first step; we next needed to isolate the Genesis Effect from external particles in order to effect the renormalization of covalent bonds.

Numerous new technologies were developed to isolate the reaction matrix from such hazardous particles as various colors and flavors of quarks, bosons, muons, gluons and assorted high-energy/low-mass cosmic particles. The greatest threat was the spontaneous appearance of quark strangelets, which initiated near-instantaneous and total annihilation of the matrix. (Refer to Starfleet Research & Development briefing 478594 for a complete catalog of the Project Genesis Sub-atomic Bestiary.)

In July 2272, we succeeded in directing the behavior of several types of fermions by altering their quantum states through the use of a Heisenberg compensator coupled with a quantum flux capacitor. The Heisenberg compensator and quantum flux capacitor also served to isolate the matrix from external particle interference, and consequently became the first integral components in the Genesis Matrix Generator.

Once it became possible to direct the behavior of subatomic particles, the next step in the development of Project Genesis was to create the Genesis Matrix, which would serve as the quantum-level template to guide the reassembly of high-energy particles into cohesive matter and renormalize their strong and weak nuclear forces.

The Genesis Matrix was crafted to simulate the geophysical structure, topography, environmental chemistry and organic ecosystems of a range of Class-M planets suitable for humanoid life, although the matrix could theoretically be reprogrammed to generate the full range of planetary types and simulate various alien organic ecosystems. These mutagenic changes are permanent.

From July 2272 to October 2282, we conducted numerous controlled experiments in our laboratory on Deneva, applying the Genesis Matrix to various types of inanimate matter, at varying energy levels. Despite some early setbacks that caused the reformed matter to disintegrate within minutes, a reformulation of the matrix in 2283 by my son and colleague, Dr. David Marcus, succeeded in long-term stabilization of matter reorganized by the Genesis Matrix.

In November 2283, it became evident that continuation of Project Genesis would require a level of funding, technological resources, and manpower that my private scientific consortium was no longer able to provide. In order to continue our work to its logical conclusion, a research grant proposal was made to the United Federation of Planets' Department of Science. Funding and official assistance was secured in March 2284, and Starfleet made available the services of the *Starship Reliant* and her crew, and relocated our team to the Regula I Space Laboratory, in orbit above the Class-D asteroid Regula, in the Mutara Sector.

Development of the planetary delivery system and the high-power Genesis Wave generator was completed at the Regula I Space Laboratory in February 2284, at which time a first-generation Genesis Device prototype was constructed. The first device was designed for a low-power, limited-range-of-effect detonation within a confined space. On March 3, 2284, at our request, the Starfleet Corps of Engineers began to excavate an underground facility within the Regula asteroid, which we confirmed was composed only of inanimate matter. The *Starship Reliant* was tasked with finding a planet devoid of all life, in a suitable orbit for a Class-M world, on which to test a full-scale

Genesis Effect. The excavation of our underground test site took the engineers ten months to complete.

In January 2285, after the sealed underground space had been sufficiently hollowed out and was confirmed to be free of gaseous particles, we initiated our first field test of the Genesis Matrix. The test was an unqualified success and transformed the lifeless, vacuum-sealed underground cavern into a thriving primitive organic ecosystem that required only the addition of artificial sunlight to sustain itself. New plant forms evolved at a dramatically accelerated rate within the new environment, a consequence that had not been anticipated during development.

Although the test versions of the Genesis Matrix included no templates for eukaryotic life-forms, they could conceivably be added in future versions of the matrix; however, given the rapid evolutionary rates of plant species within the matrix, such a course of action might be inadvisable, depending upon the genetic complexity of the animal species. Plankton and krill might prove relatively stable, whereas higher-order forms might not.

01.02 THE MUTARA NEBULA DETONATION

The final intended phase of Project Genesis was to await *Starship Reliant*'s discovery of a suitable test planet for the final prototype test. However, this effort was sabotaged by the actions of Khan Noonien Singh, who on March 22, 2285, hijacked the *Starship Reliant*, stranded most of her crew on Ceti Alpha V, and on March 25, 2285, stole the Genesis Device from our underground facility, where we had hidden it for safekeeping. Khan detonated the Genesis Device on March 26, 2285, in the Mutara Nebula.

01.03 THE GENESIS PLANET

The detonation of the Genesis Device within the Mutara Nebula resulted in the formation of the Genesis Planet from the cloud of stellar and planetary debris of which the nebula was composed. The planet coalesced within hours into a primordial sphere of molten rock approximately .47 times the mass of Earth, but with a variable gravity field of .78-G to 1.36-G. Because of its low total mass and accelerated subatomic reaction rate, the planet cooled and formed a solid crust over its mantle and molten core in less than 26 hours. Plant life-forms evolved almost immediately and spread quickly across the planet surface.

During the weeks following the formation of the Genesis Planet, erratic weather systems developed, and the planet's crust became increasingly fragile and susceptible to geothermal stressors. Alien microbes introduced into the planet's ecosystem by a soft-landing Starfleet torpedo casing, used as a burial container, evolved rapidly into eukaryotic forms, including complex invertebrate animal forms.

The planet's subatomic bonds destabilized rapidly, and finally disintegrated altogether on April 29, 2285, resulting in its explosion.

A posthumous report filed by Dr. David Marcus revealed that the planet had destabilized because he had used protomatter, an energy-rich but notoriously unstable form of matter, to energize the Genesis Wave. He had used protomatter because it was the only way he could generate an initial energy burst of sufficient power to sustain a global imprinting of the Genesis Matrix. His use of protomatter was not revealed in any of his earlier documentation, leading to the regrettable conclusion that all experimental data for Project Genesis generated after 2282 are inaccurate, fraudulent or suspect.

01.04 FINDINGS & RECOMMENDATIONS

Because of the clearly unstable results produced by the Genesis Device, the process is unsafe for the creation of habitable worlds, rendering the technology worthless for rapid terraforming.

Because of the inherently dangerous and unpredictable nature of protomatter, the Genesis Device is not reliable enough to be repurposed for military applications, which would in any event be unethical and in violation of the Federation charter; because the Genesis Wave would replace a living world's ecosystem with one generated by the Genesis Matrix, any use of this device on a living world could be described only as genocide.

For the above reasons, and because of the flawed and unethical research methods used to develop the Genesis Device, my formal recommendation to the Federation Council is that all research into Project Genesis' continued development be terminated immediately and permanently. This concludes my report.

Dr. Carol Marcus

02.00 STRATEGIC EVALUATION

Commander Stephen J. Klisiewicz, Starfleet Intelligence
San Francisco, Earth
Received via Encrypted Internal Channel 423-Sierra
09 November 2286 (Stardate 8420.1)

02.01 CIVILIAN APPLICATIONS

After evaluating the continued stability of the Genesis Cave within the Regula asteroid, this office has concluded that Project Genesis is stable at low-power levels when applied on a small scale. Although the technology has clearly proved too unstable for large-scale terraforming efforts, it continues to be a promising technology for rapidly establishing sustainable food sources in remote locations. Extrapolating from the volume of transformed matter in the project's Phase Two experiment, we believe the Genesis Effect could safely be applied to many underground locations, as well as on large asteroids or very small moons located in favorable orbits.

02.02 SCIENTIFIC APPLICATIONS

Despite the late-phase failure of the Genesis Device prototype and Dr. Carol Marcus' understandable concerns regarding Dr. David Marcus' falsification of critical data, we believe there is still substantial scientific merit to continuing research into the Project Genesis technology. The ability to reorder subatomic particles into animate matter is one that, if it could be harnessed at much lower energy levels, could yield near-miraculous discoveries in medicine, materials fabrication, and agriculture and aquaculture.

Although the energy requirements of the process currently are far too high to risk exposing living subjects to its effects, we believe that within two centuries discoveries spurred by Project Genesis research could lead to cellular-regeneration matrices that would permit the near-perfect repair of all cellular damage. Such a discovery would, in essence, allow organic sentient beings to achieve lifespans so greatly extended that they would effectively become immortal.

On a more immediate level, a technology that could transform raw energy into living plant and animal matter would revolutionize our food-production methods and represent a quantum leap forward from our current food-replication models.

02.03 MILITARY APPLICATIONS

Despite the obvious, sheer power of the Genesis Device as a weapon, this office concurs with Dr. Marcus that it would be unethical, immoral, and a violation of Federation and interstellar law to pursue any development of the Genesis Device for military purposes. Furthermore, because of the instability of protomatter, it would be unsafe to transport it as part of a live ordnance system aboard a Federation starship.

There is a serious risk, however, that foreign powers might seek to replicate Genesis Device technology and employ it against the Federation.

As a weapon of mass destruction, the Genesis Device would be one of the most lethal systems ever devised. It most likely would be deployed as a torpedo launched from a starship, from a range of not more than 1 A.U., assuming the device is used in its current configuration. Because of the payload of protomatter located in the device's core, it would be unsafe to fit the torpedo delivery system with an antimatter-based propulsion system capable of warp-speed travel, because the proximity to the warp drive's subspace field would catastrophically destabilize the protomatter, resulting in premature detonation. This lack of warp capability significantly reduces the threat of interstellar deployment of the device. (This assessment will need to be revised if, at some future time, a means is found to shelter the protomatter core from the subspace field without compromising the functioning of the system.)

Another distressing possibility would be a limited-range Genesis Device, such as the one used inside the Regula Asteroid, reduced in size to fit inside a scanproof diplomatic courier container or ship's hold. Our preliminary simulations indicate the Genesis Matrix could be reprogrammed to create a micro-ecosystem of virulent airborne and waterborne genetic pathogens that could swiftly grow and "infect" an entire bio-sphere, ultimately killing or replacing all life-forms on the planet.

The Genesis Effect for such a weapon could initially be of very low power, perhaps low enough to evade detection by existing planetary sensor nets. More important, the Genesis Device could be programmed to spontaneously tailor its pathogens to the environment in which it is detonated, creating a universally lethal effect in microseconds without requiring any prior research into the target's genetic code.

02.04 POTENTIAL COUNTERMEASURES

Unfortunately, short of destroying a Genesis Device before its detonation sequence is triggered, there currently are no known methods for shielding a ship or planet from the Genesis Effect. We are researching a system that would create an energy wave whose signature is the perfect inverse of the Genesis Wave, as a potential negation method, but because of the Genesis Device's tremendous energy level and uniquely complex wave signature, there has been no success with this method as of this time.

02.05 FINDINGS & RECOMMENDATIONS

Contrary to Dr. Marcus' suggestion, which we believe to be inspired by her grief over the recent death of her son on the Genesis Planet, we feel that Project Genesis has enormous potential civilian, scientific, and military applications, and re-quires further top-secret research within Starfleet Research & Development.

In addition, the very real risk of this technology being acquired or independently duplicated by powers external to the

Federation make it imperative that our knowledge of this technology be complete and accurate. We must not let others turn our own science against us because we are too morally repulsed to look beyond the horrors of the device's failures to see its full potential.

Commander Stephen Klisiewicz

03.00 POLITICAL EVALUATION
Xev Chiana, Secretary of State, United Federation of Planets
Paris, Earth
Received via Encrypted Internal Channel 719-Kilo
16 December 2286 (Stardate 8426.9)

03.01 DIPLOMATIC RAMIFICATIONS
The political fallout in the wake of the detonation of the Genesis Device in the Mutara Nebula can best be described as "disastrous." Aside from the expected howls of alarm that immediately were logged by the Klingon and Romulan ambassadors to the Federation, protests were declared in the Council Hall by several Federation Council representatives, including those from Deneva, Cestus III, Argelius and Mars.

Despite numerous efforts at political rapprochement with both the Klingon and Romulan governments in recent years, their ambassadors' filibusters in the Council Hall were met with little concern and silenced for the most part by Federation Ambassador Sarek of Vulcan. Despite the Klingon Ambassador's insistence on referring to the device as "the Genesis Torpedo," Ambassador Sarek made a compelling argument for the nonmilitary nature of Project Genesis.

Most of the protests entered into the record by Council representatives stemmed from their desire to distance themselves from what they perceived to be the development of a weapon of mass destruction. Ambassador Arwen of Mars, however, criticized the technology because of her mistaken perception that the Genesis Effect was designed to generate only Earthlike environments. After a detailed technical briefing by Dr. Carol Marcus, the Martian ambassador withdrew her protest.

The Klingon High Council and Romulan Senate, meanwhile, continue to demand that the Federation disclose the technical specifications for Project Genesis in order to, as they stated in a joint briefing, "maintain the balance of power in the quadrant."

In response to unambiguous refusals of their requests by the Federation President, the Klingons have threatened to resort to "more forceful means" and reportedly are tripling energy production output on the Klingon Homeworld's moon, Praxis, in anticipation of a military buildup.

The Romulans, for their part, appeared to take the President's refusal in stride, but since that meeting long-range sensors have detected a marked increase in activity by Romulan starships on their side of the Neutral Zone.

Starfleet Command has reported that the additional vessels and personnel required to police both the Klingon and Romulan borders simultaneously is presenting enormous logistical difficulties and is reducing the fleet's ability to enforce the law and conduct routine patrols within Federation territory. Consequently, Admiral N.J. Weiland of Starfleet Operations is recommending that Starfleet temporarily shift its focus from constructing Starbases to enlarging the fleet, in the interest of interstellar security.

03.02 PACIFICATION OF FEDERATION RIVALS

In order to mollify representatives from the Klingon, Romulan, Gorn and Tholian governments, the Federation Security Council officially interdicted the Genesis Planet on March 28, 2285 (Stardate 8201.5), restricting all traffic in the Mutara Sector and prohibiting all starships from approaching to closer than 10 A.U. from the planet. Only preauthorized Starfleet research vessels were permitted to approach and orbit the planet.

A Klingon bird-of-prey, captained by Commander Kruge, ambushed the Federation science vessel *U.S.S. Grissom* in orbit over the Genesis Planet on April 28, 2285, and also contributed to the destruction of the hijacked Starfleet vessel *U.S.S. Enterprise*. Kruge and his crew murdered Dr. David Marcus on April 29, 2285, on the Genesis Planet in a failed effort to obtain scientific data about Project Genesis. Kruge and all but one member of his crew, Second Officer Maltz, perished on the Genesis Planet when it exploded. Their bird-of-prey subsequently was commandeered by Captain James T. Kirk and his expatriate crew, who took the stolen vessel to Vulcan for a three-month period of exile, before returning in the vessel to Earth.

The official position of the Klingon High Council was that Kruge acted alone and in defiance of explicit orders not to violate Federation space, in an effort to enhance his political standing in the Klingon Empire by acquiring "the secrets of Genesis." The Klingon High Council denied any prior knowledge of Kruge's intent and disavowed any involvement in his actions.

In the interest of diplomacy, the Federation Security Council has chosen not to seek reparations for violations of the border treaty, the destruction of the starships *Grissom* and *Enterprise*, or the murder of Dr. David Marcus. Similarly, the Klingon High

Council has withdrawn its demand for the immediate return of the bird-of-prey stolen by Captain Kirk and his crew, choosing instead to view its capture as "spoils of war."

Further protests, however, have been filed by the Klingon High Council following the August 7, 2285, full pardons of Kirk's crew and the dismissal of all charges against Kirk himself (except for one charge of disobeying the orders of a superior officer), and their subsequent assignment to active duty aboard a newly commissioned *Starship Enterprise*, under Kirk's command. The Federation Council has taken the Klingon government's protest under advisement.

03.03 THREAT OF EXTERNAL DUPLICATION

In response to the very real risk that a foreign power—such as the Klingon Empire, Romulan Empire, or Tholian Assembly—might choose to develop its own Genesis Device for less noble purposes than peaceful terraforming, the Federation Diplomatic Corps has undertaken a major treaty initiative in an attempt to prevent the proliferation of this dangerous technology.

The Tholian Assembly has willingly entered into negotiations to suppress the technology, most likely because they expect to be technologically unable to duplicate the Genesis Effect for at least twenty-five years, due to their technological emphasis on adapting to new planetary environments through enclosed shelters due to the extreme conditions on their homeworld.

The Romulans so far have declined to sign the treaty unless they receive additional territorial concessions by the Federation along the Neutral Zone. Federation Ambassador Liz Braswell currently is developing a counterproposal that would concede no territory directly to the Romulan Star Empire but would extend the area of the Neutral Zone deeper into Federation space.

The Klingons, naturally, are resisting all attempts at diplomacy, demanding instead the surrender of all Project Genesis technical specifications and Genesis Device schematics, and refusing to consider any treaty that requires a ban on weapons development.

03.04 FINDINGS & RESOLUTIONS

Weighing the political stability of the Federation and Alpha Quadrant against both Dr. Carol Marcus' concerns and Starfleet's strategic desires, the prudent course of action appears to be to cease all public research into Project Genesis and to halt all Federation-funded research of the technology until the political climate becomes more conducive to diplomacy.

Starfleet Intelligence has been issued an Executive Order from the Federation President to initiate long-term covert operations within Klingon and Romulan territory to detect and actively sabotage any efforts by those entities to develop their own Genesis Devices.

Future inquiry into the applications of Project Genesis will be conducted under Level 9 Security Protocols by Starfleet Research & Development. Project Genesis data and technology are hereby classified as Level Ten munitions, and any publication, duplication, transmission, or possession of said data; or creation, possession, shipment, sale, or transfer of an active or inactive Genesis Device, or any of its primary components, by any unauthorized person(s) or agency will be prosecuted as treason (for Federation citizens) and espionage, and in all cases shall be punishable by a mandatory sentence of life imprisonment in solitary confinement, with no possibility of parole.

03.05 ADDENDUM—FINAL DETERMINATION

By agreement of all the parties to the Genesis Nonproliferation Treaty, all records, materials, schematics, mock-ups, and logs of Project Genesis are ordered destroyed, and active research is hereby terminated.

Xev Chiana

04.00 PROJECT GENESIS—A REASSESSMENT

Lt. David A. Mack, Starfleet Research & Development
New York, Earth
Report filed via Encrypted Internal Channel Alpha-5C
12 May 2374 (Stardate 53303.4)

04.01 INTRODUCTION

Officially, only anecdotal evidence exists about Project Genesis, although enough people are familiar with its controversial history to have kept unofficial records and theories, especially of related technologies that might someday be applied to a rebirth of Genesis. Non-Federation powers have tried to duplicate the efforts of Dr. Carol Marcus and her team, to no avail. This document is merely meant as an assessment of where Project Genesis now stands in its development cycle, because this technology is too dynamic to be ignored.

04.02 RECENT DISCOVERIES REGARDING PROTOMATTER

Pioneering work performed at the Vulcan Science Academy by Dr. Temok and at the Daystrom Institute by Dr. Glenn

Hauman indicate that the instabilities in protomatter are the result of interactions between its subatomic constituents and a nine-dimensional 5/2 spin variant on the quark strangelet, which Temok and Hauman have agreed to dub a "changelet."

Changelets affect the strong nuclear force in the covalent bonds of protomatter, and are able to breach the dimensional gap because of natural fluctuations in the fabric of space-time. According to Dr. Temok, because changelets are extradimensional, they are extraordinarily massive when compared with other subatomic particles. They appear to have a mass of approximately 21.9 GEv, placing them beyond the threshold of the gravitational constant.

Because of their already precarious position in the space-time continuum, changelets become volatile in the presence of subspace fields, which further warp the fabric of space-time, thereby permitting the negatively charged changelet to interact directly with the densely clustered protons of protomatter. The result is a catastrophic, chain-reaction annihilation of protomatter into high-energy photons.

According to Dr. Hauman, the tendency of protomatter to violently collapse in the presence of a subspace field can be counteracted through the application of a stasis field generated by a quantum flux capacitor and a Heisenberg compensator working in tandem. The compensator deflects space-time distortions from the protomatter, and at high-enough power levels can actually stabilize protomatter by suppressing microdimensional ripples in its subatomic structure that promote interaction with changelets. The quantum flux capacitor prevents subatomic constituents of protomatter from slipping through microdimensional fractures and encountering changelets.

04.03 A NEW THEORY ON THE COLLAPSE
OF THE GENESIS PLANET

It has always been accepted that the Genesis Device had a protomatter core; both it and the Genesis Matrix were stabilized by a Heisenberg compensator and quantum flux capacitor. Although the two components had been used by the Marcus team only to guide the subatomic reassembly of the target planet in accordance with the Genesis Matrix, the device's compact design necessitated that the protomatter core be contained within the stabilization field.

Conventional wisdom has always blamed the planet's rapid disintegration on David Marcus' use of protomatter; our new research refutes that. Based on our study, we have concluded that the device in fact was remarkably stable, and that its results would also have been stable had the device been deployed in the manner for which it was designed.

Dr. Carol Marcus' own briefing to the Federation indicated that the Phase Three test of the device was intended to be carried out on a lifeless planetoid or small moon. We are confident that if the device had been detonated on an appropriate target—i.e., a lifeless small moon or asteroid in an appropriate orbit for sustaining a Class-M planet—it would have produced a stable, organically rich, and eminently habitable planet. (Our findings are supported by the continued stability of Project Genesis' thriving underground ecosystem within the Regula asteroid.)

Because the device was triggered in a diffuse nebula of highly charged gas and radioactive debris, the result was a highly unstable planet. Instead of transforming a solid-core planetoid already in a stable orbit, the Genesis Effect was forced to create from loose debris an entire planet with little-to-no inherent gravitational impetus to orbit its star. Furthermore, the newly formed Genesis Planet was subject to highly erratic gravitational fluctuations caused by its situation between two gas giant planets, resulting in its greatly accelerated rotation rate and a variety of severe atmospheric anomalies, which were required by the matrix to sustain a Class-M atmosphere at a less-than-ideal distance of 1.93 A.U. from a yellow dwarf star.

Those factors, coupled with the fact that the Genesis Wave was overextended because of the vast amount of energy needed to build a new planet from gas and dust, left the Genesis Effect incomplete. The final phase of the Genesis Effect, in which the strong and weak nuclear forces are renormalized at the subquantum level, never took place because the formation of the new planet prematurely depleted the reaction's energy.

Drs. Temok and Hauman concur with our assessment and are prepared to demonstrate to the Federation Security Council that Project Genesis is a successful, viable terraforming technology, and could be a potentially decisive weapon against the Borg if its inherent tactical weaknesses can be remedied.

04.04 PROPOSAL FOR DESIGN UPGRADES

The original Genesis Device was intended to be delivered to its target as a slow-velocity torpedo released from a starship. The original research team omitted warp propulsion systems from their prototype designs because they were unnecessary during the test phase. Later evaluations of the project's military applications concluded that because the Genesis Device contained protomatter, it would not be safe to equip it with a warp drive because the subspace field would cause the protomatter to detonate.

We believe the stabilizer field for the Genesis Matrix renders its protomatter safe for transport; we therefore can devise a number of methods for protecting the protomatter payload from subspace disruption while enabling the Genesis Device to be economically deployed across intermediate interstellar distances.

First, we can produce a more compact design, at roughly 45 percent of the mass of the original device, by employing more-advanced isolinear processors and ODN circuitry. Second, we can add an additional layer of duranium shielding around the Genesis Matrix core without compromising the effectiveness of the device. Third, we can install a Mark X warp coil and antimatter core in the rear half of the casing, enabling the device to sustain a velocity of warp seven for up to ninety-two hours. Last, we can adjust the warp-field geometry to envelop the device payload without putting undue stress on its core stabilizer.

04.05 KEEPING PROJECT GENESIS FROM THE BORG

Although use of the Genesis Device as a weapon is strictly prohibited by the Genesis Nonproliferation Treaty, the Borg are not signatories of that document, and keeping Genesis from them is a more pressing concern.

If the Borg were to capture Genesis Device technology, they would be able to equip it with a transwarp conduit generator, duplicate it, and send one to every Federation planet, instantly transforming them all into Borg homeworlds.

Unless a Genesis Device can be kept from Borg detection, it will be a devasatating tactical alternative. Because of these possible consequences all efforts must be made to prevent their acquisition of the Genesis technology.

04.06 EXTERNAL POWERS DEVELOPING GENESIS TECHNOLOGY

Thanks to aggressive covert operations during the past century by Starfleet Intelligence, no other major Alpha Quadrant power has succeeded in developing a working Genesis Device. The Klingons' attempt to develop the technology as part of a military buildup is believed to have been a contributing factor in the June 2293 explosion of the moon Praxis, which caused massive environmental damage to the Klingon Homeworld.

The Romulan Star Empire withdrew from direct confrontation with the Federation following the Tomed Incident in 2311, and for nearly thirty years no Romulan vessels were detected within twenty light-years of the Romulan Neutral Zone. It is believed that the Romulans chose to pursue an aggressive expansion policy into the Delta Quadrant, and curtailed their investigations into the Genesis Effect in favor of rapidly building and deploying new starships.

The Tholian Assembly appears to have abided by the terms of the Genesis Nonproliferation Treaty.

Unconfirmed reports indicate the Cardassian Union flirted with a Genesis Device-like technology, but abandoned the research following a catastrophic accident at their key research facility. The official statement from the Cardassian Union blamed Bajoran terrorists for the explosion, but data from long-range sensor arrays indicate the explosion signature was consistent with a massive, uncontrolled protomatter detonation.

New reports, however, indicate that while the major governments of the Alpha Quadrant don't appear to be developing Genesis Device technologies, there are several terrorist factions and criminal organizations seeking to develop the technology privately. Among the organizations suspected of trafficking in protomatter with the intent of developing weapons of mass destruction are the Orion Syndicate and the Black Company, a large and well-equipped private mercenary corps.

A protomatter-based weapon also was employed by the Dominion in an unsuccessful attack on Bajor's primary star. In the aftermath of the collapse of Dominion forces in the Alpha Quadrant, other Dominion-crafted protomatter weapons might have fallen into the hands of black marketeers. Such weapons could be transformed into crude Genesis devices with the addition of a basic Genesis Matrix Generator and two components found in all transporters: the Heisenberg compensator and the quantum flux capacitor.

04.07 FINDINGS & RECOMMENDATIONS

Because the Genesis technology is, in fact, stable and safe, it would be an ideal tool for rapid terraforming. However, to avoid the political furor that accompanied the first use of the device, such a visible display of its capabilities is not advisable.

Its use as a military technology continues to be expressly forbidden by the Genesis Nonproliferation Treaty, and it is in conflict with the essential tenets of the Federation charter. Its use as a weapon also poses the unacceptably high risk that the technology will be acquired by powers hostile to the Federation—most notably, the Borg.

However, the failure of so many other parties to develop a working Genesis Device suggests that Dr. Carol Marcus has depths of knowledge unknown to both our own scientists and theirs. Including her in further research, while she is still alive, would be crucial to success.

The recommendation of this office is that further research and development to seek methods for using the Genesis Matrix to direct the creation of animate matter from raw energy, for the pursuit of peaceful applications for the fields of medicine, agriculture, and aquaculture, is tempting but inadvisable

Lt. David Mack

fifteen

Captain Picard took a deep breath and rose from his desk, the ramifications of what he had just read still sorting themselves in his brain. Now he knew why Admiral Nechayev seemed so subdued—she was frightened, much more frightened than the Dominion, Cardassians, or Maquis had ever made her. And why not? In brilliant phosphors, his screen said there was no way to stop the Genesis Effect, and the basic components were off-the-shelf commodities.

Over the years, Picard had heard rumors of Genesis but had dismissed them as exaggerated tales or a theoretical technology. But it seemed that Genesis was all too real.

Picard paced his ready room, hands behind his back. The documents mentioned torpedoes as the delivery system, but this was no torpedo barrage they were facing—this was an energy wave, sweeping across space and expanding as it went. The documents said that ignition of this device caused an energy wave which swept across a planet, causing the mutagenic changes. It was plain to see that someone had perfected the device to work without the torpedo.

They were deploying the wave itself—indiscriminately across the vastness of space.

But who? And why? Picard pushed a hopeless sigh through his clenched teeth, realizing that the answer was depressingly simple. *Conquer all the planets you want without risking a single casualty, and do it instantly! Not only will everything be just the way you like it when you get there, but there won't be any annoying locals to bother you.*

The captain tapped his combadge. "Picard to bridge."

"Riker here."

Picard crossed to his computer screen and entered a command. "Number One, I'm going to send you some reading material. Read it and disseminate it to the senior staff; send it to the *Balboa* as well. Add to the message that Dr. Carol Marcus was kidnapped six months ago. This concerns the current crisis, so tell everyone to start thinking. When Data and La Forge return, the senior staff will have a briefing."

"Yes, Sir," said Riker. "Got it. Anything else?"

"As soon as I can reach the admiral," said Picard, "I'm going over to the *Sovereign*."

Onboard the shuttlecraft *Balboa*, Data read the missive from the *Enterprise* in a matter of seconds, then recapped it orally for the others. From the sour looks around him, Geordi decided that all of them were getting sick to their stomachs hearing this, especially the old Klingon. When Data mentioned that Maltz was in the file, he perked up a bit, but then his gaze grew distant as he relived his own nightmares of Project Genesis.

Data concluded by saying that Dr. Carol Marcus had been kidnapped, which seemed to bring the mystery full circle. Sitting beside the engineer, wrapped in a blanket, Leah Brahms shivered, and Geordi resisted the temptation to wrap his arm around her.

Leah shook her head. "Maltz told me that *we* had invented it, but I didn't believe him. This Genesis sounds exactly like what I saw on Seran, down to the rapid growth of new life. I can only tell you . . . if you are on the rock which gets chewed up by this thing, you don't view it so benignly. Whoever tried to keep Genesis a secret was on the right track—they just didn't work hard enough."

"What goes around comes around," said Geordi softly. "You think you can bury a thing—forget about it—but you never can." He was thinking of his feelings for Leah as much as the promising invention turned deadly. He gazed at the slight woman curled up beside him. Her hair plastered limply to her head, grief etched in her face, and her clothes soiled and torn, Leah Brahms was still beautiful.

"It must have been awful down there," said Geordi sympathetically, unable to find the right words. "I'm truly sorry about Mikel and your team. I can't imagine—"

She gently touched his arm. "Let's hope you'll never be able to imagine it. Nobody deserves to die like that . . . in sheer terror . . . your body convulsed in pain."

Leah shivered and lowered her eyes. "You never got to know Mikel very well, but he really liked you, Geordi. I would tell him all the places you went, adventures you had, and I think he lived vicariously through you. I know I did." She swallowed hard. "We often talked about signing aboard a research vessel, but it was just one of those things we never did."

"All of this is very touching," said a snide voice behind them. "But is the Federation going to do anything about this?"

La Forge turned to see the Capellan, Bekra, looking expectantly at him. "Do you have any ideas?" asked the engineer.

"Yes." The Capellan pointed to the radiation suit. "This thing saved *her* life, and it could save everyone's, if we had enough of them."

Leah gave a hollow laugh. "The plans and components are all gone . . . lost with everything else on Seran. I'm sure I could duplicate it, but it would probably take me a few weeks—and we don't have that. It also depends upon Romulan phase-shifting technology, which is better than my poor imitation. We need to consult directly with the Romulans."

From the copilot seat came a hearty laugh. "We've got somebody who can talk to the Romulans for us." He pointed at Consul Bekra, and the Capellan shifted uneasily under the scrutiny.

Leah ignored him, and her eyes stared straight ahead. "That's not the worst of it," she rasped. "Even if you could survive when the Genesis Wave swept over your planet, you wouldn't want to live in what was left behind. You wouldn't want to be there for ten seconds."

"I agree," muttered the old Klingon.

"However," said Data from the cockpit, "somebody must plan to live on the altered planets, or else why go to the trouble of terraforming them?"

"Maybe they just don't like the Federation," said Maltz. "There are plenty of species who don't."

"We've got to find the ones who did this," said Leah softly, "and kill them."

"Yes!" agreed Maltz heartily. "A blood oath. Kahless, give me the strength to be there with you, Captain, when you rip out their hearts."

"Thank you," said Leah grimly. "That would be good."

Conversation inside the shuttlecraft trailed off after that, as the pall of death haunted their journey back to the *Enterprise*.

"The Stellar Cartography room," said a young ensign, pointing toward double doors at the end of the corridor. "The admiral is in there."

"Thank you, Ensign," replied Captain Picard. Since the *Soverign* was the model for the *Enterprise*, he could have found the right room without any difficulty, but protocol demanded the escort. "You have a fine ship here."

"Thank you, Sir," answered the young man, snapping to attention. He remained at attention until Picard strode through the doors at the end of the corridor.

The Stellar Cartography room of the *Enterprise* had been turned into a war room, with the positions and courses of hundreds of ships outlined on a sweeping, three-dimensional, holographic star chart. The image rotated slowly, updating constantly, showing fleets of ships converging on their position. Admiral Nechayev stood in the midst of the three-dimensional rendering, pointing out vessels to an aide, who made notes on a padd.

Picard waited patiently while the admiral finished her task; then she stepped down from the holograph and shook his hand. "Thank you for coming, Captain Picard. You see, we haven't been totally inactive—we've got portions of five fleets coming and more in reserve. Of course, a lot of these ships are freighters, passenger ships, and such. The official story is that we're evacuating planets because of a plague."

"I told my senior staff the truth," answered Picard, "and I let them see the documents."

Nechayev scowled, and her eyes narrowed upon the captain. Her aides cast their eyes down and tried to look busy. "You had no authorization, no right . . ."

"I don't believe we can fight this thing unless we're totally honest about what it is. And to do that my entire crew needs to know about Genesis."

"What you believe, Captain, is not the issue. And be assured I will deal with this willful breach of security after this is over," she said angrily. But then her bright eyes filled with resignation. "For the time being, though, a more important problem remains: Just how are we going to fight it?"

"I don't know, but even if you had ten times as many ships on that map, we could only evacuate a small fraction of the people in danger. I don't want to spend all day playing God, trying to decide who lives and who dies."

"Nobody wants to do that," snapped Nechayev, "but until we have a workable plan, evacuation is the only alternative."

Picard gaped in disbelief. "You would abandon Earth to this monster?"

"We're not sure Earth is in danger yet," said Nechayev defensively. "We have to collect more data."

"What about the Romulans?" asked Picard. "We've got to tell the Romulans, because it's going to hit them, too."

The breath went out of Nechayev, and her shoulders slumped perceptibly. "If you read the documents, you know we're prohibited by treaty from even discussing Genesis with anyone else. Starfleet has stuggled for years to keep Genesis under wraps. I violated seventeen regulations just showing those documents to *you*."

Picard's lips thinned. "If nothing else, those papers show that this has been a poorly kept secret. I need to be able to discuss this matter freely with my staff and other experts."

She turned her back on him and stepped once again into the revolving holographic map. Now her aides were nowhere to be seen. "So, Captain, you're saying you'll continue to disobey *my* orders and a treaty signed by all the great powers of the Alpha Quadrant in order to do whatever you see fit."

"I've proven I'll go to great lengths to save Earth," answered Picard.

The diminutive admiral froze in her tracks, apparently making up her mind about something. Then she turned to him with a tired expression on her pinched face. "Now I have to cover for you and give the order for *everyone* in the fleet to be told about Genesis. That's all right—it's better that *I'm* in the brig than you."

Picard smiled slightly, hoping that was a joke. "Under the circumstances, you couldn't get in trouble for this, could you?"

"I'm in considerable trouble already," answered Nechayev with a sigh. "I was in charge of the security for Dr. Carol Marcus. My career is basically over after this—win, lose, or draw."

"That's not fair," said Picard with all sincerity. "You've always had the tough assignments."

Nechayev flashed him a very brief smile, then resumed her all-business demeanor. "I see from your reports that you suffered some casualties."

"Yes, ten crew members lost when we had to jettison the forward torpedo module. Now I understand what was happening to it . . . and what would have happened to the ship."

"That was quick thinking, Picard. I know it wasn't easy."

The captain nodded slowly, grateful for the acknowledgment from someone who did know. "We're having a memorial service at twenty-three hundred hours. It would be an honor if you could attend."

"Certainly, Captain. Afterwards, I would like to see those projections which show that Earth is clearly in danger. We haven't been able to project that far from the data we have."

"For that, we're relying mostly on Dr. Leah Brahms and the survivors from the first planet hit, Seran. Brahms has been observing it and tracking its course the longest."

Nechayev nodded, her brow furrowed in thought. "Yes, she's the one who lived through it—in a phase-shifting radiation suit. Has fate given us one tiny piece of good luck in all of this destruction?"

"The suit's aboard our shuttlecraft," said Picard. "With her permission, we can take it, dismantle it, and start replicating it. It will be slow going, but—"

"Yes, do it." Admiral Nechayev walked back into her revolving hologram of fluorescent starships streaking across a three-dimensional star chart. "Now you've got to leave me, Captain. I've got to officially break a ninety-year-old-treaty as well as commit treason. I may hold off on talking to the Romulans until we hear the whole story."

Picard cleared his throat. "We supposedly have a Romulan spy coming on board, one of the refugees."

Nechayev scowled. "Alliance or not, they still have more spies in our midst than anyone else. I may need help dealing with them. See you at the memorial service."

"Yes, Sir," answered Picard, hurrying out the door. His escort was still in the corridor outside, waiting for him.

The shuttlecraft *Balboa* swooped through the launch door into the main shuttlebay like a bat returning home to its cave. When the craft set down and Data stilled the engines, a sigh or relief echoed inside the small craft. The *Enterprise* wasn't solid ground, but it was the closest thing to it, thought Geordi; and these people had been put through the wringer. His first priority was to get Leah Brahms settled into her quarters with a regimen of food and rest.

He would probably ask Counselor Troi to see her, because she needed help in dealing with her grief. He was troubled by her talk of killing her husband's murderers, although that was probably a normal reaction under the circumstances. However, he knew that Leah had a temper and a lot of determination. After all, she had raced the Genesis Wave through light-years of space, trying to warn as many people as she could. Geordi had been the focus of her anger, and he knew it was a force to be reckoned with.

He wondered how well Leah would be able to continue with her life, providing any of them got out of this alive. He had tried not to think of her as single and unattached, but it was impossible not to when she was so alone. But Geordi vowed to himself not to complicate her life or make her more unhappy than she already was. He just hoped he didn't get weak and tell her how he really felt.

When the shuttlecraft hatch opened, La Forge was a bit surprised to see Commander Riker waiting for them, along with a security team. They didn't have drawn weapons and obvious uniforms, but he recognized the personnel. Not far away stood another clutch of people, Dr. Crusher and a small medteam. One by one, they filed off—Leah Brahms, La Forge, Consul Maltz, Consul Bekra, and Paldor. The Tellarite lent support to the one-legged Capellan, and they seemed to have become allies. Data was last off the craft after shutting down the *Balboa's* systems.

"Welcome aboard the *Enterprise*," said Riker. "I'm Commander William Riker, first officer. We know you've been through a lot, and we were thinking that you might like to rest before we debrief you."

"I can rest in Sto-Vo-Kor!" growled Maltz, putting his hands on his hips. "How do we get this big ship turned around and find out who is responsible for this?"

"We're working on that," answered Riker. "We've got a fleet of ships trying to surround this wave, which we think is conical in shape and expanding. Once we get its dimensions, we can triangulate its source."

"We had the same trouble," agreed Leah. "You would need a fleet of ships to measure it." She staggered a bit on her feet, and La Forge propped her up.

"Commander," said Geordi, "I think Dr. Brahms needs to get some rest. Does she have quarters assigned to her?"

"Stateroom 1136," answered Riker. "But I have a quick question for you, Dr. Brahms. The captain would like to know whether we can take your radiation suit and try to replicate it. We promise not to damage it, although we'll have to take it apart."

"Go ahead, if you think it will do some good," answered Brahms wearily.

"Thank you. It's good to have you onboard. Please don't keep Mr. La Forge for long, because he has a staff meeting right now."

"I won't," agreed Leah.

Geordi nodded and quickly ushered his charge toward the door. As they left the shuttlebay, he heard Dr. Crusher ask if anyone needed medical attention, and both the Capellan and the Tellarite demanded it. He didn't really care about what happened to anyone else at the moment, because his entire focus was on Leah.

So once again, he didn't see Dolores Linton until they ran into her in the corridor. "Geordi!" she exclaimed, grabbing his arm. "You're back! Is everything okay?"

"Dolores," he said, flustered to be standing between the two women. "What are you doing here?"

"Well, after you stood me up—"

Geordi banged his palm on his forehead. "Oh, I'm sorry, I forgot all about our date."

He looked at Leah with embarrassment, but she was smiling at his dilemma. *She probably thinks that Dolores is my girlfriend!* thought Geordi with alarm.

"It's all right, I know you're busy," said the geologist cheerfully. "I looked you up and found out you had left the ship again; then I found out when you were due back."

The door opened again, and the medteam walked out, with Bekra on a gurney and Paldor limping beside him. They were followed by the Klingon and an entourage of security officers sticking close to him. Two more crew members carried the radiation suit, and Riker and Data were the last ones out of the shuttlebay.

Riker looked at La Forge with a frown. "You're still here? We've got that staff meeting, so we'll have to find somebody else to take Dr. Brahms to her quarters."

"I'll take her there," offered Dolores Linton brightly. "I haven't got anything better to do."

Geordi wanted to object, insisting that it was *his* job to protect Leah, but he couldn't make a scene in the hallway, surrounded by people. Besides, Dolores Linton didn't have anything better to do. "Number 1136," he said.

Riker smiled charmingly at the bubbly young lady. "Thank you very much, Miss—"

"Dolores Linton, geologist with the mission that's on hold." Dolores turned to Leah Brahms and smiled. "So you lived! That's great. Geordi was very worried about you."

"I bet." Brahms smiled wanly, while La Forge wanted to crawl into a hole. "Go on," Leah told him softly. "I'll see you later."

Geordi just nodded blankly, reluctant to be parted from Leah, especially when he didn't know what Dolores would say about him. Nevertheless, with Riker and Data looking expectantly at him, he knew where his duty lay. He nodded at his commanding officer and the three of them strode off down the corridor.

The android slowed down to let La Forge catch up with him. "It appears that you are making headway with Mission Specialist Linton," he said.

"Data!" exclaimed Geordi, shocked. "We're right in the middle of a crisis—I'm not thinking about that."

The android cocked his head. "But I have noticed that humans often experience their most intense love affairs in the midst of a crisis."

"Commander Riker, what did you do with the old Klingon?" asked Geordi, pointedly changing the subject.

Riker smiled. "He wanted to talk to somebody, so I sent him to see our ship's counselor. Let Deanna find out his state of mind. We already know he's the only Klingon survivor from the first appearance of Genesis, but we don't know how much good that will do us. What about the Cappellan? Is he really a spy for the Romulans?"

Geordi shook his head. "He never denied it whenever Maltz accused him of it."

"Maybe they'll both be useful," said Riker with a heave of his broad shoulders. "One thing for sure, we need all the help we can get. Now that you're back, the *Enterprise* and the *Sovereign* are headed in tandem to the next planet in danger—Persephone V."

"I know some people who retired there," murmured Geordi.

"Half of Starfleet is retired there," said Riker, stopping at the turbolift door. "Now they're all going to have to be evacuated. Being ex-Starfleet, maybe they'll obey orders and will do what they're told."

The door opened, and the commander stepped inside, shaking

his head. "I can't believe that we invented this device, and now we're fleeing in the face of it. Somebody is grabbing whole solar systems without firing a shot, and we feel good if we save a few lives before we run like rabbits. Where does it end?"

"When we stop running," answered Data, drawing the logical conclusion.

sixteen

"Sorry I'm late," said Deanna Troi, rushing into the observation lounge and seeking an empty seat at the conference table. Will Riker smiled warmly at her, and she gave him a fleeting smile. Also in attendance were Data, Geordi, Beverly, and, of course, Captain Picard.

"We've just been going over what we know about the Genesis Wave, which isn't nearly enough," said the captain, tight-lipped. "How is Consul Maltz?"

"He seems fine," she answered. "He's perfectly lucid, and he knows all about Dr. Carol Marcus and the original Genesis Project. He's an old-fashioned Klingon from another era—the kind you don't see much anymore. In fact, he kept asking me why we're not doubling back to Seran to get revenge."

Picard answered, "Admiral Nechayev has sent a small task force of *Defiant*-class ships to try to find the source. What else did our guest say?"

"He has a lot of respect for Leah Brahms and says that she's the one who saved them. He also says we should use the Capellan to contact the Romulans. He insists that Bekra is a spy."

The captain scowled and said, "We still don't know what to tell the Romulans. The admiral thinks we'll have the wave's course fully plotted by the time we get to Persephone V. Gearing up for this has been like gearing up for another war, only we don't know where the front is."

He paced in front of a cabinet full of gleaming models of other ships which had born the name *Enterprise*. "In the meantime, we're pursuing a few courses of action on our own. Commander Riker is spearheading an effort to replicate as many of Dr. Brahms' radiation suits as we can. Our thinking is that our people on the surface of Persephone V may have to stay until the last second, evacuating people. If we don't get them out in time, this will give them a chance to survive."

He continued around the table. "La Forge and Brahms will work on a way to expand the phase-shifting technology in her suit—maybe there's a way it can protect more than one person at a time. Data is going to work on a plan to stop the wave permanently, and Dr. Crusher is studying the biological data to see if we can lessen the effect of the wave, or reverse it."

"You'll need live samples for that, won't you?" asked Troi.

"I would settle for tricorder readings," answered Crusher.

"That's another use for the radiation suits," said Riker with a smile. "We can stick it out long enough to get tricorder readings."

"We?" asked Deanna doubtfully, not liking the idea that Will would be wearing one of those suits. "What's my assignment?"

"Your job," answered the captain. "This ship will soon be full of traumatized evacuees. And I want you around whenever I speak with either Consul Maltz and Consul Bekra."

"Yes, Sir."

Riker cleared his throat and tapped his chronometer. "Captain, it's time for our memorial service."

"Yes," said Picard with a sigh. "Let's adjourn. After the service, we all have plenty of work to do, but don't forget to eat and rest. Dismissed."

While the others filed out of the room, Deanna hung back to wait for Riker. She lowered her voice to ask Will, "You're not planning to hang out on a planet in one of those suits, are you?"

"It will probably be Data," answered the first officer, "although he shouldn't be down there alone. We'll see."

"I know you're a thrill-seeker," she said, "but you don't need to stand up to this."

"We need to stand up to it eventually," answered Riker, ending the conversation on an uneasy note.

Two minutes later, the same group from the briefing room filed into the Antares Theater, a small amphitheater on deck fifteen where Data had performed a few nights earlier. The hall was already starting to fill up with somber crew members, many of whom would normally be sleeping this shift. Deanna Troi doubted whether anyone was finding it easy to sleep these nights.

There was a podium center stage and a lone drummer with a snare drum; he was one of Will's musician friends from his jazz band. The commander waited patiently while the crowd settled down and latecomers straggled in. Riker opened his handheld padd and set it on the podium. Most of the audience were seated, but Deanna remained standing in the back with her captain.

There was a slight commotion and an uplift of voices around the main door, and she turned to see Admiral Nechayev rush in. Nechayev strode immediately to Picard's side and greeted him with a nod. On stage, Will wisely decided to wait a few seconds longer.

"Hello, Captain," said the admiral. "I'm glad I'm not late."

"Thank you for coming," replied Picard. "I was going to say something, but we would be honored if you would say a few words."

"I will," she answered bluntly.

When the audience had quieted again, Riker began speaking, his deep voice carrying over the crowd. "I would like to read the names, ranks, and accomplishments of our fallen shipmates in RC Three."

Accompanied by drum rolls, he read basic data about each of the dead, and Deanna recalled similar ceremonies during the Dominion war—mass funerals, no time for individual ones. When he was finished, Will looked at the captain, who nodded toward Admiral Nechayev.

"We are honored to have Admiral Nechayev onboard to speak to you." Riker nodded to the drummer, and the two of them relinquished the stage.

The stiff-backed, gray-haired woman tugged on her jacket and lifted her chin, showing off all her bars and pips as she strode toward the podium. The audience hushed as she turned to face them, except for a few scattered sniffles and sobs.

Her expression stoic, Nechayev began, "I didn't know your ten shipmates who perished, but I can tell you a great deal about them. They were selfless, devoted, loyal, well-trained, and courageous. I'm sure they weren't any more perfect than the rest of us—but when your ship was threatened, they never thought twice about risking their lives to save yours.

"We who serve in Starfleet are the front lines of the Federation, the first ones to confront threats and enemies. Yet among us is a front line—*our* first line of defense—and that is our repair and rescue crews. We all know that space is not a natural environment for our species. The only thing that stands between us and disaster is our repair crews. Their work is largely unsung, but they have saved more lives than all the admirals, doctors, and diplomats put together."

She nodded at a tearful crew member in the front row. "It's all right to cry, because your survival is a testament to their bravery. Now you need to make the most of it. We've been through wars and catastrophes before, but none of them was as devastating as the threat we face today. We must all take inspiration from those we mourn, because now *we* must be the first line of defense for all the worlds that are in danger."

The admiral took a breath and lowered her head. "I would like to observe a few moments of silence for our fallen shipmates. Not only for them—but also for the millions of innocent beings who have perished from this awful onslaught. May they all rest in peace according to their beliefs."

As the theater stilled, Deanna Troi bowed her head. She wanted to meditate, but her troubled mind wouldn't let her. She kept worrying that this was only the beginning of something much worse.

Less than seven hours later, Deanna Troi walked numbly down a corridor crammed with evacuees. They sat propped against the bulkheads, looking sullen and dispirited; a few of them barely moved their legs, forcing her to step over them. Most of these displaced people were older humans, although there were children and representatives from almost every species in the Federation. When it came to lovely shore-leave planets, Persephone V was almost as famous as Pacifica, although its greater distance from Earth made it more of a retirement colony.

"Commander!" called an older man jumping to his feet. In his desperation, he gripped her arm. "You've got to help me! I'm Captain Kellman, retired, and my daughter, Amy, is still down on the planet. She was camping in the Cosgrove Wilderness on the South Continent. I keep asking them to look for her, but nobody will help me!"

Troi slowly extricated her arm from his grip. "I'm sorry," she said. "We've got to evacuate the urban centers first—get as many people as we can. And we can't change our orbit to search for people, because the whole effort is coordinated—"

"Damn you!" shouted someone behind her. "Have you been down there? The whole thing is *un*coordinated. It's chaos!" There were grumbles of agreement up and down the corridor, and many of the strangers—who would have been dead without their intervention—began to complain.

Deanna wanted to run screaming from all of this, but she knew it was her job to listen to these unfortunate souls and let them blow off a little steam. But there were so many people—the entire ship was filling up with them—and she couldn't do any more than briefly wander among them. She could organize group therapy sessions and memorials, but she had no idea how long they would be onboard the *Enterprise*. They could be off-loaded to the nearest Class-M world that had been spared. The captain had been right—she didn't need any extra assignments, because her own job was overwhelming.

When Deanna tried to move on, Captain Kellman stepped in front of her, blocking her way. The old gray-haired autocrat was used to commanding people and having them do what he wanted. "Listen," he said desperately, "just give me a shuttlecraft, and I'll go get my daughter."

"Only the captain—"

"The captain is in hiding!" bellowed another man. "Where is he? Let him come down here and explain to us what's happening. He's a coward!" There were shouts of agreement.

"What *is* this thing that's supposed to hit the planet?" demanded a woman.

All of a sudden, there was a cacophony of noise as a dozen people bombarded her with questions and complaints. Backed up into a corner, Deanna considered calling for security, but she remembered that every security officer was busy—either on the planet surface or protecting the transporter rooms and crucial areas of the ship. Both the shuttlebay and bridge were under heavy guard while the ship bulged with ten thousand extra people, expected to go much higher.

They pressed her against the bulkhead, peppering her with demands. Captain Kellman was right in her face, insisting they give him a shuttlecraft. She could sense their panic rising, along with her own. Finally Deanna Troi exploded and gave Kellman a firm push in the chest.

"Step back and maintain order!" she bellowed. "I don't care if you were all *admirals*—I am an active-duty officer on a mission. You will maintain order, or I'll have you thrown into the brig! Is that clear?" She didn't mention that the brig was probably already full of evacuees.

Kellman gulped and stepped back. "Yes, Sir." The others followed his lead, looking chastened and depressed. A scowl firmly set on her face, Deanna shoved her way through them. She *was* on a mission, but it had nothing to do with rescuing people from Persephone V. The only one she was trying to rescue at the moment was her beloved, Will Riker.

She continued down the crowded corridor, eyes straight ahead, trying to ignore the pleas and questions of the evacuees. The way they littered the hallway and the vacant looks on their faces reminded her uneasily of the Borg, who had once taken over these same passageways.

Moving briskly, Troi finally reached transporter room one, which was guarded by three security officers wearing riot gear and carrying phaser rifles. It almost seemed as if the *Enterprise* had been overrun by intruders, and in a way it had been.

The security officers acknowledged her, and one of them pressed a panel to open the door for her. She strode into the transporter room, half-expecting it to be jammed with evacuees, as it had been earlier. Instead there were only three people there now: Will Riker, Data, and the transporter chief, a dour Andorian named Rhofistan. Both Will and Data were dressed in T-shirts and underwear, nothing else. Three hulking white radiation suits, replicas of Leah Brahms' prototype, stood on the transporter platform, looking like snowmen about to transport to the North Pole.

"Deanna!" said Will nervously. "What are you doing here?"

"You don't have to be an empath to know what I'm doing here," she answered. "I don't want you going down there, Will . . . trying to live through that thing."

"There is risk involved," admitted Data. "But we need tricorder readings and observations taken at close range. Plus we need a greater understanding of how the phase-inversion avoids the mutagenic effects."

"Data, I don't mind if *you* go down there. Just be careful." Troi walked over to Will and took his hands, gazing at him with her sultry brown eyes. "It's you, *Imzadi*. I lost you before, and I don't want to do it again. I know you're in charge of this operation, and you could send somebody else."

He enveloped her in his brawny arms and pulled her toward him. "I'll come back to you, I promise. We've tested these suits under a simulation, and they work fine. Dr. Brahms showed us the controls, and there isn't time to train anyone else. Besides, everyone else is busy."

"Okay, then I'll go with you." Troi pulled away from him and stepped upon the transporter platform, taking her place beside one of the hulking suits. "You have an extra."

"A spare," answered Riker, "in case something goes wrong."

"I thought you said they were working perfectly."

"You can help me get into it," said Will, leaping onto the platform and standing behind the suit. "We added a tricorder to all the other hardware, and it's automatically activated to record when we put on the phase-shifting."

"You know, it's supposed to be crazy down there," she said worriedly.

"I know."

Troi hugged him ferociously, not completely understanding why she was so concerned about *this* mission. Maybe it was seeing so many distraught people worried about their loved ones down on the planet. Their emotions had affected her. Or maybe it was the awful nature of this Genesis Wave, which moved so swiftly and so devastatingly. There was no defense against it—raw survival was the best one could hope for.

She heard a cracking sound, and she turned to see Data opening the back of his suit. As gracefully as if he were putting on his pants, the lanky android slipped into the imposing case. Then Data stuck an arm out at an impossible angle—as if he were double-jointed—and reached behind him to close the rear clasps.

"I think I'll need your help," said Riker with a smile as he pulled away from her. "I'll be back, *Imzadi*, I promise."

Data pointed to the transporter operator, and his voice was amplified from inside the suit. "Actually whether we get back or not all depends on you, Chief Rhofistan. We will only have ten seconds after the Genesis Wave hits before the ship has to go to warp. If we are not recovered by then, there may be no way to recover us."

"Thanks for bringing that up," said Deanna dryly.

"I'll get you back," promised the Andorian in a deep voice, his antennae shooting to attention. Thoughtfully, he considered his readouts. "We have approximately two hours before the wave hits. The question is where to set you down to do the most good. A shuttlecraft evacuation site in the capitol city of Carefree is requesting more personnel to deal with the crowds. Should I set you down there?"

"That's fine," answered Riker. He looked warmly at Deanna. "Time to put me in my shining white armor."

"You always wear that." Deanna kissed him one last time, pulling away from his lips very reluctantly. "I knew you were the guy in the white armor."

With her help, Riker managed to squeeze into the bulky radiation suit, and Troi fastened him in. The suit was a marvel of technology, and she wanted to believe it would work flawlessly. Unfortunately, she knew it was a hurried replication of a prototype, which depended upon an imitation of Romulan technology.

Riker's amplified voice boomed from inside the suit. "Chief, enter your coordinates." Troi took that as her cue to step down from the transporter platform.

"Coordinates entered," said the Andorian.

Riker finally stopped fidgeting in the bulky suit, and he stood as still as Data, making them look like two identical golems.

"Energize," ordered Riker. The gleaming white suits evaporated into swirling columns of charged particles, and the transporter platform stood bare.

"All right," said Chief Rhofistan, "now I have to get back to the evacuation."

Deanna looked at him, shocked. "You're not just watching them?"

"I can't. There are too many people to rescue. I'll shut down operations here before it hits—to pick them up on sensors. Could you please tell the officers outside that we're starting evacuations again?"

"All right." Troi walked uneasily toward the door of the transporter room, a knot twisting in her stomach. So many people were in danger—death was all around, and so were terror and fear. It was hard for her to separate her emotions from all of theirs, especially when she reached the corridor, where dozens of eyes looked up to her for hope, insight . . . a miracle. She put a pleasant look on her face and grabbed the first likely conversational group she saw, about seven or eight people.

"Come on, all of you," she said with a brave smile. "We're going to talk among ourselves about what's happening. I'll tell you what I know, but then I've got to move on to other people. I just want to get you talking."

seventeen

When Will Riker materialized in a large public square, surrounded by glittering, blue skyscrapers, a bottle pelted him, bouncing off his radiation suit. He looked at Data, who stood only a few meters away, and the android was in a crouch, fending off two brawlers who had rolled into him. Unruly lines snaked around the numerous sculptures and benches in the square, as people huddled with children and oldsters, wondering if there was any way to get farther along in a queue that seemed to have no end.

As he looked around, Riker discovered they weren't even in the busiest part of the square; that was sixty meters away, where Starfleet officers were trying to load two shuttlecraft. Other officers were attempting to push back the crowd and make room for a third shuttlecraft to land. To complicate matters, Starfleet wasn't the only outfit loading vessels in the packed square. A few intrepid entrepreneurs had opened up shop and were taking on passengers . . . if the price was right. It was bedlam.

Riker stared incredulously as one private shuttlecraft, which looked to be a six-seater, boarded about a dozen passengers. When they tried to lift off, desperate people in the crowd jumped on the landing rails of the craft and hung on. The crowd screamed and ran for cover as the distressed shuttlecraft bobbed and weaved over the mobbed square. Two of the people hanging from the rails dropped off, causing more pandemonium in the fearful crowd. Its thrusters roared, but the shuttlecraft swooped out of control, carrying too much weight.

Riker glanced over at Data, who was still busy trying to break up the fight. For some reason, the android's actions infuriated the crowd around him, and several of them attacked him, jumping on his back and legs. This had no effect on Data, who merely brushed them off as if they were lint, but more of the rioters pressed around him, trying to see what was happening with this strange apparition in white armor.

Suddenly everyone in the square screamed at once, and Riker looked up to see the stricken shuttlecraft veer straight into a skyscraper. The blue building shattered like glass, and a fireball roared from the crater, showering half the crowd with debris and flaming embers. Erupting in howls of panic and fear, the crowd ran in every direction.

The security detail near the shuttlecraft were soon firing phasers on the horde, and the officers tried to fall back to the refuge of their ships. *They'll abandon the square!* thought Riker. *Plus all these beings—thousands of them—and they don't know that Data and I are here.*

A mad rush of people suddenly plowed into the commander and knocked him off his feet. He rolled over in his bulky suit and tried to stand up, but people were pushed on top of him by the panicked crowd. Riker feared he would be trampled in the stampede, but he heard a voice in his helmet, telling him calmly, "Activate phase-shifting."

Breathless, Riker echoed the words, "Computer, activate phase-shifting!"

At once, the crowd no longer plowed into him but seemed only to glance off, and he was able to stagger to his feet. Pushing his way through the throng, Riker sought refuge behind a statue of a historical figure mounted on what looked like a giant ostrich. Data moved swiftly to his side, wrapping an arm around him and bucking him up.

"This is worse than I expected," said the android, his voice sounding unruffled yet overly loud in Riker's headgear. "I suggest we seek refuge in one of the buildings and report back to the ship. I also want to perform diagnostics on the suits to see if they have been damaged."

"Good idea," said Riker with a nod. As they lumbered off, he couldn't help but look in the direction of the Starfleet shuttlecraft, where the scene was getting ugly. With a roar of thrusters, one of the shuttlecraft managed to take off, scorching a dozen onlookers in the effort. However, the second shuttlecraft was overrun by rioters, who climbed on top of it, trying to pry their way inside. The third shuttlecraft, which had been circling overhead, simply sped away, not risking a landing.

Abandoned, the small cadre of security officers fell back from the angry mob, shooting phasers as they went. It looked as if they had no escape.

"They need help!" said Riker with alarm. "And the shuttlecraft . . . that crowd is going to smash it to pieces."

"This evacuation process does seem to be ill-advised," agreed Data. "However, we do not have any weapons, and crowd control is not our primary mission. We must leave."

"You're right." Riker felt the android grip the arm of his suit and guide him through the surging crowd. Although they were a strange sight, there was nothing on the prototype suits to mark them as being Starfleet. In this surreal scene—amidst riots and shuttlecraft wreckage—two people in white armor had a kind of logic.

As they reached the sidewalk outside the square, Riker turned back to look. He was greatly relieved to see swirling transporter beams where the beleaguered officers had been battling the crowds. They had been rescued, probably by the shuttlecraft which had fled. He saw the mob pull people out of the grounded Starfleet shuttle, while others desperately tried to take their places. At the same time, other rioters swarmed on top of the craft, ripping it apart.

"The security detail was rescued," said Riker, "but that shuttlecraft is history."

"We have two hours," said Data with a puzzled tone to his voice. "Had the crowd allowed us to proceed, we could have taken the majority of them."

"I'm afraid when people panic, they don't think that rationally. If this is happening all over. . . . This is a nightmare."

"Apparently we no longer have the problem of convincing people this is a real threat," observed Data.

Without really paying much attention to where they were going, the commander followed Data into the lobby of a grand hotel. The scene here was also chaos, with clothes and litter strewn everywhere, and people rushing madly through the plush lobby. There was a clutch of people kneeling in a corner, and they seemed to be praying. A desk clerk stood behind the counter, pointlessly operating his computer and dealing with customers in line.

Riker was aghast. "There is no way we were ever going to rescue more than a fraction of these people, even if everything went smoothly."

The android nodded his headgear. "We were unprepared for a catastrophe of this magnitude. We must reconsider the evacuation option."

"So far, it's the *only* option," grumbled Riker.

A small, purple-skinned Saurian staggered in front of them and regarded them suspiciously. He curled his beaklike mouth and asked, "Heeeey, what are you two dresshhed up for?"

"His slurred speech indicates he is intoxicated," observed Data.

"No kidding." Riker pushed a button on his helmet, and his voice boomed out into the lobby. "Do you have a room here?"

"Yesshh," answered the Saurian proudly.

"Can we borrow it?"

He looked curiously at the two people in the weird suits and shook his bulbous head. "Takes all kindsss. Sure . . . here's the chip." The Saurian produced a smaller version of an isolinear chip and handed it to Riker. The commander studied the entry key and read the number "219."

"Thank you." Riker started off, but he felt a bit guilty. "Do you have any way off this planet?"

"Sure I do!" The little Saurian proudly produced a flask and took a long drink; then he staggered off, weaving his way through the trashed lobby of the elegant hotel.

"If this were not so tragic, it would be fascinating," said Data.

"Let's take the stairs." Riker pointed to a sweeping staircase that dominated the rear portion of the lobby. He lumbered up the plushly carpeted steps and proceeded into a corridor. After checking numbers on room doors, he was glad to find that the Saurian's room was here on the second floor, and they had to climb no higher.

The hotel room turned out to be a fairly good observation point, with a balcony looking down on the chaotic square. Riker walked to the balcony and gazed at the panicked crowd below, surging from one end of the square to another. Statues had been toppled in the rioting, and the Starfleet shuttlecraft lay on its side, having been pushed over.

Persephone V had always had a reputation as one of the most peaceful planets in the Federation, thought Riker ruefully. It was supposed to be a sanctuary from the rat race, where crime was almost nonexistent. So were police, apparently. In the center of their capitol, there was no local help in crowd management. Maybe the local authorities had cast off their uniforms in hopes of getting out sooner. Probably all the important authorities—who might have been some help here—were already aboard the armada orbiting the planet.

"Commander, should I report to the captain?" asked Data.

"Go ahead," answered Riker glumly. "And don't spare him the gruesome details."

Bad news continued to pour in. Captain Picard paced the bridge of the *Enterprise*, reading the latest projections for the Genesis Wave's course. It was strongly suggested that the wave would strike Earth and the heart of the Federation before cutting a wide swath through the Neutral Zone and the Romulan Star Empire. They only had about six days before it entered Earth's solar system.

After a consultation with Admiral Nechayev, he had to talk to Consul Bekra immediately, but he couldn't leave the bridge during the evacuation of Persephone V. It was going badly, except for the million or so lucky ones who had been saved. "Disaster" was not too strong a word, judging by reports like the one he had just received from Data. They were doing the best they could, but the task of rescuing ten million people at short notice was just too daunting for the Federation alone.

A shortage of planning time had resulted in breakdowns and panic in a variety of locations. The main square of Carefree was one of the worst places, but there were other sites that had been abandoned, too. At this rate, the fleet wouldn't even meet their worst projections for the rescue mission. For every life they saved, five would be lost.

Filled ships were already going to the next planet, too. Unless they did something, there would always be a next one. The *Enterprise* was fully occupied with transporter evacuation, and he couldn't divert a single crew member to the mess in Carefree. He already had two on the surface that he would rather have back. If Riker and Data wanted someplace to observe the worst of the disaster, they were getting it.

Picard heard the turbolift whoosh open, and he turned to see Counselor Troi and Consul Bekra enter. The Capellan was limping slowly on a new artificial limb, and the scowl had deepened on his face.

"Captain!" called Bekra, moving more quickly. "I simply must protest. I was very comfortable in the private room I had, but now there are *six* people in there with me! In a room intended for *one*."

The captain cleared his throat, attempting to hide his annoyance. "There will probably be a few more people in your quarters by the end of the day. I'm sorry, but we have to squeeze as many people onto the ship as we can."

The Capellan sniffed and looked around. "It's quite roomy up here on the bridge. Tell me, when are we going to be dropped off somewhere else?"

"I haven't gotten my orders yet," answered Picard curtly. He looked at Deanna Troi, who seemed to be at a loss to help him. In fact, she looked haggard and exhausted.

"Let's step over to this auxiliary console," said the captain, leading the way to an isolated workstation on the outer ring. Despite his limp, Consul Bekra kept up with him. "You seem to be adapting to that prosthetic device," said Picard.

"Do I have much choice?" asked the Capellan. "I must say, your Dr. Crusher is very skilled, but I intend to press charges against that crazy Klingon . . . after this is all over."

The captain lowered his voice to say, "We have a serious problem. Our latest projections say that the Genesis Wave will pass through Romulan space, as well as the heart of the Federation."

Bekra shifted his eyes and looked at Troi. "You brought me here under false pretenses."

"I said the captain wanted to meet you," answered Troi wearily. "You've met. Now will you help us?"

"What makes you think I have any influence with the Romulans?" asked Bekra snidely.

"Listen," whispered Picard, "at this point, I don't care about anything you've ever done before in your life. If you want a full pardon, Admiral Nechayev will give you one. We need you to contact the Romulans—using any means you desire—and tell them the truth. Tell them what you've been through and what's happening here. We're going to contact them through official channels as well, but we wanted them to have outside verification from . . . somebody they trusted."

"They may already know about this," said the Capellan.

"They may," conceded the captain, "but we can't take that chance. We have to make sure they know. This auxiliary console has been configured for subspace communications, and I don't think you'll have any trouble operating it. We're just going to walk away, and nobody is going to watch or record what you're doing here. Feel free to contact your homeworld, too, if you like, but . . . you know what you have to do."

Consul Bekra considered Captain Picard for a few moments, then he finally nodded. "I wish to leave this ship as soon as possible. My friend, Paldor, also wishes to leave."

"We'll let you off at the nearest opportunity, when we let off the evacuees," answered Picard. "There will never be any record of our conversation."

"All right," said Bekra, looking away from them. "Leave me now."

Picard motioned to Troi for her to follow him. When they had gotten out of earshot, he whispered, "Do you think we can trust him?"

She nodded. "I believe so. I have been sensing that he had something to hide, but his mental defenses let down when he agreed to help."

"You look tired," said the captain.

"Please don't tell me to sleep," she cautioned him. "Will is down on the surface in one of those suits, and my cabin is full of refugees. Unless you've got a cot in your ready room—"

"I'm afraid not," said the captain with a wry smile. "I agree, there's no rest at the moment. Thank you for your help, Counselor."

She shook her head doubtfully. "We need a lot of help."

"I know."

Geordi La Forge paced the gleaming confines of the radiation lab on deck seventeen, feeling guilty that he had all this space to himself when the ship was crammed to the airlocks with evacuees. He hoped he wouldn't be alone much longer, because Leah Brahms was supposed to be working with him. She was late for their first shift together, which made him pace all the faster.

This situation—the two of them working alone together in a crisis—was uncomfortably like the circumstances under which he had fallen in love with Leah. Of course, that had been a simulation on the holodeck. The radiation laboratory was the same kind of close, isolated environment, removed from the rest of the ship. Geordi wasn't worried that *she* would be distracted by this—after all, the real Leah Brahms hadn't been on the holodeck—he was worried about his own feelings spilling out.

She's a widow, he reminded himself, and she's just lost everything she has in the world. . . . More than anything, he had to respect her right to privacy and grief during this tragic time. She needed a friend right now, not more complications. In many respects, he felt guilty about even making her work on this assignment, but her radiation suit was the only object to withstand the Genesis Wave so far. And she was the only person to have lived through it.

La Forge had one of the replicated suits in the lab, and he had started to study it while he waited; but he wasn't quite sure what he was looking at. What they needed were a couple of Romulan engineers who knew this phase-shifting like he and Leah knew warp engines. He could make educated guesses, and Leah had done more than guess—she had put it to use—but they had no design notes or schematics. Even Leah's records were all lost on Outpost Seran-T-One.

With a whoosh, the door to the lab opened, and Geordi turned eagerly to see his fellow engineer walk in. She was dressed in a gray engineer's jumpsuit borrowed from his department, having arrived with only the grimy clothes on her back. She looked determined and alert, if not happy to be there. Once again, he thought about how much he liked the short, chestnut-colored hair framing her angelic face, and he gave her a warm smile.

The smile faded almost immediately from his face when he saw another figure stride through the door behind her. It was the old Klingon, Maltz, and he cast a fishy eye in Geordi's direction. There was something proprietary in the Klingon's rheumy gaze, as if he considered himself Leah's protector, or at least her chaperone.

Seeing Geordi's surprised expression, Leah patted him on the shoulder. "It's all right—I told Maltz he could come along to help us. He's seen it, too."

"I must do *something*," grumbled the old Klingon. "They filled up my cabin with more derelicts like me, and it got depressing. We can not run from this enemy—we must go down fighting it!"

"Uh, yes," agreed Geordi, "but our particular mission is to find a way to let more people survive the wave."

Leah shook her head grimly. "I'll help you do it, but you won't want to live on one of these planets after you're done."

"That's just it," said Geordi excitedly. "Now we've got some really good long-range scanner data from the affected planets. They may not be pleasant—borderline Class-L—but they are livable, with thin oxygen and native plant and animal life. By replanting and standard terraforming, we can probably get them back to what they once were."

Leah shivered and looked down, and Maltz's attention seemed far away, as if dealing with an old memory. Geordi quickly added, "Both of you saw these planets when they were still forming, before the radical changes were over. The new Genesis Planets look like they're going to be stabilizing quite nicely."

Brahms turned away, and La Forge felt a pang of guilt about having been so blunt. Of course, one of those planets was Seran, where her husband and friends had been absorbed into the new ecosystem. He appealed helplessly to her. "I didn't mean anything by it . . . I was just trying to explain—"

Maltz laughed out loud and shook his head. "This is why humans are so pathetic. In trying to look on the bright side all the time, they ignore the obvious danger. Do you not see? These worlds are being terraformed to the specifications of the new owners, and they will come to claim them."

"But it won't be as easy if there are *living* people on the planets," countered La Forge. He held up his palms, beseeching Leah to forgive him. "I'm sorry, I didn't mean to be so blunt—I wish you didn't have to be here. We're just trying to save lives as best we can. We haven't got enough ships to evacuate everyone—this current mission is a mess. We need shelters that work, and we need them right now."

The woman turned around and gazed at him; her brown eyes were moist from tears, but her jaw was set in firm determination. "All right, I'll help you, but we need a lot of stuff. Start making a shopping list."

"I will," answered Geordi, snapping to and grabbing a padd. "What do you need?"

"We need those big interphase generators the Romulans have."

"Okay," said La Forge doubtfully. "That's going to be hard. We don't have that technology."

"Call up Admiral Nechayev," said Leah. "Have her contact the

Romulans. Without those big generators—the kind they use to cloak their *newest* ships—it won't work. If we can get a few, we can replicate them like we did with the suit, but we need those to stand a chance."

"Where is this admiral?" said Maltz, balling his hands into fists. "I will deal with her."

"No, I'll get on it," promised Geordi, rushing to a communications console. "What else?"

Leah stroked her chin thoughtfully. "I'll also need data on how deep into the crust of the planet the Genesis Effect goes. Maybe all we need to do is dig holes deep enough to protect the inhabitants. I know a certain geologist who's not doing much, and she'd be willing to help us."

"The more the merrier," muttered Geordi under his breath as he worked the console.

"What did you say?" asked Maltz suspiciously.

"Um, just talking to myself." Geordi went back to carefully wording a message to Admiral Nechayev and Captain Picard.

"I really like Dolores," said Leah. "I approve."

Geordi wanted to correct her impression of him and the visiting geologist, but he was done looking like he still had a thing for Leah, even if he did. He kept his attention on his work. "While we wait, you can bring me up to speed on this technology. I'd like to see how it works in the suit."

"All right," answered Leah, sitting on a stool. For the first time, she looked around the sumptuous laboratory with its miniature clean room, test chambers, and racks of test instruments.

"It has running water, too," said Leah with a wry smile. "Say, I might just move in here. There's a lot more room here than in my quarters. What do you say, Maltz?"

"Typical Federation decadence," the Klingon said, his body language at odds with his disdainful tone as he stretched out on the roomy deck. "You do your research and save your lives, while I save my strength to take lives. We will go back and kill the ones who are doing this. Right, Captain?"

"I'll be there." Leah winked at Geordi as if she were humoring the old warrior, but there was a spark of excitement in her eyes. She added, "To at least one person in the universe, I'm a captain."

"That's great," said Geordi, mustering some enthusiasm when all he felt was hopelessness. "I thought that maybe we could use a protomatter beam, so I installed one in Test Chamber Two."

"Dangerous," said Leah, frowning at the idea.

"I know, but we need it to simulate the wave in tests, don't we?"

"You want to recreate the wave?" she asked incredulously.

"Not the mutagenic part, just the energy wave that is carrying all this information."

"He is right," said the Klingon, lying on the deck, his eyes still shut. "The original Genesis Device used a detonation to expand, turning into a wave as it moved outward, circling a planet. Someone must be projecting this wave from a fixed point—a space station. It is probably hidden and hard to reach.

"A task force has been sent to look for the source," added Geordi.

The Klingon growled. "They do not know what they are looking for, do they? I understand this enemy—I knew it would come looking for me again someday, and it did. When you finish saving lives, we shall go kill it. Wake me then, Captain."

"Okay, Maltz," said Leah Brahms without a trace of humor in her voice.

"I don't much like waiting for the end of the world," muttered Will Riker. The commander sat on the edge of his bed in a strange hotel room, wrapped in a blanket; it was getting cold, and he was only wearing underwear. The climate controls in the hotel had ceased working, to go along with all the chaos in the streets. But why try to save energy now—when this world would soon be gone, replaced by something else?

"It is difficult to watch this world die," allowed Data, "especially with so little dignity." The android unplugged his tricorder from a jack on the back of his radiation suit, apparently finished with his diagnostic routines. "Both suits are still functioning within normal parameters."

"That's good," said Riker, rising to his feet. "Because I'm going to put mine back on."

"We have approximately twenty-two minutes," observed Data. "We should be receiving new projections from the transporter room very soon, and the evacuation will be over."

"Ending with a whimper, not a bang," said Riker. He stood and walked toward the balcony door, careful not to step into view, because vandals had been throwing bricks earler. All of the glass was smashed. Nevertheless, he could gaze down into the square, which echoed with plaintive voices, begging to be saved.

For the last hour, people in the square had been disappearing in random clusters, rescued via transporter beam from ships in orbit. Now thousands of residents were standing around, lifting their arms to the heavens, beseeching the fickle gods of far-off transporters to save them. Some danced; others sang, wept, or did whatever they thought might get them noticed, although both they and Riker knew it was a random process. At least somebody was doing something for the people stranded in the heart of Carefree.

"When it hits," said Riker, "I don't want to be inside this skyscraper. I want to be down there." He pointed to the square.

The wind shifted, and a whiff of something acrid hit Riker's nostrils. He looked up just as the sprinkler system in the ceiling of the hotel room came on, blasting everything with a dense spray of water and chemicals. Smoke was seeping through the closed door from the hallway. Data immediately rushed into action, grabbing the radiation suits, but even the android couldn't move quickly enough to keep them from getting drenched. Plus there was nowhere in the room to hide from the cascading liquids.

The chemicals burned in Riker's eyes, but he still managed to grab one of the suits and haul it out onto the balcony. From there, he could see that the hotel was on fire several stories overhead, where columns of black smoke curled into the sky. Riker glanced into his suit to see that it had gotten wet inside, and he also realized that they couldn't get out the doorway. It was about twelve meters straight down to the sidewalk, and that looked like the way they would have to leave.

He was jostled when Data joined him on the balcony, dragging his armor, and it suddenly became very crowded out there. "I'm considered aborting this mission," murmured Riker. "I just have a bad feeling . . . too many things going wrong."

Data cocked his head. "Transporters on the *Enterprise* will be occupied for another ten minutes and twenty seconds. Most of the rescue ships have already departed, although a few still remain in orbit. This would not be an opportune time to seek assistance."

Riker glanced down at the square and saw that the mob was milling around, arguing disgruntledly among themselves. The random transports seemed to have ceased, and so had the momentarily happy mood. Now a feeling of desperation was setting in.

"We need to get down," said the commander.

"I will jump down, and you can throw me the equipment."

Riker nodded, and Data bounded over the wrought-iron railing as easily as if he were stepping over a curb. The android made a perfect two-point landing and looked up to the human—at the very instant that an explosion blew the room door open. A fireball roared from the hallway through the room, hurling Riker and the radiation suits over the railing.

eighteen

Deanna Troi stopped in the middle of her sentence, her finger in the air, and she couldn't remember what she had been saying to the group of evacuees gathered in her office. She had an overwhelming premonition—a certainty—that something had happened to Will.

Troi looked at the chronometer over her door and noted that they were only about fifteen minutes away from the expected arrival of the wave—and their departure soon after. She knew the radiation suit was supposed to be foolproof, but so many things had gone wrong today that she couldn't rest easy for one second. She had been worried about Will before, but now she was terrified.

Patients were bombarding her with questions, but she shoved her way through them, saying things like, "We'll talk about that when I get back. Have strength! Maybe your loved ones are on another ship. We'll get lists of names as soon as we disembark."

Finally she broke out of her office into the corridor, which was hardly any better. Her shoulders and forearms were bruised from having to shove her way through the crowds which clogged the corridors of the *Enterprise*. But she lowered her head again and plowed through the dispirited, disgruntled throng. This time, Deanna was more determined than ever, because the worry for Will had turned into abject fear.

Only one turbolift was open now on this whole deck—to keep the evacuees from moving around the ship. All of them had heard about how wonderful the accommodations were in the lounge, the theater, the holodecks, or some other leisure area, and they didn't want to stay in a packed corridor. She wondered how they would like it if they knew the *Enterprise* wasn't leaving orbit until the last possible second.

Troi was slowed down by the milling crowds, who glared suspiciously at her, knowing that she had free run of the ship. But today free run of the *Enterprise* was not what it used to be; she almost looked fondly back to when it had a skeleton crew. Impatiently, Deanna tapped her combadge and said, "Troi to Riker."

After several seconds of silence, she tried again. "Troi to Riker."

A chime sounded, followed by the computer's voice. "Commander Riker is not responding."

Her jaw set firmly, Troi lifted her elbows and jabbed her way through the crowd, shouting, "Out of my way! Emergency!"

Deanna finally reached the turbolift, where the hectored guard was busy arguing with refugees. She noticed that he now had his phaser rifle leveled for action rather than slung over his shoulder, as she had seen him last time. Upon noticing her, he slapped a panel to call the turbolift for her.

"I have to go with you!" shouted a woman, chasing after Troi.

"Let me see the captain!" shouted someone else. "You don't understand—"

The counselor hated having to turn a cold shoulder to their fervent pleas, but they were safe—and Will was not. When the turbolift door opened, she dashed inside, leaving the guard to fend off the evacuees who tried to follow her. He snapped and barked at them, using his rifle to push the mob back. Deanna was grateful when the door finally shut, leaving her alone in the conveyance. It seemed oddly peaceful inside the cocoon of the turbolift.

"Transporter room two," she ordered, hoping to get as close as possible.

When the turbolift door opened at her destination, an armed security officer tumbled backwards into Deanna, pushed by a surge of refugees trying to get on. Operating instinctively, Troi picked up the man's phaser rifle and quickly fired a shot over the crowd's head. That stopped them for a second, long enough for her to make sure the phaser was set to stun. When the horde pushed forward again, she drilled a big Ardanan in the front row, and he tumbled across the threshold of the turbolift, unconscious.

"Back off!" she shouted. "Make way! That's an order!"

She wanted to see how far this mutiny would progress—if it even was a mutiny. The sight of the ship's counselor wielding a weapon and firing at will into the crowd did have an effect, and they finally made a slight path for her.

Before she left the turbolift, Troi bent down to make sure the security officer was all right. The young ensign seemed groggy but coherent. "Can you get to your feet?"

"Yes, Sir."

"I'm keeping your weapon," she told him. "I want you to call for backup on this deck and get yourself to sickbay."

"Yes, Commander," he answered. "Thank you."

Phaser rifle leveled in front of her, Troi strode off the turbolift, motioning people to get out of her way. "If necessary, we won't hesitate to use force to maintain order!" she shouted.

Most of the panicked crowd backed away from her, but a few distraught evacuees regaled her with queries and demands. "My children are in school!" shouted one worried man.

"All your questions will be answered," she told them. "Now let us do our jobs and rescue as many of you as we can. If you cause us to delay, maybe *your* loved one is the one we'll miss. Get out of the way!"

Moving steadily down the jammed corridor, Deanna finally reached the transporter room, where there was now only one security officer on guard. Since the door was open, she could see why— the other two officers were busy trying to move people off the transporter platform and out the door. But where exactly these new arrivals were supposed to go was hard to tell.

She muscled her way into the transporter room, shoving people out of the way with her phaser rifle, until she reached the operator's console. The tall Andorian was busy working his instruments, bringing groups of eight haggard evacuees in at once. The security officer moved them off the platform just as another wave took their place.

"Chief Rhofistan," she said, "have you heard from the away team? Riker and Data."

"No," he answered, never taking his eyes off his instruments. "I'm due to pick them up exclusively in another two minutes."

"I think they're in trouble," said Troi. "They haven't answered my hails."

"Maybe they're out of their suits for some reason," said the Andorian. "Their only communications systems are inside the suits."

"They're not wearing their combadges?"

"No, that signal wouldn't get through the shielding in the suits. Excuse me, Commander." The transporter operator had to ignore her while he brought up another group of dazed survivors. Deanna spent those few precious seconds looking around the crowded room, and she finally found what she was looking for. Discarded in the corner was the third radiation suit, the spare one.

When the transporter chief looked up again, she asked him, "Do you have two spare combadges?"

"Sure." From a drawer, he fished out two standard combadges and handed them to her. They usually kept a few spares on hand to give to passengers to make it easier to lock onto them with the transporter.

"I'm going to put on the extra radiation suit and go down to the surface," she told the chief.

He raised a snowy white eyebrow, and his antennae twitched for a moment. "Are you sure that's advisable?"

"No, but I'm doing it anyway. Set me down exactly where you set Riker and Data down. But do what you can to get all three of us." Troi hefted the phaser rifle. "I think I'll take this with me, and my combadge."

"The combadge won't do you any good inside that suit," said the transporter chief. "But I'll route your communications through. Are you staying to take the readings?"

Deanna swallowed dryly. "Let's say for the sake of argument, I am."

"I have to turn off the phase-shifting a split second before I transport you," said Rhofistan. "I'll control that from here, but I didn't want you to be surprised. The suit checks out—you're good to go."

Having helped Will into his armor only a couple of hours ago, Deanna remembered fairly well how to get into it. First she stripped off everything but her undergarments; then she cracked open the back and climbed in. Troi was unprepared for the way the gel material molded itself to her body, but the disconcerting sensations soon passed—to be replaced by the strangeness of being encased in the bulky cocoon. Good thing I'm not claustrophobic, she thought. In fact, Troi was reminded of the meditation chambers on Betazoid—hardly bigger than coffins.

One of the security officers helped her close her rear clasps, then he went back to work. "One more group to bring up," explained the transporter chief, his voice booming in the headgear.

Deanna waited impatiently inside the armor, listening to her own labored breathing and thumping heart. Finally the last group of refugees arrived and stepped numbly off the transporter platform. Troi tried not to think about the ones waiting in line behind them—the ones who would not make it to safety.

As security officers tried to deal with the new arrivals, Troi lumbered onto the platform and situated herself on the pad. She knew time was running out—she could see it in the anxious faces of the security detail and the transporter chief. If she had any sense at all, she wouldn't be doing this, but she had never had any sense where Will Riker was concerned.

With a wave of her phaser rifle, she ordered, "Energize."

A moment later, Deanna Troi materialized in the middle of a huge public square, filled with people, trash, and the wreckage of a couple of shuttlecraft. She instantly whirled in every direction, looking for Will and Data, but she couldn't see them in the mass of people rushing to and fro.

Then she remembered that she had a tricorder, sensors, and all kinds of goodies built into this suit. Of course, she didn't have any training in using it, but she assumed its computer would take orders.

"Computer," she said, "locate any radiation suits like this one."

"Please clarify the request," answered the computer.

"Activate comlink. Troi to Riker. Troi to Data!" She waited, but her hails met with stony silence. Before she could think of another order to give, her attention was distracted by columns of dark smoke spewing from one of the glittering skyscrapers bordering the square. *I need to find some kind of high ground*, thought Deanna, *so I can see over all these people.*

As she lumbered along, wielding her phaser rifle, Troi got a few blank stares, but most of the inhabitants were lost in their own worlds. Unless they were in denial, as a few jovial souls were, they were facing death for the first and last time in their lives. She could feel the fear and desperation—it was as palpable as the dark smoke that hung in the sky.

She jumped when she heard a voice in her headgear. "Chief Rhofistan to Troi."

"Troi here," she answered, relieved that the transporter operator was keeping tabs on her.

"I just wanted to let you know that we've stopped evacuations, and we're on Yellow Alert. The captain has given word that we should be ready to pull out any second."

"But I haven't found them yet!" she said with alarm.

"You know we can't stay here," said the chief. "After it hits the planet, we only have ten seconds before it reaches the ship. I'm under orders to get you after six seconds, even if we can't find the other team."

"All right," rasped Troi, knowing it would do no good to argue with him—he had his orders. Captain Picard had already shown that he was prepared to sacrifice lives to save the *Enterprise* and all aboard, even if that meant losing his first and second officers.

How could she find them in all this chaos? She suddenly realized that she had the equivalent of a signal device in her hands, and Deanna pointed the phaser rifle toward the sky and sent one brilliant streak after another into the sky. Many of the startled inhabitants shrunk away from the strange white golem who was blasting off a phaser as if it were New Year's Eve, but she didn't care about that. She *wanted* to cause a commotion and attract some attention.

It seemed like forever that she wandered in the square, shooting her phaser, but it was only a couple of minutes. Finally, a figure came bounding toward her across the park, leaping over people's heads. His leaps were so huge and effortless that he looked like a man jogging on Earth's moon. Troi stopped firing, knowing it could only be one entity—Data. He wasn't wearing his radiation suit.

"Counselor Troi," said the android, bounding to a graceful stop. "I am surprised but gratified to see you."

"Where is Commander Riker?" she demanded.

"He was injured in that fire." Data pointed to the black smoke spewing from an elegant skyscraper. "He is conscious now but unable to walk. I believe his leg is broken. The problem is that our radiation suits were also damaged, and we were unable to contact the ship."

A voice burst into her ears over the comlink in her headgear. "Picard to Troi."

Deanna held up a finger, motioning Data to wait. "Troi here, Captain."

"You're on the planet surface?"

"Yes, Sir."

"The wave is moving faster than we anticipated. You have less than two minutes. We can't seem to contact Riker and Data."

Troi took a deep breath and looked around the dying city. In this suit, it would take her two minutes to walk across the crowded square to reach Will, and probably another minute to get out of the suit. So she made a difficult decision. "I'm staying on the surface to take readings, but I've got combadges for Riker and Data. Beam them up now, but don't forget *me*."

"We won't, Counselor. Good luck. Picard out."

She turned to Data, about to explain, but the android was holding out his palm. "My hearing picked up the conversation. You are very brave, Commander."

"Just get Will to safety," she said as she handed over the two extra combadges. "How do I work this suit?"

"Say, 'Computer, phase-shifting on.' Tricorder operations are automatic." With that, the android turned and bounded off, leaping twenty meters at a time, sailing over the desultory crowd.

"Computer, phase-shifting on," ordered Deanna. She held her breath, expecting some change, but nothing felt different inside the suit. Deanna had a moment's panic that the phase-shifting wasn't working, and she would be dead with all of these poor, dispirited souls.

"Computer, what is the status?" she asked with a gulp.

"All systems functional, interphase mode activated," answered the computer. "For a Betazoid, your vital signs are quite elevated, indicating severe stress or illness."

"Never mind about me; I'm okay." She had more pressing con-

Breen ship, disabling and capturing it. Of course, all the Breen crew had vaporized themselves, since they never allowed themselves to be captured. Jagron had moved swiftly up the ranks after that, gaining command of this D'deridex-class warbird, but he had ambitions beyond the command of a single vessel.

Despite his relative youth and a family background of low nobility, Jagron looked every centimeter the part of a Romulan commander. He was tall and slim, handsome in a hawklike way, and arrogant to a fault.

"That's enough fussing," he said, brushing off his valet's hands and straightening his own stiff collar. "It's just a meeting."

"But with the Praetor, Sir," said the old valet in hushed tones. "And the Proconsul."

"Yes," replied Captain Jagron with a frown. "All this firepower . . . for what?"

"You'll know soon, Commander."

Still frowning, Jagron strode from his quarters down the hallway to the transporter room, where he was met by his top aides, Centurion Gravonak and Intelligence Officer Petroliv. The tall and stately Petroliv was also his lover, but they had taken considerable pains to hide that fact from the rest of the crew. They always treated each other with cool professionalism.

"My Liege," said Gravonak, bowing like the toady he was.

"Are we still in the dark about the reason for this gathering?" asked Jagron as he strode into the transporter room.

"Not entirely," answered Petroliv. "We're sure it has something to do with the massive fleet movements we've been observing in the Federation."

"Movements *away* from the Neutral Zone," added Gravonak, sounding displeased that, unlike his colleague, he had nothing new to report.

When they reached the transporter platform, all three of them climbed aboard. A very nervous transporter operator cleared his throat. "I'm sorry, Commander Jagron, but the protocols call for every commander to bring *one* aide, no more."

Centurion Gravonak folded his hands in front of him, as if expecting the intelligence officer to step down. Commander Jagron gazed from the stuffy first officer to his beautiful intelligence officer; he had already made his decision, but he wanted to make it look as if he were deliberating.

"Gravonak, return to the bridge."

"Sir?" asked the centurion as if he hadn't understood. But Jagron was not going to humor him with another request. He simply motioned to the transporter operator, who sent the commander's molecules and those of his lover into the bowels of another warbird only five kilometers away.

They were met on the *Terix* by Commander Tomalak, who smiled pleasantly at the new arrivals. An old veteran, Tomalak could afford to be more personable than the usual Romulan commander. He had seen almost everything in his long and distinguished career, and he never let you forget it. Jagron respected, envied, and hated Tomalak, but he was never anything less than cordial to the venerated commander.

"Welcome aboard, my young colleague," said Tomalak, grasping Jagron's shoulder. "You're the last one—even the Praetor was here before you."

Jagron shrugged, not explaining that he had planned it that way. "Are we supposed to be guarding the Neutral Zone or sitting around in a conference room?"

"You're jaded at rather a young age," observed Tomalak with amusement. He led the way out the door. "The Praetor and the Proconsul—this is undoubtedly the most important meeting you've ever attended."

Jagron motioned to his intelligence officer, Petroliv. "Why could we bring only one aide?"

"Apparently the number of people who are allowed to know about this will be kept small."

"Do you know?"

Tomalak stopped and shook his head, a scowl on his craggy face. "No. And I don't remember ever hearing of a similar meeting in all my decades of service."

They said no more until they reached the briefing room, which appeared to be a small classroom near a row of laboratories. A large viewscreen dominated one wall of the room. Already seated were two more commanders, Horek and Damarkol of the *Livex* and the *G'Anohok* respectively, plus their aides. The Praetor and the Proconsul were not in evidence.

After a few quick pleasantries, Tomalak said, "Our most distinguished guests will be joining us soon. They wanted us to watch some video logs first. I am told these were sent to us by the Federation." After finding a seat, he said, "Computer, begin playback."

Jagron had never pretended to have seen as much in his life as Tomalak and these veteran captains had seen, but his jaw was hanging open a few seconds into the presentation. In one harrowing scene after another, they watched as an eerie wall of flame destroyed planets, moons, stars, nebulas, cities, mountains, skies— everything that stood in its way. "Destroy" was not quite the right word, Jagron decided, because planets and suns were left in the wake of this awful wave. But they were drastically altered.

When the horrendous images finally ended, a Romulan scientist came on the screen to explain what they had just witnessed. Although Commander Jagron didn't understand half of what he said, he grasped the gist of it perfectly well. A secret Federation weapon, which had been outlawed by every power in the Alpha Quadrant ninety years ago, had been unleashed in a new attack. This mass destruction was happening in the Federation right now. The only thing which had stood up to it so far was phase-shifting technology copied from the Romulan Star Empire.

The image of the scientist blinked off, leaving a blank screen and equally blank expressions among the audience. "That's not the worst of it," said a voice behind them. Jagron turned to see the round face and pudgy body of Proconsul Woderbok, head of the Senate. "If the Federation cannot contain this Genesis Wave, it will cross the Neutral Zone and strike deep into our territory, endangering dozens of inhabited worlds."

"No," whispered Commander Damarkol. She might have once been beautiful, but now the commander was gray and wizened. "How can they do this to us? What's the matter with those fools? Can't they control their own weapons?"

"Apparently, they don't know who unleashed this attack," answered the Proconsul, "or who perfected the Genesis Device to be employed in this manner." He went on to explain about Dr. Carol Marcus and her abduction.

Commander Horek sneered in disbelief. "How do we know this is even *real*? Maybe it's some kind of trick to make us move our fleets . . . or abandon our worlds."

"It has been verified by one of our operatives in the area," answered the Proconsul, "as well as our own long-range sensors. Believe me, we *wish* this was a hoax, because the reality of it is staggering."

Commander Tomalak looked ashen. "What are we supposed to do?"

"You will receive your orders from the highest source. Please rise for the Praetor." Everyone in the briefing room jumped to their feet, and the stocky Proconsul stepped back from the doorway to allow a bent, gray-haired man to enter. He wore the regal charcoal and lavender robes of state, bedecked in elaborate insignias, medals, and ribbons, all of which connoted this order or that society. Although the Praetor was elderly, a spark of anger and intelligence burned in his hooded eyes.

"Sit down, Commanders," said the Praetor in a gravelly voice, and they all did so. "If it were only the Federation in danger, we would do nothing to help these pathetic fools. However, this may be the gravest threat our empire has ever faced. I am ordering you to go to the coordinates which are being sent to your bridges as we speak. Proceed at maximum warp—you will receive free passage through the Federation. If hailed, just use the code word 'Genesis.' Upon reaching the Starfleet vessels *Enterprise* and *Sovereign*, you are to hand over your interphase generators to their scientists."

Commander Damarkol opened her mouth as if she wanted to speak, but she held her tongue, apparently realizing she would be interrupting the Praetor. Commander Jagron now saw the need for all this firepower. If anybody other than the Praetor had ordered them to go into Federation space and relinquish their interphase generators—the guts of their cloaking systems—they would have resisted. When the news came from their supreme leader, they all realized how truly grave this crisis was.

"In short, you are to assist Starfleet in any way they see fit to use you," rasped the Praetor, the mealy words twisting his lips into a scowl. "You're only the advance party. The Third Fleet is being mustered as we speak, but the Federation is in dire need of our technology now. We are in dire need of your courage. Go with the speed of the bloodhawk. You are dismissed."

They stood again as the Praetor shuffled out of the room. Tomalak sighed and said, "If the *Enterprise* is on duty, that's a small token in our favor."

"We should have destroyed the Federation years ago," muttered Damarkol, striding out the door.

Horek sneered. "Those fools. They set out to do terraforming and end up creating the most horrendous weapon in the galaxy!"

Jagron didn't trust himself to say anything profound, so he kept his mouth shut. From the corner of his eye, he saw the pudgy Proconsul motion to him. "Stay a moment, Commander Jagron. I have news from home."

This seemed odd, but Jagron kept an indifferent look on his face while the others, including his intelligence officer, filed out of the classroom.

It wasn't until the door shut that Proconsul Woderbok stepped closer to him. "You're looking well, Commander."

"A message from home?" asked Jagron doubtfully.

The Proconsul snorted a laugh. "I sincerely doubt if I know any of your family. You're not of the same bloodlines as the others. Why, you're almost a commoner."

Jagron maintained his stoic expression, because this was hardly news. There was some reason why the Proconsul wanted to see him. And why he needed him.

"You're not of noble birth," said Woderbok, "but you have distinguished yourself by your actions. This mission is one more opportunity for you to take the initiative. There's something that needs to be done, and I can't ask one of the others to do this. In fact, I can't ask *you* to do it."

Jagron nodded. "You want me to steal this Genesis Device."

The Proconsul smiled, increasing his double chins. "Hypothetically, if someone were to come into possession of such a device, it couldn't be known to anyone. He would have to cover his tracks and make sure no one knew, especially not the Federation. He would have to take full responsibility, if caught."

The pudgy man drew closer, his voice a whisper, "If this person were successful in smuggling the device back to *me* . . . well, the stars are the limit for a young man with such initiative. He would have backing from the highest levels."

"I can't even tell the other commanders?" whispered Jagron.

"No. Their careers are on the downward path—they have no ambition beyond sitting in their command chairs. They would argue with me. Or you. They don't understand that this Genesis Wave makes their mighty warships obsolete. I need somebody who will be *bold*—with no thoughts of treaties or alliances."

Commander Jagron shook his head slowly, running through the possible pitfalls in this risky plan. "It may be hard to hide it from the other commanders, and I won't fire on them."

The old politician smiled and put his hand on the commander's padded shoulder. "You leave that to me. Copy me on your dispatches, and I'll know when the time is right to *withdraw* the others and leave you in a position to snatch the prize. And the glory."

Jagron tried not to smile, but the corners of his mouth tilted slightly upward. He was already one of the youngest commanders— maybe he could be one of the youngest senators.

"Maybe we'll have ill fortune, and you'll never get an opportunity to grab it," said the Proconsul with a shrug. "So be it. However, a rich future awaits us if we're successful. As you have seen, Genesis means food for multitudes, a convenient way to terraform planets, and a painless way to destroy our enemies. It would be a shame if the only ones to possess this technology were the Federation."

"Besides," said Jagron, "they used our phase-shifting technology without permission."

The old Proconsul laughed. "Yes, Commander. As usual, right and justice are with the Romulan Star Empire."

Captain Picard and Admiral Nechayev stood on the observation deck of Starbase 393, watching a stream of refugees disembark from the *Enterprise* and file down the extendable docking port into the space station. The *Sovereign* was docked at another pylon, disgorging its passengers as well. The starbase was beginning to look like a Paris tube station during rush hour, except that the people milling about had no place to go.

Picard had never seen the admiral so despondent, not even after other missions had gone awry. Although she tried to mask her feelings, Nechayev looked about ten years older, and there was a sadness in her eyes that he had never seen before. Normally she was the type who could give a suicide order, lose all hands, and never show a scintilla of regret. But the Genesis Wave had Admiral Nechayev gazing deeply into her soul.

"I can't say I'm sorry to see the evacuees go," remarked Picard, just trying to make conversation. "But we can be justly proud of all the lives we saved."

"What about all the lives we *didn't* save?" she muttered. "Did you read the final casualty reports from Persephone V?"

"No. I didn't see much point in it."

"You're wise, Captain. I wish I hadn't read them." Nechayev rested her elbows on the railing and looked down at the sea of people below them. "We lost more people in three minutes than we lost during the entire Dominion war."

"Don't be too hard on yourself, Admiral; we did all we could do."

She gave him a withering glare. "*You* may have done all you could, but I didn't. It's not that I didn't move quickly enough once I knew the threat was real. I did. But I erred six months ago when I didn't make full disclosure about the abduction of Carol Marcus. I should have put Starfleet on alert right then and there."

"If you're going to have twenty/twenty hindsight," said Picard, "we should have handled Project Genesis differently ninety years ago. We should have known that we couldn't sweep technology like that under the carpet."

Nechayev narrowed her gaze at him. "We were virtually at war with the Klingons back then. We were trying mightily to keep the peace with a stubborn, hostile power. You and I know how difficult that is—we failed with the Cardassians. So we appeased everyone and hushed it up. As with most appeasements, it only delayed the inevitable."

"Speaking of Klingons," said Picard, "I kept Consul Maltz on board at Leah Brahms' request. He might also be helpful in dealing with the Klingons when they arrive. Plus we kept the specialists we had on board from our aborted mission. They're proving to be helpful."

"That seems like a long time ago, doesn't it? When it's only been a few days." The admiral rose to her feet and stuck out her chin. "The Klingons have started arriving, and they're taking over much of the evacuation. But we have to find someplace to make our stand."

"I agree," said Picard. "We can't keep running, saving a fifth of the population here and there. Once we get the interphase generators from the Romulans, Brahms and La Forge think we can arrange shelters big enough to protect large groups of people and animals. Our latest long-range scans show that the planets revert to a livable state sooner than we thought."

"The task force has already skirted around Seran," said the admiral, lifting her chin. "Soon we'll have another front. Maybe they can find the source of the wave . . . and shut it down."

Picard nodded, unable to add anything to that fervent hope.

twenty

Captain Landwaring of the *Defiant*-class starship *Neptune* peered curiously at the dark boulders, debris, and dust cluttering his viewscreen. According to the charts, this was the Boneyard, a vast asteroid field—the remains of some cataclysm when the universe was new. It had never been explored, except with sensors, because it was too dangerous. There were trillions of rocks in there, ranging in size from Earth's moon to the tiniest dust particle. With the naked eye it was impossible to pick out much detail—it looked like an avalanche frozen in midfall. Landwaring did notice several large asteroids that were shaped like rubber dog bones.

According to the latest projections, *this* was ground zero— where the Genesis Wave began. Of course, here the wave was hardly bigger than a laser point and undetectable by their sensors. It was nothing like the destructive force it became light-years from here.

The five *Defiant*-class vessels had small crews but the speed and firepower of much larger ships. To do a physical search of the Boneyard would take them a lifetime. They had come fully armed, ready to fight to the death with a ruthless adversary—and all they found was a galaxy's biggest rock pile.

The *Neptune* observed the Boneyard from a cautious distance of two hundred thousand kilometers. Even so, the captain felt inexplicably nervous.

"Probe three reporting back," said his ops officer, a young blond woman named Herron. "No life-forms reported, although there are amino acids, proteins, and other building blocks."

"That kind of residue is commonly associated with the wave," said his science officer, Mitchell. Normally the *Neptune* didn't have a science officer, but on this mission it did. So far, the mousy fellow hadn't been much help.

"That residue often occurs in regular space dust, too," said Ensign Herron.

"What about signs of a power source?" asked the captain. "Electrical interference? Fluctuations?"

"All over the Boneyard," answered the ops officer, shaking her head. "Half of those rocks must be magnetically charged, and the other half are kelbonite, which distorts the readings. There could even be fake, hollow asteroids in there—we couldn't spot them with a few probes."

"It's a good haystack in which to hide a needle," conceded Landwaring. "Is anybody here a hunter?"

No one volunteered to have ever been a hunter, and the captain went on, "Sometimes you have to flush the game," he explained. "You know, fire a couple of wild shots and see if you can roust anything from the brush."

"I advise against firing willy-nilly into there," said the science officer.

"Why?"

Mitchell hemmed and hawed for a second then came up with, "Well, you're liable to send that debris flying in all directions."

"And so would a wandering comet or a meteorite," answered

Landwaring. "If you have a better idea of how to proceed with our search—the fastest way possible—I'm listening."

The science officer hung his head. "I know these are dire circumstances."

"They sure are," said Captain Landwaring. "Tactical, open up a secure channel to the task force."

"Yes, Sir," answered the bald-headed Deltan, working his board. "Channel open."

"To all ships in Task Force Javelin," began Landwaring, stepping behind the tactical console. "I've decided to fire a brace of torpedoes into the Boneyard, to see if we can stir anything up."

The captain reached over the Deltan's shoulder to enter a target, his best guess. "We're transmitting targeting information to you. On my mark, fire torpedoes in firing pattern delta nine. Remember that we can't fire and forget. We have to change position—just as we did with the probes—because the Genesis Effect has been known to follow the deuterium trail back to the firing ship. Rendezvous thirty thousand kilometers dead to port. Keep all logs running, and look for anything . . . I mean, *anything*. Landwaring out."

He nodded to the Bajoran male on the conn, Jorax. "Set new course. Be ready to go to full impulse as soon as we launch."

"Yes, Sir,"

On ops, Ensign Herron said, "Captain, all ships report targeting complete, per your orders."

"Course is set," repeated Ensign Jorax with a nervous glance over his shoulder.

It was clear that none of the crew would care to have his job at the moment, thought Landwaring. While they were groping around here for answers, whole worlds were being lost forever.

"Alert the task force. Hold for my mark." The captain lifted his hand, then brought it down decisively. "Fire."

"Torpedoes away," said the Deltan, looking up at the viewscreen, where two streaks of light shot outward from the ship, headed toward the asteroids.

"Going to impulse power," said Jorax on the conn. The image on the viewscreen blurred and took a few moments to refocus as the *Neptune* sped away. They had done this routine so many times with the earlier probes, their actions were almost automatic.

Seconds later, they had stopped and were again watching the endless, ageless sprawl of debris called the Boneyard. Without warning, ten violent eruptions tore through the asteroid field, like a string of firecrackers going off in a pile of dirt. Rock and debris were blasted outward and inward, turning the targeted area into a ricocheting demolition derby.

A minute later, it was relatively peaceful again in the Boneyard, except for slowly expanding clouds of dust and clumps of debris hurtling outward.

"Anything on sensors?" asked Captain Landwaring, leaning over Herron's shoulder.

She frowned curiously at her readings. "I'm detecting vegetable matter."

"Vegetable matter?" asked Landwaring curiously.

"It's true," said the science officer, Mitchell, who peered at his own readouts. "But it looks old. Probably lichens on the rocks, still there from eons ago when this field was a living planet."

The ops officer suddenly sat up. "There's something metallic out there, Sir! It appears to be spherical in shape."

"Spherical?" asked Landwaring. "You mean, as if it were manufactured?"

She nodded her head. "I've isolated it—I can put it on visual."

"Do it." The captain folded his arms and gazed expectantly at the viewscreen overhead. Thus far, they'd had nothing of interest to look at, and he was eager to see this metallic sphere which had lain hidden inside the Boneyard for who-knew-how-many years. When the image cleared, he gasped with surprise. It looked like a charred, dented escape pod, revolving slowly as it sped through space.

"What's the size of that thing?" he asked.

"It's approximately four meters in diameter," answered Mitchell. "There are no lifesigns on board, and it doesn't seem to be producing any power. But I am picking up a bit more of that vegetable matter. Maybe it's old foodstuffs."

"Conn, take us within a hundred kilometers of the sphere," ordered Captain Landwaring. "And get a tractor beam on it. Just to stop it. Don't bring it aboard. Keep shields up as much as you can."

"Yes, Sir," answered Jorax, working his console.

While he was doing that, the captain prowled behind the row of secondary stations. "Tactical, what are the other ships reporting?"

"Same thing we're seeing," answered the Deltan. "That sphere is the only thing of interest."

"I'm locked on with tractor beam," said Jorax on conn. "The sphere has stopped moving."

It had even stopped revolving as it hung in the darkness of space, bathed by the eerie glow of their tractor beam. Landwaring peered curiously at the relic on the viewscreen and ordered, "Tell the other ships to converge on our position. Shields up."

He wanted to believe that this find was significant, but there were plenty of logical explanations why an escape pod had become lodged inside an asteroid field. After all, they didn't call it the Boneyard for nothing.

"Mitchell," he said to the science officer. "I want you to do an EVA inspection on that object, while we take another look around for anything that got shaken loose. Take the shuttlepod. Herron will pilot for you."

The young science officer gulped. "You want me to go outside and do a hands-on?"

"Yes," answered the captain in his coldest tone. "You can start earning your keep around here."

"Come on, Sir," said Ensign Herron, pointing to the door. "I'll be right there in the shuttlepod."

"Sapor, take the conn," ordered Landwaring, motioning to the auxiliary consoles where relief personnel were waiting. "Come on, let's move quickly," he said. "They're not paying us to sit on our hands. While we're messing around here, that thing is eating its way through the Federation."

The shuttlepod was the smallest self-propelled vessel to carry Starfleet markings, except for one-person escape pods. The clunky little craft didn't have warp drive, and its range was limited, but it was all they had room for on the *Neptune*. Nevertheless, Eileen Herron liked piloting the little sprite, and she was the best on the ship.

Peter Mitchell sat down beside her, wearing a thin, low-pressure environmental suit, and he gave her a pout that was part disdain and part fear. "I shouldn't have to do this. Don't we have security officers or something?"

"You know, science officer isn't a desk job out here," answered Eileen. "And the *Neptune* isn't a big cushy starship. We have a small crew, and everybody has to do as many jobs as they can. Besides, we don't know you, and the rest of us have been through hell together. So you have to prove your mettle."

"Prove my mettle," echoed Mitchell doubtfully. He hefted an armful of tricorders, tools, drills, and sample bags. "Okay, let's do it. At least I get to ride in Eileen's Buggy."

"Oh, you heard them call it that," said Herron with a grin. "Nobody can touch me in this thing. How close do you want me to get?"

"How long is the tether?"

"We usually do fifty meters."

"Okay, make it thirty. Then I can get all the way around it."

"Hold on." The ensign applied thrusters, and the shuttlepod shot out of a small opening in the underbelly of the *Neptune*. With a few quick, sure maneuevers, Herron homed in on the aged sphere floating in space. The closer they came to it, the more it looked like space junk, although it appeared mostly intact. She was amused at how it seemed to be about the same size as the shuttlepod, although of a completely different shape.

She applied reverse thrusters then looked at her instruments with a smile. "Thirty-two meters away. Is that close enough?"

"Good flying," muttered Mitchell, peering at the sphere which filled the main viewport. "I don't see why we can't bring this thing onto the ship for study at our leisure."

"Just make a quick appraisal of it," said Herron impatiently. "Take some readings, a core sample, a few souvenirs—just do your job. I don't think anyone will be shocked if it doesn't have anything to do with why we're out here."

"I know what to do," Mitchell said huffily. "Prepare to open the hatch." He put his helmet over his head, and Herron helped him tighten the seals. Both of them checked the readings on the tether.

"Go get 'em, Tiger," she said with a thumbs-up. The pilot grabbed an oxygen mask from a panel overhead and put it over her face. Then she belted herself into her seat. Force-fields would keep most of the atmosphere inside the shuttlepod, but it never hurt to be safe.

"Ready?"

He nodded, and she cracked the hatch open. With a whoosh, a bit of the air flew out, and Mitchell fumbled anxiously in the sudden weightlessness. Finally he managed to extricate himself from his chair and float out the open hatch. He quickly attached his tether.

Once the science officer got hooked up, he oriented himself fairly well. Taking a small harpoon gun from his bag of tools, he shot a grappling hook at the sphere. On his first attempt, he hit the relic and got a solid hold with the molecular bonding. After tugging hard on the rope, he set out, pulling himself easily hand over hand in the microgravity of space, his tether trailing behind him.

From her pilot's seat, Ensign Herron shut the hatch, having decided that the mission was going smoothly so far. On her instrument panel, she saw that Mitchell's vital signs were a bit elevated, but that was normal. Checking her sensors, she concluded that this part of space was about as boring as it got, even if the source of the Genesis Wave lurked nearby. With no sign of the deadly weapon, it felt as if they were the victims of some mass hoax.

Gazing out her viewport, she noticed that Mitchell had reached the mysterious sphere and was taking tricorder readings. Then he moved very close to the relic, as if he were listening to something inside. Or perhaps he was trying to read markings on the hull. Herron thought about asking Mitchell what he was doing, but she didn't want to interrupt him. He obviously wasn't having any difficulty with his assignment. In fact, he moved around the sphere touching and feeling its surface as if he knew its intimate workings.

Then he astounded her by pulling or pushing something that opened a hatch. At any rate, a dark cavity suddenly appeared on the surface of the sphere, and Mitchell stuck his hand into it.

Now Herron got on the comlink. "Mitchell, what are you doing?"

"I've got to go inside," he replied insistently. Without any further leave, the science officer popped into the sphere and was gone.

She hit the comlink again. "Shuttlepod to *Neptune*."

"Go ahead," said Landwaring. "How's it going?"

"Well, Mitchell is being awfully brave," she reported. "He just went inside the thing."

"Really," said Landwaring, sounding impressed. Then he grumbled, "I didn't clear him to do that. Can you see anything?"

"It looks awfully dark in there, Captain." Herron shook her head. "I'm only thirty meters away, and it doesn't look like anything but space junk to me. I don't see how this could be connected to the Genesis Wave."

"Do you think we could beam it aboard?" asked the captain.

"Only if we took it apart, and I don't know if it would be worth the effort. This old museum piece will still be here if we need it later."

There was movement around the pod, and a helmet emerged, followed by the rest of the environmental suit. The ensign sat up in her chair. "He's coming out."

"Reel him in," ordered Landwaring. "Unless there's something pertinent we should investigate, I want you to get back here."

"Yes, Sir. Shuttlepod out." The ensign gave two taps on the companel. "Herron to Mitchell, I'm going to bring you in. All right?"

The hooded figure waved to her and hefted what looked like a bag of old leaves. Slowly he removed the grappling hook from the sphere. Herron activated the winch to retract the tether; then she put on her oxygen mask. The ensign watched with amusement as Mitchell's body drew closer; he looked like a kite floating at the end of its string.

A few seconds later, she sprang the hatch, and the suited figure climbed back into the shuttlepod. His movements stiff and jerky, Mitchell deposited his equipment and samples behind the seats; then he settled into his chair. His chest went up and down in the suit as he caught his breath. Herron knew what it was like to read-just to gravity, so she let him have his moment of reorientation.

Finally, Mitchell removed his helmet and smiled at her, looking somehow more at peace and more handsome than he had before. This trip had been a confidence builder for him, she decided.

"Is there anything unusual?" she asked. "Anything we should report back to the ship before we leave?"

"No," he answered, staring straight ahead. "It's dead. Really old. I don't think this escape pod, or small craft, was ever manned. Maybe it was released by mistake."

"What's that stuff in the bag?" asked Herron, glancing behind the seat. Now that she saw the dried plant life at close range, it looked dirty and gray, like old clumps of Spanish moss or mistletoe. "Are you sure we should bring it back to the ship?"

Mitchell gazed meaningfully at her, his words calm and soothing. "It's inert, and it's probably the only thing that will tell us the age of this craft. It's definitely not Federation. It must have been a survival pod of some sort, because they had a kind of hydroponic growing system. That's the remains of it, a plant that's been dead for a long time. It's no more harmful than your grandmother's pressed flower collection."

She blinked at him, amazed. "How do you know about my grandmother's pressed flower collection?"

He shrugged. "Every grandmother has a pressed flower collection. So did mine." He boldly touched her arm. "It's just one more thing we have in common."

Herron knew she should slap him, but the move had caught her by surprise . . . and in an oddly receptive mood. In fact, her skin seemed to burn where his mere fingers touched it, even through a heavy glove. Why had she never noticed how desirable he was?

"What do you say to calling the captain, and telling him that neither one of us feels well. We're both going to need to go lie down in our quarters."

She smiled slyly and punched her companel. "Shuttlepod to Neptune."

"Landwaring here," came the response.

"There's nothing major to report," said Ensign Herron, gazing at the handsome man beside her. "Mitchell just says it's real old and real dead, so we're on our way back."

She coughed and tried to sound sick. "But I don't feel well, and neither does Mitchell. We're going to need to go to our quarters and lie down when we get back."

"What's the matter?" asked Landwaring with concern.

"I don't know, maybe it's something with the air in the shuttle-pod. It got a little thin when we opened the hatch. It's all right now. I'll run diagnostics when we get back."

"All right," said the captain begrudgingly. "I guess you've both earned a rest, but don't expect it to be a long one. Sometimes an EVA can leave you a little nauseous."

"I'm sure that's it," answered Herron, barely containing her excitement over being alone with Mitchell. "Shuttlepod out."

twenty-one

Maltz snored peacefully in a corner of the radiation laboratory, snuffling and grunting to himself, while Geordi La Forge and Leah Brahms poured over equations and charts on their situation monitors. These documents represented the release patterns, speeds, and trajectories of the Genesis Wave once it hit a planet, and it couldn't be more devastating. They continued to sift through data gleaned from Commander Troi's jaunt on Persephone V, and it felt as if they needed months to get a hold on this thing, when all they had was hours.

La Forge couldn't help but glance at his beautiful colleague every now and then, just to make sure she was really here beside him. It wasn't that she was a distraction—her presence was more reassuring than anything else. If the universe could drop her here beside him, then maybe it wasn't as cruel as it seemed to be at the moment.

However, Geordi didn't care much for her Klingon chaperone. He understood survivors' syndrome and how the two of them might have bonded in that shuttlecraft, but he was still a little jealous. Leah and Maltz were a crew, albeit tiny, but he wasn't part of it.

Still he and Leah worked as smoothly together as they ever had, in reality or simulation. She was immersed in the task at hand, and Geordi was basically assisting her. He was in awe of her intellect and drive, although the urgency of the situation made the atmosphere around the lab unusually grim.

Other teams on nearby ships and elsewhere in the Federation were wrestling with the same problems. Some of them reported different solutions or variations on the phase-shifting plan. Since the Romulans were already on their way with the interphase generators, it was definite that phase-shifting would get the first trial under fire. The irony was that Leah had created the vaunted radiation suit, but she didn't have a lot of faith that the same technology could protect thousands of people at a time. Despite her dedication and hard work, it was clear that she would have preferred to be with the task force that was hunting down the perpetrators of this horror.

While Leah continued poring over equations and charts, La Forge checked on dispatches from Data. In addition to his bridge duties, the android was sifting through incoming correspondence from their colleagues. He rejected the preposterous and unworkable, and the stuff that just rehashed what they already knew, forwarding anything he thought might be helpful. Unfortunately, that wasn't a lot.

As Leah had surmised, the Genesis Effect only extended a certain distance into the crust, since it retained its terraforming characteristics and was programmed to move fast over a planet that met the right criteria. This had brought many suggestions for using mines, caverns, underground storage tanks, missile silos, and the like for shelters. Unfortunately, the wave triggered earthquakes and volcanic eruptions as a side effect. Plus it wasn't always predictable how deeply into the crust it went. It was probably dependent upon the composition of the bedrock.

The effect on stars, nebulas, and miscellaneous objects in space was more devastating and unpredictable, resulting in total reconfiguration. Even in Leah's radiation suit, Geordi wouldn't care to be caught in a starship when that wave hit it. Oddly enough, despite the horrendous upheaval, a suitable planet was the safest place to be.

"Anything new?" asked Leah, glancing at him from the corner of her eyes. Although she didn't appear to be paying that much attention to him, she always seemed to know exactly what he was doing.

"No," he answered glumly. "A correspondent from Alpha Centauri would like us to put everybody in transporter suspension while the wave passes through."

"That would work, except how do you protect the transporter stations themselves?" She shook her head glumly. "Unless we stop the wave itself, we're just killing time . . . along with a lot of planets."

"But the same technology saved you," said Geordi, hating to sound like a broken sound chip.

"Oh, it may save *lives*, but if you think you're going to save anybody's *home* with this, you're sadly mistaken. You're still going to have to evacuate these people."

"If we can evacuate them at a normal pace, that might not be such a bad trade-off." La Forge took a deep breath and tried to tone down his rhetoric. "If I've learned one thing in my decade on the *Enterprise*—if you can't do anything else, you buy time."

Brahms closed her eyes and rubbed her forehead. "I'm sorry, Geordi—I don't know why I'm so negative. Well, I do know why, but I'm trying hard *not* to deal with it."

"If you want to talk, I'll listen. Or you could see our counselor."

"I've seen your counselor, and she has enough patients to last her a lifetime. Every day, we pick up more."

"We're letting them off, too." La Forge shook his head in exasperation. "I don't know what to tell you. The loss of a spouse . . . that's something I've never gone through. It must be awful."

"I didn't love him anymore," she said softly, as if admitting it for the first time.

"What?" asked Geordi hoarsely.

"I mean, he was a huge part of my life—my husband, my colleague, my partner—but he felt more like a partner than a husband. And I think he was seeing somebody else." Leah sighed and looked down. Now her short brown hair framed a face that had lost its cherubic innocence; it was an adult's face full of character and experience.

"He certainly had the opportunity," she said with a disdainful laugh. "Because I let him go his own way whenever he wanted. I just didn't care enough."

Geordi didn't trust himself to say anything, or even make a sound, so he just nodded slowly. He wanted to take her hand and assure her that she never needed to lack for love as long as he was alive, but he wasn't courageous or uncouth enough to do it.

Leah sniffed and rubbed her nose. "Now that he's gone, of course, I see all the good about Mikel. And the bad. I see my life for everything it was, and everything it wasn't. I need to try harder at living—to balance myself with work. I can't think of any other reason why I was spared."

Trembling, Geordi extended his hand and was about to reach for hers, when the door whooshed open. The old Klingon was instantly on his feet, brandishing a knife. "Who goes there?"

It was Dolores Linton, dressed in work overalls. She stepped sheepishly into the lab and glanced warily at Maltz. "Hi, Leah. You asked me to come at noon?"

Brahms dabbed a sleeve at her eyes and jumped to her feet. "Dolores! Thanks for coming. Is it that late already? I had forgotten what time it was."

"It happens." The geologist shrugged cheerfully. "Hi there, Geordi. You still owe me—"

"I know." He waved helplessly at her. "I heard you were heroic on the lines in Persephone V."

She smiled. "I used to be a bouncer. That's how I put myself through the academy."

Brahms made the introductions. "Consul Maltz, this is Mission Specialist Linton. She's on our side."

The Klingon nodded.

Leah motioned Dolores over to the situation monitor and tapped her finger on the screen. "We've got a lot of geology data, but we're not exactly sure what we're looking at. In open air, the interphase generators should work against the wave, and I'm not sure how far either one of them extends into the ground. I don't want it to come up through our feet and get us."

"Interphase generators?" asked Dolores.

Geordi jumped to his feet. "We really should spend some time bringing Dolores up to speed on the plan."

Maltz laughed out loud, and everyone turned to look at the grizzled old Klingon. "What is to explain? Throw down some sneaky Romulan devices, and hope for the best! This is just the kind of reaction you would expect to get from the Federation."

"We've sent a task force to Seran," said Geordi defensively.

The Klingon waved derisively and sat down, having said his piece.

Dolores Linton glanced around at the desultory expressions in the room and put her hands on her hips. "When was the last time any of you were out of this room?"

"Um—" Leah shrugged and looked at Geordi, who also shrugged.

"That's too long," insisted the geologist. "It's lunchtime, and the ship is relatively clear of refugees. I say we talk over food."

"Good idea!" barked Maltz, headed for the door. "We need our strength to confront the enemy. Have you ever tried rokeg blood pie, Mission Specialist Linton?"

"One of my favorites, Consul Maltz." She stepped back to allow the lanky Klingon to exit first, and he seized the honor.

"Oh, great," muttered La Forge to himself, "a double date."

"Pardon me?" asked Brahms, moving toward the door.

The engineer cleared his throat. "Nothing. I thought you were getting somewhere . . . talking about your feelings. Then we got interrupted."

"I wasn't getting anywhere," she answered. "Besides, this isn't the right time to dwell on personal issues, is it?"

"No," said Geordi quietly. "I suppose not."

A padd in his hand, Captain Picard paced across his ready room, reading the reports from another world that had fallen, Sarona VIII. It could have been much worse. Although the Klingon fleet showed up with less than eight hours to spare, they had very efficiently saved four million lives, killing a few dozen rioters in the process. Unlike Starfleet's rescue attempts, they reported no sites abandoned or overrun.

"Maybe we've found the right party for that job," Picard muttered to himself.

His handheld device beeped, picking up an intraship transmission from the bridge. He glanced at the padd and saw that it was a coded message from Admiral Nechayev. It read simply:

"We stand at Myrmidon. The Romulans will meet us there at fifteen-hundred hours. Need-to-know basis at present."

Picard nodded to himself, half-expecting this news. Myrmidon was moderately populous—almost fifty million—and it would be hit in about twenty-six hours according to their forecasts. That would be cutting it close, but wherever they tried to mount this operation, it would be cutting it close. This information was on a need-to-know security basis, and he knew someone who needed to know.

He tapped his combadge. "Picard to Mot."

"Mot here!" said his favorite barber. "What can I do for you, Sir?"

"Can you come up to my ready room for a moment?"

"A trim, Sir? A shave?"

"No, you don't need to bring anything with you. It's not business.

Picard out." Mot was the unofficial head of the Bolian contingent on the ship, which hovered between ten and twenty in number at any given time. He had gone home at the height of the Dominion war, but he had come back to the *Enterprise* a year ago to reestablish his business.

The blue-skinned humanoids with the bifurcated ridge in the center of their faces were some of the most personable, loyal, and competent members of his crew. Picard would gladly take more Bolians aboard the *Enterprise*, if he could find them.

Myrmidon was a good choice. Although not the Bolians' ancestral homeworld, it was declared their spiritual home five hundred years ago—after an ancient artifict, the Crown of the First Mother, was discovered there. A former paramour of his, Vash, had tried to steal the relic, so Picard knew all about it.

The Crown of the First Mother bore a striking resemblance to the royal jewelry depicted in the Orezes Codices, the Bolians' most sacred text. Its location and rediscovery also fit in with the origin stories and predictions. After numerous archeological expeditions to Myrmidon, the Bolians found they had much in common with a long-dead race who used to inhabit the planet, the Bolastre. There were intriguing indications of a common ancestor.

Although the artifact was never proven definitively to be related to the Bolians, they were very happy to accept Myrmidon as their main religious shrine. It was a beautiful planet, by all accounts, and Bolians had relocated there in record numbers until now there were almost fifty million inhabitants. It was all about to tumble down—sacred archeological sites and modern cities alike. He only hoped their new plans wouldn't result in a worse disaster than they had already witnessed.

His door chimed, jarring him out of his worries. "Come."

Mot bustled in, and he was his usual jovial self in the face of what must be considerable personal anguish. The portly Bolian snapped to attention. "Good afternoon, Captain. Mot reporting."

The captain put his hand on the blue-skinned barber's shoulder and said, "You haven't asked for any favors, Mr. Mot, but I know you must be thinking about Myrmidon. You have family there, don't you?"

The smile vanished, and the barber gulped. "Yes. My parents, in fact. Almost all of us on board have relatives there. We have big families."

Picard nodded sympathetically. "Keep this under your hat, Mr. Mot, but Myrmidon is where we're making a stand. We're going to try the phase-shifting plan there."

The barber put his hands together in applause. "Oh, thank you, Sir! Thank you!"

"Don't thank me, thank Admiral Nechayev. But we're keeping this on a need-to-know basis for the time being. I think all the Bolians on the ship need to know."

"I agree," said Mot with relief. "But why the secrecy?"

Picard leaned forward, his voice low. "I'm not the admiral, but I know she's concerned about how some of the past evacuations have gotten out of hand. We don't want to raise anyone's hopes, because there may be extenuating circumstances. We might not be able to pull it off. As soon as possible, we'll alert the populace and the rest of the crew."

Mot nodded thoughtfully and cast his eyes downward, increasing his double chins. "Thank you, Captain, for telling me. However, I should warn you—my people believe strongly in assisted suicide."

"Yes, the double-effect doctrine. I'm familiar with it." The captain frowned deeply, not having considered this complication. That was all they needed—mass suicides—as they were trying desperately to save lives.

"Any act that relieves suffering is acceptable, even if that act has the effect of causing death," said Mot. "The philosophy and history behind it are very complicated, but that's the kernel of it. We're a very religious species."

Oh, well, he supposed they all had to get acquainted, providing they did it quickly. Right now, the room was big enough that the various groups could ignore each other, except for the blue-skinned Bolians, who were eagerly making friends wherever they could. The captain looked back at his party to make sure they were accounted for. There was Commander Riker, Counselor Troi, Commander La Forge, Dr. Leah Brahms, Consul Maltz, and Mr. Mot, the barber.

The only one who even seemed remotely glad to be here was the old Klingon, who bounded in front of the captain. "I am taking my leave, Sir, to report in. I may be reassigned, but I would like to stay aboard your vessel until that happens." He glanced pointedly at Leah Brahms.

"Certainly, Consul, you're always welcome."

The Klingon strode off, waving his hands as if he were greeting old friends, although his fellow Klingons regarded him warily. Maltz paid them no mind as he began to introduce himself in loud tones.

Riker grinned. "Captain, I think I know one of those Klingons. Can I go over?"

"Go ahead, Number One." He turned to his staff. "All of you, feel free to mingle."

"I'll just see how my people are holding up," said Mr. Mot, puffing out his chest bravely.

"Captain Picard!" called a stern male voice.

The captain whirled around, expecting to see an admiral with some complaint to air. Instead he saw the regal gray uniform of a Romulan commander, topped by a craggy face etched with cruelty but also honor and intelligence. It was Commander Tomalak, an old adversary from numerous encounters, none of which had proven fatal. He was accompanied by a much younger commander—a tall, thin, cadaverous sort.

"What is going on here, Picard?" asked Tomalak. "Can't you people be trusted with your own toys?"

The captain scowled and lowered his voice. "Believe me, I never believed in Project Genesis until now. Our intentions were good, but we failed to foresee the consequences."

The old Romulan nodded sagely. "Now that sounds like the Federation we know and love. Captain Picard, this is a rising star in our fleet, Commander Jagron of the *D'Arvuk.*"

Picard shook the hand of the hawk-faced Romulan. "It's a pleasure."

"The honor is all mine," said the young commander with a polite nod, his alert eyes never leaving Picard's face. "Your career is the stuff of legends."

"That's because the Federation writes most of the legends," said Tomalak with a sneer. "Although in this case, the legend is more notorious than proud. I don't think our alliance is going to last very long if this disaster destroys several of our worlds."

"It's not going to get that far," vowed Picard, although he didn't know how they were going to stop it before then. "When do you turn over your interphase generators to us?"

"Your efficient Admiral Nechayev has us dismantling them right now," answered Commander Jagron. "How can you possibly replicate enough?"

"Apparently, there are a lot of facilities on the planet," answered Picard, hoping that was true.

The noise level of the conversation trailed off, and Picard saw several Starfleet officers hurry toward the door. He turned to see Admiral Nechayev stride into the sumptuous lounge, accompanied by her padd-carrying staff. She looked charged with energy, which was a welcome change from the last time he had seen her, and he wondered if she had gotten good news from the task force.

The small woman stopped in the center of the lounge and said loudly, "Honored guests, generals, captains, commanders, thank you for attending this gathering. In the days to come, there won't be much time to get to know each other or share a convivial drink, so make the most of it. In twenty-four hours, the beautiful planet floating beneath us will be transformed forever. But it will still be here, and so will *we*. This time, we will not retreat!"

This sentiment met with shouts of approval, especially from the Klingon contingent. Picard glanced at Leah Brahms, who shook her head and looked very troubled. She said something to La Forge, and the two of them moved away from the crowd to continue their conversation in whispers.

Nechayev continued, "Our Romulan allies are contributing the most important part of our new defense, and we can't even begin to express our gratitude to them. Our Klingon allies have proven themselves to be the champions of the rapid evacuation. They have already saved three times as many lives as Starfleet itself has been able to save. In this operation, they will provide logistical support. We also have representatives from Myrmidon herself, and we welcome the chance to hear their concerns."

The admiral motioned to the Romulans. "Some of you are still reading data sheets about the Genesis Wave. If any of you have any questions, please don't hesitate to ask myself, my staff, or our experts: Dr. Leah Brahms and Commander Geordi La Forge."

That rudely interrupted the private conversation of La Forge and Brahms, and they nodded hesitantly at the crowd of hard-bitten Klingons and Romulans.

"I have a question!" growled a stocky Klingon, striding forward. "Why do you not eliminate the beasts who are doing this to you?"

"We're trying," answered Admiral Nechayev. "We've dispatched a task force of five *Defiant*-class starships to locate the source, but so far they've been unsuccessful. I assure you, General Gra'Kor, we have talked about opening another front against our unknown enemy. If we continue to be unsuccessful, I will be happy to give you that assignment."

The Klingon grunted with satisfaction and looked at his aides, who also seemed satisfied with this response.

Captain Picard felt a light tug on his sleeve. He turned to see

Counselor Troi, who leaned close to whisper, "I don't believe she's being entirely honest."

"Really?" whispered Picard. He listened more closely to what the admiral had to say, but she went on to simply recap much of what he already knew.

Finally Nechayev grabbed a filled glass from an aide, held it aloft, and concluded. "Although the impact of the Genesis Wave has been tragic, it has brought the great powers of the Alpha Quadrant together in acts of bravery and altruism. We will never forget your courage under these trying circumstances. We salute you, our allies."

"Hear! Hear! Bravo!" and similar calls echoed throughout the lounge. No one was more appreciative than the Bolians in attendance.

While conversational groups formed all over the room, Nechayev turned to address her aides. Her instructions sent most of them scurrying off, then she motioned to Picard. "Captain, could I see you for a moment?"

"Certainly," he said, taking his leave from Commanders Tomalak and Jagron. Deanna Troi stepped in to keep the Romulans occupied.

Admiral Nechayev led him along the observation window until they were far away from anyone else's hearing. Picard realized he was about to be told a confidence, and he could guess what it was.

"Something wrong with the task force?" he asked softly.

"How did you know that?" Nechayev stopped to stare at him with frank amazement.

"I have a Betazoid on staff. What happened to them? "

"We've lost contact," said the admiral glumly. "They stopped checking in about eight hours ago, and they haven't answered our hails either."

"Where were they? Is there any sign of them on sensors?"

She kept her voice low. "Not now. They were investigating a large asteroid field called the Boneyard, where we *think* the wave might originate. We haven't seen any sign of them since, but with all the space traffic . . . our tracking systems are overloaded. Everybody with a spacecraft is flying it, making an escape or picking up passengers."

The diminutive admiral sighed. "I suppose it's good that the private sector is starting to kick in. I hear Earth is beseiged with Ferengi vessels, offering expensive passage out. Of course, the Ferengi would pick the richest, most populace planet, and give themselves plenty of time."

The captain nodded gravely, still troubled by the news that the task force not had only failed, they had disappeared. "What are we going to do about the missing ships?"

"All of our forces are committed here," said Nechayev, motioning toward the yellow-green planet shimmering below them. "Or they're involved in other evacuations. We're facing a ruthless enemy, and they're not going to make it easy for us. If we don't hear soon, I'm going to give the Klingons this information. Maybe they can spare a ship or two. There's really no time for us to question our strategy now—we'll have to leave that to the survivors."

Her stern expression softened into thoughtfulness as she gazed out the window at the endangered planet. In a confidential tone, she added, "I have something else to tell you."

"Yes, Sir?"

"I'm going to stay on Myrmidon with the populace during the . . . transformation. A show of confidence."

"Sir?" said Picard, trying not to sound alarmed. "Is that really necessary?"

"I think it is," answered Nechayev. "We have to be able to show our confidence in order to win their confidence. We have plenty of technicians who must stay behind, too, and I want to show camaraderie with them. Besides . . . I have to do it for myself. If I can live through this, I'll be able to convince others that they can live through it. That there's hope."

"How will you get off the planet . . . afterwards?" asked the captain.

"Our scientists think the Romulans can cut through the wave in a cloaked ship and beam us off Myrmidon. If they can't or won't, I'll have to wait several days until the effect diminishes. It's not a perfect plan."

"But it is a noble gesture. Perhaps I should . . ." he began.

"Don't even think about it, Picard," she answered curtly. "Although I'm going to make a call for Starfleet volunteers to stand with me, I really don't want a horde of people. Besides, you have to make sure the *Enterprise* survives. If I don't get out, my aides will put through a field promotion for you—to admiral—so that you can take over this operation. That won't be doing you much of a favor, of course. For that, I'm sorry. But you're here, you're able, and you know as much about it as anybody."

"Admiral, eh?" said the captain distastefully. "I can assure you, we will do everything in our power to make sure you survive and get back to your desk as soon as possible."

"I'm certain," said the admiral with a fleeting smile. "Just don't volunteer when I make my call. That's all, Captain."

"Thank you, Admiral." The captain stepped away from the observation lounge window to allow others access to Admiral Nechayev. Despite the massing of ships and the arrival of allies, he was worried. The disappearance of the task force showed that their mysterious enemy was more formidable than they imagined.

Admiral Nechayev appeared energized by her plan to risk her life in solidarity with the people, and she was sure of her reasons. But Picard could see the disaster in the making. If admirals and dignitaries died horrible deaths—not to mention fifty million Bolians—then confidence in Starfleet would disappear. The rest of the evacuations would be more insane than they were now. Picard would be left to oversee a chaotic stampede stretching halfway across the quadrant, plus the destruction of more planets and billions of people, including Earth. And the ultimate enemy would remain anonymous and untouched.

We have to succeed on Myrmidon, he told himself in no uncertain terms.

Will Riker did indeed know one of the Klingons at the reception, from having served with him aboard the *Pagh*. Dermok was now first officer on the *Jaj*, and the two of them relived old times. The other Klingons bombarded Maltz with questions, but the old warrior held his own, sounding alert and arrogant. When Maltz began to sweep his hands through the air and gruffly relate his tale, Riker and his friend had to stop to listen. No one could ignore a Klingon in full storytelling mode.

First came his heroic escape from Hakon, complete with jailbreak, Romulan spy, and the Genesis Wave bearing down on them. In a hoarse whisper, Maltz told about their final contact with the Pelleans—a mighty, spacefaring race who were now gone forever. He praised the young human who had saved him to spread the alarm, Dr. Leah Brahms.

"Saved by a human!" said General Gra'Kor with a sneer. "You still have much to answer for, Maltz."

Steel and a hint of madness glinted in the old Klingon's eyes. "What do you mean by that?"

The stocky general growled. "I mean, you and that idiot, Kruge, let the Genesis Device escape our grasp when you had the chance to seize it! And protect it. You let a bird-of-prey be captured and piloted by a ragtag band of humans. You haven't tried hard enough to get to *Sto-Vo-Kor*."

There were audible gasps, and the other Klingons moved away from Gra'Kor and Maltz, who proceeded to size each other up. For the first time, Riker realized that it was no accident that Maltz had been living on Hakon—he was an outcast.

The old Klingon finally laughed—a howling, roaring shriek that sliced through the genteel conversation and brought every eye to him. He finally sneered in the general's face and said, "Is that the best you can do? That insult is ninety years old, and I hear it every day of my life."

Maltz pounded his chest. "I *know* I am going to *Sto-Vo-Kor*, because I have sworn a blood oath against this cowardly weapon and the demons who unleashed it."

"*Qapla'!* *yIntagh!*" cheered the younger Klingons, catching Maltz's infectious spirit.

Maltz drew his *d'k tahg* and pointed it menacingly at the general's ample stomach. "So if you stand in my way, you will either get killed, or you will usher me to *Sto-Vo-Kor*. I do not care. I have been alive long enough. This beast has come after me *twice*—wrecking my career each time—and this time I intend to finish it!"

Now every one of the Klingons was cheering Maltz and slapping him on the back. General Gra'Kor grinned and pounded the old warrior's shoulders with his beefy fists. "I misjudged you, Maltz. I will sing your praises at the High Council! Nothing will stand in the way of your blood oath. What will you require?"

"A ship," said Maltz boldly.

Gra'Kor nodded. "Will you be captain?"

"No, I have a captain—a partner to my blood oath. I am content to be first mate."

"Getting a ship may take some doing," said the stocky Klingon, tugging on his beard. "Ships are scarce at the moment. But I will do what I can. In the meantime—"

"I would like to stay on the *Enterprise*." Stealing a glance at Riker, the old Klingon leaned forward and said, "They need a Klingon to keep reminding them of what is important. They think it is saving lives, and I know it is taking lives."

"Well said!" barked Gra'Kor, lifting a mug of ale. "We drink to your success! *Qapla'*!"

Maltz nodded and sheathed his knife, tears filling his rheumy eyes. Riker had the feeling it had been a long time since a gathering of his fellows had praised the old Klingon.

"Leah, please!" insisted Geordi in a tight whisper. "You can't leave now." He pulled her away from the dignitaries in the Saucer Lounge and hustled her along the starboard window, hardly noticing the beautiful starscape.

"I'm going to leave as soon as this operation is over," she said fiercely. "That's only twenty-four hours from now."

"But why?" asked La Forge, certain he was sounding shrill and possessive. But he couldn't let her walk out of his life without a fight, even if he couldn't tell her why.

Leah sighed with exasperation. "Because my life's been destroyed, because I don't know what I'm doing, because I'm not a member of your crew. All those things, Geordi. I know you're being sweet—wanting to give me a new place to call home—but I'm not ready for that. I just need to wander for a while. I think I should tell the captain."

"But we need you," insisted Geordi, hiding much more than those four words conveyed.

"Why?" Brahms shook her head and gazed wearily at him. "If this idea works, anyone can set it up. If it doesn't work . . . Well, I'm not sure I can save the Federation single-handedly. I don't want that responsibility." She started walking off.

"But if there's a new idea . . . one that works better?" begged Geordi, grasping for words that would keep her beside him.

"I'll see you in an hour on the surface," said Leah Brahms. She turned and strode quickly from the Saucer Lounge. Several pairs of eyes watched her go, including Captain Picard, who pointed to her and said something to his Romulan companions.

La Forge turned back to the observation window, gazing at the endless vista of space. To his bionic vision, darkness was mostly coolness, and this space looked as chill as the emptiness in his heart.

twenty-three

For an hour, Deanna Troi wandered the streets of Neprin, the most populous city on Myrmidon. It was a glorious city—with towering triangular and conical shaped buildings, many of them constructed with the widest part of the triangle at the top. The smaller buildings were almost all domes, either geodesic or smooth, with breathtaking inlaid mosaic that sparkled in the sun. There was not a single conventional box-shaped building in sight. Not surprisingly, blue was a favorite color, and the Bolians seemed to have discovered more shades of blue than anyone else in the galaxy. The architecture reminded her of the stylishness that the Bolians exhibited in everything they did.

Interspersed tastefully among the buildings were small, parklike areas. At first, Deanna thought these parks were decorated with strange, bulbous statues. But upon closer inspection she realized the "statues" were in reality gigantic vegetables up to four meters tall and shaped like artichokes. Citizens often stopped during their travels to cut off a bit of the giant plant to eat as they walked, although Deanna did not partake.

She was supposed to be interviewing the residents, gauging how much work Starfleet would have to do to convince them to stroll into a building or an empty field and calmly watch the Genesis Wave roll over them. But she couldn't bring herself to talk to the Bolians, who gazed upon her Starfleet uniform as they might gaze upon a figure in a dark hood, carrying a sickle. Her presence represented the destruction of everything they knew, plus the loss of their greatest religious shrines. Many of them were still in denial, going about their regular business. Others flashed her furtive glances as they scurried away, probably to catch a shuttlecraft or transport off the planet.

Ferengi and Bolian hawkers stood on the street corners, offering passage off Myrmidon for exorbitant prices. A thousand strips of latinum seemed to be the going rate. Although Deanna hadn't dealt much with money, she knew that was a lot.

"Starfleet's plan is a hoax!" one of the hawkers shouted loudly. "There's no way to survive this thing. Look at what happened on Persephone V! Their plan is unproven and risky!"

Troi thought about stopping to refute his claim, but their plan *was* unproven and risky. So she walked on, feeling terrible about her cowardice. She couldn't bear to speak to the Bolians, because when she looked at them, all she saw was death. It was the same horrible death which had claimed millions on Persephone V. She could envision their bodies being ripped apart, screams still frozen on their lips, as their flailing limbs sank into the churning morass this planet would soon become.

With a start, Deanna realized that *she* should really be under a counselor's care herself, after what she had witnessed. But there weren't enough counselors to go around.

Feeling despondent, she continued to walk down the sidewalk, gazing at the magnificent buildings, none of which would be here this time tomorrow. She shuffled past one of the geodesic domes, which was covered in a mosaic of inlaid gold, and a kindly voice said, "My child, rest a moment. You look weary."

Troi stopped and turned to look at an older Bolian woman standing in the doorway of the domed building. She was dressed in flowing blue robes, like some kind of cleric, and the counselor realized that she had stumbled upon a place of worship. A sign over the door said it was the "Sanctuary of the First Mother."

The woman looked so kind and helpful that Deanna felt her reticence to speak slipping away. "Hello," she said, "I'm with the fleet that's orbiting the planet."

"I assumed as much," said the old Bolian with a smile. "You look particularly upset, when *we're* the ones who should be upset."

"But you're smiling," said Deanna in amazement.

"Yes, because I can gaze at the Crown of the First Mother whenever I want. I know this awful scourge will not destroy us."

"But—" said Deanna helplessly.

"Come inside, Child, and cast off your bonds of worry." The old woman took her hand and gently pulled her inside the beautiful dome. "What is your name?"

"Deanna Troi. I'm a counselor. . . . I help people."

"That's wonderful," replied the old woman. "Then we're in the same business."

"And your name?"

"Just call me 'Mother,'" she answered with a smile. They walked slowly through a vestibule which was lined with beautiful murals depicting an archeological dig and the discovery of Myrmidon's most famous relic. Deanna saw the story unfold as they strolled through the vestibule—first the discovery, then the mass pilgrimage, ending with the construction of this great city and others. The last murals showed happy Bolians dancing and feasting under flowered garlands, with a blazing golden crown.

Instead of being consoled by these vivid images, Troi was only more distressed. Centuries of joyous work and progress were about to vanish in a matter of seconds, and there wasn't anything any of them could do about it.

Pushing open a pair of gold-inlaid doors, Mother led the way into a vast sanctuary, which was filled with Bolians on their knees, muttering prayers aloud. All of them faced a small cabinet, which was lit by its own internal fires. Overhead, the inside of the dome seemed to sparkle with an unearthly light, and Deanna realized it was sunlight filtered through a clear ceiling. It seemed as if the entire room was suffused with a holy glow.

"Is that really the Crown of the First Mother?" asked Troi in a hushed voice.

The woman smiled wistfully. "I'd like to think it is, but I don't know for sure. There are sanctuaries like this all over the planet, and one of them contains the genuine relic. The rest contain copies identical of the original. We did this to thwart thieves, but it has been a blessing in disguise, allowing every citizen to feel as if he has personal contact with the greatest of our treasures. Shall we move closer?"

Troi nodded, and Mother led her down an aisle of worshipers to stand at the side of the case, so they wouldn't block anyone's view. Deanna peered inside at an unexpectedly simple piece of golden jewelry, which had the same triangular motif she had seen in the Bolians' architecture; each of the crowning points was an upside-down triangle. Whoever had made the copy—if this was a copy—had done an excellent job, because the relic looked as old as the universe but undiminished in beauty.

"Now do you feel peace?" asked Mother.

Troi shook her head. "I wish I could say I did. But, Mother, I've seen the Genesis Wave. I know what it can do."

"Faith can conquer mountains," said the woman. "I heard a human say that once."

The Genesis Wave can also conquer mountains, Deanna thought glumly. She looked around, realizing that the domed building was about the size of a standard starship; then she suddenly had an idea. "Tell me, is the sanctuary always as crowded as this?"

"Yes, and I expect it to get more crowded as the day goes on," answered the holy woman. "No offense, Deanna Troi, but our people place more faith in the power of the Crown than in all the might of Starfleet."

"Maybe they have the right idea," said Troi, hope stirring in her heart for the first time. "Do you have the locations of all the sanctuaries like this on the planet?"

"Yes, in my office, on the computer."

"I need that information right now," said Troi.

Will Riker gazed with satisfaction at the platform in transporter room two. Every spot on the pad was occupied, not by a person but by a complex machine about two meters tall, with emitters, injectors, nozzles, and power taps all over it. In addition to those eight interphase generators, another dozen waited in the cargo area, and the transporter chief and cargo handlers were beaming them down to the surface as quickly as the replicators could produce them.

"Everything going as planned, Chief?" he asked.

"Yes, Sir," answered the dour Andorian. "This is the last batch consigned to the planetary factories—all the rest are headed to the sanctuaries."

"Great. Let me know when you're done with the generators, and we'll start sending down crates of gel-packs. Keep up the good work."

Riker strode from the transporter room, headed to the forward torpedo module, which was being replaced with spare parts contributed by other ships in orbit. He didn't think they would need quantum torpedoes, because they hadn't done any good so far against the Genesis Wave, but he was determined to replace the module while they had the chance. Something told him this would not be the end of their battle with their unknown foe, and he wanted to be ready.

* * *

"The power source is going to be our biggest problem," said Geordi La Forge, gazing at a field of gigantic vegetables that would serve as their testing ground. "I don't know if the gel-packs can handle the surge."

"Of course not," sneered a senior Romulan engineer whose name was Duperik. "I could have told you that."

"Then why didn't you?" asked Leah Brahms impatiently.

"This was *your* idea," said the Romulan. "Nobody consulted us until just now. These generators draw a lot of power, which is their biggest flaw. If we could erect your shelters near power stations—"

"We could," answered Brahms, "but then we would have to protect the power stations as well, and we can't protect all the underground cables and transformers. One breakdown along any of the lines would kill us." She groaned with exasperation. "How many more hours?"

"Twenty," answered Geordi, checking his chronometer. "We only have to maintain power for the first onslaught of the wave, about ten minutes. Let's run the test, and see how long the gel-packs can power it."

He waved to the dozen or so technicians who were assisting them, one of whom was Dolores Linton. "Start the monitoring equipment. Check the power couplers. Get the emitter and the dampening field ready."

For several minutes, there was frantic activity in the field, as the technicians double-checked the various pieces of equipment. Their test was a larger version of the test they had run aboard the *Enterprise* in the chamber. Two interphase generators and their power packs had been set up in the center of the field, which was a bit less than one hectare in size. They assumed they could cram almost sixty thousand people in an area this size—and many more if they used buildings of multiple stories. Two generators were being used, with the second one intended as a backup in case the first one failed.

They would measure how far the protective phase-shifting field extended and how effective it would be in guarding the giant vegetables from the protomatter beam. Geordi knew it was awfully late in the process to see whether this plan would work, but this was the first chance they'd had to try it. If the test failed . . . He didn't want to think about that, because they didn't have a backup.

While the Romulan was checking one generator, La Forge was checking the other, when he felt a comforting hand on his shoulder. He looked up, hoping it was Leah, but instead it was Dolores Linton, smiling at him. He felt a pang of guilt, because he'd been awfully cavalier about her feelings for him. But he resented the fact that Leah thought the two of them were involved. Nevertheless, he reached up and squeezed her hand warmly.

"You know, you don't have to be here," he said.

"What?" said Dolores cheerfully. "Do you think I'd miss a chance to get off that ship onto solid ground?"

Geordi smiled. "Maybe if I ever gave you that tour of the ship, you'd appreciate it more."

"Maybe." Dolores glanced over at Leah Brahms, who was some distance away, tinkering with the protomatter emitter. "Leah told me that she's leaving . . . and that I should take care of you."

La Forge grumbled and turned back to his work. "Is that so?"

"It's too soon for her, Geordi. Too much has happened. Besides, she doesn't realize how you feel about her."

"I know," he said, grabbing a spanner from his tool belt and making a slight adjustment. "I've been a perfect gentleman."

"Yes, and some of us are getting a little annoyed about that."

He turned to look at her, and Dolores was gazing hard at him, having made a joke that wasn't a joke.

"Okay," he said boldly, "when this is all over, a tour of this ship it is. Starting with my quarters."

"That's more like it!" replied the geologist enthusiastically. "Now save the day, will you?" Dolores squeezed his shoulder one more time and walked away.

La Forge watched the muscular young woman's easy stride, wondering what on Earth was wrong with him. It was a good thing Data wasn't here to see how inept he was—he'd never hear the end of it. Yes, he was still carrying a torch for a traumatized widow who seemed to prefer the company of a grizzled old Klingon. But then, it was a torch he was used to carrying.

A few meters away from him, the Romulan finished his adjustments to the second interphase generator, and he stood and walked over to La Forge. "I'm still not sure it will work, but you might as well try it."

"Thanks for your vote of confidence." Geordi was finished, too, having set the device to the optimal settings they had discovered in the lab. On the edge of the field, a transporter beam deposited half-a-dozen swirling columns of light, who formed into half-a-dozen Starfleet officers, one of whom was Admiral Nechayev.

"The brass is here," said La Forge, motioning to Duperik to follow him. He and the Romulan walked up to the admiral and her aides, several of whom looked frightened to death.

"Is everything in readiness, Commander?" asked the admiral solemnly.

"Yes, we were just about to do our first test."

The admiral frowned and looked at her chronometer. "You're a bit behind schedule."

La Forge didn't argue with her, or mention that the schedule was absurd—along with this whole idea. Instead he clapped his hands loudly and yelled, "Come on, let's do it! Everyone to their places!"

A ring of technicians formed around the estimated area of protection, and all of them were manning tricorders, monitors, or remote controllers. "Ready?" called Geordi.

All around the field, assistants acknowledged that they were ready, and La Forge nodded to the Romulan. "Activate generator number one."

Duperik pressed his control device and reported, "Phase-shifting activated. Power levels holding steady."

Nothing in the field looked any different to normal sight, but Geordi could see the oscillating ripple of wave after wave of energy pulsing outward. Some of the huge vegetables seemed to quiver, like asphalt in the summer sun.

He pointed to Leah on the emitter gun. "Give it the protomatter. Begin countdown. All monitors on!"

Brahms shot a narrow beam into the rows of giant vegetables, and it seemed to pass right through half-a-dozen of them before terminating in a dampening field on the other side. Geordi kept his eyes on his chronometer, because there wasn't any doubt that the phase-shifting would cover the distance for a short period of time. The question was whether the gel-packs could power the generator long enough to brave the worst of the Genesis Wave's effects.

La Forge saw a couple of the technicians in the circle move forward, as if the field were shrinking. He sidled over to the Romulan and asked in a whisper, "Is power holding steady?"

"No," answered Duperik. "The power has dropped by twenty-two percent, but the generator is still working. We make good equipment, don't we?"

"There are still five minutes left to go," said Geordi worriedly. The last thing he wanted was for this test to be a failure—in front of the admiral. "Activate the backup generator."

"Are you sure?"

"Yes."

The Romulan engineer did as he was ordered, and the test continued. "Are you planning to use two generators at each site?"

"I don't know yet," answered Geordi, his eyes on his timepiece. "Maybe backup gel-packs would be better. We'll have an engineer at each site."

"Not a Romulan engineer, you won't," said Duperik pointedly. "We're not staying around for this fiasco."

"Just keep that to yourself," whispered Geordi.

The minutes seemed to drag by, but the giant, artichokelike vegetables were suffering no ill effect from the protomatter beam. Geordi barely breathed until he was finally able to shout, "Time! Stop protomatter!"

Leah Brahms turned the emitter off and stood at attention, gazing at the azure sky as if her mind were light-years away. Everyone else shouted with joy, congratulating each other with hugs and slaps on the back.

Admiral Nechayev actually cracked a smile as she walked over to La Forge. "Well done, Commander! This means we can approach the Bolians with confidence and go to the next stage. Our latest plan is to use their religious sanctuaries as shelters, because they seem to be flocking there anyway. Send your settings and results to the *Sovereign*, so that we can distribute them to all the teams."

"Yes, Sir," answered Geordi, wishing he felt more confident than he did. He stole a glance at Leah Brahms, who was slowly walking toward them. Her face was a stoic mask, but he could see the fear in her dark eyes.

Nechayev was still holding court. "This also allows me to put out a call for volunteers among Starfleet officers—to stand with us here on Myrmidon."

"With *us*?" asked La Forge hesitantly.

"Yes," answered the admiral. "My aides and I are staying here with the populace. This will reassure them of our faith in the plan."

Now Geordi knew why her aides had looked so frightened when they first arrived. They were going to voluntarily remain on the planet and endure the Genesis Wave.

"Admiral," said Leah Brahms, "I would like to leave immediately. My work is done—I can't do anything else here."

"Certainly, Doctor. You can return with us to the *Sovereign* right now."

Geordi's heart sank to the bottom of his heels upon hearing Leah say she was leaving. Now it was definite. Without thinking, except that he wanted to make her feel as badly as he felt, he blurted out, "Admiral, I'd like to volunteer to stay with you on Myrmidon."

"Geordi!" said Leah, aghast. "Are you crazy?"

"Doctor, that will be enough," snapped Nechayev. She turned to La Forge with gratitude and respect on her usually stern face. "That will mean a lot to everybody if you stay, Commander."

"Then *I'll* stay, too," said Dolores Linton resolutely.

Now it was Geordi's turn to look aghast, but he couldn't very well berate her for doing what he was doing.

"Tell us your name." Nechayev nodded to one of her aides, who had already entered La Forge's name on his padd.

"Dolores Linton, mission specialist, geology."

"Ah, yes. You should be on Itamish III. Hopefully, we can get you back there without delay when this is all over. Your bravery will not go unnoticed."

Nechayev motioned to her entourage. "We'd better get back to the ship, because we have a lot to do. Dr. Brahms, you're with us." She tapped her combadge. "Nechayev to *Enterprise*. Seven to beam up."

Leah gave Geordi a final look, and it was hard to tell whether she was angry or mournful over his rash decision. She just shook her head and gazed solemnly down at the ground. In a swirl of glittering molecules, the admiral, her entourage, and the love of his life were gone.

Will I ever see her again? wondered Geordi. If he were a betting man, he wouldn't have bet on it.

The engineer sighed and looked at Dolores, standing resolutely beside him. "You didn't have to do that," he whispered.

"Neither did you." She mustered a brave smile. "I told you, I'd rather be on solid ground, even if it's not so solid. Besides, the test went great! What could go wrong?"

"I'm going to make sure nothing goes wrong," vowed La Forge. He tried not to look at the Romulan engineer, who was shaking his head as if the people in Starfleet were absolutely insane.

twenty-four

On the bridge of the *Enterprise*, the mood was somber as they listened to a fleet-wide message from Admiral Nechayev, calling for
volunteers to stay on Myrmidon and tough it out. The admiral
could be persuasive, thought Will Riker, but not persuasive enough
to convince him. It helped that she had specifically asked for no
more than one or two volunteers per ship.

When the message was over, he looked at Captain Picard and
asked, "What do we do if we get volunteers?"

"We let them go," answered Picard from his command chair.
"One or two at the most. But I'm under orders *not* to volunteer, and
I hope none of my senior staff do either."

"You knew about this?"

"I'm afraid so," said the captain grimly.

"At least it sounds like she wants to keep it to a small number," said
the first officer. "Do you think some of our Bolians will want to stay?"

"I don't know," answered the captain. "Although we haven't
been ordered to take any evacuees, I intend to make an exception
for Mot's parents and other family members of our crew."

"That is odd," said Data, seated in his usual post at the ops console. "A Starfleet vessel has just come out of warp twenty thousand kilometers from here—"

"Why is that odd?" asked Riker, glancing at a viewscreen that was full of Starfleet, Klingon, and Romulan vessels. They were lined up in orbit like hover-taxis waiting at a spaceport.

"It is the *Neptune*, *Defiant*-class. She is part of Task Force Javelin, which has been reported missing."

Now Captain Picard whirled around in his seat and stared at the android. "Are you sure about that?"

"Yes, Sir. Warp signature matches. Here is the ship on visual." The viewscreen overheard switched from a view of ships in orbit to a single, squat starship floating in space. Its running lights blinked oddly, as if shorted out, and there were scorch marks along its hull.

"Hail them." Picard jumped to his feet and peered at the image on the screen. "Tactical, get me Admiral Nechayev."

"She's already on the comlink, Sir."

Picard nodded and pointed to the screen, where Nechayev's dour face appeared. "Hello, Admiral," he said. "Did you see who just arrived?"

"The *Neptune*," she answered. "You had better take a closer look, Captain."

Picard turned curiously to Data, who shook his head. "They do not answer our hails. Sensors show no lifesigns onboard. Their shields are up, which may be affecting our sensor readings."

"A ghost ship?" asked Riker in amazement. "How did they know to come out of warp right here? Who set the course?"

A troubled scowl on his face, the captain turned back to the admiral. "Did you get that, Sir?"

"Our sensors show the same thing," answered Nechayev. "We can get the override codes and turn off the shields from here, but I'd like the *Enterprise* to investigate. If the *Neptune* is spaceworthy— and she just came out of warp—we have to fly her out of here. You know what will happen if we leave her behind. If she can be saved, assign a skeleton crew and tell them to await orders."

"Yes, Sir," answered Picard. "What about possible survivors? The other missing ships from the task force?"

"All hell is going to break loose here in seventeen hours," answered Nechayev grimly. "We can't worry about anything else but Myrmidon. I'll inform our allies, although they have their hands full. That reminds me, Captain—I'm going down to the planet now . . . for the duration. It's time to muster support among the populace. Contact the *Sovereign* if you need me, and they can patch you through."

"Yes, Sir."

Nechayev glanced at the readouts on her terminal. "We've already got two volunteers from the *Enterprise*, so you're off the hook. That would be Commander La Forge and Dolores Linton, who are already on site."

"Geordi La Forge?" asked Riker with surprise. "He volunteered?"

The admiral nodded. "I'm sorry if the request wasn't put through officially, but Commander La Forge volunteered personally to my face. I couldn't say no. It was very brave of him, and it's gone a long way to calming fears down there. Give me a report on the *Neptune* as soon as you can. Nechayev out."

The captain took a deep breath and let out a sigh, while Riker stomped across the bridge. "What was La Forge thinking? Did any-body—" He stopped and rubbed his forehead, realizing there was nothing anybody could do.

"Number One, you and Data are on the away team," said Picard, getting back to business. "You'd better take Dr. Crusher, too. Tell her, it's likely the crew is dead, but she should be prepared for casu-alties."

Riker nodded. "I'll put Krygore in charge of engineering."

"Good choice," said the captain.

Data bounded out of his seat and started for the turbolift, with

Riker following. At the turbolift door, the first officer stopped and turned around. "Captain, if the *Neptune* is shipshape, Dr. Crusher would be a good choice to command her. I'll put together a decent crew for her."

The captain scratched his chin thoughtfully. Riker figured he might appreciate an excuse to get the doctor out of harm's way. Deanna would also be a good choice, but she was already occupied on the planet's surface.

"I'll consider it," answered the captain. "Let's find out what happened to the ship first. Conn, set a course for the *Neptune*, half-impulse, and take us within five kilometers."

"Yes, Sir."

Riker's eyes drifted to the viewscreen, where a scorched starship floated in the blackness of space, its shields and running lights flickering eerily.

Pulling the strap of her medkit over her shoulder, Dr. Beverly Crusher charged down the corridor on her way to transporter room two. She was relieved that she could still move freely in the corridors, since the *Enterprise* had been spared from picking up evacuees on Myrmidon. Although most of the populace was supposed to stay on and brave the Genesis Wave, many thousands were being evacuated on the support ships. But the *Enterprise* had been held in reserve for other jobs, such as this investigation of a deserted ship. After abandoning whole worlds right and left, it almost seemed quaint to be worried about one little ship.

When she reached the transporter room, she found Riker and Data already waiting for her. "Hello, Doctor," said the first officer, checking his tricorder. "Ready for a little jaunt off the ship?"

"Just when I finally get sickbay empty," said Crusher in mock anger, "and you give me something else to do. Did we run out of security officers?"

"Yes, as a matter of fact," said Riker. "They're all down on the surface."

"What's the story with this ship?" asked Crusher.

"The *Neptune* has been missing for almost thirty hours," replied Data. "It was part of Task Force Javelin, and its last known whereabouts were near Seran, the first planet stricken by the wave."

"So what is it doing here?"

"Exactly," answered Riker. "We're not picking up any lifesigns, but you never know. It's a small ship, so it shouldn't take much time to explore."

"Which is good," added Beverly, "since we don't have much time."

Riker led the way onto the transporter platform. "If it's spaceworthy, we have to fly it out. You may end up in the captain's chair before the end of the day."

Crusher said nothing, but the prospect of having her own ship in the middle of this crisis wasn't all that unappealing. She was feeling a little frustrated in sickbay, where the action had fallen off considerably since they had unloaded all of their evacuees. So far, her review of the biological data collected on Persephone V hadn't borne any fruit, and it felt as if she would need weeks to understand what was happening to these planets.

Riker motioned to the tall Andorian on the transporter console. "Have you got the coordinates, Chief?"

"Yes, Sir," answered Rhofistan. "I'm putting you on their bridge."

"That's fine. Are their shields down yet?"

"Just went down."

Crusher looked puzzledly at the first officer. "There's nobody on this ship, but it has shields up?"

"Just one of many mysteries," answered the commander. He motioned to the transporter chief. "Energize."

A few seconds later, their swirling molecules coalesced on the bridge of the *Neptune*, which was deserted as expected. Beverly looked around, thinking that it reminded her of a smaller version of the bridge on the old *Enterprise*-D. Although no one was here, most of the consoles blinked and beeped as if they were functioning, and the viewscreen showed a disconcerting view of the *Enterprise*-E, sitting just off port.

While Data consulted his tricorder, Riker strode to the ops console and checked the readouts. "I want to see if there's any record of someone setting a warp course and then beaming off just before it engaged."

"Is there?" asked Beverly.

Riker pressed the membrane keypad several times and shook his head. "No. All the logs for the last two days have been wiped."

Data peered intently at his tricorder. "There are still no signs of life, but there is inert organic matter scattered throughout the ship."

"Organic matter?" asked Riker.

"Vegetable matter," answered the android. "Perhaps foodstuffs. There are only three main decks—this one, an upper deck for crew quarters, and the engine room below. I suggest we split up."

"All right," agreed Riker, "but let's use the Jefferies tubes, in case there are malfunctions we don't know about. Data, you take the engine room. While you're down there, take a look at the warp and impulse engines and see if they're in good shape."

"Yes, Sir." Data immediately strode toward an access panel at the rear of the bridge and opened it with an effortless tug. As if he were leaping down a manhole, the android took a single step and was gone.

"Doctor, why don't you take the crew quarters?" said Riker. "You can check on sickbay, too, and see if it's functional."

"They have a sickbay on this little ship?" asked Crusher, impressed.

"I'm going to check out the shuttlebay," said Riker, heading after Data. "I want to see if they've still got their shuttlepods. Let me know if you see anything unusual."

"Yes, Sir." A moment later, Beverly Crusher was alone on the deserted bridge of the *Neptune*, and her footsteps clacked as loudly as gunshots as she walked across the deck. It wouldn't be a bad ship to command, she decided, although she would like to know what happened to the previous captain and crew.

Slinging her tricorder and medkit over her shoulder, the doctor descended into the Jefferies tube. After finding a junction that curved upward, she climbed for several meters until she reached an access panel, which she pushed open. A moment later, Crusher was standing in a nondescript corridor with doors lining only one side. Something smelled funny—like spoiled food.

Consulting her tricorder, Crusher homed in on the strange smell and found a mound of leaves rotting in an open doorway. At least it looked like leaves, or maybe the remains of an old Christmas tree. Tricorder readings couldn't identify the pile any better than her eyes could, and Beverly stepped over it to enter the crew quarters.

There was nothing unusual in the simple stateroom, which was obviously meant to be shared by two crew members. She walked over to a desk and looked at the collection of framed pictures, depicting two human children and two elder adults. The adults in the pictures were no doubt the children's grandparents, but where were the parents? The eerie quiet of the ghost ship was beginning to get on her nerves, and Crusher found herself talking aloud, just to hear a voice.

"Where did everyone go?" she asked the pictures on the desk, but their smiling faces divulged no secrets. Beverly opened a desk drawer and found a clean, pressed uniform inside.

"This is all wrong," she muttered.

She was startled by a rustling sound—like leaves stirred by a breeze—and she whirled around to see a shadow pass the open doorway. Gripping her tricorder, Beverly dashed out of the room into the corridor, expecting to see the owner of the shadow.

But there was no one there.

"Now this is getting to me," said Beverly, shaking her long, auburn tresses. "I'm imagining things."

this was their spiritual home—a holy place—and it couldn't be destroyed without reason. Either the outsiders were mistaken about the Genesis Wave, or it was the will of the First Mother.

Unfortunately, there was no way Starfleet could demonstrate the horror of the Genesis Wave, and there was no way for the populace to get a taste of it before it actually hit. By the time they knew how bad it was, they would be dead.

The door creaked open behind him, and he turned to see his mother walk out, carrying a plate of his favorite treats, *bazoban* bars. He mustered a smile for his parent, who was grinning broadly at him, but it was difficult to feign happiness. While she baked his favorite foods, while his father searched the closet for his favorite peg-jumping game, the minutes were ticking away. Already they had only twelve hours left, and his parents still could not fathom the seriousness of the situation.

It had been so long since Mot had seen his parents that he hadn't wanted to interject doom and gloom into their reunion, but the doom was very real. As soon as his father returned from rummaging through the closet, Mot was going to level with his parents—and force them to make a decision. He could slap himself now for not having come months sooner to visit them, but like most young people, he was selfish and wrapped up in his own life. Mot vowed never to let that happen again.

"Eat! Eat!" his mother encouraged him, shoving the plate of goodies under his nose. "It's your favorite."

"I know," he said, grabbing one of the fruity bars and shoving half of it into his mouth. Mot hadn't gotten to be as large as he was by being a slow eater. He chewed ruminatively as he watched the river flow by.

"How is that nice Captain Picard?" asked his mother.

"Fine," answered Mot. "He never complains about his haircut. Of course, he doesn't have much hair. Things have been peaceful on the *Enterprise* for many months now . . . until this."

"Your sister says she is doing well in her new position," Mother continued. "I'm certainly glad Bolarus isn't facing this problem. It isn't, is it?"

"No," answered Mot with a grunt of relief. He didn't say that their unknown enemy could always unleash the Genesis Wave again and again, until there was nothing left of the Federation but misshapen planets and old legends.

The door opened again, and his father came out with a dusty box in his hands. He looked older than Mot remembered, his once gleaming blue skin now pale and mottled. "Look, Son, I found it!" he claimed joyfully. "Your game of Tubes and Gutters! How about a quick match?"

With a heavy sigh, Mot set the plate of *bazoban* bars on the arm of his chair. "Mother . . . Father . . . we've got to talk and decide what you're going to do. You're lucky, in that you have more choices than most. Because I'm a member of the *Enterprise* crew, you can be evacuated from the planet."

His father laughed. "Leave Myrmidon? Do you know how long we worked and saved to move here? Coming here has been a dream for all of our lives, hasn't it, Mother?"

She nodded wistfully. "Yes. Nothing, except you children, has ever made us happier. Look at the beautiful view we have! Here there is enough room and land for everyone. You only have to be here for a few days to realize that *this* is truly the chosen planet."

In exasperation, Mot jumped to his feet, knocking the plate of *bazoban* bars onto the patio with a clatter. Guiltily, he bent down to pick them up, but then he realized that *he* would have to be the adult here. Mot rose to his feet, leaving the food on the floor.

"Don't pick it up," he told his mother sternly. "In twelve hours, those crumbs won't be here. That river won't be here. The cottage won't be here, and *you* won't be here. Unless you're evacuated or go to a shelter, you'll be dead. To tell you the truth, I don't even know if the shelters will work, but it's the only way we have to save as many people as possible."

The big Bolian knelt down and clasped his parents' hands. "Please! Take this opportunity to come with me back to the *Enterprise*. I don't want to call my sister and tell her that you're dead . . . and that I could have saved you, but didn't."

His mother smiled benignly. "If it's the will of the First Mother to change our world, then we will change with it."

"No!" shouted Mot. "It's not the will of the First Mother—it's a weapon! A truly horrendous weapon."

"Is there much suffering?" asked his father.

Mot well knew where that line of thinking was headed, and he wanted to head it off. "No, death will be very swift. You needn't worry about that. But the thing is, you don't have to die! If you refuse to be evacuated, will you at least go to the sanctuary in Genroh and wait there?"

The elder Bolians looked at one another and then at their little cottage, and Mot could tell they were still undecided. He screwed up his courage and added, "I'll go with you. I'll wait with you, too . . . until it's over."

"You won't leave with the *Enterprise*?" asked his father with surprise.

"Not if you're staying here."

His mother squeezed his hand. "My son, we'll all go together to the sanctuary."

With that, Mot breathed an enormous sigh of relief and wrapped his arms around both of his parents, tears welling in his eyes. At long last, when the hug was over, his father picked up the old dusty box and asked hoarsely, "Now . . . how about a game of Tubes and Gutters?"

Maltz paced the now-empty radiation lab on the *Enterprise*, which he had made his home since the ship began filling with refugees days ago. He hadn't realized that staying aboard the *Enter-*

prise meant staying alone, and that Leah Brahms would disappear. In fact, everybody on the ship was so busy that they were ignoring him. He thought momentarily about wreaking havoc, which would have been easy enough to do, but Starfleet was already in a more chaotic state than it had ever been. It seemed cowardly to kick them when they were down.

Besides, he might need their assistance to fulfill his blood oath. He certainly needed them to be reunited with Leah Brahms, wherever she was. The old Klingon had spent a lot of time alone in recent years, and he was content with his own company. He had also learned to be patient.

Maltz went to the replicator, wondering if it could produce a mug of ale. Finally, he rejected that idea, thinking he might need his wits about him; he settled for carrot juice, a Terran delicacy for which he had developed a taste. He was enjoying his glass of juice when the door whooshed open. In strode the tall first officer named Riker, and Maltz jumped to attention.

"You must be getting bored," said Riker.

"A bit," admitted Maltz.

"General Gra'Kor has asked for you to be reassigned to him. Are you ready to go?"

"Am I ready to go!" barked the Klingon happily. "Does a *targ* have spikes?"

Riker smiled. "Come on, let's see if we can squeeze you onto the transporter."

They exited the laboratory and strode down the corridor, which seemed oddly quiet. "Where is everyone?" asked Maltz.

"On the planet, getting ready for the wave."

"How does it go?"

Riker frowned. "All I know for sure is that there are more interphase generators down there than in the whole Romulan Star Empire. I think we'll save lives, but I wish I knew for sure."

"How much time is left?" asked the Klingon.

Riker checked his chronometer. "About six hours."

They reached the turbolift, and the first officer told the computer their destination. "Is Leah Brahms still on the planet?" asked Maltz.

"No, I was told she was over on the *Sovereign*. She didn't want to stay on the planet."

"She has good reason to stay alive," said Maltz darkly. "Did your task force have any success finding the beasts who are doing this?"

"No," muttered Riker, "although one of the ships turned up . . . deserted."

"No sign of the crew?" asked the Klingon puzzledly.

Riker shook his head as the turbolift door opened. He strode out, and Maltz followed, smiling to himself. When vengeance would be wreaked, *he* would do the wreaking, not the Federation.

They reached the transporter room, and the cargo handlers moved aside enough boxes of gel-packs to make room on the platform for Maltz. Riker extended his hand, and the old Klingon gripped it forcefully.

"I hope you find peace," said Riker.

"I hope I find war," answered Maltz with a grin. "Tell Captain Picard he has a noble vessel and a fine crew, plus good hospitality."

"I will." The first officer nodded to the transporter operator. "Do you have the coordinates for the *Jaj*?"

"Laid in," answered the tall Andorian on the console.

"Energize when ready." A second later, the grizzled Klingon was gone.

He materialized in a much darker, smokier transporter room, where it was no less crowded. Only here it was jammed with confused Bolian evacuees, who never thought they would find themselves aboard a Klingon warship. With a few shoves and grunts, armed guards kept them moving quickly into the corridors.

"Consul Maltz," said the transporter operator. "Wait here—the general is coming."

Maltz moved out of the way and stood in the corner, waiting patiently until the stocky general arrived.

"Maltz!" Gra'Kor growled magnanimously as he strode into the room, slamming his palms on the old Klingon's shoulders. "I called in some favors. Are you ready to see your ship?"

"My ship!" echoed Maltz in an awed tone of voice. "It's been a long time since I had a ship."

"I know," said Gra'Kor, his brusque manner softening. "I'm sorry I said the things I did. A warrior shouldn't have to suffer ninety years for one mission gone wrong."

"But you were right!" insisted Maltz. "I have not tried hard enough to get to *Sto-Vo-Kor*. But now that I have another chance to face my greatest enemy, I know why I have lived so long."

The general nodded sagely. "Do you know that the Federation has failed to find the source of this scourge?"

"Yes. Fate is saving them for me."

"You have a good crew of experienced warriors," said Gra'Kor. "I tried to pick those who have had dealings with humans, but I don't know if they will follow a human female."

"They will follow this one," Maltz assured him. "What is the name of our ship?"

"The *HoS*. She is an older attack cruiser but still valiant. Her captain and first mate were promoted to larger ships, so she is perfect for your purpose. But enough talk—you must go. What is the name of the misguided human who invented this disaster?"

"Carol Marcus," answered Maltz through clenched teeth. "If she yet lives, it will not be for long." He bounded back onto the transporter pad, pushing two startled Bolians out of his way. "Thank you, General."

"*Qapla'*!" said Gra'Kor with a salute and a toothy smile.

"I will see you in *Sto-Vo-Kor*," promised the old warrior seconds before his molecules disappeared in a shimmering curtain of light.

* * *

Leah Brahms paced about three steps, then turned and paced three steps in the other direction, which was all the room she had in the quarters she shared with five Bolian evacuees on the *Sovereign*. Admiral Nechayev had treated her like a pariah ever since she came aboard, shunting her off with the refugees, who were just as miserable as she. They might have wondered what this human was doing in their midst, because there weren't many non-Bolian residents on Myrmidon. They had to conclude that she wasn't part of the rescue effort.

In their abject fear and misery, the evacuees talked very little to each other, and none of them talked to Leah. She considered speaking to them, but she didn't trust herself to say anything positive. They certainly didn't need to hear that the world they left behind, and probably most of their friends and relatives, would be reduced to sludge in a few hours. She didn't really want to tell them that she was responsible for a desperate plan which had a good chance of getting everyone on Myrmidon killed.

Now Brahms knew why Admiral Nechayev's name was spoken in hushed and fearful tones. The woman's wrath was worthy of a wronged Klingon. Leah had been banished to this purgatory for a slip of the tongue, calling Geordi "crazy" for staying. The punishment didn't seem to fit the crime, but she had no idea how to get out of it. More than likely, she was destined to be offloaded like so much cargo at the nearest Bolian spaceport, along with the rest of the refugees. It was an ignominious ending to what she had thought was a distinguished career.

Of course, decided Leah grimly, *where else do I have to go? What else do I have to do? My life's over, my marriage is over, my career's over, and the only friend I have left is about to kill himself. Perhaps I should have stayed on the planet and taken my chances.*

A chime sounded at the door, and one of the Bolians said hoarsely, "Come in!"

A young ensign with a padd in his hands stepped inside and looked around. "Which one of you is Leah Brahms?"

"I am," she answered.

"Come with me, please." He motioned to the corridor, then stepped out to wait for her.

"Where are we going?" asked Leah as she followed him.

"You're being sent somewhere else." He checked his padd. "The *HoS*."

"The *HoS*? What is that?"

"A Klingon ship." They walked briskly down the corridor, which was also packed with refugees, until they reached the turbolift.

Hmmm, thought Leah glumly, *I must really be in the doghouse if the admiral is shipping me off to a Klingon vessel.* She finally decided that it couldn't be any worse than being cooped up on the *Enterprise.* Nevertheless, Leah spent a few irrational moments envisioning a brutal prison ship where she would spend her final days.

Moments later, she found herself in a frantic transporter room, where Bolian evacuees were being beamed aboard while crates were being shipped off at a rapid pace. The ensign conferred briefly with the transporter chief, and they made room for her on the transporter pad.

"Are you ready?" the chief asked her.

"Whatever," she answered with a shrug. "Remind me not to run afoul of Admiral Nechayev again."

"Never a good idea," agreed the transporter chief as he plied his controls. "Energizing."

A moment later, Brahms materialized on a dark, smoky bridge, where half-a-dozen sullen Klingon warriors stared suspiciously at her. She was about to ask what she was doing here, when the raised command chair in the center of the bridge swiveled around, and a rugged but familiar face grinned at her.

"Captain on the bridge," said Maltz.

Brahms looked around, wondering which one of them was the

captain, but all eyes were still focused on her. She felt an odd mixture of dread and elation.

Maltz rose to his feet and looked down at her. "What are your orders, Sir?"

Now it was Leah's turn to grin. "You did it, Maltz! You got yourself a ship!"

"I got *us* a ship. I've already laid in a course for Seran and the suspected origin point of the Genesis Wave. I assume you will want to leave orbit immediately."

Leah hesitated, thinking about Geordi and Dolores on the planet's surface, but there wasn't anything she could do for them, short of kidnapping them. They had volunteered of their own free will, and she had now been given an opportunity to exercise *her* will.

"Yes," she said, "take us out of orbit."

When her unfamiliar crew was a bit slow to move, Leah told herself to act more like Admiral Nechayev. "Move it!" she yelled. "I've got a blood oath to fulfill!"

That made them jump, and she turned to Maltz and said, "I've got to familiarize myself with this ship. Why don't we begin with the engine room. I think I'll feel more comfortable starting there."

"Yes, Sir," answered the old Klingon snappily. "You heard Captain Brahms! Second Officer Karuk, escort the captain to the engine room and answer all her questions fully."

"Yes, Sir," said a young officer, who still looked puzzled about how he could end up serving on a Klingon vessel under a human female. These were strange times indeed.

"Don't worry," Brahms told him, "the *HoS* is going to go down in history. And in glory."

The young officer gave her a smile and nodded to his fellows, as if to say they were going to be all right. Leah decided he was awfully young to die, but millions who were even younger had already perished. At least everybody on the *HoS* would die for a purpose.

*   *   *

Deanna Troi nearly gagged at the musky smell of all the animals crowded into the Sanctuary of the First Mother, along with their owners and what seemed like half the city. Starfleet had been so worried about saving the Bolians that they hardly thought about saving animals, but the residents of Myrmidon were sure thinking about it, as they brought livestock and pets by the dozens. There were fur-bearing animals, milk-giving animals, primates, birds, reptiles, even insects—some of them in cages, many on leashes, and others running between people's legs. It was like a land-bound Noah's Ark.

Mother, the stocky woman who ran the sanctuary, welcomed all who came for protection, two-legged, four-legged, or six-legged. To make room, volunteers had removed the pews and every stick of furniture, except for the display case which contained the Crown of the First Mother. It was sitting in a prominent place, right on top of the interphase generator. Although people and animals were crammed shoulder-to-shoulder in every square centimeter of the domed building, Mother pushed her way through the throng, assuring everyone that they would be saved by the grace of the First Mother . . . and her Starfleet assistants.

Troi finally had to make her way outside to get some fresh air, even though there was less than an hour left before the Genesis Wave hit. To her surprise, she saw the sky had turned a salmon shade, streaked with crimson clouds. It was dusk, a suitable time for the great transformation which was about to come. The counselor was only supposed to stay for another half an hour before returning to the *Enterprise*, but it felt as if she were deserting her comrades on a sinking ship.

She toyed with the idea of gutting it out on the planet, but once again she talked herself out of it. Deanna had witnessed that awful cataclysm once, and once was enough. Besides, she didn't think she could bear to see the beautiful city ravaged, as she knew it would be. Even if millions of lives were saved as planned, Myrmidon would be changed forever.

Unable to calm her nerves, she walked briskly through the now-quiet streets, just as she had done many hours earlier. Deanna felt vaguely guilty about leaving Mother and the sanctuary, but there wasn't anything she could do there but get in the way. Her idea to use the sanctuaries as shelters had been a good one—it would work, as long as everything else worked. If the interphase generators failed, at least the people would perish in a comfortable place that gave them peace. It wasn't much consolation, but it was all she had.

As she wandered, she heard the sound of voices rising on the twilight breeze. It sounded much like the chanting and praying that was happening inside the sanctuary, but she knew these worshippers had to be outside by the way their voices carried.

Following the chanting sound, she came to one of the parks with the giant communal vegetables. Gathered in the center of the clearing was a group of Bolians numbering about thirty, and half-a-dozen others were lying on the ground, sleeping. That was odd enough to make her stop to watch the proceedings. The Bolians were passing a large horn around, drinking a dark liquid from it. With a start, Troi realized that the sleepers on the ground were not sleeping—they were *dead*. The dark liquid was poison!

Without thinking, she charged into their midst and shouted, "Stop! Stop! What are you doing?"

A large Bolian glowered at her. "This is none of your concern! Haven't you brought enough disaster upon us?"

"Go away! Leave us in peace!" shouted others.

"But you don't have to die!" she insisted. "There's safety in the Sanctuary of the First Mother. Come with me, and I'll—"

She never saw the rock sailing through the air. It hit her in the head with enough force to knock her to the ground, and Troi lay there unconscious, blood streaming from her forehead. Those bent on suicide went on with their grim task, believing they had done the Starfleet officer a favor by sparing her undue suffering.

twenty-six

"Captain," said Data from the ops console on the *Enterprise*, "the last of the Klingon fleet is leaving orbit."

Picard looked up at the viewscreen in time to see a huge *Negh'-Var*-class warship bank away from the planet and careen into space, thrusters burning. The Romulan ships had pulled out fifteen minutes earlier, and the skies over Myrmidon were returning to a semblance of normal. But it was only a semblance, Picard knew, because there was nothing normal about the awesome force which was bearing down on them. Very soon those peaceful skies would turn an electric shade of green, and the fiery curtain would raze Myrmidon as it had razed every other object in its path.

"Any sign of the wave?" asked Commander Riker, pacing behind the command chair.

"Yes," answered the android as he scanned through information on his console. "The outmost planet of the solar system has already been transformed. This is only an estimate, but I would say we have twenty minutes until contact."

Captain Picard rubbed his chin thoughtfully. They had been

through this before—on Persephone V—but this time it was different. This time they had hundreds of Starfleet personnel down on the planet. The *Enterprise* had contributed La Forge, Linton, Mot, and four technicians to the effort. This would be either the greatest success in the history of Starfleet or the greatest disaster.

He heard his first officer say, "Riker to transporter room two."

"Rhofistan here," came the reply.

"Has Counselor Troi come back to the ship yet?"

"No, Sir. She hasn't reported in or asked for transportation."

"Stand by." He tapped his combadge. "Riker to Troi." There was no response, so he tried again. "*Enterprise* to Deanna Troi."

Again there was no response, and Riker looked beseechingly at the captain. "Can we beam her back?"

"Go ahead."

"Transporter room two, lock onto Deanna Troi's combadge and beam her back immediately," ordered Riker.

"Yes, Sir," responded the chief's voice.

Riker looked relieved to have issued the order, until the chief's voice sounded again. "Sir, there's been a problem."

"What kind of problem?" asked Riker impatiently. "Didn't you beam her back?"

There was a pause that seemed to last an eternity, then came the response. "We beamed back the person wearing her combadge, but it turns out to be a Bolian child about eight years old."

"What?" bellowed Riker. He looked worriedly at the captain.

"Go ahead and investigate," said Picard. "But I don't want to lose anybody else. Get back here in time."

The first officer nodded and charged toward the turbolift. After he was gone, it was the captain's turn to pace nervously across his bridge. He felt like contacting Nechayev, La Forge, or somebody on the planet, but what good would that do? It was far too late for second guessing, and last-minute heroics didn't work against the Genesis Wave. From all reports, the vast majority of Bolians had either found their way to shelters or had been evacuated. They had done all they could.

Then why did he feel so lousy?

At least Picard took consolation in knowing that Beverly Crusher was safe aboard the *Neptune*, which had left orbit about ten minutes ago. He had also gotten a promise from Captain Tomalak that he would replicate and reinstall the interphase generators on his ship, so that he could use cloaking again. As soon as it was safe, the Romulan had promised to come back to retrieve the admiral, La Forge, and the others.

Still, none of it seemed to be enough.

"Data," said Captain Picard, "take over the conn. Mister Perezo, you take over ops."

Swiftly, the two officers reconfigured their consoles so that they had switched responsibilities. The captain looked at the calm, efficient android and was very glad to have him on the bridge at the moment.

He walked behind the android and bent over to whisper in his ear, "Mr. Data, I want you to get us out of here before that wave hits, and I don't care who is—or isn't—on board. Don't wait for my order. Do I make myself clear?"

Data turned to regard him with those cool yellow eyes. "Yes, Sir."

Now, thought Picard, *I have done all I can.*

Will Riker strode purposefully into the transporter room and looked at the chief, who pointed to a small, blue-skinned person sitting on the edge of the transporter platform. The female child was still wearing the gleaming Starfleet combadge in the center of her blue tunic. He told himself to be patient and remember that he was dealing with a child, who was probably frightened and disoriented.

He walked over and knelt down in front of her. Smiling, he

pointed to the insignia badge. "That's a very pretty pin. Where did you get it?"

"I want to go home," she whined.

Riker clenched his teeth and tried to stay calm. "Listen, I'm not mad at you, but I know that pin belonged to somebody else. You can keep it, but I just want to find her. She's a good friend of mine."

"Will you take me home?" asked the child. "I miss my mother."

"Yes, as a matter of fact, I'll be glad to take you home. But I need to find my friend, too. Can you show me where you were when you found that pin?"

"I didn't find it," she answered. "My mother gave it to me."

Riker nodded slowly. Now it was making sense. Some distraught parent had hit upon a clever way of saving her child, if not herself. He clapped his hands together. "Let's go try to find my friend, and your mother."

He stood up and lifted the child to her feet, then he took her hand. "My name is Will. What's yours?"

"Dezeer."

"A pretty name," said Riker, mustering a smile. He steered her toward an empty pad. "Why don't you go stand over here, and I'll stand just over here. And the nice man will take us home."

He motioned to Rhofistan. "Do you have the coordinates where you picked her up?"

"Yes, Sir. But I'm not picking up any other life-forms around there."

"That's all right," muttered Riker grimly. "We haven't got a lot of choice." He glanced at the child to make sure she was still standing in the center of the pad, and she was. "Energize."

Tricorder in hand, Geordi La Forge circled nervously around the two interphase generators he had set up in the lowest part of a dry riverbed. For at least the twentieth time, he checked all the couplers, power connections, and gel-packs. Although most of the shelters were in the religious sanctuaries, Dolores Linton had convinced them to put a few in open air. She had determined that the seasonally dry riverbeds offered the greatest chance for success—she liked the low altitude and the sandy, porous soil, which allowed for good penetration of the phase-shifting pulse.

Plus the riverbeds held a lot of beings, as demonstrated by the huge throngs of baying animals and praying Bolians. It looked like a scene from one of those old Biblical epics—with a whole nation stuck in the desert.

Geordi stopped and glanced at Admiral Nechayev and Dolores Linton, who were conferring with some nervous Bolian dignitaries. Dolores and the admiral had become fast friends in the last few hours, and La Forge figured that her career was going to take a major leap forward . . . if they survived. Dolores had been such a stalwart and cheerful presence that Geordi was beginning to feel very fond of the geologist. He hadn't stopped thinking about Leah Brahms for one moment, but he had decided that Dolores was a real keeper.

Although he had no idea where Leah was, at least she was safe. At the moment, it seemed highly unlikely that he would ever see her again. He looked up at the sky, which was just beginning to turn a rosy shade as dusk hit this part of Myrmidon. A cool breeze blew across the dry river, rustling the tall trees and grasses which grew there. It seemed altogether too beautiful of a day for this world to end.

The conference with the Bolians broke up, and Nechayev and Linton waded through the crowd to get back to Geordi's position at the generators.

Dolores lowered her voice to say, "We assured them that they were going to die quickly, and with no pain. Of course, I don't think any of us are going to die."

"We'll know soon," said Nechayev. "I've just received word that the wave is moving through the solar system and should hit here in about ten minutes. I've ordered the fleet to leave, although one or two ships will stay until the last minute. The Klingons and Romulans are already gone."

"Is the *Enterprise* still in orbit?" asked La Forge.

The admiral gave him a slight smile. "What do you think? I can always count on your captain to take the risks nobody else would."

"What are you worried about?" asked Dolores.

Nechayev sighed. "I don't know, but my career has taught me to believe strongly in Murphy's Law. Besides, we need someone to alert us when the countdown has started."

"Right." Geordi noticed that he was wringing his hands nervously, and he quickly dropped them to his side. With a smile, Dolores grabbed one of his hands and gripped it tightly. He could feel her pulse throbbing in his palm, and he realized that her cheerfulness was a brave act.

"As soon as we have two minutes left, we'll start the countdown," said the admiral. "I can't begin to express my gratitude for the two of you staying here. Suffice to say, it's good to be among comrades at a time like this."

There was nothing left to say, and all three of them gazed anxiously at the deepening auburn sky.

Gripping the little girl's hand, Riker tried not to drag her through the deserted streets of the capitol, but it was difficult not to hurry when time was running short—less than five minutes by Data's latest estimate. The Bolian child, Dezeer, was crying and fearful, and Riker couldn't blame her. He might be crying soon too if he couldn't find Deanna. It didn't help that darkness had descended on the great city, and every building and side street looked the same.

They stopped at another intersection, populated only by leaves and bits of trash which skidded along the sidewalk. "Does this look familiar?" Riker asked. "Is this where your mother gave you that pin?"

"I don't know," she answered, looking sorrowful.

Riker gritted his teeth. "Do you know this part of town? Please take a look around. Do you know where we are?"

Wearily, the child gazed at the triangular-shaped buildings and broad thoroughfares. Finally she nodded and pointed. "Yes. My school is down there."

"Good!" exclaimed Riker. "Now try again—do you know where your mother was going when she left you?"

Dezeer nodded. "To the park, I think."

"To a park," repeated Riker. "Do you think you could take me there? I would love to see your park."

"Where is everybody?" asked the child, puzzled.

"They're probably in the park, having a party. Why don't you take me there, and we'll have a party with your mother and all your friends."

The little girl nodded, and for the first time, she took his hand and led him down the deserted street.

"One-hundred-twenty . . . one-hundred-nineteen . . . one-hundred-eighteen . . . one-hundred-seventeen," droned the voice of the computer over the shipwide intercom. Captain Picard turned and looked at the viewscreen, where a small magenta dust cloud glimmered in the firmament. He watched, transfixed, as the dust cloud seemed to implode, forming into a gaseous ball a split second before it was obliterated completely by a seething, fiery curtain of green. Although he had seen it before, the awesome sight made him shiver. Now that the dust cloud was gone, nothing stood between the Genesis Wave and Myrmidon.

The captain tapped his combadge. "*Enterprise* to Riker."

"Riker here," came a breathless reply.

"I'm sorry," said Picard, "but we need you to return."

"Captain, we've just reached a park where there are a lot of dead bodies. I need to look through them."

"Dead bodies?"

"It must be the site of a mass suicide," answered the first officer. "Take the girl back, but give me another few seconds."

Before he could reply, Data spoke up urgently. "Captain! One of the Starfleet ships has returned, and . . . they have opened fire on the shelters!"

"What?" barked Picard. "Which ship? Hail them!"

The android looked up, a glimpse of shock in his yellow eyes. "Sir, it is the *Neptune*. Dr. Crusher does not answer our hail. I will put it on screen."

Captain Picard stared at the viewscreen, where the once-derelict ship was firing torpedoes and phasers in rapid succession. On the planet's surface, bright flashes indicated where the deadly weapons were wreaking their toll. Picard gripped the back of his command chair, hesitant to order the destruction of Beverly's ship.

"Eighty . . . seventy-nine . . . seventy-eight . . . seventy-seven," continued the computer, calmly counting down the destruction of Myrmidon and the fifty million souls who dwelled there.

twenty-seven

The first explosion blew up a mammoth chunk of the riverbed, along with scores of innocent Bolians. There were smoke, dust, carnage, and wailing everywhere, and Geordi instinctively dove on top of the interphase generators in order to protect them. That was his first instinct, but the second one was better. Without hesitation, he threw the switch to initiate phase-shifting, even though they were over a minute early.

Then he cowered in the dirt, as the unexpected onslaught continued. Lifting his head, he squinted through the smoke and chaos to see both Admiral Nechayev and Dolores Linton lying on the ground, amidst dozens of other casualties. He fought the impulse to dash to their aid, because he had to stay with the interphase generators and power packs. As horrible as this was, the real horror was yet to come. Some of the Bolians were fleeing from the deadly explosions, running out of the field of protection. He tried to yell at them to stop, but his ragged voice was lost in screams, chaos, and explosions.

* * *

Captain Picard rousted himself from his momentary hesitation and pointed to Data on the conn. "Pursue the *Neptune*, full impulse. Tactical, target phasers on their impulse engines and fire at will."

"Yes, Sir!"

He slapped the companel on his chair, and his voice boomed over the ship. "Transporter room one, as soon as we get into range, lock onto the life-forms on the starship *Neptune* and beam them aboard. All security personnel, report to transporter room one and take the crew of the *Neptune* into custody. Use force if necessary."

Riker! he thought in a panic. He had forgotten about his first officer. "Transporter room two, lock onto Commander Riker and the Bolian girl right now and beam them aboard.

"Thirty . . . twenty-nine . . . twenty-eight," droned the voice of the computer as the Genesis Wave streaked ever closer.

Riker heard the explosions ripping through the city, and his small companion screamed in fear. Now he wasn't gentle at all as he lifted the girl and hauled her from corpse to corpse, looking for anyone among the bodies who wasn't Bolian.

He finally spotted her by her mane of dark hair, splayed outward from her bloody face like a black halo. Clutching the girl in one hand, he fell on top of Deanna's unconscious body, trying to protect her from the blasts. In that same instant, all three of their bodies dematerialized in the shimmering haze of the transporter beam.

Mot and his parents huddled in the vestibule of the sanctuary and tried to ignore the jostling, weeping, and wailing all around them. They could hear the distant explosions, but they couldn't figure out what they were. Mot had feared that some residents might commit suicide, but they weren't likely to blow themselves up. He also couldn't tell if the technicians had switched on the phase-shifting, but he certainly hoped so.

"Is it starting?" his mother asked fearfully.

"I don't know," answered Mot, wrapping his arms around his parents and squeezing them tightly. "Whatever happens, we'll be together."

From the vestibule, they were able to see the starlit sky through the open doorway, and Mot watched it intently. Even though it was just shortly past sunset, the sky seemed to be growing lighter, as if the sun were coming up in a roaring blaze. He watched in awe as the sky turned a mottled shade of red, then a sickly green, and then a dozen other colors in a bizarre kaleidoscope effect. The ground began to tremble, and the wails and chants increased in volume.

"Yes, it's happening!" said Mot. He kissed the top of his mother's head and then his father's. "I love you both!"

"We love you, Son!" rasped his father, burying his face in Mot's broad chest. All around them, the sanctuary shuddered, and the wind howled with an unearthly force. Mot closed his eyes and gripped his loving parents, certain that the next moment would be their last.

"Captain, we are leaving orbit," declared Data, taking the initiative Picard had charged him with.

On the viewscreen, the *Neptune* soared toward the planet, no longer firing indiscriminately but in flames. Their phasers had stopped the rogue ship, but there was no telling how much destruction she had wrought before being stopped.

Picard wanted to rush down to the transporter room and find what had caused Beverly and her crew to lose their minds, but he couldn't tear his eyes away from the planet. A pulsing wall of flame ripped over the yellow-green plains and the blue rivers, turning them into great pillars of steam and ash. The whole planet quivered and throbbed like a sun going nova. He tried to imagine there being hundreds of pockets of survivors, but it hardly seemed possible. It could be days before they knew how many had been saved, if any.

The last image he saw on the viewscreen was the fiery wall engulfing the tiny *Neptune* like a monstrous tidal wave crashing over a rowboat.

They had made their stand on Myrmidon, but there was no way anyone could call this a victory. In a few more days, Earth would fall, and they still had no idea *who* was doing this to them. Or how to stop it. The Genesis Wave rushed onward, undiminished, its voracious appetite still eager to consume more worlds, more solar systems, and more lives.

To Be Continued in
Star Trek: The Next Generation
The Genesis Wave
Book Two

Coming in April from Pocket Books

Editor's Acknowledgment

The editor would like to thank David Mack, who is less fictional than some might presume, for providing THE GENESIS REPORT that makes up the bulk of Chapter Fourteen.